CW00701632

For Paula, Always.

FOR THOSE WHO ARE WITHOUT SIN

D. B. Cooper

This is not a true story.

1

DEATH

G erald was dying, and he knew it. They all knew it. Pretty much everyone knew it, and for him it wasn't going to happen soon enough. At least that's what he said – to himself and, at times, to the rest of his family. He'd had enough of this world and was looking forward to moving onto the next one. With his chest heaving with each breath, he looked up desperately towards the ceiling of the small, white bedroom and prayed.

'Dear Lord, please take me now. I can't stand it a moment longer. Take me away from all this, please. What have I done? Do I really deserve this? Was it me? Could I really be responsible? Oh God, please forgive me. Take me now. Just let me enter the next world and leave this all behind.'

Gerald's mind was swimming in confusion as his synapses fired randomly and his neurones started the inevitable process of shutdown. As he lay in bed, his mind replayed scenes from his past. Confused images of his family appeared to him mixed with random frames of his life's experiences. These were mostly memories of closer, happier times.

'Oh God. Please let me start anew,' he said to himself. 'Let me start a new life in the power of your Kingdom. There they are... I will miss you all... will you miss me?. You will won't you?... You will learn to stand on your own two-feet? Won't you? You must... learn... learn to get on... to live together... You will, won't you? It will surely be worth it... In the Kingdom of Heaven... The glory of the Lord... Oh God!'

The walls in Gerald's bedroom seemed to pulsate in unison with each of his laboured breaths. The room had once reflected the taste of a younger, fitter and healthier man, decorated with an immaculately manicured and spotless white carpet with carefully matched furniture. Even the meticulously chosen crucifix was carefully placed some years earlier above a happier bed.

But to look more closely, past the younger man's intent revealed an attention to detail that faded over time. The bedroom ceiling and walls were now tarnished with nicotine stains, long-hanging cobwebs and the ignored scuff marks of every-day life. The carpet was worn, marked, and stained - and a closer inspection of the crucifix revealed it covered thick with dust. This was a room neglected. This was a man neglected.

As Gerald drifted in and out of consciousness, he reflected on his life.

'How had it come to this?' he thought to himself. 'Eighty-five years old. A life spent defending my country, building a career, a home and a family, and I'm left like this. How could this have happened? Abandoned by my friends. Shunned by my Church... and exploited by my family... But then again, at least I have Sheena. I'm sure she cares, really... She has my best interests at heart... And Sean has been good as well. He looked after the house. Maybe I should count my lucky stars after all.'

Each of Gerald's shallowing breaths condensed onto a diminishing patch inside his oxygen mask. It wouldn't be long now. He yearned for Kitty, his long-passed wife, to make all of this all right. She would understand his fears. She would know what to do.

'Why did you have to go before me?' Gerald asked. 'For seven long years, I have had to endure this cruel world without you. Why didn't you warn me? Why didn't you tell me what it would be like?'

Kitty was Gerald's confidant, his protector, his translator and his defender. Since her sad passing, Gerald had found it increasingly difficult to make sense of the world. Together for over 60 years, Kitty was the only one who really understood him. She recognised that the way he viewed the world was not like other people. She knew that he approached things very differently from most people. Perhaps today, Gerald would have been diagnosed with Asperger's Syndrome or considered mildly autistic, but he was born in simpler times when these things were largely unheard of, so he had lived undiagnosed and untreated his entire life. He knew he was different, and those who came into contact with him also knew. Gerald was very different from everyone else.

As a child, Gerald would often spend hours alone in his bedroom rocking back and forth by the window while staring out into space. He was socially awkward, and found it difficult to engage with people, unless encouraged into his favourite subjects of aircraft and aerospace. He could be fantastically focused when he wanted to be. Working in his uncle's greengrocer shop he would carefully stack the apples, oranges and other fruits in the window display so they were geometrically and symmetrically perfect. Beautiful in fact. A mathematical marvel in fruit. So protective would he be of his creation that he would refuse to allow any customers the pleasure to buy them and have his artwork spoiled – much to the displeasure of his uncle.

Kitty however, was Gerald's buffer – his interface to the world. She allowed him to interpret the world in a more socially acceptable way. Kitty was born into a large but poor Catholic family in 1920s Ireland, in a small terraced house in Tipperary, where she was raised with nine brothers and sisters.

They were deprived but hard-working and proud. She was expected to polish her brothers' and sisters' shoes each night and line them up on the narrow stairs, ready for the next morning. That, and find a husband. As the eldest, she was destined to be the first to move to England on her quest. After spotting and then 'accidentally' meeting Gerald at a church dance, they soon became inseparable and married in what some people outside of the Catholic community might have called haste. Despite the wagging tongues of the parish, there was no shotgun element to Gerald and Kitty's matrimony, and contrary to expectations, they remained completely dedicated to each other for the next sixty-five years.

Naturally deferential but something of a social climber, Kitty became an expert at translating the peculiar way in which Gerald expressed himself. At parties and social gatherings, he would often be seen leaning towards her and, not-so-surreptitiously, whispering in her ear. Kitty would then skilfully introduce a new subject into the conversation, which instantly allowed Gerald to go through the tick-list in his head of points and anecdotes he had relating to the subject. Most people witnessing this behaviour for the first time would stare as it played out. The braver ones might even try and interrupt Gerald in mid-flow. This, of course, was pointless as Gerald would simply stop, stare quizzically, and restart from the top. Kitty's displeasure with the interruption would, of course be made very apparent.

The strange thing is that people eventually became used to the two of them and their ways. Most of their social encounters were either family-based affairs via Gerald's brothers or his sister or through Church gatherings, where his peculiarities were largely accepted. He really didn't stand out that much at that time. Many men returned from the Great War with terrible physical and mental injuries. Missing limbs were a common sight at social events. Shell-shock was a well-known disorder but was left largely untreated, while alcoholism and mental health problems remained unmentioned throughout the parish. As time progressed, more of Kitty's siblings arrived from Ireland, and their social circle expanded, but it was still largely confined to the Church community.

Gerald's passion for engineering, and all things aviation-related eventually paid dividends. He joined the Air Training Corps, where he could immerse himself in his obsession. His attention to detail and powers of focus made him a top student and marked him out early for fighter training. Too young to enter the Battle of Britain, he saw action over England and France, supporting the D-Day landings and the push towards Germany, and then later providing air cover during the migrations in the Middle East. Gerald was a skilled spitfire pilot. He loved the security that he found in the detail and process of the pre-take-off checklist and safety procedures. He enjoyed the sense of oneness with his aircraft. In the air he was free to be whoever he wanted to be. There were no constraints.

Though he was not exactly socially accepted by his Royal Air Force (RAF) compatriots, he was at least respected. When the rest of the squadron drank in the officers mess or one of the local watering holes, Gerald was usually found with his head buried in a technical manual. In battle, however, Gerald was always front and centre. He was calculating and methodical in all his engagements. Never flustered, he would plot his attack with minute precision, either appearing high and out of the sun, strafing enemy bombers with his machine guns, or more unusually, from behind and below.

In the event that an enemy fighter responded to the attack, Gerald could turn his Spitfire faster and more tightly than any other pilot in the squadron, pulling the enormous G-forces to barrel-roll out of the attack. He could pivot the aircraft and its guns against the enemy with such speed that the German pilots were often hit before they knew what was happening. Gerald's skills were recognised with the Distinguished Flying Cross, not to mention his eight confirmed dogfight kills.

By the end of hostilities, Gerald's reputation preceded him. It wasn't uncommon for the maintenance teams to compete to service his aircraft - simply so that they could claim to be part of his latest sortie. His reluctance to accept promotion was not simply down to his desire to stay in the air. He was in fact, terrified of leading men. Give him a complex technical challenge and an oil-stained manual, and he was on expert territory, but to understand and lead a squadron? Understand their emotions? No. Gerald knew his limitations, and he knew never to compromise them.

By the time he was demobbed, Gerald was very well known in flying circles, but it was hard for him to find a pilot's position at the end of the war. The newly formed British Overseas Airways Corporation (BOAC) was the first airline to put a passenger jet into commercial service, and Gerald was eventually able to secure a place to train on their new deHavilland Comet. Graduating top of his class, he was all set up for a successful career as a commercial pilot, a position Kitty was only too happy to share with the other wives and mothers at the weekly Catenian meeting. She was extremely proud of him and very keen to use his newfound position to elevate herself in her social circles. She had certainly come a long way from cleaning shoes in a rundown tenement in Tipperary.

'I just wish he was fucking dead,' hissed Sheena to the other two.

'I'm sick and fucking tired of putting up with his demands. I have had seven years of his bitching and griping, and I'm sick of it. I want him gone. Send him off to meet Mum. Now wouldn't be soon enough.'

Sean and Michael eyed Sheena wryly. They were used to these outbursts. Experience had taught them to hold back and not to engage. Despite their differences, the two brothers each saw a sister they knew very well. Sheena – eldest daughter – apple of Gerald's eye and chief troublemaker. She never made anything easy. Standing five feet three tall, her dominance in this and most situations belied her small stature. Her skin was cooked to a deep ebony from too many foreign holidays, and sat beneath a shock of raven hair that reached down to just above her shoulders. Too dark to be natural, it was a dense mass such that one could neither see her dark brown eyes, nor much of her face from beneath her fringe and the dark tresses that fell down on each side of her head.

Dressed in clothes just a little too large for her, perhaps reflecting a lack of confidence, she cut a sometimes sad figure. In her younger days she had attracted a great deal of male attention. Her Mediterranean good looks were a magnet to would-be lotharios all over the world and she had her pick of the fresh-faced youth at university, at least for the one year she attended. She also had the ability to attract married men - a status she found to be 'variable,' at least until their wives found out. But now, sadly, her lifestyle had not permitted a graceful transition into old age. Too many late nights. Too much red wine. Too many cigarettes and too much of having her own way had seen to that.

'Look, he must be in his final hours now,' said Sean coldly as he checked his watch. 'The doctor said he wouldn't make it past yesterday, so it must be soon.'

Sheena scowled and lit another cigarette. Failing to inhale, the smoke billowed up around her face and through her hair, sliding upwards to settle stickily against the kitchen ceiling.

'Don't you need to be somewhere else?' She said.

Sean ignored her.

'You don't know what it's been like, Sean,' she continued through the smoke. 'He does nothing but make countless demands all day and night. Wanting this, wanting that. I have been run off my feet seeing to his needs. No one else helps.

7

None of you are ever here. It's just me. Just me for the last seven fucking years, and I've had enough.'

As much as Gerald doted on Sheena, the feeling wasn't reciprocated. She had spent much of her life getting into one difficult situation after another, then later running to her dad for help. School expulsions, love-struck boyfriends, jealous girlfriends, teenage pregnancy, and abortions were all quietly and efficiently dealt with by her father. After dropping out of university, she rushed headlong into a hasty marriage only to be followed by a not unexpected messy divorce some months later. Each time, Gerald was there to clear up the debris. Strangely though, he never appeared to help his other children in the same way. Even the youngest, Louise, never received the same special treatment. It might have been because he saw something of himself in Sheena. Perhaps her emotionally-driven lifestyle resonated against his unemotional demeanour. It was hard to tell the reason for their special connection. Interestingly, Kitty and the other four children seemed to go along with this arrangement without comment or complaint. It was woven into the fabric of the family. There was an unspoken expectation that Sheena always came first in Gerald's eyes. What Sheena wanted, Sheena got. And as far as Sheena was concerned, today was going to be no different.

Having run into financial difficulties while living in Leeds, Sheena, under the pretence of, 'I'm going to look after Dad now,' chose to move in with her father soon after Kitty had died. Her version of 'looking after' was pretty light-weight, but she certainly took advantage of the rent-free accommodation and the extensive free time her new role afforded her. Ok, she made sure Gerald ate three meals a day, albeit ones requiring only a few minutes in the microwave. She would run errands and shop for extra groceries for him – as long as he provided the cash. However, as Gerald grew older, his need for care also grew. He developed nasty ulcerous sores on his legs and Sheena didn't want to be involved in the messy business of treating and dressing them, so a rotating regime of nurses was recruited. Naturally, Sheena saw an opportunity, and tried, unsuccessfully, to broaden the nurses' remit to accommodate more of Gerald's needs. As Gerald aged further, however, Sheena's responsibilities expanded unavoidably, and she began to feel increasingly pressured. She hadn't signed up for this, but she realised that she had painted herself into a corner. Even though her brothers and sister would help out where and when they could, they were either too unreliable or lived too far away to provide anything meaningful. So there appeared to be only one way out. And today, Sheena was going to make sure it happened.

Standing around the table in the small kitchen of the mock-Georgian semi, Michael shuffled awkwardly on his feet and tried to avoid eye contact while Sean looked straight at his sister.

Sean, the third eldest of the five children and middle brother, wasn't about to pander to Sheena's latest outburst, nor was he prepared to believe a word that she said. He had known her far too long to let her get away with that. It was better, perhaps, to allow her to let off steam and then gradually persuade her around to his way of thinking. Chip away at her. Wear her down gradually. Relentless, that was his way. She was an ally he could always make use of, but best not to let her know.

With pale, thinning hair, parted in the middle and left long as would a faded 1970's rock-star, Sean showed all of his fifty-eight years. Having survived alcoholism and then heroin addiction in his youth, he was now far from a picture of health. And though he continued to attend the AA meetings regularly and swore he had not touched a drop nor chased a dragon in many

9

years, his stooped demeanour and persistent cough made him look old before his time.

But to see Sean as weak was a mistake that many people had made. For beneath that pale, dour and rather vulnerable-looking exterior lurked a steely character. A chartered surveyor by trade, Sean found that his job gave him access to many people on many different levels which, under the guise of 'client visits', allowed him to supply Grade-A narcotics to those in the city that wanted them. Sean had been supplementing his income for years and had developed a widespread reputation for being able to provide the best quality gear at very short notice, especially for his VIP clients. Capable of unspeakable acts of ruthlessness and manipulation, Sean was not one to be messed with. Sheena and Michael had also discovered, first-hand, Sean's ability to close down a situation quickly and brutally when he saw fit.

'Oh yes. Of course. You have been waiting on him hand and foot for seven years,' he repeated with more than a hint of sarcasm. 'You must be exhausted... It must be at least three weeks since your last holiday'.

Sheena whipped her head around towards Sean. She pulled her lips back over her teeth, ready to lash out, thought better of it, and re-directed her anger into dragging hard at her cigarette.

'Well, what are we going to do?' She said insistently. 'He's still upstairs, rasping away.'

'Sheena!' exclaimed Michael, 'Please have a little respect for Dad. You of all people should feel something... something... more...'

Michael's words trailed off as Sheena's volcanic stare ground into Michael's train of thought. He looked up, stalled, and then tried to continue.

'More,' he continued weakly.

Visibly flustered simply by Sheena's presence, Michael

failed to find his thread. He stopped, looked apologetically down at the floor, and retreated back into his shell.

Michael. Eldest son. Filled to overflowing with parental expectations. Sadly, always destined to fall short. Disappointment was etched on his face from years of trying to live up to his parent's standards. He'd had it quite tough as a child. As Catholic as they were, Kitty and Gerald weren't really prepared for a new addition. While Kitty loved the idea of having a baby she tended to view children as something of a fashion accessory. Even though she had nine younger siblings, the singular hard work of looking after a newborn child had largely evaded her. Michael's arrival was a big surprise, and at first she struggled to cope.

Michael was a smart but slightly peculiar child. Like his father, he sometimes found it difficult to relate to other people. But Kitty and Gerald never recognised his introspective and artistic nature. Often they tried to show him off, get him out of his shell, and parade him for their friends and family, which only made things worse. Over the years, they heaped increasing amounts of pressure upon him. They wanted him to reflect well on them in the community. This meant he was expected to excel at everything. Which of course he could never do. So he was doomed. He did pretty well at school, but was not a sociable child. He had a few friends, but even those relationships were mostly temporary, lasting no more than a few months each time. He enjoyed drawing and art and eventually developed a talent for architecture. Family pressure led him to join a busy local practice, where he eventually rose to become Junior Partner.

Marrying Megan in haste provided a welcome escape from his stifling parents, but it was also a serious mistake. Having four children in as many years was never going to bring Michael out of his self-obsessed shell. He found it difficult to connect with his kids, and they found it increasingly difficult to relate to him. After only a short time, he gave up, but they also pretty much gave up on him. This may have been suitable for all of them at the time, but it sowed the seeds for dysfunctionality and repressed animosity.

A strange combination of insularity and sensitivity, combined with a rather selfish streak, led Michael to explore some of the more esoteric, cult-like religions. This was the death knell for his career and his marriage. Rather than changing nappies and feeding his children, he preferred to spend his time at religious retreats and communes, searching for meaning. Much of that meaning was found, temporarily at least, in the arms of other faith-seekers, oddballs and hangers on. He grew a long, straggly beard and began to walk barefoot everywhere. For a while he sported a battered straw hat atop a worn t-shirt and faded cut-down jeans. His behaviour became more and more eccentric and he was quietly 'let go' from his job. With nowhere else to go, he moved into the garage of the family home, living like a strange semi-detached guru figure in his own personal wilderness. In retrospect it was probably a cry for help. Probably an undiagnosed nervous breakdown. But given that Michael's natural behaviour was difficult to understand at the best of times, a few steps further down that route came as no surprise to anyone.

The inevitable divorce from Megan failed to give Michael the freedom he hoped for. He still had responsibilities. But he had an answer for his problems. Avoid them. He was largely absent for the upbringing of his four kids. He missed all birthdays and anniversaries. School open-days were a one-parent affair, and family holidays were things other kids enjoyed. Megan did her very best to hold down part-time jobs and a full-time household with no support from Michael. Inevitably the kids suffered. Not in the classic deprived and abandoned way but in a more subtle 'absence of guidance'. Even as infants they were left to their own devices. They were allowed to do whatever they wanted. And that they did. School absenteeism, drugs, brushes with the law, and the regular intervention of

Social Services all featured. Most parents would have been shocked by some of their behaviour, but while Megan did her best to cope, Michael refused to acknowledge anything. His head stayed firmly buried in the sand.

Deeply tanned from his regular naturist pursuits, Michael was extremely slim, skinny even, borderline undernourished, but probably more from choice than circumstance. Vain, bouffantly maned, with a once dark but now greying shock of proudly worn hair, one could see his similarities to his father. His large Romanesque nose sat beneath his soft blue eyes and tight cheekbones. Michael was very concerned about his appearance, or perhaps more accurately, the effect his appearance had upon others. Especially the opposite sex. And although he appeared not to have the funds to dress exactly how he wished, he made a very respectable, if slightly effeminate effort with what he did have.

Today he was wearing tight-fitting 70's style slacks and a body-sculpted vertically multi-coloured striped shirt, open well down on the neck revealing a little bling and a carefully tanned torso. The cuffs of his shirt were turned up enough to reveal a variety of leather, cotton and metal wristbands on one arm hinting at his hippie past, and a cheap plastic watch on the other.

As the eldest brother, Michael always felt as though he should take the lead on matters, especially like this. But he almost always failed. Not having the ferocity of Sheena, or the cunning and guile of Sean, Michael always found himself outplayed. Nonetheless, he saw himself as the natural heir to Gerald's crown... He, of course, would make the best use of his parents legacy, wouldn't he? He had the best credentials to administer the estate, did he not? As a respected architect, he was honest, truthful, reliable and trustworthy. No, surely he was the most deserving and righteous of his siblings. He must be. He was the eldest.

Unfortunately, Michael's expectations were not shared

with Sean and Sheena, who, for the most part, viewed him with undiminished disdain. While Sean kept this to himself, Sheena could never contain it. They certainly did not see him as the heir apparent to their father's throne. They didn't think he deserved any special benefit or treatment. In fact, if they could cut him out completely, all the better.

'How about we go upstairs and see how he is getting on,' Sean suggested, hoping to avoid witnessing another mauling.

'What? And just stand by as he twitches and gasps... and clings on even longer?' Sheena retorted.

'He is still your father, Sheena,' said Michael. 'What will you feel when he's gone? Won't you be sad? Won't you regret anything?'

Ignoring him, Sheena took a final drag on her cigarette before stubbing it out in the overflowing ashtray. She marched out of the kitchen followed by a swirl of acrid, blue smoke. The trick walked through the hallway and past the living-room before heading upstairs. Dark rectangles where pictures and paintings had once hung against the hallway walls, were etched into the now-faded wallpaper. Stubborn depressions now resided in the living-room carpet where the furniture once stood. Echoes of a sideboard, a table, even two sofa's and perhaps an occasional chair in the bay window were now all gone. Sitting awkwardly in their place stood three white plastic garden chairs, barely facing one another.

The trio made their way up the stairs and into the master bedroom where they stood awkwardly around the bed. Gerald had almost no profile under the sheets. He seemed to be melting into the very fabric of the bed. He gradually opened his eyes and slowly looked up to see them looking down upon him.

'How are you feeling, Dad?' asked Michael tentatively.

Gerald's eyes swivelled towards his eldest son, focusing somewhere between the three of them while his breath condensed on the clear plastic oxygen mask covering his nose and mouth.

'Mmmmmuunnnnnnnuufff,' he said.

'Oh, for fuck's sake,' moaned Sheena.

'Wait, wait', urged Michael.

'Mmmmmmnnnnnuuurff,' continued Gerald.

'He's trying to say something.'

'Crrraaeennnnmmmmmfff,' Gerald mumbled, his arm jerking below the bedsheets.

A long bony hand emerged from beneath the sheets and extended an even longer bony finger towards the three of them.

'What?' asked Sheena.

His finger pointed directly at Sheena and curled inwards, beckoning her closer to him.

'He wants you,' Michael whispered, still shocked by his father's wizened face and arm.

Sheena stood rigid, and for once, she didn't reply. She moved not a muscle.

'Sheena!' Michael and Sean exclaimed together. 'Look...' Michael twisted his head towards his father.

'I think he wants to say something to you... Go On.'

Sheena's trance broke and she moved around the bed and sat closer to her father. Gerald wrapped his hand around her arm and used it to pull himself upwards towards her. At the same time, and with an enormous effort, he removed the oxygen mask from his face. The mixture of oxygen and water hissed out of the plastic container around his head, leaving thin trails of moisture on his forehead.

Sheena moved forward.

'I can't hear anything,' complained Michael.

'Shhh!' snapped Sean, trying hard to listen.

Gerald's lips moved imperceptibly.

'What's he saying? I can't hear what he's saying,' whined Michael.

'For Christ's sake... I'm trying to listen,' hissed Sean.

After what seemed like an age, Gerald's lips stopped moving. The tension in his body slowly left him, his shoulders relaxed and he slumped back, exhausted, onto the bed.

Sheena sat rigidly next to him, staring ahead at the bedroom wall.

'What did he say?' pressed Sean.

Sheena's face was ashen. Her eyes continued to stare blankly straight ahead, with her mouth agape, and her hands gripping the bedsheets as though clinging onto a spinning room.

'Are you alright?' asked Michael. 'You look terrible.'

Sheena did not respond.

'What did he say, Sheena?' Sean was almost shouting now, but it was of no use.

Slowly, she slid down off the edge of the bed and onto the carpeted floor in a motion that involved no bodily effort but just the effect of gravity. She slumped down like some unwanted doll on a child's bedroom floor.

'Oh my God, Sheena... Are you alright?'

Sean fell to his knees over Sheena's limp form.

'Get some water,' Sean ordered... Michael didn't move.

'Michael... Water...'

Michael was silent. He was no longer looking at Sheena or Sean. His eyes were fixed on the body of their father, now lying dead on the bed in front of them.

The beige Toyota Prius glided slowly around the corner of the close and drew carefully to a halt. David opened the car door, carefully exited the vehicle and, blissfully unaware of the events unfolding inside, headed towards the family home. It wasn't the elegantly located, detached, double staircase, six-bedroom house of his youth, but a rather smaller, faux Georgian terrace to which Kitty and Gerald had downsized after the children had left.

Dressed casually smart, perhaps in a style just a little too young for him, David was dapper and elegant in a 'fifties-schoolboy-on-vacation' kind of way. His checkered country jacket was nicely set off with brown corduroy trousers and a cravat under a plaid shirt. Where one would normally expect to see country brogues, David sported red converse trainers, ankle high with red and yellow striped socks atop. Angular in feature, and perhaps over-slim from 20 years of strict veganism, he cut a metropolitan figure. His hair was swept back elegantly over his greying temples while his permanently attached glasses gave him a bird-like, academic look.

David was your typical middle child. Neither was he at the forefront of his parents' attentions, nor the baby of the family either – so he was never afforded any special privileges. A ponderous child from the outset, he looked at life objectively and unemotionally. At school he would often be found in the Maths room, poring over textbooks and absorbing number theory and gaming strategies. At the age of ten, his well-organised poker school had to be disbanded not just because he was fleecing his schoolmates, but because his teachers owed him so much money.

Unexpectedly, David possessed considerable skills with the opposite sex too. While not conventionally good-looking, he was very well-read and could be erudite, funny and very charming. He had that rare ability to make whoever he was talking to feel like they were the only person in the room. All of this was completely calculated of course. He assessed every person he met or wanted to meet in terms of a poker player. If you could be of any benefit to David, you became the centre of his world, at least for a short time. He would be interesting, knowledgeable, flirtatious, teasing and exciting. These traits did not come naturally to him. Each was a learned activity. He practised like a possessed magician in the mirror to hone his craft, repeating key phrases and gestures until they were perfected. And over the years he became an expert. If he chose to, he was able to switch on his cool charm effortlessly and draw you into his exciting world. If he assessed that there was no benefit to be gained from your acquaintance, he wouldn't acknowledge your existence.

Anyone meeting David for the first time would, from his measured movements and his careful pondering of each word he spoke, perhaps not guess that he was an accountant. His refinement and precision of words and actions allowed him to observe and analyse all around him and predict the probabilities of upcoming events, and their exact chances of occurring. This aptitude for the penetrating analysis of both numbers and people made him every casino owner's nightmare. He had grown into an expert card counter and roulette data miner. He had been escorted many times out from gaming clubs by burly club 'assistants', for balancing the odds a little too much in his favour. Now an expert poker player, David was very much in demand by underworld figures to play on their behalf in high-stakes games. Such was his reputation, that he regularly travelled to pit himself against the very best in the world. So far, he had managed to avoid any misunderstandings, but after a couple of close calls, he recognised that his luck was beginning to run thin.

All this glamour and intrigue was, however, just an entertaining side-line in his increasingly complex web of financial illusion. David's main thrill was to day-trade stocks and shares. He loved the excitement and intrigue of the pre-investment analysis and discovery, as well as the hard-nosed, rough-and-tumble of day trading. His phenomenal intellect was able to model his entire portfolio position in his head on a moment-by-moment basis – reading the market fluctuations as a series of waves and eddy currents moving through his brain. Imperceptible adjustments in the FTSE, Hang-Seng and the Dow Jones were somehow streamed broadband-like into his mental model and sorted, impacted, concluded and closed with phenomenal speed. He was able to multi-task his positions with the combined power of a quantum computer memory merged with an Einstein-like intellect.

Now all of this would have been admirable had it not been for David's one major failing. Of course, he preferred to engage in the more exciting pursuits rather than completing his clients' tax returns or maintaining their accounts. Who wouldn't? But that wasn't it. No, David's failing was that he never ever risked his own money on anything. Every aspect of his extra-curricular life was carried out exclusively with other people's money, whether they knew it or not. Preferably, if they did not, and this made life very complicated for him. While his cool, calculating mathematical intellect was able to model his client's position, his angles were deteriorating rapidly. A mixture of currency fluctuations combined with some extremely risky investments had put his financial empire under a considerable strain, and while he would show no physical indication of the pressure, it was chewing him up inside.

David made his way to the front door of the family home only to find it off the latch and slightly ajar. He pushed gently at the door to reveal the hallway of the house. He stepped in.

'Hello?' he called.

Nothing.

'Hello,' he repeated. 'Anyone home?'

Silence.

'Strange?' he thought. Surely there must be someone home. The call he had received was urgent. Dad wasn't expected to last much longer.

David looked into the kitchen and the lounge/dining-room and, finding nothing, he moved upstairs. As he entered the bedroom he encountered a scene of disarray.

Sheena sat in a crumpled mess on the floor, with her legs tucked beneath her. She faced the bedroom wall with a thousand-yard stare etched on her now pale and drawn face, an unlit cigarette lying on her lap. Sean stood by the window leaning forward with each arm outstretched on the riser of the window frame; he also with a burning cigarette hanging limply from his lips. Michael was upright, but with his legs curled up, foetus-like, against the wall, gently rocking forward and back. Gerald's body, was so small that David could hardly see it under the bedsheet. Gerald lay face up, eyes and mouth open, mummy-like.

Sean looked up. 'He's gone...'

'Oh, shit. Shit. Shit. Shit.' cursed David, 'I didn't get a chance to say goodbye... Shit. How long?'

'Minutes.'

'Shit. I should have left earlier. Damn it. Why didn't you phone me earlier?'

'How were we to know? We called as soon as we could,' replied Sean.

David looked around the room again, looked at Sheena and raised his eyebrows quizzically towards Sean.

'Dad said something to Sheena before he died. Michael is just overreacting as usual,' replied Sean.

'What?'

'Dad whispered something before he died'

'What was it?'

'God only knows. But just look at her.'

David moved over to place his hand on his sister's shoulder. She didn't move. Instead she raised her palm rapidly towards her brother to deter any physical contact.

David backed off towards the doorway again, trying to comprehend what had just happened.

'He's gone. He's really gone. What are we going to do?' asked Michael, mournfully.

The doorbell rang, piercing the silence. Just once. All that was necessary. David made his way downstairs to let his younger sister Louise in. Louise – the youngest of the siblings and the baby of the family. Pretty, petite and looking younger than her 45 years. Her blonde wavy hair fell down her back, supported by a small but curvaceous frame. She was very much her mother's daughter, but in a more modern manner. Dressed in a tight-fitting skirt, heels and a silk blouse, with her face immaculately made-up, she looked classical and elegant in a sophisticated and European way.

'Louise,' cried David with joy in his voice. 'Thank goodness you're here.'

Louise smiled expertly and moved past her brother.

'How is he? He's Ok isn't he? He is still with us, Yes?' she said.

She hurried through the hallway glancing upstairs as she did so.

'He is Ok? Does he need anything? Who's looking after him?' she continued.

So many questions. Louise, as with most of the others, liked to get her own way. She was another one that wasn't prone to compromise. A sister to Sheena, yes, and closer to David than she realised, but a much different model than her elder sister. Louise truly loved her father and wanted the very best for him, even now, in his last days. But no matter how much she tried, she felt she could never make the others feel the same way as she did. Her attempts at kindness always seemed to fall on barren ground, and she could never understand why.

Always the baby, she was spoiled rotten as a child. She had the benefit of coming into this world just as Gerald's flying career was reaching its zenith. He was flying 747's long-haul to Australia, Indonesia and the Middle East and was a candidate to pilot Concorde. The family was able to move to a large and imposing house in the most expensive part of town. As a baby, she was loved by David, Sean and the many older cousins in the extended family. Never really wanting for anything, Louise enjoyed an idyllic upbringing. She used to spend hours playing with the family and cousins in the garden and at the local park.

Always surrounded by friends and relatives, she never really had to fend for herself. Always looked after, she never had to fight her own battles. Someone else was usually there to do it for her.

As a child, Louise was always excited to see Gerald for several reasons. Firstly, he would bring home wonderful presents from his trips away which included exotic dolls from the Far East or beautifully bound picture books with fabulous inlays and ribbons. She especially loved the fancy chocolates that he brought from his European trips. But secondly, because it was only when Gerald arrived home that Louise was permitted to play with her toys. Until he crossed the threshold she wasn't allowed to open her toy box to play with any of her many dolls or games. She was allowed to read or play in the garden during the summer, but her toys were only ever allowed out whenever Gerald was home which was strange because Gerald and Kitty rarely actually played with Louise or any of her toys. That was generally left to David whose patience and attention to detail were legendary, or Sean, who would rather spend time teasing her. Like many parents of their era, Gerald and Kitty were more involved in their own lives than that of their children. It was not so much that children should be 'seen and not heard', but more to be a socially respectable addition to a family that wanted to get on. In the main, the older siblings were expected to look after the younger ones, feed and clean them, keep them entertained, and make sure they were presentable when the family was on show.

Louise, despite the regular estrangement from her favourite toys, developed an astonishing lack of patience. Her temper could be explosive if she ever felt she was being denied some-thing unnecessarily or that she had to wait for something when it was promised. Admittedly this eruptive nature was worse as a teenager when tantrums were a common feature in the household. As an adult, however, she had learned to control her frustrations. She had found that it was far more effective to be steely and determined and use her guile and sexuality to get what she wanted.

Sadly though, this expertise had taken Louise some time to develop. After several short-lived romances in her teens, she met Dan, a man ten years her senior, who became the love of her life. She threw herself into the relationship and dedicated herself to him. But for Dan, Louise was just a first-class opportunity to exploit the family for his own benefit. Grooming her to wear more revealing outfits, he encouraged her to be more flirtatious. He liked to see how far he could get her to go. Louise, in wanting to please her man, was prepared to do almost anything for him.

Dan and Louise moved into a basement flat together while she was just out of her teenage years, funded exclusively by Gerald and Kitty, of course. But after only a few months of heavy partying, experimentation with all manner of alcohol, sex and drugs, and after several monumental arguments, Dan left. Louise was heartbroken and vowed never to allow herself to trust one person so deeply in future. Gerald and Kitty were there to pick up the pieces, and before long Louise moved back into the family home, while Dan disappeared with several thousand pounds of cash and jewellery, never to be seen again. Dan's betrayal shaped Louise's relationships for the rest of her life. She was never again able to extend the same level of trust to anyone else. She became harder and more sceptical of people's motives.

'Is he upstairs?' asked Louise quietly.

'Louise...' said David.

'I'll just run up and see him...'

'Louise...' David placed his arms on his sister's shoulder and looked hard into her eyes.

'He's dead.'

Suddenly, a swelling, wailing animal sound began to emanate from the top floor and down the stairs. The wail was a kind of blood-curdling scream that starts low, quietly and insistently and rises in pitch, volume and intensity until it filled every part of your being. David and Louise looked at each other with stunned stares, as if they were being eviscerated. They rushed upstairs together to find Sheena and Sean head-to-head in the middle of the room, grappling with one another. Sheena, screaming a banshee wail at the top of her voice that would burst eardrums, her head flailing as if it was separated from her body. Breaking free, she grabbed a porcelain statue of Mary, Mother of Christ and hurled it through the window. Before anyone could react, she grabbed the crucifix from above Gerald's bed and threw herself headlong at the opposite bedroom wall, using the cross like a knife, stabbing her way into the wall while wailing and punching at the plasterwork.

Louise and David had witnessed many tantrums from Sheena before, but this was something else. She was completely out of control. Michael continued to rock back and forth in the corner while Sean, his face bloodied from Sheena's long, sharp nails, tried once again to restrain his elder sister. In the end it took all three of them to subdue her. Her face was bruised and her nails were split and broken. Hair, makeup, blood, and saliva were strewn across her face, and her breathing was short and laboured. Gasping for lungfuls of air, a picture of pained anger lay across her face.

'Call the doctor...' ordered David.

'Who for?' replied Sean, looking at both Gerald and Sheena.

'Ok, Ok. Don't worry. I'll do it,' said David, and he headed back downstairs to make the call.

'I'll help,' added Louise, seizing the opportunity to distance herself from the madness.

Sean waited a few moments for the pair to leave. He looked out of the window, then cautiously sat the now calmer Sheena down in the chair next to the broken window. Gently, he brushed her hair from her face and pulled his chair closer so he could look into her eyes, and, trying hard not to grit his teeth, he quietly asked.

'Sheena... What... Did... He... Say?'

The priest cycled in an unsteady fashion up the hill and towards the close. Beads of sweat ran off his prematurely balding head, down his brow, over his puffing cheeks and down his neck. Every now and then his wire-framed glasses slipped awkwardly down his nose as he pedalled, and he had to reach up to push them back onto the bridge of his nose. His heavy black jacket combined with his dark trousers, solid black boots and thick socks were probably not the best clothing to cycle in, given the hot weather, his padded frame, and general lack of fitness. Nonetheless he pushed on upwards towards his goal.

Connor had been the local priest for more years than he cared to remember. Raised in Ireland, he accepted his calling at an early age after a childhood immersed in the Catholic faith. Having commenced his training in his teens as a monk, Brother Connor, as he was always known, had an extra special calling; an extra enthusiasm for the faith and all its rituals and traditions. Even before he was ordained into the clergy, he was an enthusiastic supporter. He loved the pomp and ceremony of the Catholic Mass, the weight and feel of the vestments, the smell of the incense, and the protocols for sharing Holy Communion. He enjoyed the day-to-day practices and procedures his position asked of him as well as the preciseness and minutiae of his role. But above all, he loved two things more than any others. Firstly, the performance of the Catholic Mass, which he took as his regular opportunity to perform 'on stage' in front of his rapturous audience. And secondly, the frequent and personal confessionals he undertook with most of the parish. He couldn't help immersing himself in the mixture of gossip, tittle-tattle and embarrassing revelations they revealed. He loved discovering who had done what to whom and what they had done back. He took great delight in knowing all the intimate details in families, between couples and groups of friends. He took extra delight in trying to subtly manipulate the outcomes within his congregation. The drama was always so exciting for him. He found the details of knowing everyone's business gave him a great sense of power.

Connor cycled around the corner and into the close. Leaning his bicycle against the hedge, he rang the doorbell. Standing and waiting, he began to bite his nails. His fingernails were bitten down to the quick and were ingrained with dirt. He shuffled from one foot to the other as he waited, and he adjusted himself in his underpants when he thought no one was looking.

'Hello, can I help you?' asked Louise as she answered the door.

'Brother Connor, Louise,' replied the priest.

'Oh, right,' replied Louise, surprised that he still knew who she was, 'How can I help you?'

'Your father? Gerald? I understand that things are moving on...' His words tailed off in implication. 'I was asked to administer the last sacrament?'

'Oh. Who told you that?'

'The Lord moves in mysterious ways,' he said as he made his way into the house.

Michael, Sheena, Sean and David were sitting awkwardly in the lounge. Sheena and Sean were both smoking again. Michael flinched slightly as the priest entered, while David chose to find something very important on his mobile phone.

'What's he doing here?' said Sheena coldly.

'He's come to perform the Last Rights,' replied Louise.

'Well he's too late. He's dead,' replied Sheena.

'Dead?' Connor looked perplexed.

'Yeah. You're too late once again Father. He died twenty minutes ago,' continued Sheena.

'Oh my word, I am so sorry. It may not be too late. Can I see him?'

'I think it is... But if you really must,' said Louise.

Louise took Brother Connor up to the bedroom. There were still very obvious signs of the earlier struggle – splatters of blood on the carpet and walls, water soaking into the carpet, porcelain remains under the newly broken window and more plastic chairs askew in the fireplace.

'Tsk...' tutted the priest as he put down his things.

Gerald's eyes and mouth were still wide open. The priest leaned over to him, closed them and opened his small black bag.

'It is permissible to apply the Sacrament of Anointing after death,' he explained.' As long as it is only a short while.'

'Did he want you to do this?' quizzed Louise

'Oh yes, very much,' replied the priest, 'It's what he wanted. He made his wishes very clear.'

'Oh, ok,' said Louise.

The priest took out his vestments and stole and placed them on the bed. He then took out a Bible, his aspergillum and a small bottle of holy water. He placed them all carefully on a cloth on the bed in front of Gerald's lifeless body. He slowly dressed in the vestments and stole, then unscrewed the bottle of holy water and poured a little into the aspergillum. He then carefully replaced the screw top.

Once prepared, he began to perform the Last Rites.

Louise could hardly bear to watch.

No sooner had she made a step towards the door than Sheena came hurtling into the room, screaming and flailing at the priest. Before he knew what was happening or was able to react, she had grabbed him by the back of his holy garments and with powers beyond all imagination, and like a creature possessed, pulled him backwards out of the room and down the stairs. She acted with such violent force and speed that he seemed not even to touch the floor as she forcibly ejected him from the house and onto the pavement outside.

'And you can keep your Last Rites to yourself, you lying fucking hypocrite,' she screamed.

The others rushed after them and followed them out onto the street. Louise couldn't help but notice that both Michael and Sean were grinning from ear to ear and that they had made no attempt whatsoever to stop their sister.

2

FUNERAL

Gerald's casket was constructed from a beautiful solid oak and furnished with gold-plated handles, each of them buffed to a super high shine. All the elements of Catholic ostentation were on display here. This was the last opportunity to demonstrate wealth and power, so no expense was spared. If you couldn't fill your relatives with admiration now, then it was never going to happen. If this rich man were to get into Heaven, this might be his best, albeit last, opportunity, without the necessary assistance of camels and needles.

The coffin was covered from head to foot with beautiful flowers. 'GRANDAD', read the largest and most obvious of all the wreaths. Whether those words and flowers were a true reflection of the grandchildren's love and respect or more of a manifestation of the struggle for control of the casket real-estate, it was hard to tell. However, some kind of accord must have broken out to permit the flower arrangement in its pride of place.

The lead undertaker opened the door of the hearse and stepped out. Dressed in a sharp black suit with a subtly vertically striped waistcoat, tipped off with a neat black tie against a crisp white wing-collared shirt, she was the perfect example of the 'Caring Lady Funeral Director' the advertising had promised. She put on her top hat and strode, Dickensian-like, towards the front door, with her cane clacking against the road as she made her way up the driveway.

Inside, there was a lot going on. Various parts of the family were scattered across different rooms in the house. Each of Gerald's children seemed to have their own group of disciples around them. The call had gone out to the many cousins, aunts and uncles across the country, and the response had been incredible. Dozens had descended from all corners of the world to attend. Sheena's camp was in the kitchen, smoking hard and drinking strong coffee. Michael's coterie had found space in the dining room and were eying up what paintings and furniture remained. Sean's crowd were in the garden, vying with Sheena's sect who straddled the threshold of the kitchen door. While the two groups had strong coffee in common, Sean's friend's taste in nicotine was much more of the spicy, roll-up variety. David and his latest girlfriend were trying hard to keep up appearances and gather followers by flitting from one group to the next. Louise was upstairs in her old bedroom with her immediate family and a couple of close friends trying to summon the courage to face the growing crowd downstairs.

Gerald's youngest brother, his wife and two of his three kids were standing in the living room. His sister, Libby and her seven children were busy drinking tea and trying to avoid all the smoke in the kitchen. Richard, Gerald's eldest brother was in the dining room with his wife Jeanie and their four grown-up children. The hallway was full of various cousins, second cousins, second cousins once removed, twice removed, and maybe even three times removed. Plus there was a wide variety of friends from the airline and from the Church. Like most large Catholic families, they usually only got together for chris-tenings, marriages and funerals. Funerals were their favourite. Funerals always presented the greatest risk for incident and the greatest potential for drama.

By some coincidence, while preparing the various groups to leave the house, the five siblings found themselves alone, together, in the living room. Together for the first time since it had all happened only three weeks before. In all the turmoil since Gerald's death, they hadn't really been alone together. Even the funeral arrangements were largely a tick-box exercise that Sheena and Sean had executed as quickly as possible.

As David entered the living room, they each found themselves together, alone and without any backup. A silence fell upon the room. Here they were, together. This was it. No one said a word. None of them even made eye contact. Perhaps there was nothing to say. Perhaps they were each afraid. Instead, the five just stared collectively into the space in front of them - momentarily imprisoned in their own thoughts. The awkwardness hung uncomfortably in the air as though each of them was expecting one of the others to announce something, but it was mixed with the type of uneasiness usually reserved for strangers in a crowded lift. Michael and Sean each clung onto the back of the last remaining sofa in the house. Sheena, who was dressed head-to-toe in black, stood still in front of the fireplace. Louise and David, standing by the window, failed to gain the support they were looking for from each other's expressions. So the awkward silence prevailed. And then prevailed some more.

The sorcery was broken by the loud 'rappetty-rap-rap' of the undertaker's silver-topped cane on the front door.

'I'll get it,' said Sean, with more than a hint of relief in his voice.

'I'll gather my lot,' Louise interjected, almost cutting Sean off.

'Me too,' said David quickly.

'Ok, let's go,' said Michael.

Sheena walked out, leaving the room empty and still silent.

'No, No, No. That's not what I wanted,' complained Sheena as the funeral cars headed towards the church.

'We each have to drop one of these into the grave. You know...once the priest has finished doing his stuff. We have to show... show, show everyone how we're... special'

She waved a small bouquet of red roses.

'Special?' scoffed Sean. 'Special how?'

Sheena and Sean travelled together in one car, while the others took to the remaining cars.

'Don't you get it?' continued Sheena. 'This isn't Dad's funeral. This is our funeral. This is about us and how everyone sees us. We have to maintain the right image. We have to make sure we do the right things in the right way. It's how Dad would have wanted it.'

'You mean we have to do things in a way that makes you look good,' said Sean.

Sheena just looked at her brother with disdain, and added nothing.

'Is that why you're dressed the way you are?' asked Sean.

'What do you mean?' said Sheena.

Well, it's just possible that people could get the wrong idea.'

'What do you mean? What idea?'

'When did you and Dad get married?' Sean's lips curled up a little. 'Are you his widow, now?'

'Oh fuck off, Sean. You know as well as I do that what Dad and I had was special. And without Mum here. Well, it just falls to me, doesn't it?'

She smoothed down the lapel of her matt black coat.

'There's a part that needs to be played. And anyway, we both know the others aren't really interested.'

'Hmmm,' Sean nodded vaguely.

'What about that scene of yours in the bedroom?' he asked.

'Scene?'

'You know what I'm talking about... Dad said something to

you didn't he, before he...you know. Whatever he said, turned you into stone, ...and yet the next minute you're throwing that priest out into the gutter.'

'Oh that? That was nothing.'

'Really? What did he say?'

'The priest?'

'Yeah. The priest. No, of course not the priest. Dad. What did Dad say?'

'Oh, nothing much, and anyway, it's between him and me. Look, about the teddies. I made sure just our teddies are in Dad's coffin.'

'What? You did what?'

'I made sure that only our teddies are being buried with Dad. But keep quiet. No one else knows. They all think there are five in there with him. But there are only two. Our two.'

Sean really had no interest in what the others thought. To him the teddy-bear arrangement was childish and ridiculous. There had been a huge debate about it. Michael and Louise were particularly insistent. They wanted one each of their favourite childhood toys to be buried with their Dad, but Sean couldn't care less. In the other more practical elements of the funeral, like the coffin design, the flowers, or the order of service, there was very little interest. But the status brought by the teddy bears took on an enormous significance. Sean knew when his sister was being evasive. He'd leave it for now, but he would not forget. He was, however, more interested in managing the overall outcome to his benefit. He played a longer game. He had a plan, but he needed Sheena's help in bringing it to fruition.

'Just yours and mine, eh?' he added, playing along.

'Yes, but don't tell the others.'

'Ok. That's good,' he added, 'But what do you want to do once this charade is over? Have you thought about... you know, Dad's wishes?'

'Oh yes, everything is in place. And we'll prepare the

remembrance packs like we said. That should be enough of a distraction,' said Sheena.

'Excellent. And you're certain everything else is in place?' pushed Sean.

'Certain.'

The column of large black cars drew up as the crowd gathered outside the church. There were friends, extended family, acquaintances, and many members of the local parish attending. They assembled together on the wide gravel driveway, forming large groups and chatting. The occasional daring soul might venture between two groups by crossing no man's land. This was usually done with a flourish and the expectation of an open-armed welcome. All the more humiliating of course, if it was not forthcoming.

St Mary's was a large, traditional church in the centre of town, with huge pillars and buttresses supporting a cavernous roof, capable of holding hundreds of worshippers. Today it would be full. The decoration was extravagant, with large amounts of gold-leaf and mother of pearl adorning much of the vestry and the altar.

Brother Connor was waiting outside to greet the family. He approached Sheena and Sean.

'Hello my dear. So lovely to see you on this sad, sad day.'

'Lovely?' replied Sheena.

'And it's so good of you to bring your husband and children to pay their respects.'

'But I don't have a...' replied Sheena, but it was too late; he had moved on.

Ah, Sean, Michael. Lovely to see you on this sad, sad day,' repeated Brother Connor.

As they shook hands, Brother Connor wrapped his left

34

hand over Sean's right, clasping it in a friendly but self-assured ministerial manner.

'What was all that about?' quizzed Sean. 'He seems way too cheerful.'

'Weird,' said Sheena.

'And he could have cleaned his cassock', added Sean, as the priest passed by.

'Yes, and he doesn't seem to have seen a razor for some time, either,' commented Michael.

As the crowd waited patiently, Gerald's coffin was carried from the hearse into the nave and along the arcade of towering columns, finally positioned just in front of the altar. A picture of a much younger Gerald, in his RAF uniform, was placed upon the coffin, nestled amongst the floral tributes.

The crowd followed the coffin down into the church as a melancholy dirge was played in the background. Sheena and Sean took the lead while the rest of the siblings and their families respectfully moved down the aisle to find their seats. The crowd was reticent to sit at or near the front and avoided the first few rows, innately understanding that they were reserved for close family only. Inevitably, a gap appeared in the seating arrangements. Seeing this, Louise instinctively began to organise the different groups forward so that they were closer to the family.

Black was the colour chosen by most of the mourners. But not all. Some chose to wear brighter colours – Blues, greens, and even one or two purples. Many adhered to this seemingly unwritten rule. Had any mourners asked Gerald, they would have realised that he would have absolutely loved it if they wore any colour but black. Sadly, these wishes hadn't been passed on, and so a sea of dark colours prevailed.

As Brother Connor stepped up into the pulpit, the organ music faded away and the assembly quietened.

'Blessed be the God and Father of our Lord Jesus Christ, the Father of mercies and the God of all consolation, who consoles us in all our affliction,' he began. 'Life is changed, not ended. Death is a passage to a new and fuller life, and ultimately the resurrection and eternal union with God. We are gathered here today to pray for the repose of the soul of our friend, dearly departed Gerry. And it is wonderful to see so many of you here to join together in our remembrance of him.'

'Gerry?' whispered Sean.

'Gerry,' continued Brother Connor, 'was a dedicated Christian, a husband to Lillian and father to Michael, Stella, Sean, Declan and Beau.'

'What?...' said Sean. 'What is he talking about? Who the heck are Lillian, Stella, and Declan?'

'Let us pray,' continued Brother Connor.

'In your hands, Oh Lord, we humbly entrust our brethren. In this life you embraced them with your tender life; deliver them now from every event.'

'This isn't right?' whispered David. 'It's 'deliver them now from every evil. What is he talking about?'

Sheena ignored everything and stared directly ahead, expressionless.

Brother Connor continued. 'We selfishly want to hold on to Gerry. It brings great pain to let go. Living in the resurrection and hope of our Lord Jesus Christ, in the trust of a loving God and in the promise of eternal life, we commit his or her body to its place of rest. We will continue to mourn Gerry, but his laughter will warm the Kingdom of God.'

Moving down off the pulpit and walking around the coffin, Brother Connor began to sprinkle his holy water.

'We will continue to love Gerry, but God will now take care of him. We will continue to carry him in our thoughts, but he will be kept safe in God's hands.'

David and Michael looked across at each other, almost open-mouthed.

As Brother Connor continued, he shook the holy water vigorously over the coffin.

'Receive him in the arms of your mercy, Oh God, into the blessed rest of everlasting peace, and into the glorious company of all your saints.'

Suddenly, there was a high-pitched crack and the top of the aspergillum flew off, hit the floor and rolled across the marble altar.

'Oh my good God,' hissed Sheena. 'Did he just do that on purpose?'

The noise of the lid was followed by the splash of holy water hitting the marble floor and a muted laugh from someone at the back of the church. Brother Connor carried on regardless, ignoring what had just happened, and continued to wave a now empty container around the coffin.

'What kind of a priest is this? Does he have any idea what he is doing?' said David.'

'Good God,' moaned Sean.

'You did explain to him that this was a funeral mass, not a stand-up comedy, didn't you?' asked David.

Brother Connor pressed on.

'We will continue today's Mass by singing hymn number 217 in your Hymn books - How Great Thou Art.'

The congregation rose and, with a stuttering start, after realising that the hymn being played was number 317 not 217, made a reasonable effort to sing – some more enthusiastically than others. By the end of the hymn, Brother Connor had lost none of his concentration or solemnity. He soldiered on through the entire service. By the time the Mass was complete, it had descended into something of a farce, with muted laughter and embarrassed looks between many of the mourners. Things did not improve as the ceremony moved outside to the graveside for the final blessing and the committal.

'Unto Almighty God, we commend the soul of our brother departed,' said Connor. 'We commit his body to the deep; in sure and certain hope of the Resurrection unto eternal life, through our Lord Jesus Christ.'

'To the deep?' David was incredulous. Sheena remained stony-faced, almost physically biting her lip, while Sean, finding the whole thing very amusing, tried to stifle his growing laughter. Louise was embarrassed for everyone.

Finally, the moment came when the siblings were required to come forward and drop their single rose onto the coffin. This was the moment Sheena was waiting for. She grasped her single rose and stepped forward, tears conveniently welling beneath her dark sunglasses, and in a dramatic flourish, dropped the flower into the grave. She beckoned the others forward, and each of the four siblings took their turn to say goodbye. Some more self-consciously than others. Once they had finished, Brother Connor began to clap loudly and enthusiastically while bellowing, 'Well Done. Well Done.'

'Why did we ever choose him?' asked Sean as they walked away.

'I have never been so embarrassed in my entire life,' said Sheena. 'What the hell was all that about? It's not as though he doesn't know all of our names. I think he screwed it up on purpose. What a total embarrassment. Did you hear the people laughing?'

'I've never seen him be so useless. He's never been like this before. Do you think it might have something to do with, you know, what happened?' asked Sean. 'I mean... with what you did?'

'He deserved, it,' replied Sheena, icily. 'If this is his revenge for that, he has no idea who he's messing with.'

'Well, wasn't it you that wanted him for the service?' asked Sean

'No', said Sheena, 'I thought it was you?'

'Didn't you say it was part of Dad's wishes?'

'No, never. I don't remember him saying anything like that. It was you who always insisted we use him.'

'I only agreed to Brother Connor because he's been the family priest for so long,' said Sean. 'Dad knew him quite well, didn't he? Didn't you tell me he'd performed many funeral services before? I distinctly remember you saying that it was one of Dad's wishes.'

'What a total fuck-up that was,' said Sheena as she walked into the restaurant. Her tears were now dried, and her demeanour was largely restored.

'Well, he was trying his best,' said Louise.

'It was a complete embarrassment. We are the laughing-stock of the Parish. I don't know if I'll ever be able to look at any of the Catenians again,' continued Sheena. 'All that people were talking about at the wake, was how Brother Connor made such a mess of the whole thing. And add to that, he has the gall to come and drink our whiskey and eat our food afterwards.'

'Yeah. He didn't seem phased at all. In fact he seemed to be quite enjoying himself,' said Sean.

'Good grief...' said Sheena.

The siblings had gathered at the Little Drummer Boy restaurant after the formalities of the wake had been completed and the guests had had their fill of Gerald's hospitality. Instead of eating the buffet at the wake, Sean and Sheena wanted to get together at the restaurant afterwards to discuss things. Given that they were named as joint executors, the rest of the family wanted to know what was to happen next.

'Is Michael coming?' asked Louise to David.

'I hope so,' replied David. 'We're all supposed to be here, right?'

'Yes, but normally Michael would fuss about the restaurant seating and would want to talk to the chef about the ingredients and all that stuff,' said Louise. 'He didn't say anything back at the hotel about meeting here. Sean, is Michael going to be here?'

Sean looked at Sheena.

'Well I didn't invite him, did you?'

'No, well, we thought it would be better without him,' answered Sheena.

'Really? Why?' asked Louise.

'Well, er, you know how fussy he can be about things, and er, how difficult he can make matters when they don't exactly line up with what he wants. We thought it would be easier at this stage without him.'

'Oh,' said Louise, 'but you will keep him in the picture about things, won't you?'

'Of course,' replied Sean and Sheena in unison.

As they gathered around the table, David took Louise to one side.

'Don't you think that Michael should be here?' he said. 'Things are going to be agreed here, and he needs to know. It doesn't seem right. He should be here. They can't just exclude him.'

'I know,' replied Louise. 'It does feel a bit odd. Let's see what happens. We can always speak to him afterwards.'

Once the meal was finished, during which Sheena drank enthusiastically and David pushed his food around his plate, Sheena opened the discussion.

'I thought it would be good for us to get together here, and for us to let you know what is going to happen next. We have an appointment at the solicitors office next week to read the will. Dad had some very specific instructions that he wished for us to carry out. We need to be there by 3 pm sharp on Tuesday so you know what they are.'

'Which solicitors?' asked Louise.

'What instructions?' added David.

'You know, the family one,' said Sean. 'Taylor, Otley and Snyde. On the High Street.'

'In the meantime,' announced Sheena. 'I will be staying here to make sure all the paperwork is prepared properly.'

'Here?' said Louise.

'I'm sorry, I don't understand,' asked David. 'What instructions? What paperwork? Aren't the solicitors dealing with all of that?'

'Well, yes, but it will just be easier for me if I stay in the hotel suite while things settle down, and then I can be close to deal with things. Dad shared some specific instructions with Sean and I as to what will happen next.'

'Hotel?...Suite?' said Louise.

'Can I see a copy?' asked David

'A copy of what?'

'Dad's specific instructions.'

'Oh, Sean has them, don't you, Sean?'

'Not right here,' said Sean. 'I'll bring them with me when we meet at the solicitor's.'

'But what do they say?' asked David

'Well...things about what happens next. You know, after Dad had passed on.'

'Such as?'

'Well, er,' replied Sean, 'He wanted us to send out some memorial boxes to everyone.'

'Memorial boxes? What kind of memorial boxes? Memorial of what? And who are they going to be sent to?'

'I don't remember Dad saying anything about memorial boxes, or even any other wishes,' added Louise, 'Surely everything he wanted would be written in his will.'

'And who is paying for this hotel suite? Dad?' asked David.

'Only indirectly,' replied Sheena, 'But anyway, there is so much to do. Dad was very specific about his wishes.'

'Only to you and Sean, it would appear,' said David.

'What about Mum and Dad's furniture?' asked Louise, 'What has happened to that?'

'Dad said that Sheena could bring her furniture into the house while she was caring for him,' explained Sean.

'But the house is virtually empty,' said David. 'There's nothing there, just some plastic garden furniture. Where has everything gone?'

'He didn't want it anymore, so he told us to get rid of it.'

'Get rid of it? Get rid of it how? Do you mean you sold it?'

'Dad wanted Sheena to bring her furniture into the house in place of what was there,' said Sean. 'He was very clear that the contents were to be Sheena's and that she should be allowed to live at the house for at least two years. He left a signed note to this effect.'

'Two years? I think we all should see this signed note, don't you?' said David testily. 'The trouble Sean, is that both you and Sheena have each had your fair share of financial challenges in the past, haven't you? We need to be certain that you are up to the executors job? I mean, some of the company you keep leaves a lot to be desired.'

'People in glass houses...' replied Sean.

'Isn't it you, David, that we should be concerned about?' said Sheena. 'Surely it's only a matter of time before some of your 'friends' catch up with you... and then what?'

'Well that's only because the people I have to deal with aren't confined to an iron lung.' David countered.

'Oh yes...Keep digging your hole, David. Perhaps you'll discover gold, or oil or something else,' sneered Sheena.

'Stop!' cried Louise. 'Look, all this sniping isn't going to help anyone. You carry on, and I suggest that we discuss it all when we meet at the solicitor's.'

'Sure,' said David. 'But in the meantime I think Sean should send us a copy of Dad's wishes so we all know exactly what he wanted. Surely things will be clearer when we all see his will.

'I don't know, Louise', I'm worried about Sean and Sheena,' confessed David, 'They've always said that they are the executors, and we have always believed them, but how do we know? For all we know, it could be Taylor, Otley and whoever that Dad asked to do it.'

Louise and David were sitting together at the Little Drummer Boy after the others had left. They were still trying to come to terms with things.

'True,' said Louise. 'We'll just have to wait until next week.'

'Sean is acting very strangely, you know?' said Louise. 'He seems to have taken on a very authoritative air recently...He's very cocky. I'm worried that whatever power he thinks he has, is going to his head.'

'Yes,' said David. 'The fact that they didn't invite Michael along today is very suspicious to me. Why didn't they want him there? And as for the furniture and the hotel suite. My God!'

'I'm worried about what might have happened even before Dad died. You saw what Sheena was like on that day,' said Louise. 'The way she acted with the Brother Connor... I mean.'

'I've seen her pull some crazy stunts in her time, but that was something else. She was like something possessed.'

'I don't know what's going on, David and I'm really worried. I saw Dad pass cheques amounting to thousands of pounds to her in the last few months. She was supposed to be his carer, but I didn't see much caring going on. I suppose we have both been remiss about the furniture. But I just didn't notice it going until it had gone. I just arrived one day and it had disappeared!'

'Into Sean's back pocket, I expect,' said David. 'You know this is what they've both been waiting for, don't you? They've been circling Dad ever since Mum died. Don't you remember that time Dad was in the hospital?'

'Yes, I remember. I also remember the look on their faces when they came back from visiting him. They thought he wasn't going to make it. I've never seen either of them look so happy.'

'Didn't Sheena get thrown out of the hospital?'

'Yes. She kicked up such a fuss with the doctors about how they were treating his sodium deficiency. Do you think she has ever had his best interests...'

'After all he did for her?'

'Yes...I know. And now they're going to have control over his will... And what was all that about her staying in the house for two years? Who thought of that? Dad's wishes? Pfaah..'

'They're both acting a bit power crazy, aren't they?'

Louise and David stared glumly at each other, trying to make sense of it all.

'What about Michael?' suggested David.

'What about him?'

'Couldn't we speak to him before next week? You know, to let him know what is going on and perhaps persuade him to help us understand things a bit better. That might give us a bit more leverage? The balance of power and all that?'

'Perhaps. But you know how fickle he can be.'

'It's worth a try, though, right?' said David.

'Ok. But if they're the executors, they can do whatever they like?'

'Well, not really. It's the executors responsibility to discharge the will in accordance with the deceased's instructions.'

'Yes, but what about these 'Special Instructions' they keep talking about? You know, Dad's wishes they keep mentioning?'

'Yes, that is strange. I never had any conversation with him about any wishes he might have, did you?'

'Only that he didn't want anyone to see him in the funeral parlour... And that never happened, thankfully. But nothing else.'

'Well if they're making it up in the, 'It's what he would

44

have wanted' kind of way, then we'll have to do something about it,' said David. 'I'm sure the solicitor will make sure things are done properly. Shall we give Michael a call and let him know what is happening?'

'Yes...But be careful. You know how close he is with Sheena.'

David pulled out his mobile phone and dialled his brother.

'I didn't know you had your phone with you. I never bring mine to funerals. I'm always too scared it might go off in the middle of the service,' said Louise.

David smiled as he waited for an answer.

'Hello,' answered Michael.

'Hi Michael. It's David. I'm just here with Louise.'

'Hello. What's up?' said Michael.

'We just had a chat with Sheena and Sean about Dad's wishes. Do you know anything about them?'

'Dad's wishes?' said Michael, 'I don't know what you mean. Where are you?

'We're in The Little Drummer Boy restaurant. We've all just had a meal with Sean and Sheena after the wake. We thought you were going to be here, but they told us you weren't able to come,' said David.

'I don't know what you're talking about,' said Michael. 'We're all at home now. What do you mean you've had a chat with Sheena and Sean?'

'In the restaurant. Sean and Sheena invited us to come and discuss things. We thought you'd be here.'

'I don't know anything about it. I wasn't there. And you have discussed Dad's wishes?'

'No, No, No. It's not like that. Sheena wanted to speak to us. She told us that you couldn't make it to the restaurant, and told us about the will reading next week. So, since you didn't make it, we thought we'd give you a call to try and discuss it with you,' said David.

'So you're ringing to tell me what you have decided without me?'

'No. Nothing of the sort. The will is going to be read at the solicitors next Tuesday at 3 pm. You know Dad's solicitors, Taylor, Otley and Snyde?'

'This all sounds very peculiar. Why would you think I'd not want to be there?'

'We didn't, Michael... That's why we are ringing now.' David placed his hand over the phone and grimaced.

'Ok, Ok...This is most peculiar,' said Michael. 'I'll be at the solicitor's. But I have never seen Mum or Dad's will, have you?'

'No,' said David. 'But Sheena and Sean are talking about "other wishes" that Dad had made clear to them or written down. Have you heard of anything like that? You know, things like what to do with their furniture and possessions and how he wanted to let Sheena stay in the house for two more years.'

'What?' said Michael. 'Sheena wants to live in the house for two years?'

'Yes, that's what they've said.'

'But how are they going to execute Dad's estate if Sheena is living in the house?'

'Exactly.'

'I really should have been there,' said Michael, 'This is the first I've heard about all this.'

'Well, we were hoping that you might want to hold fire until next week when we can all ask questions.'

'Sure. But I'll speak to Sheena first.'

'No... I mean, I wouldn't do that now,' said David. 'She's staying in a suite in the hotel. She says she's very busy with the paperwork. She probably doesn't want to be disturbed.'

'Is she now?' replied Michael. 'Well, I'm sure she'll want to speak to me.'

The line suddenly clicked, and Michael was gone.

'Shit,' said David.

Louise's phone rang just as she was closing her front door to head out. Dressed in her trademark chic skirt, jacket and heels and fumbling with her keys, she had to grope around in her handbag for her phone.

'Hello, it's Sean.'

'Oh, Hi Sean, How are you?'

'Fine, fine... Do you have a minute for a chat?'

'Sure. Just let me get back into the house... Give me a moment.'

'Ok...'

Louise let herself back in while still clasping the phone to her ear. She moved into the large, beautifully furnished living-room and settled herself on the large white damask sofa.

'Go ahead,' she said.

'Well, I just wanted to have a chat after we spoke at dinner last week. I wanted to clear a few things up,' said Sean.

'That would be helpful, Sean. Both David and I have been a bit worried. Have things been straightened out?'

'They've always been straight, Louise.'

'I'm sorry? What do you mean?'

'Well, we need to make a few things clear. Dad put Sheena and I in charge of his will, not you or David. There are certain grey areas that he left to us to sort out.'

'Grey areas? What kind of grey areas, Sean? I don't know what you are talking about.'

'Well, let's just say that there may be some things that come out about Dad's estate. Other things... to consider... As I say, grey areas.'

'Ok, I understand there might be some things he wanted you to do... I remember you mentioned the memorial boxes. I don't know what they are, or what they are for, but fair enough if Dad wanted them put together.'

'It's more than that. And you and David just need to

remember that Sheena and I are running this, and you would be best served if you kept your opinions to yourselves.'

'What? You're beginning to frighten me now, Sean,' said Louise.

'Look. Dad conveyed all his wishes to me and Sheena before he died. He was very detailed and very specific in what he wanted.'

'Yes, you said...His special instructions... You're going to share them with us tomorrow, right?'

'Well, yes... but it's more than that... There are some things that may need to happen. Things that need to be done. And I don't want you and David making life difficult...Understand?'

'Sean, you are really beginning to frighten me now... I don't know what things you are referring to. Did Dad confide in you in some way? What did he say? What is it he wanted you to do?'

'Let's just say we don't want you and David washing the family's dirty laundry in public. It would be much better if you were to just sit back and let Sheena and I handle it.'

'But Sean, you are my brother. I have known you all my life. If there are things that have happened or need to happen, I'm sure that we can sort them out together, as a family. You don't need to be so threatening, you know. I'm scared about what might happen.'

'Louise, I'm not threatening you. I'm just saying that there are certain things, I don't know, like... perhaps what happened when you were with Dan, that you wouldn't want to become public knowledge. You know what I mean, right?'

'What are you trying to say, Sean? What has Dan got to do with any of this?'

'Well, you wouldn't want any of that stuff to become public, now would you?' added Sean.

'What!' exclaimed Louise. 'How? How do you know about that? Who told you? I mean... Do you have...You couldn't. You wouldn't...'

'I know a lot of things,' said Sean. 'All it takes is the click of a mouse button.'

'Oh my God, Sean. Those things are private, and it was a long time ago. I can't believe what you are threatening. You are my brother... My own flesh and blood.'

'All I'm saying is that it would be better if you and David were to just let Sheena and I do what we need to do with Dad's will. Then everybody will be happy.'

'I thought I could trust you Sean,' said Louise.

'You can trust me Louise. Just to let you know, I have spoken to David too.'

'You haven't told him anything, have you?' asked Louise.

'No no no. Not about you... But we've had a chat, and he is very amenable to our plans now.'

'I can't believe this...Have you threatened him as well?'

'He knows exactly what is good for him. And if you have any sense at all, you will too.'

'I can't believe this is happening,' cried Louise. 'After Dad died, all I wanted was for us all to get on and be a proper family again together. Now you go and spring this on me. I don't want Jim, or any of the kids to find out about about this. He's under enough pressure at work as it is. He doesn't know anything. You promise not to...'

'Just keep your mouth shut, do what we ask, and no one will be any the wiser. I'll see you at the solicitor's tomorrow afternoon.'

The phone line clicked, and Louise was left staring at a blank screen.

3

WILL

Taylor, Otley and Snyde had been the family's solicitors for many years. Somewhat down on its heels, and old-fashioned, the place seemed just a little worn out. The office furniture comprised mainly of old melamine from the late 1970s and 80s. Cheap wood-pulp desks were pinned together with small plastic blocks that loosen over time, leaving them rather unsteady. The carpet had seen better days, and those surfaces that were not covered in legal boxes and papers of various kinds had a thin layer of dust on them. The office was full of people, but there was no real buzz about the place. Office staff went about their daily business, going through the motions, but seeming to lack any real enthusiasm or passion.

The five siblings waited in a dingy corridor for Mr Otley to see them. His secretary, Miss Dench, timidly brought them coffee in small, thin plastic cups, while they waited.

'Jeez...It's impossible to hold these without searing your fingers, or drink it without it removing the skin from your lips,' said Michael, shaking his free hand.

The intercom on Miss Dench's desk beeped. She flinched slightly and reached for the intercom button.

'You can let them in now, Miss Dench.'

Leaving their coffee behind, the five of them proceeded into a rather small, cluttered office with piles of papers everywhere and with only two chairs in front of a reddish-brown teak veneer desk. Mr Otley had placed the desk at a specific angle in the room so that the space in front of it reduced towards the window. Anyone sitting on the chair nearest that window would have no room for their legs.

'Do come in. Do come in,' he ushered, as the five of them stepped into the room. 'Miss Dench... Can you get me some more chairs please.'

Mr Earl Otley, the solicitor, was in his mid-forties, not tall, not small, dressed in a grey suit that was a little oversized for him, and wearing a shirt and tie that would not have been out of place in one of the old office pictures that adorned the creaking shelves behind him. He was slight in stature, completely bald apart from some sprouting hair just above his ears that his razor must have missed. His domed head was large and prominent, yet his facial features were small and insubstantial as if embarrassed to be there. He wore small horn-rimmed glasses that he moved up and down from the bridge of his nose to his large forehead as he needed.

'I am so pleased to see you all,' said Otley as he shook everyone's hand. 'Please take a seat.'

Miss Dench had found some dusty black plastic chairs and passed them to Sean and Michael who managed to squeeze them in so that they could all be seated.

Otley sat down and puffed out his chest.

'As some of you know, my name is Earl Otley,' he continued. 'I have been a partner here at Taylor, Otley and Snyde for about eight years, and I have had the pleasure of dealing with your family's legal matters for at least fifteen years. I am so sorry to hear about your father's passing. He was a wonderful man, a real pillar of our society and a real friend to the partnership.'

Louise and David looked across at each other and raised their eyebrows.

'I have had the pleasure of representing your father, Gerald and your mother Kitty, on a number of occasions, and I'm glad to say that they were very pleased with the work I was able to complete for them.

Sean stifled a yawn.

'We are here to read the last will and testament of your late father, Gerald, a sad task. But one I am duty bound to carry out, here and now...'.

'Please just get on with it,' whispered Sean under his breath.

'Your father had some very specific wishes when it came to how we looked after his will,' continued the solicitor.

Sean and Sheena's ears pricked up.

'He first entrusted his will with us nearly twenty-five years ago, and came to renew it the last time only six months ago.'

'Six months?' asked Louise

'Yes. He always liked to have his papers stored in a partic-ular manner, so when he wanted to change it, it often required a lot of work.'

'What do you mean, stored in a particular manner?' asked David.

'I can show you.'

Otley got up and sidled over to a large safe in the corner of his office. He fiddled with the combination and pulled open the heavy door.

'This is your father's last will and testament.'

He placed onto the desk an ornately carved box made from wood and ivory and inlaid with pearl, about eight by five inches, and wrapped tightly in a purple and black ribbon. On the box and around the ribbon could be seen a very small and delicately carved set of inscriptions that were almost impossible to read.

'Wow,' said Michael. 'That is very unusual.'

'Yes,' replied Otley. 'And your father insisted that this container and only this container be used to store it.'

The five of them peered over to take a closer look at the box. Otley's tone became more dramatically sombre now.

'You will notice the bronze and clay seal on the top that prevents the box from being opened without the proper authorisation. Your father insisted that that the seal be of the strongest and the most durable material that could be found; one that would protect his final wishes until the time came.'

The solicitor raised himself up to his full height and pushed out his chest.

'And I can tell you that the authorisation is mine to give, and the time is now'

The solicitor gave a thin grin. Clearly, he'd been rehearsing this dialogue for some time.

Sean stifled a laugh and tried to turn it into a cough.

'Now, the only way we can open this box is to break the seal on top,' he continued. 'And to do that we'll need something a bit more powerful. So if you don't mind... '

From behind his desk Otley produced a large metal mallet and a heavy-looking chisel.

'I think these should do the job... Now would you like to do it or shall I?'

Michael held his hand out and nodded towards the solicitor.

'Ok, then it's up to me,' grinned Otley.

Otley moved some of the piles of paper that decorated his desk and placed the box in the centre of the table against one of the heavier piles.

'Right. Here goes... Stand back...'

Sean and Michael both ducked their heads away, Louise covered her eyes with her left hand while David put both of his hands just above his eye-line. Sheena, fully concentrating, kept staring forward at the box.

Otley positioned the chisel head against the top of the seal, took a deep breath and swung the metal mallet down hard. There was a loud metallic clang combined with a toe-curling crunch. Bright blue sparks shot out from the box and pieces of metal and clay flew in different directions across the room. All six in the room briefly ducked for cover.

'Wow, I wasn't expecting that,' said Sheena as she turned back.

'No. Neither was I,' said Michael. 'What was that made of? Metal? Wood?'

The force of the strike had broken the seal into several parts and opened the box beneath. They all peered into the newly open box. Inside sat a small envelope.

David collected up the pieces of the seal from around the room and put the seven pieces back on the table. After a few attempts he managed to arrange them roughly back together, jigsaw-like.

Mr Otley opened the envelope and pulled out a few sheets of paper.

'Ok,' said Mr Otley, 'I shall now read what your father has said.'

The solicitor cleared his throat.

'This is the Last Will and Testament made by me Gerald Joseph Allen. Being of sound mind, I wilfully and voluntarily make this declaration. I revoke all earlier Wills. I appoint my daughter Sheena Allen and my son Sean Allen to be my executors and trustees.'

Sean and Sheena nodded to each other.

'In my will, my estate shall mean all of my property of every kind, wherever situated, and any moneys or investments in my ownership and made under my name... My trustees shall hold my estate upon trust to retain, postpone or sell it, and will pay any debts, funeral and testamentary expenses.'

Mr Otley looked up momentarily and then continued. 'I give my residuary estate for such to my executors and only my executors, as shall survive me, in equal shares and if either of them shall fail to obtain a vested interest leaving issue who survive me then such issue shall take by substitution such failed share by the other party.'

'What?' said David. 'Do I understand that right? Everything goes to Sean and Sheena?'

Otley looked closer at the pages.

'Yes... It would appear that that was your late father's wishes,' he said.

'Oh my God' said Louise. 'He's given it all to them.'

'That can't be right...You said...' said Michael as he looked at Sheena, '...there must be more to it.'

'This is bullshit,' added David.

The hubbub in the room rose as the three siblings tried to come to understand what had just been said.

David snatched the papers from Otley to take a closer look.

'Yes...that's what it says... Everything goes to them. Sean and Sheena... What the fuck.'

'There is one more thing,' said Mr Otley. 'Your father had his estate valued at the time he last updated his will. He was very keen to ensure that the two elements were properly tied up.'

Otley reached for another file on his desk.

'As of six months ago, your father's assets came to a total of 6.7 million pounds.'

'What?' said David and Sean in unison. '6.7 million pounds!'

'Holy shit... I didn't realise it was...' said Sheena.

'Oh my God,' cried Louise.

'Your father had a significant portfolio of assets. Just look here... A house in France, one in Bermuda and two more in South Africa – Cape Town and Johannesburg, I believe. He also invested shrewdly on the stock market and built up a wide range of holdings valued at over two million pounds just six months ago. I suspect they are worth more than that now.'

'Holy fuck,' said David, 'I never knew he had anything like that.'

'Did any of us?' asked Louise. 'How could he have possibly made that kind of money and not told us? And the properties... Where did they come from? Why did we not know about them? Is anyone living in them? He never visited them... He never took us to any of them...'

'Well,' said Otley. 'It would appear your father made some very good investments over the years and his assets grew gradually. I think he liked to collect things. He wasn't really a spender.'

'Other than on Sheena,' commented Michael.

'Oh, you can talk... People in glass houses,' replied Sheena.

'It's all accounted for here,' said Otley, pointing to a binder in his hand.

'I presume that you will be able to take care of this now. But please remember, if you need any advice, financial or otherwise, you know where to find me...'

'Does it say anything else?' said Louise, pointing at the will. 'What about this idea of Sheena staying in the house for the next two years?'

'Which one? She's got five to choose from,' sniped David. 'This is just ridiculous.'

Otley looked at the papers again.

'No, there's nothing about that. That's it,' he replied.

'No special instruc...' continued Louise.

'...Louise,' interrupted Sean. 'We can talk about all that later.'

Louise bristled.

'You said we were going to be talking about that today. You were going to show us what Dad wanted done, but all we've got is this terrible slap in the face' she said.

'It's what he wanted,' said Sean.

'It's what he wanted? It's what he wanted!' shouted Louise, 'How the hell can either of you know what Dad wanted? Were

you with him every day looking after his needs? Did you cook
for him? Feed him? Wash his clothes? No... You just spent the
last six years in the kitchen, smoking and drinking coffee, and
from what I can see, spending his money. You call yourself a
carer, Sheena, but I never saw any caring from you. All I saw,
and all I ever saw was you deceiving and manipulating
everyone to get your own way. And taking... taking money
from a frail old man, God knows how many times. And now
look what you have done. Don't you think I don't know what
is going on... Do you think you can get away with this? This is
theft on a grand scale. I don't know how you two did it, but
I'm going to find out, and when I do there will be hell to pay.'

'And You... You... What have you done?' yelled Louise,
pointing at Michael. 'We expected so much more from you...
You are the eldest. Why haven't you shown some backbone for
a change and stopped this? You knew what was happening
Michael?...Didn't you? Didn't you...?'

'Of, of... Of course not,' stuttered Michael, 'How... How
could I have possibly known anything about any of this?'

'What happened when you spoke to Sheena last week
Michael?' pressed David, 'We never heard from you after that,
did we? What did they say? Eh? What did they do?... What
did they offer you Michael?... What did they threaten you
with?'

'Yes, how much did they pay you Michael?' said Louise.
'We trusted you all, and now you have all deceived us. Just
when we needed you to be strong, you are weak, so weak...
Isn't that always the way? How could he have done this... and
six million pounds?'

Louise began to sob.

'Hold on... Hold on,' interjected Otley, 'Let's not allow
things get out of hand here. Clearly, the will is valid and legitimate, so there is no need to go about threatening anyone.'

'Legitimate? Really?' said David, 'Perhaps from where you
are standing, but from here things look very much in need of

some threatening. And anyway, Mr Otley, when did you last speak to these two before today? Hmmm? I bet you have, and recently, as well. I reckon you are part of this little charade as well.'

'I very much resent your tone,' said Otley, 'Everything we do here is above board and to the letter... Just because the co-executors wanted a pre-meeting with me. Well... That is not illegal.'

'A pre-meeting? Oh I get it now. How much did they offer you? How can we believe that Dad's will is even valid? How do we know that it hasn't been tampered with?' said David.

'Well... Well, you can see that the seal was untouched. How could anyone have known what was inside?' replied Otley defensively.

'That seal, yes. But how do we know there aren't other identical boxes? This whole thing stinks to high Heaven,' said David. 'You two have been lying and cheating and manipulating things since Mum died, and this is the result. Michael will do anything you tell him, Sheena, and as for you, Motley, well, I have no words... You can be assured that we won't be taking this sitting down. You will be hearing from our own solicitors, and when we have enough evidence, you will be hearing from the police.'

'Six point seven million pounds,' squealed Sheena. 'I can't fucking believe it. I had no idea. Did you?'

'No of course not', replied Sean, 'He never mentioned anything like that.'

'He didn't say anything when, you know?' Sheena made a passing motion with her hand.

'No. Of course not,' said Sean.

'The others weren't happy now were they?'

'No, but if we'd known, then we'd probably have done

things differently, eh?' added Sean. 'I mean I know you bought a car, I paid off my mortgage and had Holly's teeth straightened, and of course you've had a few holidays haven't you, but Six point Seven Million Pounds... Woweee!'

The two siblings were sitting in a small cafe opposite the solicitors office, celebrating their success. Sheena wanted to go for something stronger, but Sean had to keep his AA pledge.

'How on earth did he manage to amass such a fortune? How did he do it? Five houses, Sean. France, Bermuda and South Africa... My God,' said Sheena.

'Well. I suppose he did travel a lot when he was younger.'

'And his salary from BA was very good.'

'I guess, I know he flew to South Africa a lot. Maybe that was when...'

'Plus all those stocks and shares,' said Sheena, excitedly. 'Christ, if I'd known I would have pleaded for more.'

'It makes you think though, doesn't it? It's way too much. I mean even on a Captain's salary. I mean, I don't see how he could possibly have made so much. And why the hell didn't he tell us about it? Do you think Mum knew?'

The two of them looked at each other and tried to make sense of it all. Their plan had worked, albeit in a way that backfired spectacularly, and at a scale neither of them could have foreseen.

'He did help us out a lot though, didn't he?' said Sean.

'No more than one would expect from a loving father,' replied Sheena stirring her coffee.

'No more? I think he did a lot more, especially for you. He bailed you out of university... Twice. Made sure Roger didn't cause any problems after you split up, and didn't he help you out with that Eastern European adoption stunt you pulled a few years back? Then there were the medical expenses...'

'Don't you say another fucking word,' snapped Sheena. 'You also benefitted handsomely. Not only your mortgage, but what about Marilyn? And then there were the others, weren't there? What were their names? Stefanie... Gia, to name but two? Probably others too. Am I right? They didn't come cheap, now did they?'

'Ok ok... We've all benefitted from his generosity,' said Sean, 'I mean even Michael got bailed out of that dodgy cult he got mixed up in. Didn't you go a few times too? You know, that Children of God thing? What a bunch of weirdos they were. And Michael went even weirder. Didn't he live out of his garage, sunbathing all the time and wearing that battered straw hat and his cut-down jeans with his arse hanging out?'

'He wasn't exactly an angel either, now was he? He left a trail behind him too, even though he was married to Megan. A few shotguns involved there, I reckon. They didn't come cheap either, and you know what? Every time. Every time Dad was there to help him out.'

Sean chuckled and nodded his head.

'And what about the others?'

'The others? I'm sure David was helped out with some of his debts early on, and when he needed it. So he's got no reason to be angry. They both did ok. And none of them had to care for him like I did. Nobody saw how difficult he was, especially near the end. I was at his beck and call twenty-four hours a day.'

'Didn't Louise get herself into something tricky with Dan a few years ago? You know, when they split up? There was something going on there. I never really got to the bottom of it, but I'm pretty sure Mum and Dad stepped in again. I reckon Louise swore Mum to secrecy.'

'But Otley was right,' said Sheena, 'Dad was very careful with his money. He never bought anything for himself really, now did he? But to the rest of us he was always helpful, I guess.'

'Well in a way. You always seemed to be at the front of the queue,' said Sean.

'Maybe I was. But I always had to work for it. He was there to help you out?'

'Yes, but there was always a price, wasn't there?'

'A price? Oh... yes... I see what you mean. Did he do the same to you?'

'Oh my God, yes,' said Sheena. 'Once he was involved, well I couldn't make a single move or do anything without his say-so. He wanted sight of everything I did – who I saw, when I saw them, what we did, when we did it. It was ridiculous. I even had to keep a daily diary for him.'

'Yes. Yes. Yes. The diary. You as well? Did you have to report in to him every week, when he would go through his list, and you couldn't speak while he was going through it because if you did he would go back to the very beginning again and it would take forever?'

'Yes... He hated it when I did that.'

'Did he make you go to Mass every week too, and confession?' asked Sean.

'I went in secret. I didn't tell anyone. I'd go during the week when there was no one else around.'

'And he'd know if you hadn't been, wouldn't he?'

'I'm sure he had the confessional bugged. Either that, or Brother Connor was on his payroll.'

'I came to hate it so much. Not just the Mass and the endless confessions. I could deal with those, but there was always the nagging feeling that you were forever indebted to him, and no amount of remorse or repentance would ever satisfy him.'

'Like you owed him. Always?' asked Sean.

'Yes. That was it. I found myself resenting him,' said Sheena. 'I always felt like he was ticking everything off gradually from my account, like some earthly St Peter at the pearly gates. He made me move my job so I could be nearer to him when he wanted me. He made me list my friends and all my acquaintances and demanded to know when I saw them and what business I did. It was just relentless. He never ever let go did he?'

'Never. Not Ever. He caught me out a few times. He had that second sense of knowing when I wasn't being completely honest... And boy did I suffer.'

'It got so bad for me that I just ended up telling him what he wanted to hear,' sighed Sheena. 'I used to tell him whatever came to mind in the end. I just made it up. I couldn't give a damn.'

'Turned out profitable though, didn't it?'

'I can't believe it,' exclaimed Louise. 'They have screwed us. I just spoke with Michael, and he as good as admitted that Sheena bribed him to keep quiet at the reading.'

Louise and David stood together on the pavement outside the solicitors.

'That's why he was so quiet,' said David.

'So they swindle us out of over six million pounds, and he gets a few thousand to keep quiet. He's just so weak.'

'I guess with Michael on their side they can push the probate through quickly, regardless of what we say or do, right?'

'It looks that way. I think that slime-ball Otley was in on it too. Did you see his face? He was as guilty as sin.'

'We can't even oppose the probate process can we? Three against two, plus with Otley and Snyde on board. They really have fucked us,' sighed Louise.

'Do you think the will was actually Dad's?' asked David.

'I have no idea. I recognised his signature at the bottom, so it must be. They couldn't have opened that box contraption without breaking the seal now could they?'

'I don't know how they did it, but I can't believe that Dad would have wanted them to have the lot.'

'And so much money too. Did you have any idea?'

'None. It was a complete surprise to me. If they'd just tried to swindle us out of the house, then perhaps I could have understood it, but this...'

'And to hear how much he was worth and all those properties... France, South Africa... Good God,' said Louise.

'We've got to do something... We can't just take this lying down.'

'I know. But what?'

'We need leverage of some kind to force them to reveal what they did, and how they did it.'

'Such as?'

'Well, if we can produce evidence that Sheena or Sean took money from Dad's accounts, which I'm sure they did, before he died, well that would be embezzlement wouldn't it? We need to get hold of Dad's bank statements. At least that would prove what they've been up to.'

'Good idea. What about Michael?'

'Oh Michael... He's going to be harder. We need to pressure him to come over to our side.'

'Money?' said David, rubbing two fingers of one hand together.

'Hmmm maybe,' said Louise. 'But I think we're going to need something even more persuasive. I think I'll start by having a word with Megan and some of the kids. He hardly ever speaks to them. They might have something we can use to convince him.'

'And Otley?' added David. 'What a piece of work he is. I think I should get some of my friends to pay him a visit. You couldn't swing a cat in that office, but I'd really like to see if you could swing a solicitor.'

Louise laughed.

'If they go through with this, I'm not only going to wash our dirty linen, I'm going to take it to the launderette and hang it up in the park with spotlights shining on it. They have so many skeletons in their closets. They wouldn't survive the embarrassment.'

'Even for over six million pounds?' said David.

'Maybe... but six million pounds worth of skeletons.'

'You know, none of this would have happened if Dad had just been, you know... normal,' said David.

'Yes, I know what you mean. It wasn't really a conventional upbringing, now was it?'

'I was always scared of him,' said David. 'Especially when I was younger. If I did something wrong, no matter how insignificant, he would make me kneel up on the table for hours making them red and swollen. Sometimes, if I had been rude, Mum would forget to pick me up from school, so I had to spend hours outside Father Matthew's office until she picked me up. It was Dad who decided that.'

'It doesn't sound too bad.'

'You weren't there... It was creepy. I never actually saw anything, but I remember hearing him caning boys in his office. He used to take ages over it and he used to enjoy it. He would ramp up the fear as they were made to wait outside his office. Then they had to listen to the screams of the boy inside. It was mental abuse. Some boys even pissed themselves, and one or two passed out from the fear. Just terrible.'

'Do you think he ever?'

'No, nothing like that. He was more of a sadist than a pervert. I think he just really enjoyed scaring the shit out of us.'

'Did Dad make you report to him every week?' asked Louise.

'The weekly confessional? Yes, he did. He made me keep a diary too and tell him everything that was going on in my life. Everything I did and everyone I saw. I wasn't allowed to miss anything out.'

'Why did you do it?'

'Well, I had to. I mean...'

'What?' asked Louise.

'Well, he would threaten to tell my friends or the rest of you what I had done wrong even if I hadn't done it. He even said he would report me to Father Matthews, and I didn't want any of that treatment. You were lucky, the school had changed a lot by the time you were there.'

'Aaah, I thought so. Dad did the same to me. It was like he kept a running account. Whenever he decided I owed him something, he'd make sure that he controlled my every move. I thought it would stop when I left home, but that didn't work. It just got worse.'

'Oh my God,' said David. 'I had the same thing. I was so relieved when I left for university. I don't think Mum and Dad even knew where I was going. I just packed my stuff and left. Boy, did I live to regret that. After a few short months, I had to crawl back for help. Things got out of hand at Uni, and I never heard the end of it. It was like he was on my shoulder telling me what to do for every hour of every day.'

'Yes. The same for me. He was such a control freak. That's exactly what it was like,' said Louise. 'I thought it was normal until I met Dan. I thought all families were like ours. You know, spying on each other, reporting in each week and having to tell your Mum and Dad everything. To be honest, all that stuff didn't help with our relationship. He couldn't stand the interference.'

'Do you think he did it with the other three?' asked David.

'Of course he did. He had perfected it by the time we came along. Mum knew, but never did a thing about it.'

'Do you really think she knew?'

'Knew? She was his first victim. You know how spooked she would get when she thought she wasn't doing what he wanted. She would run around after him like a woman possessed. I'm surprised her nerves weren't even more shot to pieces.'

'Oh my God. Poor mum.'

'Do you remember we always had to wait for him when we were going out? You know, with Mum at the bottom of the stairs hinting loudly, "We're going now Gerald..."'

'I bet she paid for that.'

'I bet she did. Then he would appear at the last minute after spending hours in the bathroom making himself, well whatever.'

'She just became more and more jittery as she got older, didn't she?' sighed Louise.

'Nothing we can do about that now,' said David. 'We need to do something to stop Sean and Sheena from getting away with this.'

'Ok. Well if you're going to put the frighteners on Otley, I'll speak to Megan and the kids to see if there's anything we can persuade Michael with,' replied Louise

'What else?'

'I think we should hire someone.'

'Like who? What for?'

'A private investigator. Someone who can dig up some real dirt on Sean and Sheena.'

'Good idea. But it'll be expensive.'

'There's seven million pounds at stake here David, I think it'll be worth it.'

'Do you know anyone?' said David.

'No, but I'll ask around. There's bound to be someone who can help.'

'We should get them to look at the validity of the will too, and whether Dad was in any way coerced into signing everything over to them.'

'Yes, and the bank accounts.'

'You're right. Did you notice how little was in Dad's current account? I reckon they've been siphoning it off for years. They just weren't aware of all of the other assets he had.'

'That would explain their faces. That's why they were so surprised. That's it. They were just trying to get away with bleeding Dad dry and stealing the house and its contents from us. They had no idea it was this big.'

'Big mistake... And it's going to backfire on them soon enough. If it had just been the house and a few thousand pounds, and with Michael quiet, we probably wouldn't have done anything. But with this amount, they know they've got a fight on their hands,' said David.

'Or maybe they don't, yet. I know we made a scene in there, but perhaps it would be better to play along with it for the time being... until we have more information and evidence on them.'

'It was you that made the scene.'

'Ok, fair point,' said Louise. 'But thinking about it now, we're probably going to be more successful if we play along for now.'

'Run with the foxes, hunt with the hounds?'

'Exactly.'

'Ok. Speak to you later.'

4

THE RED HORSE

The old Freedport Hotel was a classic folly in the finest of English traditions. Built by an aristocrat who clearly had more money than sense, it loomed high out of its surroundings like a weird medieval castle sprouting from the centre of a suburban housing estate. Its flint and lime-rendered walls stretched upwards for more than 60 feet, finishing with a large turret at the top of each corner, while its thin, archer-friendly windows were complemented by the artificial moat and the mock portcullis. In order to enter, one had to make your way across the drawbridge, through the gatehouse and into the large keep on the far side of the central green. Built in the 1960s, The Manor Castle, as it was originally known, was clearly designed to make a statement. The Earl of Dreyfuss was a fanatic for all things medieval and Old-English, though his grip on authenticity could be considered tenuous at best. He filled his folly with as many ancient objects and paraphernalia that he could find. Suits of armour lined the hallways, while mock sixteenth and seventeenth-century paintings looked down disappointingly on visitors. There were heraldic shields and tapestries, stuffed animals, the heads of beasts supposedly slain in the outlying woods, as well as many examples of medieval weaponry on the walls. The mad old Earl even managed to find a suit of armour for a horse and have it mounted in what is now the hotel's reception. Sadly, the whole enterprise was something of a folly for the Earl. None of the items he collected had any authenticity or any real meaning. He was something of a cultural magpie and though the Manor Castle became a centre for trendy young Horse and Country journalists to report upon when it was first built, unfortunately, its lack of legitimacy and the untimely demise of its original owner made the place something of a local laughing stock. The story goes that the poor Earl fell madly in love with an American oil heiress and built the place to try to woo her into marriage. It was said that while the faux charm of the place appealed to her new-world sensibilities, the appeal of the Earl fell on less welcoming ground. After only six weeks in the Manor, she went back to Cincinnati with her entourage, leaving the Earl bereft. Rumour has it that one night, broken-hearted and grief-stricken, he threw himself off the South Tower and drowned in the moat below. However the smarter money remembers him putting the place up for sale and leaving for London, not long after. Now the hotel, with all that history and drama behind it, and having later been converted to a beautiful 32-bedroom five-star hotel, was a favourite with wealthy tourists and local businessmen alike, all wanting to get their slice of the Old English experience. All for a New English price, of course.

Sheena arrived first. She was escorted to the private dining room by a footman, dressed in tunic, doublet and hose and sporting a Robin-Hood style felt hat. Sheena had to wait only a few minutes before Louise and David were also shown in.

'Oh, hi', said Louise cheerfully.

'Hello,' replied Sheena coolly, as she poured herself some coffee. Louise gave her a kiss on the cheek.

'Michael and Sean coming?' asked Louise casually.

'Yes, Yes, Sean is on his way. Not sure about Michael, but he said he'd be here when I spoke to him.'

'It's been a difficult couple of weeks, hasn't it?' said Louise, trying to warm the atmosphere.

'Difficult? It's been a nightmare,' replied Sheena.

'Well, I'm hoping that we can all get things settled today. I'm sorry that we had to challenge the probate,' said Louise.

Sheena looked up from her coffee preparations.

'Yes, well, I'm sure that we can clear everything up here and then we can move on. Dad did want us to get things done, you know. He left it in our hands.'

'Yes, I know.'

The door burst open and Michael swept into the room like he was on fire.

'I'm not late,' he declared.

'No, No... we haven't even started,' replied Louise. 'And Sean isn't here yet anyway.'

'Well... I didn't want you starting without me,' said Michael as he made his way to the tea and coffee. He looked around hurriedly. 'What is this place like? They haven't even got any green tea,' he complained.

'There's some just there,' said Sheena pointing her long red fingernail. 'Are you feeling alright? You look very hot and sweaty, and your skin...'

'I'm fine... Fine I said,' said Michael as he grabbed a bottle of fizzy water, ripped off the top, and downed nearly all of it in one go.'

'Easy!' said Sheena

'Don't you tell me what to do,' snapped Michael, with sweat still pouring off his face. 'I just want you all to know that I'm not going to be pushed around by anyone anymore.'

Michael sat at the large table and started drumming his fingers on the tabletop while his right leg twitched up and down rapidly.

'Come on... Come on... Let's get on with it...'

'Are you feeling alright Michael?' asked Louise. 'You really don't look very well. Would you like some more water, or perhaps some ice?'

'I said... Let's just get on with it,' he growled.

'We can't,' said David tersely. 'Sean's not here yet.'

'Well, where the fuck is he? We were supposed to have started by now.'

'He's just coming,' said Louise, looking out of the window. 'I can see him crossing the courtyard now.'

'Does he think I've got all the time in the world... Does he? Does he?' he barked.

'Calm down... There's no need to be so aggressive. I'm sure we can get everything underway once he gets here,' said Louise.

'Taking me for a fucking mug...'

At that moment Sean arrived through the door in much the same manner as Michael, swinging the huge oak door wide open letting it bounce off its hinges with a huge bang.

'I don't care if you think I'm late,' he announced loudly, as he strode in.

'Hello, Sean... How are you?' asked Louise.

'And don't you say another fucking word. We've heard enough from you and him already,' said Sean, as he looked intently at David and Louise.

'Sean,' said Louise. 'Oh my God are you feeling alright? You're sweating too. And your eyes... They're all bloodshot.'

'Oh, my they are', added Sheena looking closer, 'What have the two of you been up to... You both look as sick as dogs.'

'Let's just get on with it shall we.' said Sean, as he sat down at the large conference table next to the open French window. Louise noticed small specks of blood coming from his nose as he took one heavy breath after another.

Sheena began. 'So look... I'm sorry that things took a bit of a wrong turn at the solicitors. We were as surprised as anyone by what Dad has done, and what he wanted. None of us could have imagined that he was worth so much and I think everyone was shocked. I hope that we've all had some time to get used to things a bit now, and we'd like to proceed with executing Dad's will to everyone's satisfaction, if that is alright.'

'Fan-fucking-tastic,' sneered Michael as he pushed back on the heels of his chair.

Sheena ignored the comment and continued.

'I know that you two were unhappy with how things worked out before, and you have put a caveat on the probate and I can understand why. I'm sorry that we didn't get off to a good start, and I'm hoping that we can clear things up here and move forward together.'

'With or without you,' added Sean, mirthlessly.

'So to that end,' continued Sheena. 'Sean and I have prepared an affidavit that I hope will allay all your fears. We thought we could go through it with you here.'

'Does it change anything?' asked David.

'Does it change anything?' mocked Sean.

Sheena continued, 'Mr Otley has prepared...'

'Otley!' snapped Michael, 'That slime-ball.'

'Look, do you want me to do this or not?' pleaded Sheena, 'I'm trying to bring some peace and order here. If you two just want to mess around, then I'll leave you to it. This affidavit enhances what Dad put in his will so that hopefully it makes more sense to everyone.'

Sheena passed the papers to Louise, David, Sean and Michael. They took a moment to read through the document.

'And this is how you want to proceed?' asked David.

'Yes. Otley was good enough to prepare it for us so that things are clear between the five of us.'

David began to read the document aloud.

'Dad was very thorough and methodical and in control of his affairs, and of course he set out the ways in which we were to carry out our responsibilities as executors. We have followed his timetable and instructions in this regard, to the letter.'

He continued, 'He had numerous conversations with us regarding his will and how his estate was to be administered. He was very clear as to how, and the order in which, his wishes are to be carried out, and had left papers relating to each action, in order, in his bedside cabinet.'

'What papers?' interrupted Michael loudly.

'He was very clear that...' replied Sheena

'Where's the evidence?' interrupted Michael again. He was now standing up at the table looking even more angry.

'He wrote...' said Sheena, trying hard to continue.

'There isn't any fucking evidence is there? This is all just part of your swindle... You and him.'

Michael pointed to Sean who was also now standing up. David tried to continue.

'Dad wanted Sheena to stay in the house for at least two years, so she could adjust to this new period in her life. She has suffered more than most of us because she put her career on hold to look after Dad and missed out on other opportunities,' continued David.

'What a crock of shit,' replied Michael. 'You never suffered a moment for Dad. Not even close to the rest of us. You were always looking for a way out. Career on hold? What career? You just spent your life banging your boss.'

David tried to press on.

'During the course of Mum's illness I spoke with Dad every day and visited him at his house several times a week...'

'Only to screw money out of him,' sneered Michael.

'To offer practical help where needed... I have received several unsolicited gifts from Dad... I believe these gifts were his way of thanking me for all the time and care I had given him and my mother and I accepted these gifts in this spirit.'

This was too much for Michael.

'You were never there... neither of you. Unless it was to

collect a cheque or remove a painting,' he roared. 'All you ever did was sponge from him. This is a FUCKING JOKE...' Michael's voice was now thunderous and he banged his fists down hard on the table.

'I've seen nothing but you lot clambering over each other to get your snouts in the trough. Nothing but lies, blackmail and bribes in this family.'

'Michael. Calm down,' insisted Sheena, trying to inject some order. 'Glass houses, Michael... Perhaps you're forgetting...'

'I don't give a fuck about glass houses. No one in this family is without sin. Every one of us took advantage when we wanted to, and by God, we are all going to pay the price.'

Michael's whole head was now covered in sweat, his collar and armpits were stained, and his eyes were a deep bloodshot. Foaming spittle bubbled from his mouth.

Sean suddenly turned against Michael.

'Sin, Michael? Sin?' raged Sean. 'You talk about sin, but what about you and your family, eh? Megan, your kids and us? You have never thought of anyone but yourself... ever.'

'At least I'm not a fucking thief and a low-life drug pusher,' screamed Michael.

'No, you're a nasty, cheating little scumbag who would leave his children out on the streets for thirty pieces of silver.'

The two brothers were now screaming at the top of their voices from either side of the table, snarling and raging at each other.

'Stop it... You two... Stop it,' cried Louise. 'You're really scaring me!'

'At least I didn't screw my own brother over a crappy business deal, now did I,' screamed Michael.

'Yes, you fucking did...'

Michael swiped at the table, and pulled hard at the table-cloth toppling the centrepiece and the highly ornate candlesticks over, letting them fall to the floor. Reacting quickly, Sean leapt onto the table, snarling like a man possessed, and lunged viciously for his older brother. Louise screamed and leapt out of the way, while David and Sheena retreated to the corner of the room. Sean crashed across the table and slid onto the floor. He got up, seemingly unhurt, and with some kind of super-human strength, ripped the medieval shield from its fixings on the wall above the fireplace, and with both hands held it over his head, as if to throw it.

'Stop... Stop... Stop!' cried Louise.

The brothers now faced each other on the table, snarling and spitting like rabid dogs. Sean swung the shield around his head and brought it cracking hard against Michael's left shoulder, sending him spinning backwards into the wall.

'You were never any good at anything, anyway,' he taunted. 'You failed at everything you ever tried... You're a failure... Nothing but a pathetic fucking failure.'

Impervious to the pain, Michael jumped up and levered a huge medieval axe from the wall. Spitting like a viper, he swung it around his body in a large V motion, towards his brother. As he closed in, Sean jumped to one side and the axe slammed into the centre of the table, sending shards of wood in every direction. Louise screamed again.

'You are nothing but a drug-pusher and a nasty little pimp,' howled Michael as he pulled the axe from the tabletop with an ear-splitting snap of oak. Sean, by now had dropped the shield, and seeing a rapier hanging from the wall, moved to grab it. He swung it hard at Michael, missing his head by millimetres.

They faced each other once again, each gasping for breath, both with sweat, snot and spittle pouring from their face, nose and mouth. Their eyes were so bloodshot now that their pupils were no longer visible. Their pallid complexions shone white against their scarlet eyes, like two rabid wolves.

'This is insane,' shouted Louise from the far side of the room. 'Just stop... Someone is going to get killed.'

'Well one of us is,' cried Sean as he held the sword across

his body. 'And it's not going to be me...' He made a series of wide swings with the blade, cutting across in front of his body sharply from top left to bottom right, switching the blade in the air. Michael quickly leapt from the table onto the floor, narrowly avoiding the blow.

'Stop... Stop... STOP!' implored both Louise and Sheena together.

Sean jumped down, span around the table, and lunged again in a stabbing motion, this time hitting his target and striking his brother deep in his back. The sound of ribs snapping and muscle tearing cut through the rest of the noise in the room. Although injured, Michael did not cry out in pain. Instead, he leapt up, fury filling his face, and began to spin the axe rapidly as he moved even closer towards his brother. The room was filled with the deep grunts, snorts and heavy breathing of two men possessed with murderous intent.

Michael's curving axe head flew by Sean's face a second time, just catching his nose as it went, and ended by embedding itself in the wall behind him. Blood began to pour from the wound, turning his face bright crimson. Oblivious to any injury, he moved to try and finish the job, and pushed Michael backwards hard with both his hands whilst still holding the sword. Michael, caught off balance, stumbled backwards towards the full-length window. As he fell backwards, and with what seemed like superhuman strength, he brought the axe upwards and across his body in one huge powerful arc, catching Sean perfectly on the side of his neck, decapitating him in a single blow. Sean's head span off his shoulders with an elegant ease, removed from his body like a loose tyre from a speeding racing car, pirouetting and bouncing across the room.

The effort of swinging the axe further knocked Michael off-balance, and with blood gushing from his shoulder, he stumbled backwards, catching the edge of the low window parapet with the back of his heels. This motion and his momentum pitched him backwards and over the stone ledge, sending him upwards and outwards into the thin air beyond the ramparts, and abruptly dropped two floors to the paving stones below. The sound of twisting and snapping bones reverberated loudly around the quadrangle as he hit the ground.

'Oh My God!... What have they done?' shrieked Louise. 'My God! Sean... Michael...'

'Sean... Sean...' screamed Sheena. But it was too late. Sean's headless body was lying slumped across the table, blood pumping from a now unoccupied neck, his head having come to rest on the floor on the far side of the room. As the two sisters screamed for their brothers, David curled himself up on the floor, foetus-like, with his head lowered and and his hands wrapped around his knees, rocking forwards and backwards, mouth gaping open, looking intently, as the inhuman eyes of his brother's severed head stared up at him.

A further high-pitched scream came from the courtyard below as someone discovered Michael's now lifeless body, twisted, warped and distorted on the unyielding concrete below.

'So, let's go through it again can we?' said Detective Inspector Somerset. 'You came here to meet your brothers and sister?'

'Yes,' said Sheena, drawing deeply on another cigarette. 'As I said, we were here to discuss the contents of our father's will. The five of us were meeting to agree on future arrangements. And then...Michael... arrived and he was, he was, just so angry... furious in fact... with everything and everyone. At first I thought he was upset because he thought he had been badly treated... And then Sean arrived... and... he was as angry or... I guess... even more angry... And then... they just...' She put her face into her hands and began to sob.

'Could Sean have been angry about the will?' asked DI Somerset.

'No. Not a chance,' said David. 'Sean had no reason whatsoever to be unhappy.'

'But Michael did?' asked the Inspector.

The room was a complete mess. Thinking there had been a terrorist attack, the police had arrived astonishingly quickly, but a little too enthusiastically. Snipers had been deployed to the battlements to train their sights on the body in the courtyard, and the window from which he had fallen. Tactical officers stormed the compound, first to eliminate any potential hijackers and then to isolate and secure what they thought were hostages. They moved all the guests they could find into one room, while they searched the rest of the building. When they burst into the dining room, they were confronted by the macabre scene. Sean's headless torso was lying in an enormous pool of blood, slumped over the dining table. The shield lay in one corner with the long sword, while the contents of the dining table were strewn everywhere. David, Sheena and Louise were found cowering in a corner beside a heavy oak cabinet. Sean's head was still staring lifelessly from the polished wooden floor.

'We were here to try and sort out our differences,' said Sheena. 'But for some reason the two of them were just completely unreasonable. They were spoiling for a fight from the moment they arrived.'

'Have they ever fought before?' asked the Inspector.

'No, of course not... Nothing... Nothing like... this,' said Sheena.

'Who started it? Who was the instigator?'

'Well it's hard to tell... they were both so... well, unlike anything I've ever seen before. They were like, possessed... The way they both acted, they would have fought anyone.'

DI Somerset sighed. He was a policeman of some experience, with over 20 years in the force. He was tall, slim, fair-skinned and with bright blue eyes. His hair, thinning a little and greying prematurely at the temples, was the only indication of his extensive world-weariness. Somerset had witnessed some strange and troubling incidents in his time, but this one was extraordinary. Two brothers fighting to the death in a fit of rage, and in such a violent and bloody way – in a public place – and in broad daylight. It was downright weird. Baffling, in fact.

'What about their eyes?' asked Somerset.

'I know, I've never seen anything like it before,' replied Sheena, drawing again on her cigarette.

'And they were sweating profusely,' said David. 'Both of them... That was unusual.'

'Have either of them been involved with illicit drugs, ever?' asked the Inspector.

Louise and David looked at each other.

'No, of course not,' said Louise, defensively. 'They'd never be involved in anything like that.'

'Oh come off it, Louise,' replied David. 'We all know what Sean was up to. Even you can't deny that. I mean, it was obvious. I think we need to be honest with the police officers.'

'Er, ok,' replied Louise. 'I suppose you are right. I'm sorry Inspector. It's a bit of a habit, you know, protecting my family. As far as we know, Sean did do some dealing. Mostly coke to his friends and to some of his clients. But we never had anything to do with it.'

'But Michael, he'd never touch anything,' added David. 'He really took care of himself. He was very fussy about what went into his body. He'd never take any illegal drugs.'

'Ok. Thank you,' said Somerset. 'We'll have to wait for the toxicology report, as well as investigate what Sean was into,' said Somerset.

'Have you ever seen anything like this before, Inspector Somerset?' asked Sheena. 'What kind of drugs do that to a person? Do you think that they took something, or were given something that could have made them act that way?'

'It's hard to say at this point. It truly is a strange one. But we'll know more after the post-mortems.'

'Oh my God... You're not going to do that are you?' said Louise.

'I'm sorry. I'm afraid we have no choice... One more question. Did either of your brothers have any weapons training at all? I mean fencing or, I don't know, medieval re-enactments of any kind?'

'What? ' said David. 'Weapons training?'

'Only, the way your brother's, er, and I'm sorry to say it like this... his head... was, ...er, removed. Well it looks pretty professional.'

'Oh, Jesus,' cried Louise, clamping her hands over her mouth and turning her head.

'Oh I'm sorry. I didn't mean to...'

'It's ok,' said David, putting his arm around his sister.

'I can't believe what has happened,' said Sheena. 'One minute we were a happy family, and the next, all this happens...'

'But you said that you were here to sort out your differences? Correct? What differences were those?'

'Well,' said Sheena. 'Our late father's will had found in favour of Sean and me, and we were hoping to put any difficulties that, well, you know... that arose because of that... behind us.'

'I see,' said the Inspector. 'What difficulties were those?'

Sheena looked pained. 'Well, because our father had bequeathed us his estate.'

'All 6.7 million pounds of it,' added David.

'To you and Sean?'

'Yes,' replied Sheena awkwardly. 'And I think Michael felt left out of the whole thing.'

'He wasn't alone,' added David.

'6.7 million pounds you say? Well that's a considerable amount of money for you and Sean to share,' said Somerset.

'You've lost an ally now, haven't you? A co-conspirator...It's not quite the same now is it?' pushed David. 'What will happen to his half now? I wonder what his wishes might have been...'

'Do you know?' asked Somerset.

'Of course not,' replied Sheena, icily.

The Inspector continued his questioning.

'Michael was the eldest brother, right? Would any of it have gone to him? Or would it all go to you?'

'I don't know,' snapped Sheena, 'All I know is that two hours ago we were trying to sort things out and now two of my brothers are lying dead,' Sheena snapped.

'I wouldn't be surprised if it all goes to her now, Inspector,' added David.

Somerset's phone buzzed in his pocket.

'Hello. DI Somerset... Yes... Look I'm here at The Freedport Hotel. You know, the Old Manor Castle. Yes... double mur... homicide... Look, I can't just drop it now can I? I'm talking to the family... Yes witnesses. Can't you find someone else? Ok... Ok... Well put them in a cell and I'll try and get finished here as soon as I can.'

The inspector hung-up the call and looked indignantly at the phone screen.

'Look, I'm sorry about that, but something important has come up. I'm going to have to leave my officers to finish up with you here. But I will need to speak to each of you in more detail later.'

'What could be more important than this?' asked David.

'I know. I know... I'm sorry... It's just that we are pushed for resources at the moment.'

'So what happens now?' asked Louise.

'Well, once the SoCo's have finished their work, we can clear your brothers' bodies for removal. I'm sorry to say that they'll have to be kept at the hospital morgue until after the post-mortem's. We'll need to take full statements from you all, as well as any other eyewitnesses, and then there's the toxicology report. Oh, and we'll need your clothes as well.' The detective sighed again. 'It's all going to be a huge amount of work.'

'I see,' said Louise. 'Well I'm sorry if we have inconvenienced you in any way. Please don't let us keep you from your more important work.'

'No... I'm sorry,' said Somerset. 'I didn't mean it like that... Look, my officers will take care of you all. They can arrange for you to go home if you wish, either separately or together. And I can assign a special liaison officer to each of you, in case you need to... you know... talk to someone. But please don't do anything unusual, like go anywhere without letting me know first, Ok?'

'Excuse me, Sir,' interrupted one of the SoCo's. 'Do you have a moment please?'

'Not really,' said Somerset, 'I'm needed down at the station right now.'

'This is important sir', pressed the policewoman.

'Ok... Ok... Hurry up... What is it?'

'Well, er...' hesitated the Police Officer, 'Only that we found one of these on each of the deceased.'

The policewoman held out a latex-covered hand to reveal what looked like two small red earthenware objects.

'What the hell are they? asked Somerset.

'Looks like two small clay horses,' said the police officer. 'As I said Sir, one was found on each of the deceased.'

Somerset looked closely at them. Do you recognise these at all?' asked the Inspector. 'Could these have belonged to your brothers?'

'No. I don't think so,' said Louise, looking intently at them. 'I've never seen them before.'

'Me neither,' added Sheena and David in unison.

5

HERSCHEL

Babbage peered through the bedroom door. Ahead of him was a scene of some disarray. Clothes were strewn on the bedroom floor. Empty tins and take-away containers were left open with their contents half-eaten. Glasses occupied nearly every surface. Books left opened at various pages, half-read on the floor, on the desk and on the bed. At least three laptop computers blinked soullessly into the semi darkness. Crockery and food wrappings were strewn everywhere, decorating the expensive carpet. An open pizza box lay with the remainder of its hurriedly eaten contents on the bed next to a prone figure, half-submerged, under the duvet. Babbage stepped stealthily into the room. He looked left and right at the detritus in front of him. Bending down to take a short sniff at one of the half-eaten slices of pizza, he snorted at the pepperoni and shook his head. Suddenly, a long groan emanated from beneath the duvet cover. The intruder jumped back momentarily, before advancing carefully again. He was interested in the mozzarella and gently licked at the pizza cheese by the bed before grimacing again on the spicy sausage. Undaunted, he moved nearer to where the occupant was lying with his head just poking out from the covers. The interloper jumped up expertly onto the pillow to look more closely at the sleeping inhabitant. He looked intently at the features and put his face right next to his. After a moment or two he sat, then settled down, snuggled in, closed his eyes, and began to purr.

'Oh Babbage... Can you not give me a moment's peace?' groaned the voice from beneath the duvet. Babbage ignored it. The voice turned over, sighed, and realising it was pointless, decided that no more sleep was to be had, and that it was probably best to face the day. Rising slowly out of bed, he looked at the clock, sighed, lifted the tabby cat into his arms to give him a gentle stroke, and set him gently back down on the bed. Babbage jumped straight down from the bed and wrapped himself around his owner's legs.

Damien Herschel was a man with a noble background, not that you might deduce this from the state of his bedroom. Tall, slim and elegant, with a slim nose, deep hazel eyes and a shock of dark, wavy hair; he cut an impressive figure. Herschel was an only child. He was born in Cyprus into an English aristocratic family but orphaned at the age of seven when his parents died in a horrific ocean cruiser accident in the Mediterranean. Schooled at Harrow and Oxford, he excelled at the psychological and analytical sciences, and possessed an emotional intelligence far beyond normal expectations. His ability to connect and understand people, and understand their thoughts, and what their motives might be, became legendary at school. He could easily stay four or five steps ahead in any argument without breaking a sweat. He dominated the debating society at Harrow, such that opposing teams gave up trying to outsmart him and had to rely on ugly brute-force, which did not make for a pleasant outcome.

While the levels of intelligence and empathy Herschel possessed would make most people very sociable and approachable, with Herschel it tended to push him towards being all-knowing and arrogant. His ability to get under your skin and hit the emotional nerve was fine-tuned and could put people off, especially when used with his rapier timing and accuracy. Herschel soon learned that he had to temper his outstanding insight so as not to unnerve people. To disguise his extraordinary abilities, and not appear to be a total freak, he taught himself magic and hypnosis. This provided at least a focus for his talents, and allowed his eccentricities to become part of his act and therefore more socially acceptable. It allowed him to integrate better with others, but never really afforded him the gregarious adoration he secretly craved. Something of a loner, Herschel's wide circle of acquaintances never really developed into any close friendships as he grew up. People tended to be wary of his extraordinary abilities, and would give him a wide berth. Plus, his unpredictable demeanour and his habit of being disarmingly direct made it difficult for him to make lasting connections.

Herschel dressed quickly and ran his fingers through his hair. Today's attire was dark chinos, brown brogues, and a checked plaid shirt. A dark country jacket hung on the door for later.

'Ok Babbage,' he said. 'Let's get you fed.'

He walked out of his bedroom into a large landing. There were at least three other bedrooms on this floor, and a spiral staircase leading down another two floors. This townhouse arrangement suited Herschel perfectly: nice and central, with enough room to pursue his many interests, and enough floors to hide away when he wanted time to think. Herschel walked down the stairs, past the first-floor which revealed several darkened rooms filled with racks of computer servers blinking endlessly into the gloom. He skipped down the last few steps and rode the bannister into the black and white marble hallway, and then into the large, brightly lit kitchen.

'Morning Damien,' came a voice from the far side of the kitchen. 'If you can still call it morning... Eleven Forty-nine...Just.'

'Morning Mrs C. How are you?'

Mrs Cambridge, Herschel's housekeeper, sat up at the breakfast bar, reading the newspaper and drinking coffee.

'I thought I wouldn't disturb you. Let you sleep in a bit. You know.'

'Yes, thank-you. Babbage didn't think that way though.'

'Oh, did he wake you? I don't know how he could have got in. He's always after food that one. Oh well.'

Mrs C's gaze returned to her newspaper. 'Would you like some coffee, Damien?'

'That would be lovely, Mrs C.'

'Well, the machine is over there. The coffee is on the side. You know what to do...'

She waved a long finger towards the far side of the kitchen.

'Ah,... Right... Yes.'

Herschel moved over and began to prepare his coffee.

'And don't worry about your room, I will get to it today. Yes, I will...'

Her voice tailed off.

'My word, have you seen what they're planning to do with the Gardbourne Centre? Again? Yet another council plan that won't survive the summer. I don't know why they bother. The place has been falling apart for years. Every year they come up with another plan for what they're going to do with it and every year they do nothing. The place is just a depressing eyesore. They should just knock it down. Start again... Do you need some help?'

Herschel was bashing at the coffee machine, pressing buttons randomly, without success.

'Look... Come here... All you need to do is, put this in there, like that, put your cup underneath and press the button... and hey-presto.'

Dark black coffee began pouring from the machine into a china cup.

'I don't know, Damien. What would you do if I weren't here to help you, eh?'

'You're right Mrs Cambridge. I don't know how I'd survive,' replied Herschel, smirking.

'Now, I'll make a start on your bedroom once I've finished reading this... They should really just knock it down you know, and start again.'

Mrs Cambridge settled back on her stool, and continued reading. Norma Cambridge had been Herschel's housekeeper for as long as he could remember. She kind of arrived and took over just after he had moved in all those years ago. Tall and angular, she possessed very long limbs that perfectly accompanied her extended features. Her short dark hair was usually neatly waved against her features in a 1920's flapper kind of way. She never wore dresses or skirts; always slacks, usually from a bygone era, and usually in lurid colours and designs, as if borrowed from a pair of 1970's curtains. She was very helpful to Herschel, especially at first, making sure that everything was in order and in its place. Her children had grown-up and left home, and Herschel presumed that she needed someone else to fuss over. Though, these days she spent more time at the breakfast bar reading the newspapers and phoning her friends than she did pushing the hoover around. But Herschel didn't mind. He liked that she was always there. She always made sure Babbage was fed, and she turned the lights on in the evenings, even though the computer systems did that automatically. It was almost as though she came as a package with the Townhouse. But more importantly, he could trust her. Herschel had long ago decided that Mrs Cambridge was either a trained MI6 double-agent who saw everything, acknowledged nothing, and relayed all the sensitive intelligence that passed though the building back to her Soviet handlers, or she had absolutely no idea of what any of it was. Herschel preferred to think it was the latter.

'Any post, Mrs C? Any messages?' asked Damien.

Norma looked up quizzically. 'Er... yes. Somewhere... Now what did I do with them? You know, I don't know why anyone bothers with post anymore. It's all electronics and WhatsUp messages these days isn't it? Hold on... No, I think I put some stuff on your desk. Ignore the catalogues. You're probably not interested. And now you come to mention it, there were a couple of calls. I think they left messages. But I forget what they said. They'll be on your fancy machine upstairs.'

'Ok. Ok. Thanks,' said Herschel.

Herschel took his coffee back upstairs, past the server rooms and across into his main office. His office was a kind of mix between GCHQ and a tastefully decorated Pall Mall gentleman's club. It was a classic blend of traditional Rococo, Romantic and Neoclassical tables, sofas and chairs and paintings juxtaposed against bleeding-edge technology – much of which was not yet available to governments, let alone the public. One side of this studio was adorned with posters and photographs of well-known fictional and non-fictional criminals: Charles Manson, Harold Shipman, Jeffrey Dahmer, Ted Bundy, the Joker and Lex Luthor, to name but a few. Herschel's main desk was a large polished walnut affair with a dark mahogany inlay, but with a sculpted high-tech chair in front of it. On top lay a huge curved monitor that provided a single 7ft by 4ft workspace. Flicking quickly through the post, most of which he dropped straight into the bin, Herschel waved his hand in front of the huge monitor and brought the device to life.

'Messages,' he commanded.

'Three messages,' declared the computer.

'Play,' said Herschel. The first message began to play immediately.

'Hello, Herschel. This is Detective Inspector David Somerset. How are you? It's been some time, I know, but I would like to pick your brains on a case we're looking at. A brutal double murder, with some very strange overtones.'

As DI Somerset spoke, the computer monitor displayed a series of visual analytics and metadata that provided a wealth of extra information to Herschel – more than perhaps the caller would have wanted to reveal. A whole web of photographs, video, audio analysis, plus graphical and textual information, was displayed in real time as the message was replayed. Pictures of DI Somerset continued to show alongside what must have been his wife and children, his friends and a number of other relatives, as well as his military and police records. Links to historical phone-records and geo-location information were sorted and displayed in multiple windows in an instant. There were even some predictive analysis suggesting what the caller might want to do, or where he may be found next. Herschel quickly flicked his eyes over the content as the Inspector continued.

'We're struggling with motive on this one. Each of the victims was also the perpetrator, and they were brothers, so it makes it a bit difficult to track and trace. And the means were, well...brutal. Could you take a look at it as soon as possible? I'd really appreciate it. You have my number.'

Herschel smiled. 'Next message,' he said.

'Herschel. 'C' here... I wanted to thank you for your insights last week on Operation Dandelion.'

The voice was clipped and plummy. This time the monitor showed only a single picture of a middle-aged man in a suit and tie staring straight out of the screen.

'Your breakdown and analysis of the Persian situation was first-class. We managed to extract at least twenty operatives through the route you suggested. Well done. Keep up the good work, and if you're anywhere near my club next week, give me a call and I'll stand you lunch. Take care, and thanks again.'

The message ended and Herschel swiped away the picture of 'C' on the monitor.

'Next,' he said.

The audio clicked, and was preceded by some static and rustling.

'Er... Hello? Is this Mr Herschel? I wonder if you can help me. My name is Louise Aitken...'

Before she had even completed her surname, Herschel's screen was full of pictures of Louise, Sheena, Michael, David, Sean, Gerald and Kitty, plus many others, with multiple overlays showing CCTV footage, audio thumbprints as well as the police and medical data for each of the siblings and their families.

'Tssk.' Herschel pursed his lips as images and informatics flew across the screen simultaneously to form a broad web of characters with a huge amount of supporting data behind them.

Louise continued, 'And I have been given your name as someone who might be able to help me and my family in a time of great need. Two of my brothers recently died in a terrible accident...'

The AI swung the pictures of Sean and Michael to the foreground and highlighted their Police and phone records.

'And the police seem to be unable or unwilling to help find out who was responsible. We are at our wits end, Mr Herschel. I am very scared, angry, and, well, desperate... and I have been told on good authority, that you are the best there is when it comes to solving particularly delicate and problematic cases.'

'Hmm... I wonder,' muttered Herschel.

'...Which... I think this is... Please, Mr Herschel contact me as soon as possible. You're the only person who can help... I'm afraid the police are just useless.'

'The police are just useless,' complained Sheena.

'Well, they are trying their best,' replied Louise.

'They haven't got a clue. Can't you see that? We've been over the same questions time and time again and where has that got us? No - fucking - where.'

Sheena was in no mood to be patronised. It had been over a week since Sean and Michael's demise, and the remaining siblings were expecting answers.

'What is this place anyway?' asked David. He looked around the windowless, beige room, furnished with a single small table, four black plastic chairs and the standard police microphones and recording machines.

'I think they call it an interview room,' said Louise.

'Well, I don't see a two-way mirror... It feels more like a cell in here,' said Sheena. 'They're not going to interview us again, are they? Surely, we can't still be suspects. I have just about had enough of this.'

'Did DI Somerset say what he wanted?' asked Louise.

'Nope. Just to meet us at the police station. I have to agree though, I would have thought they would have provided slightly better accommodation than this. This place gives me the creeps,' said David.

The door opened and a uniformed officer and Detective Inspector Somerset entered. Somerset tried hard not to drop the huge bundle of papers and files under his arm.

'I'm so sorry to have kept you,' he puffed as he heaved his pile of assorted papers onto the table. 'Only we're pretty much up against it still.'

'Up against what?' asked David.

'The, er... The accommodation.. This erm... room,' said Somerset. 'Only all our family rooms are being used at the moment. You know, the demonstration, yesterday? We just don't have enough to hold everyone. So, sorry again. Have you been looked after?'

'No... Nothing,' complained Sheena. 'We've been in here nearly forty minutes and we haven't been offered as much as a drink of water. I feel like a convict.'

'No, no, no... It's nothing like that,' said Somerset. 'It's just that we have so much on at the moment... It's hard to...'

'Why are we here, Inspector? Do you have anything you can share with us?' asked David.

'Well, yes. There have been a few developments.'

Somerset rummaged through his pile of papers on the table, and after some time found what he was looking for. He opened a thick folder...and looked at the first page.

'But before I... er... right... Now, is it alright if I check a few things with you?'

Sheena sighed. '...More things?'

'Er, yes... Firstly, let me introduce you to Sergeant Stevens here. He is our Positive Action Co-ordinator. He works closely with the investigation teams on cases like this. He investigates from a heterogeneous perspective, ensuring that resources are allocated, employed and opportun-ised in line with our public diversity statement.'

'Heterogenous? Opportun-ised... Diversity?' scoffed David. 'What on earth are you talking about?'

'And he needs to determine if the deaths of your brothers could have been classified as a hate crime.'

'A hate crime?' asked Sheena. 'What on earth are you talking about?'

The Inspector continued, 'It's part of our internal proce-dures. The Home Office demands that all violent crimes reported to us are fully investigated by our P.A.C. So he will need to ask you a few more questions related to hate crime, so we can complete this...'

The Inspector pulled out a wad of paper nearly a half an inch thick.

'Once we get that out of the way, we just need to cross check with the HCAP, and then, we should be good to go.'

'The HCAP?' questioned David drily.

'The Hate Crime Action Plan. Once we have all of that completed, we can move on and share what we have discovered.

'Do you not think that perhaps when our two brothers

were swinging at each other with medieval axes there might have been some element of hate involved?' asked Sheena.

'Er, yes, Ma'am,' said Sergeant Stevens. 'Perhaps you're not aware... A hate crime is a prejudice-motivated crime which occurs when a perpetrator targets a victim because of their membership, or perceived membership, of a certain social group, or race.'

'Good grief,' sighed David.

'Is it possible that either Michael or Sean could have viewed each other in that way?' asked Somerset

'Oh, for fuck's sake... This is getting us nowhere,' said Sheena, getting up to leave.

David jumped in. 'Look Inspector Somerset, I don't know how it is you go about solving a crime, but it's not going to get solved by us filling in yet another ridiculous form.'

Yes, I know... It's just,' said the Inspector.

At that moment his mobile phone rang. He grabbed it and fiddled with the buttons.

'Hello. Somerset... Yes... Herschel... Excellent. Where are you? Where? Really? Ok... Excellent. Shall we meet you there?'

'Did I just hear you say Herschel?' asked Louise.

'Yes'

'Damien Herschel?'

'Yes. That's right. He's here. He's going to take a look at the case for us.'

'Oh, Thank God for that,' sighed Louise.

'Who are you talking about?' asked Sheena.

'Damien Herschel. I spoke to him earlier. Well, I left a message really, about him helping us with the case. He's a private detective. He came recommended,' explained Louise.

'Well, I wouldn't call him a private detective,' said Somerset. 'He's more of a Complementary Investigator. He usually works with us on complex cases like this one.'

'The ones you can't solve?' added Sheena.

'Well, I wouldn't put it that way. It's just he has access to a greater range of resources than we do.'

'Is he here... Can we see him now?' asked Louise.

'Ah, there you are... Come in, come in,' said Herschel.

He was sitting at the far end of a large mahogany table in the police station executive conference room when the three siblings and DI Somerset walked in. Being on the sixth floor, the meeting room had a magnificent view across the city. Herschel was staring intently at the display on his laptop as they came in. He gently closed the lid as they sat down.

'How on earth did you...?' asked Somerset, looking around the room.

'Would you like some coffee?' said Herschel calmly.

'Please,' replied Sheena, David and Louise in unison. Herschel looked at Somerset and flashed his eyes towards the freshly prepared coffee pot on the side cabinet.

'Oh... right,' said Somerset.

'This is more like it,' said David, as he looked around the room and out of the large picture window.

'So, let me introduce you to Herschel,' said DI Somerset. 'This is Damien Herschel. We have asked him to help us with this case because he is an expert in a number of modern investigative techniques and procedures, especially in the fields of serial killers, hostage situations, and international relations. He comes highly recommended by the Metropolitan Police as well as a number of international agencies.'

'Which we don't talk about,' said Herschel.

'Er, no... Anyway,' continued the detective, 'I thought it might be useful if Herschel took a look at the evidence we have gathered so far, and try and give us his angle on what happened with your two brothers last week.'

'Mr Herschel,' said Louise.

'Please call me Damien, or just Herschel.'

'Herschel...' repeated Louise, 'I left messages for you about this case. Are you here because of me or because the police asked you to be?'

'Good question,' replied Herschel, 'It's always interesting to get involved in a case when you get two different backgrounds from two different sources... It's... intriguing. Mrs Aitken?'

'Louise.'

'Louise... And this must be Sheena and David, correct? You advised me of a terrible accident at the Manor Castle last week. You called it an accident, correct?'

'Well, yes,' said Louise. 'In my eyes it was terrible set of circumstances that resulted in an accidental...'

'Where one of your brothers accidentally had his head removed from his shoulders by his elder brother wielding an axe?'

'Yes,' said Louise. '...But when you say it like that.'

'Some accident... And you, Inspector Somerset, contacted me to say there had been an unusual double murder at the Freedport Hotel, where two brothers had killed each other in some kind of rage-fuelled attack. Correct?'

'Yes,' said Somerset.

'Yet, from what I can gather, these two brothers had very little love lost between them. Is that right? One, a rather well-known drug dealer, was to inherit the vast majority of his father's estate at the expense of the other brother. Yes? Two brothers, who some years ago, went into business together.'

'So what? What's that got to do...' said Sheena.

'So what?' interrupted Herschel. 'Well there seems to have been quite a lot of 'What'... That business did not succeed now did it? One brother, Michael, right? Spent most of his time driving around in a newly acquired sports-car, while the other, Sean, was it? Yes? Directed most of the business expenses up his nose? Please tell me if I am off the mark here in any way?'

'Herschel... Please,' said Somerset. 'These are their brother and sisters. They were there at the... the incident'.

'Yes Inspector, I shall come on to that... These two loving brothers seemed to have something of a motive, if not a driving vendetta against one another, perhaps. Their business empire, funded by some shady third-party character, supposedly in an iron-lung, never really got off the ground now did it? Well, it never really had the chance...'

'Do we have to listen to this? I thought you were here to help,' said Sheena.

'I'm just stating the facts of the incident as I have become aware of them. Though, unfortunately not all of the facts have seen the light just yet. Let's look at the incident in question. The witness reports, and by witnesses, I mean you three, say that the two men were raging at each other from the moment they arrived?'

'Yes. They were out for each other's blood,' said Louise.

'And no-one else?'

'Well, its hard to say, but they were both so fired up that I think they could have gone for anyone.'

'Both of them?'

'Yes... What do you mean?' asked Louise.

'Would either Michael or Sean have gone for someone else if the other had not been in that room that day? Do you think Michael would have attacked you?' Herschel looked directly at Sheena. 'Would Michael have had a motive of any kind to harm you?'

'If you mean, would he have attacked me because of Dad's Will? No, of course not,' said Sheena.

'Really? How much do you stand to inherit with both Sean and Michael dead?'

'I don't have to sit here and put up with this,' said Sheena. 'We have all been interviewed at length by the police, and regardless of the will or anything else, there is no way that I, or my brother and sister could have known what they were going to do. I mean, you weren't even there, were you Hershing... Hernmann ... or whatever you call yourself.'

'But you can't deny that you are likely to be the biggest benefactor of Michael and Sean's death, right?' continued Herschel.

'No, I can't,' yelled Sheena. 'But it didn't mean I wanted them fucking dead. If you want to know, I'd give all of the inheritance back in an instant if it meant I could have them back... All of it.'

Sheena hit the conference table with both palms and began to sob. Louise put her arm around her.

'And you two don't come out of this unscathed, you know,' continued Herschel. 'Following the reading of your father's will, where you were both unceremoniously cut out of his estate, have you not attempted to coerce and influence the outcome by threatening the family solicitor, Mr Otley, isn't it?'

'Well now... hold on. I wouldn't call it threatening,' replied David.

'Demanding an outcome in your favour with an underlying promise of violence if it's not carried out? If you don't call that threatening, what would you call it?'

'I wouldn't trust that Otley as far as I could throw him. What a slime-ball,' said David.

'Perhaps not. But you should all be aware that Otley was only too happy to take money from any side to feather his own nest. I wouldn't be surprised if he was taking money from your father as well at some point.'

'Creep,' said Louise.

'So,' continued Herschel. 'I ask myself, which of you is without sin? Who would cast the first stone? Who would benefit the most from Michael and Sean's deaths? And you know what?...' Herschel paused as the three siblings viewed him suspiciously.

'...I can't tell. You know... I really can't tell. Perhaps you're each as bad as the other? Perhaps you deserve each other.'

'Herschel!' exclaimed DI Somerset.

'I'm sorry but sometimes I am asked to look at these cases...and normally they're pretty straight forward. Over 90% of murder victims know their perpetrators, which in this case is obvious, but which of the two of them was it? That's what makes it interesting. It's amazing how small and petty jealousies can grow inside a person over time... into nasty black motives for murder...And normally it's pretty obvious who is responsible. I mean, given what we know, the finger of suspicion weighs heavily against you Sheena, now doesn't it? Yet, I can't help but think that Louise and David cannot be free from any responsibility in this matter.'

'You know, I don't know why we bothered contacting you, Mr Herschel,' said Louise. 'I had hoped that you could help us work out what has happened here, but instead, all you seem to want to do is make accusations. If you're not willing or not able to help us, then I will thank you for your attention and wish you good-day.'

'Yes. Go stick your investigator nose somewhere else,' echoed Sheena.

'That, I may well do,' replied Herschel. 'You know, I really think I could...'

'Damien. Stop! Pay attention,' said Cassandra. 'There's more to this than you think. These people need you... Be nice.'

Herschel stopped mid-sentence, and stared upwards and left, towards the ceiling corner.

'You think you could... what?' asked Louise

Herschel took a long pause, then raised two fingers upwards and then to his chin, deep in thought.

'What? Is something happening here?' asked Louise. 'Is everything alright? Only...' She looked towards Somerset quizzically.

'I'm sorry,' said Herschel, 'You are right. I'm not helping like this. Maybe I have been looking at this the wrong way. Forgive me... Please... One moment...'

He moved over to his laptop and opened it up, typing quickly on the keyboard.

'Ahh... Yes... of course,' he continued. 'That's it.'

'What? What are you talking about? What just happened?' asked Louise.

'Mmmm... Yes... I thought so,' continued Herschel, ignoring everything around him.

'Hold on Herschel,' interrupted Sheena. A moment ago, you were accusing us of all kinds of things and now you go all quiet. What is going on?'

'Of course,' said Herschel, still looking at his screen. 'North Korean... or perhaps Russian. Probably not Chinese.'

'What the hell are you talking about Herschel? Explain yourself,' burst Somerset.

Herschel came back into the room.

'Yes... Look, I'm sorry about all that before. It was a bit of a mis- communication on my part. I think I may have something that you will find interesting.'

'What?' asked Sheena.

'Well, I have the analysis from your brothers' blood samples and they really are quite interesting.'

'We didn't find anything unusual,' said Somerset, 'just some traces of cocaine in Sean's sample and that wouldn't have caused this.'

'No, but I had a wider range of tests run. Have you ever heard of Arythmodref? Well, more specifically, Arythmodref-P?' said Herschel

'No, what is it?' said Somerset.

'It's a powerful designer drug – pretty much unknown in the West at the moment. More commonly developed by either North Korea or perhaps Russia. What they have managed to do is combine LSD and Fentanyl, a powerful opioid, in such a way as to be almost untraceable. Very clever really.'

'And you have found this Arithmo... whatever, in Sean's blood sample?' asked Sheena.

'No. I've found it in both of your brothers' blood samples. In minute, but similar quantities.'

'How could it have got there?' asked Louise.

'Oh easily. It's tasteless and odourless. They wouldn't have known. It could be put in a drink, in an aerosol, on a surface of some kind like a steering wheel, or a door handle, or anything they might touch... though that's pretty risky...'

'Oh my God? Was it Sean?' asked Louise.

'No. This is weapons grade material. It's not something a little local pusher would come across. It's not designed to give a high, it's designed to cause rage in soldiers and make them fight much, much harder, and more fiercely... You know... without any fear. Usually it comes as red liquid or a paste that can easily be administered. But my research indicates that the North Korean's had difficulty in getting the dosage right. Too little and nothing would happen, but too much, and well...'

'And is that what caused them to become so angry and aggressive?' said Louise.

'Yes. But the North Koreans had difficulty in directing that rage towards the enemy rather than each other. Look, let me show you.'

Herschel pressed a few buttons on his laptop and a crystal clear picture appeared on the large monitor on the wall behind them. The video showed an outside compound containing two monkeys.

'What are they? Gibbons?' asked the Inspector.

'Baboons... Much larger. These two are brothers. You can see how attentive they are. Grooming and cleaning each other.'

The screen showed the two baboons moving around together, happily stopping to share food, then lazing around, hugging and grooming each other on the far side of the compound.

'These two lived together like this for at least six months without any problems,' added Herschel.

A few moments later the screen showed a few drops of a red liquid being added to the monkeys' drinking bowls.

'Arythmodref-P,' said Herschel.

'I can't bear to watch,' said Louise.

The screen showed both of the monkeys go to the water containers to take a drink. Within a few minutes their moods changed and they became agitated and disordered. They began to strut and march up and down on each side of the compound, baring their teeth and howling in an aggressive, combative manner. A few minutes later, the two brothers squared up against each other, pushing and shoving each other, becoming increasingly aggressive.

'Look at their eyes,' said Somerset pausing the playback. The baboons were salivating heavily and each had bloodshot eyes.

'Just like Michael and Sean,' said David.

'Shall I go on?' said Herschel.

'No...I really can't watch,' pleaded Louise as she turned her head away.

'Please,' said David.

The video continued. The two baboons circled each other, shrieking and posturing for some minutes, until one of them, with no real reason, bounced from the side of the concrete wall of the compound and leapt upon his brother, sinking his huge teeth into the back of his neck. The attacker ripped a huge chunk of flesh from his rival, who in turn span around and buried his teeth into his adversary's hind quarters. Blood gushed from each of the wounds.

'Err... Perhaps we should skip on,' suggested Somerset.

'Yes, of course,' replied Herschel. He waved his hand in front of his laptop and moved the display forward to reveal the aftermath of the confrontation. Remains of the two baboons were scattered around the compound. Pieces of flesh, blood, brains, sinew and bone hung from the wire cage walls and were smeared over the floor.

'Good God,' said Somerset, 'And all that is down to this drug?'

'Yes, I'm afraid so,' said Herschel. 'And I'm surprised that it has shown up here. So unless any of you have been to North Korea recently.' He looked up. 'And you haven't. There is no way anyone could have acquired this substance.'

'It's horrific,' said Sheena.

'Who could have done such a thing? And why? Who would want Sean and Michael dead? What possible benefit could there be?' asked Louise.

'That,' replied Herschel, 'Is the mystery I am going to solve.'

'What about the clay animals?' asked Louise

'Clay animals?'

'Yes. Didn't you say Inspector, that some clay animals were found on Michael and Sean?'

'Yes. That's right,' said Somerset, 'They were trinkets that they shared, right?'

'Shared?' said Louise. 'We've never seen them before. We have no idea what they are.'

'Do you have them?' asked Herschel.

'Not here. But I have a picture of them.'

The Inspector pulled out two A4 photographs from his pile of papers.

'Here. We surmised that they were just trinkets that they kept as part of a family bond. Are you saying they're not?'

'These are nothing we have ever seen before Inspector,' replied David.

'Let me have a closer look,' said Herschel. He looked closely at the photographs. 'Are these covered in blood?' he asked.

'No. That's their original colour. They each had one in their pocket.'

'Red Horses.'

'That was excellent work on the Arythmodref-P,' said Cassandra.

'Thank you,' replied Herschel, 'Even though I do say so myself. The police only ever test for the most obvious compounds, but my little friend in Tel-Aviv is so much more enterprising and thorough.'

'So, do you think its presence negates the siblings as suspects?' asked Cassandra.

'Perhaps so. Though it's difficult to get over the obvious motive for Sheena. But then, why would she want Michael dead too?' asked Herschel.

'Maybe he was in the way? Maybe he knew too much about what was going on?' replied Cassandra.

Back at the Townhouse, Herschel had taken some time to think more deeply about the siblings' reactions to what he had shared. He searched for some common thread to tie it all together.

'On reflection, I don't think they had anything to do with it,' continued Herschel. 'The witness reports say they weren't involved in the fight and that the two brothers were simply out to kill each other.'

Herschel paused again. He was deep in thought, sitting in his office chair in front of his monitor, looking upwards and to the left.

'There is no way they would have access to such a powerful narcotic like that. Even in the unrefined form in which it was prepared; you'd have to have military or international connections. And even then, it's very new and extremely scarce.'

'But what if you had run a whole load of military exercises, only to find that it didn't work the way you wanted it to? Then perhaps you'd be more open to selling it?' said Cassandra.

'Maybe. The trouble is of course that it's almost completely untraceable. It's not radioactive, it's not toxic in the traditional sense, and it's not deadly.'

'But it is deadly,' Cassandra emphasised. 'Just not directly. Is this the first time it has been used in this country?'

'Yes, looks like it. Let's hope it's the last.'

Herschel paused again, still deep in thought.

'What about the Red Horses? Did Somerset send them over?' asked Cassandra.

'He did.'

Herschel lent back on his chair, his feet up on his desk, pulled one of the figures from his pocket and held it between his thumb and forefinger. 'No traces of designer drug on these. And no fingerprints or DNA either.'

'Not even of the brothers?'

'No... Exactly.'

'So a message then?'

'I think so. But I'm mystified as to what. They're just clay animals. There's nothing special about them. You could probably buy them at any toy store in the country... I'll do a more in-depth search against their provenance, but I don't expect anything to result.'

'So, symbolic then?'

'Almost certainly. But of what? The family don't seem to be interested in equestrian pursuits and the brothers certainly weren't. So there's no connection there. Their children are all grown up..and there are no small grandchildren, so the toy angle is a bit of a blind alley.'

'How about we look a bit more closely at the symbology?' asked Cassandra.

'Ok... Sure... Good idea. Fire away.'

'Well, let's think about this,... I've spent some time in the Hive... and have come up with some interesting material,' said Cassandra. 'Shall I proceed?'

'Yes, of course,' replied Herschel

'What is the symbology of horses? What image do they

project? What do you think about when you think of a horse? Courage and freedom? A majestic beast being made of power, nobleness, courage, independence, freedom, endurance... heroism?'

'Yes...I'd say so,' said Herschel.

'The horse is an essential part of our history, mythology, and folklore. It is man's most loyal companion in battle. Communities have admired them throughout history, sometimes even raising them to actual deities. Historically, horses have enjoyed more respect than some humans. They have been symbols of wealth and power for their owner, and so have often been revered and protected.'

'Didn't some ancient clans bury their horses with their dead kings?' asked Herschel.

'They did, yes... Horses motivated the ancients to move forward, succeed in their ventures and become the best version of themselves for their time. So to them, the horse symbolised development, improvement and modernity. I guess, it's a bit like a flashy new car for us. When tamed, the horse symbolised one's mastery over a large and powerful beast. Skill over the animal symbolised control over primal urges and appetites and so implied self-restraint. As a wild animal, the horse is inclined to a promiscuous life, but if tamed, then this animal is a perfect example of loyal, trusting, and mature relationships.'

'Interesting,' said Herschel. 'What else?'

'Well,' continued Cassandra. 'Equine symbolism, is manifested often in the European Celts as a Sun God. And the Goddess Epona, the horse-mother, was worshipped right across the Roman Empire.'

'I see,' said Herschel.

'Celtic druids had a ritual in which the one that would be named King, slept inside the skin of a sacrificed horse. And in the Celtic zodiac, the horse symbol identified with people that love attention, admiration, and have a noble stature.'

'Nothing wrong with that. What about wider?'

'Hmmm... Well, in North America the horse was considered a spiritual being by Native Americans. It represented independence, freedom and was their token of war. They viewed the animal as a symbol of motility, strength, power, and stamina. They had a deep respect for it. Tribes with the most horses were also the most likely to win the battles. It was believed that great wealth came from those who owned the most. The Blue Horse as part of Native American symbolism speaks of a chieftain from the Oglala Lakota tribe that saved white people in distress, even though he battled the white man for over 50 years. This Blue Horse was born from the first horses that the Indians were able to catch and ride.

'So, is the colour of the horse significant?' asked Herschel.

'Yes, it can be. The Native Americans that rode horses were believed to have divine power – and it was their custom to paint the horse in a variety of different colours to increase its magical powers.'

'Wow. Powerful stuff. What about elsewhere?'

In China and Japan the horse was considered to be an animal of courage, integrity, perseverance, and power. A divine being, in fact, and it was believed that the Gods entered the world riding them. Chinese mythology depicts white horses delivering the Buddhist sutras or Holy Scriptures to man for the first time, thus introducing religion to the area. While in the Chinese zodiac, the symbolism of horses was powerful, as it conveyed a spirit full of nobleness and faithfulness.'

'Hmmmm, Ok. So universally viewed for its power and nobility... Anything else?'

'This is interesting. There is a lot of horse symbolism in the Bible, and colour seems to play an important part. A white horse is a sign of death in the Bible, and a black horse means death but with the addition of evil, malevolent and destructive characteristics. Having said that, a black horse combined with a white horse is often presented biblically, as a symbol of both life and death.'

'How very binary. They always like to cover all the bases, don't they?'

'So it would appear. In the Bible, the horse is often a figure of purity and holiness, but in the book of Revelations it is believed that Jesus Christ will, at the End of Days, return to earth riding a white horse – symbolising Gods return to earth to bestow justice upon an evil world.'

Suddenly, there was a loud knock at the door.

'Hello... Knockety, knock knock... Can I come in?' Mrs Cambridge pushed open the door and poked her head around.

'I just want you to know that I've finished for the day... Oh, is everything alright? Only I thought I heard voices. Damien, you weren't talking to yourself again were you?'

Herschel looked around coolly.

'Ahh, Mrs Cambridge. There you are. Thank you for reminding me. Well, you know how I like to talk out a new case to myself.'

'I do, I do... I just get worried for you, upstairs here, all on your own, rabbiting away. It's not healthy you know.'

'Trust me Mrs C, I'm perfectly used to it. Now, you said you were off, did you? Ok. Thanks for everything.'

'Well, I didn't have time to finish the laundry. You'll have to put out anything that needs drying. And, er, the dishwasher is still full... Ooops... But at least I did a bit of the ironing for you today. And the surfaces are done. Well, more or less...'

'Thank you Mrs C. I don't know what I would do without you, I really don't... Now, if you don't mind...'

'Ok, Ok... I'll leave you to your philosophising... Don't forget to feed Babbage. And don't forget to eat... See you tomorrow... Byeee.'

Herschel waited until she had closed the door and he was sure she had gone.

'Domestic Occupational Challenge,' he said.

6

CHURCH

The Cathedral spire loomed majestically above the distant skyline, rising high above the horizon; its form commanding all the land around. With its twelfth century gothic towers, large and ornate stained-glass windows, expansive pointed arches, ribbed vaults, huge flying buttresses and extraordinary detailed decoration, the Cathedral dominated every other architectural feature in the area. The Grade 1 listed building was dedicated to Saint Eligius, patron saint of horses, goldsmiths, metalworkers and coin collectors. Bishop Eligius earned his reputation as the chief counsellor to the French Merovingian dynasty in the seventh century, and worked tirelessly to convert the pagan population of French Flanders to Christianity. Legend has it that one day, while on his travels, he came across a very distressed horse that would not allow itself to be shod. Eligius, believing the animal to be possessed by demons, removed the animals foreleg, before re-shoeing it and miraculously re-attaching the leg to the horse. And so, his reputation and path to canonisation was sealed. The Cathedral was built in his honour over a 150-year period following the Norman conquest. Once completed, it was eventually compared against the grandeur and architectural standards of some of the world's finest works of architecture, including St Peter's Basilica in Rome, Notre-Dame in Paris, as well as Cologne and Salisbury cathedrals.

The Cathedral was built to the glory of God, and was expected to be as beautiful, imposing, and grand as the wealth and skills of the local people could make it. Its elaborate and complex architecture served to emphasise the elaborate and complex liturgical rites performed beneath its vaulted beams. The Cathedral soon became the central point for all acts of confirmation and ordination, as well as a meeting place for large numbers of clergy and others, and not just for those in the city, but across the entire region. St Eligius' had been inaugurated alongside the Trinitarian order of monks, who now had a number of small chapels within the Cathedral dedicated to their fellowship, so they could attend Mass privately. Local businessmen and wealthy families became patrons and, over the years, endowed the Cathedral with funds for successive enlargements and numerous building programs. All in return for a space for a family crypt in the church basement, or a well-positioned plaque in the nave, or perhaps an even better placed plot in the graveyard.

The Cathedral was also a place of pilgrimage. World-weary travellers were welcomed by the fraternity and along with fifty or so other travellers, were allowed to lodge in the draughty dormitory, set three bunks high and lit by a single naked bulb within the airless crypt at the back of the church. Pilgrims were expected to make their own arrangements for food and drink. They had at least a choice of one of the three cold showers in which to wash, which they could access via the heavy, wooden entrance door that opened directly onto the courtyard of the petrol station outside.

Brother Connor stood by the black railings at the main entrance to the Cathedral, and looked up. The gothic walls seemed to go on forever. His eyes rose past the buttresses, over the roof and up the extended spire, right to the very top where the golden statue of St Eligius, astride his steed, surveyed the land below. This house was built to show the power and the majesty of God in all his glory. Brother Connor looked down and drew in his breath. He walked briskly past the main Cathedral door and down a side alley into a courtyard where he found a large black door at the far end. The sound of brass on the oak door echoed loudly around the quadrangle. Connor stepped back slightly, surprised at its loudness. He dropped his head a little and looked up at the entrance, slightly flustered, while gently stepping from one foot to the other. After what seemed like an age, a small, elderly woman pulled the door open. She had trouble moving it, and Connor had to help by pushing from the outside before he could step inside.

'Can I help you?' said the woman, looking at the priest over her small, opaque glasses.

'B... Brother Connor,' blurted the priest. 'I... I have an appointment with the Cardinal Stonehouse.'

'Have you now... What time?' was the reply.

'T... Two o'clock,' replied Connor, realising he was being scrutinised.

'You're a bit early.'

'Yes, I know. But it's not every day one gets to meet a Cardinal.'

'It is if you live here,' laughed the woman. 'Ok... Come in, come in. The Cardinal is still busy in meetings. So you'll have to wait.'

She stepped back and motioned towards the entrance. The priest stepped into the large ornate hallway, painted with bright yellow walls and a wide black and white tiled staircase reaching up and around a huge glass centrepiece that hung from the ceiling a full forty feet above.

'Wow,' said Connor.

'Wipe your feet, and follow me,' said the woman. Connor obeyed, scraping each side of his newly shined shoes carefully on the mat.

Before he knew it, the old lady had scooted up the stairs. Her sprightliness caught Brother Connor unawares and he had to move fast just to keep up with her. As he hurried after her, he could not help but admire all the interior decoration. The staircase was adorned with pictures of venerable clergy from at least the last five-hundred years. Each was male. Each was white. Each looked rather dissatisfied with life. Most just scowled out from behind the veneer, surrounded by the most popular and expensive trappings of their position at the time. Many clutched at a copy of the Bible. There was always a crucifix either around their neck, or close by on a surface nearby. There was an abundance of elaborately decorated gold cloth, ceremonial swords, orbs, sceptres, bejewelled crowns, magnificent purple galeros, as well as many starched white mitres. Even though the portrait painters of the Middle Ages and Renaissance period used allegory and symbolism in their paintings, all that meaning passed Brother Connor by as he hurried through. All he could see was wealth and power. And power and wealth.

At the top of the stairs, he followed his fast-moving muse down a further corridor which was adorned with glass cabinets filled with what he took to be gold and silver trophies and trinkets. He had never seen such ostentation before. The chapel in the orphanage never had anything of this sort. And of course, his own church could never have boasted such golden riches. As they reached the end of the long corridor, the woman turned elegantly on her heels.

'Wait here,' she said crisply, pointing to three well-worn chairs set against the oak panelling of the corridor wall, each with velvet maroon coverings. 'The Cardinal will see you soon.'

Brother Connor couldn't help notice that one of the cushions was split and was determined to disclose its earthy looking contents onto the floor, while the other cushions appeared empty and sagged with a halo despondently in the centre of the seat. Looking around, the priest was amazed by the ornamentation and opulence that surrounded him. Just in this simple corridor were treasures and artefacts that would have astounded any and all of his compatriots back in Ireland. There were golden encrusted crosses, silver fishes, coins large and small, beautifully bound books – all presented in glass cases – and probably not having been touched for years. This was nothing like any of the churches he had known in Ireland.

The Cardinal kept Brother Connor waiting of course. But he didn't mind. He happily amused himself by studying all the exhibits in the cabinets, wondering as to their possible use – how the Church might have come to acquire them, and even sometimes, when he allowed himself, their value. At one point he even found himself wondering if they would miss a piece or two? Shaking his head and silently castigating himself, he moved away to look at some of the portraits. He tried to imagine what it must be like to be surrounded by that much wealth. He wondered what must it feel like to have that much power and riches, and be able to show it off. But also to have the confidence to display it back to those who have paid for it.

After waiting for some time, the door in front of him opened and a young, good-looking priest appeared, dressed in his black cassock, a dog collar, a silver crucifix, and a simple red cincture around his waist. The priest was slim, dark-skinned, of medium height, and walked with a casual elegance that matched his expensive haircut. He held the door open and gracefully swept his left hand across in front of him to usher a young couple out through the door. The young man had his arm around the woman's shoulders. She was sobbing into his shoulder. Brother Connor watched as the priest accompanied them away and down the corridor. With the door left open, Brother Connor could peek inside the room beyond. It was lushly carpeted with a deep vermillion pile, and with a pair of large arched windows which cascaded bright light into the room through crisp, clean, net curtains rustling slightly in the breeze. In the middle of the room, he could see a large mahogany table at which a second priest was leaning over, fingertips on the table-top, peering hard at some papers. Beyond him, Brother Connor could see a set of floor-to-ceiling shelves packed with ancient-looking books of all sizes and colours. Some were stored behind wire mesh, while others appeared to be padlocked into their covers. Beside the book-shelf was a large drinks cabinet containing many decanter bottles with what looked like Port, Whiskey and Brandy. Above the cabinet was an enormous painting of St Eligius pulling a three-legged white stallion by its reins. The lower half of the steed's leg was lying near the bottom of the painting, partly obscured by vegetation. The white stallion was exquisitely painted with pink tack and a pale blue saddle. Connor looked at it with awe and admiration.

'Beautiful,' he mouthed.

The first priest now re-appeared, walked up the imposing corridor, smiled, nodded and re-entered the office, shutting the door carefully, yet firmly behind him. Connor, still standing, found himself staring awkwardly down at the polished floor-boards. He noticed his hands. They were still ingrained with dirt, despite all the scrubbing he had done. He wished he could have cleaned up his fingernails and the red-raw cuticles that surrounded them. Oh well, he thought, it was too late now. The door swung open again suddenly, and the same stylish young priest looked at him.

'Father McIntyre?'

'Yes,' replied Brother Connor.

'The Cardinal will see you now.'

Connor was shown through the ante-room into an even larger office, equally as ornate with a high carved ceiling and walls lined with the kind of religious paintings a local priest would kill for. At the far end was large mahogany desk, behind which stood the Cardinal.

'Father,' called the Cardinal. 'So good to see you. I'm so sorry to have kept you waiting... Come, come...'

The Cardinal beckoned him down into the cavernous room towards him. Cardinal Stonehouse was in his early 80's, tall, angular and long-limbed. He tended towards precision and accuracy in his movements, and wasted no energy. His steely blue eyes pierced into the priest, assessing every tiny detail. The Cardinal looked as sharp as a tack. He was dressed in a white cassock with a full length bright red ferraiolo cape that reached to his ankles, and his grey hair was neatly cut beneath the three-peaked biretta on his head. On his right hand he wore his gold episcopal ring, set with a large purple amethyst, whilst on his left he wore his Cardinal ring bearing an inscription of the crucifixion alongside another large gemstone, this time a sapphire.

'You may leave us,' instructed the Cardinal. Brother Connor stopped, turned and began to head back out towards the door.

'No... No... No,' said the Cardinal, chuckling to himself. 'I meant Father Silvano here,' as he pointed towards his accomplice. The urbane-looking priest stopped, nodded, turned on his heels and headed swiftly out of the office. As he left, he spun and reversed out of the room, closing the double doors in front of him, like he had done it a hundred times before.

'Please take a seat,' said the Cardinal as he pointed towards one of the chairs in front of his desk. 'I'm sorry about all of this ceremonial regalia. I would normally prefer a simpler outfit, but I have an investiture to attend later this afternoon.'

The Cardinal stopped looking at his papers, paused momentarily, raised and turned his head, and looked intently at the brother, as if assessing his very soul.

'Excellent,' he said, 'I'm so pleased, Father McIntyre, that you could take time out of your busy schedule to come and see me.'

'B... Brother...'

'Excuse me?'

'Brother Connor... Everyone calls me Brother Connor.'

'Oh really? That is unusual. Why is that?'

'Oh... Well, you see, your Eminence, I... I started my ecclesiastical life in a monastery, in Ireland. I spent my first years under the Order of St Benedict and... and it wasn't until later on that I was fortunate enough to take orders. But by then, the Brother Connor title had kind of stuck, and I liked the sound of it, It made me feel part of the family... so...so it was easier not to change... so everyone still calls me Brother Connor.'

'Oh, I see. How very unorthodox, but humble of you. Brother Connor... Yes, I like that. You were brought up in Ireland, then?'

'Yes. I was raised in St Vincent de Paul's orphanage, just outside Dublin.'

'Ah yes... I think I know it.'

'Yes, no doubt, your Eminence. The nuns have always worked hard to look after the children there.'

'Quite so. And their teaching led to a calling?'

'Very much so, your Eminence. Though at first I wasn't permitted to join the Holy Orders. So instead I dedicated myself to the Lord at Ellis Abbey, the Benedictine Monastery nearby. But after twelve years, I was invited to take holy orders and join the Sacerdos.'

'Well congratulations... You are obviously doing great work. Would you care for a drink?'

The Cardinal pointed towards another well-stocked cabinet. 'I have some very nice Redbreast single malt here if you would care to join me?'

'That's very kind of you, your Eminence. Thank you.'

'And do you?' The Cardinal pointed towards a small wooden box filled with cigarettes.

'Oh, no. Not for me, Sir.'

'I hope you don't mind if I do... Another of my many vices for which I am sure I shall pay, some day.'

With the drinks poured, the Cardinal gestured for Connor to sit on one of the two large vermillion sofas in front of the marble fire-place. And with the Cardinal sipping at his whiskey and drawing deeply on his cigarette, they sat down to talk.

'So... I'm so very sorry to hear of this terrible business in your diocese,' said the Cardinal. 'The passing of dear Gerald, not so long after his wife. And now I hear of the terrible death of two of his sons. Is that right?'

'Yes, your Eminence. Sean and Michael. Do..Do you know them?'

'That's right... Yes I know the family... Well I say, know, I met Gerald and Kitty once or twice at some memorial events. Charming couple. They were quite devoted to each other, and to the Church.'

'That is true. They were, Sir.'

'Unfortunately, I wasn't able to attend Gerald's funeral. I hope it went satisfactorily.'

'I think so,' said Brother Connor. 'He had a very good turnout. The parish and many friends and family were there.'

'They were active in your parish?'

'Yes Sir, very. Every Sunday, and most holidays. They were committed Catenians, and supported the parish with their time when they could, and always with generous contributions.'

'Very good, very good... What about the rest of the family? There are five siblings, is that right?'

'Well, yes, at first. All five of the children would attend, but as they got older, we saw less and less of them.'

'They were all confirmed though?'

'Oh, yes.'

'So what happened with the two brothers? Michael and Sean, you say?'

'It's hard to say, Sir. There was some kind of incident at a local hotel, and the two of them died. Rather violently, I'm afraid. They say one was... was,' Connor lowered his voice, '...decapitated... And the other fell from a second-floor balcony.'

'Was it an accident?'

'I'm afraid I don't know, your Eminence. The police are still investigating.'

'Have you spoken to any of the siblings?'

'No I haven't. I last saw them at Gerald's funeral.'

'Hmmm... And what about the two brothers. What were they like?' asked the Cardinal.

'Well, Michael was an architect and Sean was a surveyor.'

'Did you ever see them at Mass? Were you ever asked to officiate in any way?'

'No, not really. Not after their teenage years. Though they both married in the Church, but I never saw much of their children. I think there were difficulties with both marriages. I don't think Sean's children were even baptised.'

'That is a shame. What about the other three children? The sisters and the other brother? You haven't seen them either?'

'No Sir, I haven't. But David, Sheena and Louise were there when it happened.'

'Really? Oh my goodness... They witnessed this terrible event? Oh, the poor things. I presume you have offered them solace or spiritual guidance?'

'I will do Sir, though I'm not sure my presence would be welcomed by all of them.'

'What do you mean?'

'Well... It's just that Sheena, the eldest sister, seems not to care for me, nor have much respect for the clerical collar.'

'Really? Well that is a shame, too.'

'Well, she is the feisty one. She can be something of a handful when she feels like it. She is a professional, though I have never been quite clear what at. She was married, but only for a very short time. No children. And from what I understand, her attendance at church dissipated at a rather early age. She was involved in some er, shall we say, alternative communities for a while. Nothing ever lasted though. She seems to flit from one thing to another.'

'Oh, I see. She finds it hard to settle?'

'Yes, I think so. She was Gerald's carer for the last few years of his life, and lived with him, but I believe she relied a great deal on him for his support, so we can only speculate as to what might happen now.'

The Cardinal frowned. 'It's quite troubling, isn't it? What about the others?'

'Louise, the youngest, seems to be respectful of the faith, but she is very aloof. She has brought up a family, but they only ever attend Mass when they have to. She certainly seems to be the peacemaker in the family, but she can display some of the more robust elements of her sister when she chooses to.'

'And the youngest brother?'

'David? Well, he is something of an enigma. He lives some distance away from the rest of the family. He seems to be always searching for something. He became involved with a religious cult of some kind too some years ago. I couldn't say if he still is, but needless to say, he doesn't attend Mass any longer. He is the most sensitive of them all, and may be the one to find this whole incident the most difficult to deal with.'

The Cardinal stopped for a moment to think. He took another drag on his cigarette and blew the smoke towards the fireplace then sipped his whiskey.

'Well, this is a sad state of affairs now is it not?' said the Cardinal. 'I know they are all adults, but to lose their father and two of their brothers in such a short space of time. That must be such a shock.'

'Yes, your Eminence.'

The Cardinal looked at Brother Connor's now empty glass. 'Would you care for a top up?'

'Well Sir, I... I don't really know.'

'It's a fine Irish Whiskey is it not? Go on... No-one will be any the wiser.'

Brother Connor hesitated again, and then nodded. The Cardinal refilled their glasses and sat down again, pausing to think again for a moment.

'...I wonder, Brother Connor, if you could do me a small favour?'

'Of course. Anything, your Eminence. Just ask.'

'Well, I think we need to take this family more closely under our wing. They have clearly suffered an enormous shock and would probably benefit from some pastoral care, don't you think? Perhaps we can help with their spiritual fortitude in this time of intense challenge and temptation.'

'Temptation?'

'Yes. Temptation... Did you know that Gerald was a very wealthy man?'

'He was?'

'Oh, so I am led to believe. So it is possible that money could be at the root of this particular evil.'

'But surely you can't think that any of them had anything to do with this?'

'I think there is more to this than meets the eye, my son. I sense that the family are in deep spiritual danger. I truly believe that their souls are in mortal jeopardy. They are a flock that needs our attention and I think you are well positioned to lead them onto the righteous path. Is that something you can do? Can you help me save this poor family? Can you do that for me?'

'Of course, your Eminence,' said Brother Connor, 'What is it you would have me do?'

'Do any of the siblings ever attend confession?'

'No Sir. They have sadly all lapsed.'

'Ok. I understand. Then I think subtlety will be the best path here... I think it would be best to keep a close eye on them. Try and gain their confidence. But at the same time try and understand what makes them tick, and well, try and get a sense for... for what their intentions might be. You know? Do you understand me?'

'I think so Sir. You'd like me to get closer to the family, father?'

'Yes. But try not to make it obvious. The path to the Lord is a mysterious one, is it not? And we don't want to put any more pressure on them than there already is.'

'I understand.'

'And keep me informed, won't you?'

'Of course, your Eminence'

'Excellent... And it goes without saying, we will keep this between ourselves, won't we.'

'As you wish, your Eminence. I am at your disposal.'

'Perfect. Thank-you.' The Cardinal stood up, stubbed out his cigarette and moved back to the sofas.

'Shall we pray together?'

'Oh,' replied Connor. 'I would be honoured.'

'No, the honour is all mine... Please follow me.'

The Cardinal walked behind his desk and opened a small concealed door and gesticulated for the priest to follow him. Through the door, the pair descended down a small, dark and dusty wooden staircase that led to another small wooden door at the bottom.

'This is one of the many passageways that run throughout the Cathedral and its grounds,' said the Cardinal. 'They were used in the past mainly by, well, shall we say, people who wanted to keep their movements away from prying eyes. You can very easily move around unnoticed if you know how they are connected. I just use them to surprise Mrs Ames, the housekeeper occasionally,' the Cardinal chuckled.

The Cardinal opened the wooden door and the pair stepped out into a small chapel located to one side of the transept. The Cathedral was closed so the only natural light entering the building came from the sunset streaming through one of the magnificent stained-glass windows at each end. One depicted Jesus' temptation in the wilderness, while the other showed an image of St Eligius holding a golden monstrance, and wearing his full bishops robes. The inscription below the window read, *"I pray god saue thee and seint Loy. Now is my cart out of the slow pardee*". The Cardinal beckoned the priest forward and they walked round to the altar. Each of their steps echoed through the building. Cardinal Stonehouse showed the Brother to a pair of small red cushions in front of a row of small wooden pews.

'This is my favourite place to think, pray and find some sanctuary from the challenges of office,' he said. 'It has a certain special ambience here, especially at the end of the day.'

Brother Connor just nodded in agreement. He was still looking down the length of the Cathedral and at its over-whelming height, power and majesty.

'A little different from a parish church outside Dublin, eh, Brother?' asked the Cardinal.

Connor just nodded once more and tried not to let his mouth drop open again. The Cardinal faced the altar and the enormous crucifix with the classical image of Jesus high upon it. He made the sign of the cross. Connor followed. The Cardinal nodded his head in respect and genuflected. And in the light of the sun disappearing over the horizon as the earth spun slowly on its axis, and with dozens of candles burning brightly in the chapel, the two men knelt to pray.

7

THE BLACK HORSE

'Glad you could make it,' said Sheena sarcastically, as Louise arrived at the restaurant. 'Where is David?'

'Ok, Ok, I'm sorry,' said Louise. 'Let me sit down... I'm sure he'll be here soon... Nice table.'

'He's always late, that boy. I honestly don't know why I bother sometimes.'

'Stop getting so upset. Play nice. He'll be here. He always is.'

'Ok, Ok... So, what do you think of that Herschel guy? A bit up himself, don't you think?'

'No doubt, but he was smart enough to work out what happened to Sean and Michael. More than the police ever did.'

'Do you think he'll discover who the killer is?' asked Sheena.

'Well, I think we've got more of a chance with him than without him. He seems to be very, well... connected, now doesn't he?'

'I don't trust him. I didn't like the way he insinuated that I might have been involved.'

'He insinuated that we all could be involved, and to be honest Sheena, he does have a point. You are the one who will benefit the most from Michael and Sean not being here any longer.'

'You don't know that,' snapped Sheena, taking another mouthful of her wine. 'And neither do I. Oh, Jesus... It's all just so mixed up.'

'But you can't blame him for eliminating each possible suspect, can you?' said Louise. 'I mean, we must all be suspects at the moment, right?'

'But where would any of us be able to get hold of that weird drug?'

'I know, I know. Look, Herschel's just doing his job, right? I think, in the end, he'll be beneficial for all of us. Have faith, and I'm sure he'll help us all get to the bottom of this.'

The three siblings were to meet at the Olive Ranch restaurant, a favourite haunt of Sheena's. It was an attractive, family-run Italian restaurant that sported a large terrace with fabulous views over the city. Sheena had secured the best table, over-looking the edge of the balcony, under the gnarled and twisted stems of cultivated vines, arranged to form a covering of natural foliage. With the addition of a pale awning to protect them from the sun, the table provided a beautiful, uninter-rupted view across the rooftops. Sheena was on her third glass of Chablis and her fourth cigarette by the time her sister had arrived.

'I'm not sure I share your trust in him,' said Sheena, 'Don't you think he's just a bit, well... weird?'

'Yes. He does have a certain way about him. But he's smart isn't he, and connected.

'And weird...'

'Ok, ok, I get it. But for now, given that the police have neither the resources nor the ability to help us, he's the best we've got.'

'Hi. I'm sorry I'm late,' said David as he joined the two sisters. 'Traffic.'

'Traffic? Hah!' mocked Sheena, 'More like, you couldn't get out of bed. Look at the state of you.'

David sat down at the table. His normally neat and tidy visage was absent for once. Where he would usually be scrupulous about his tight, tucked-in, college-boy look, today his jacket looked very loose, and his crumpled white shirt was hanging out over his belt, while his chinos were baggy and creased. Even his usually shiny brown brogues appeared duller than normal.

'Oh my God David... Are you ok?' said Louise. 'You look terrible. You're all disheveled. Are you feeling ok?'

'Yes, I'm fine. Don't worry about me,' replied David. 'I've had a little trouble sleeping lately. That's all. It's all the stress of this...'

'But your skin...your face David. You're... yellow... Look,' said Louise. She took out her makeup compact and put it in front of his face.

'Your skin doesn't look right David, and your eyes are really sunken. I mean, those dark rings,' added Sheena.

'Well, I haven't been feeling myself lately, that's true. I'm sure it will pass,' replied David, hurriedly.

'I think you should see a doctor, David,' continued Louise. 'You really don't look well. Have you lost weight? I mean you're thin enough as it is, but you look like you could do with a good meal.'

'Can we just get on with this, please?' said David. 'Have you ordered?'

'No, not yet,' replied Sheena.

Sheena waived the waiter over and the three of them ordered. Louise and Sheena ordered salads from the waiter and Sheena ordered a second bottle of Chablis.

'Can you tell me what is in the Smashed Chickpea and Avocado Salad?' asked David.

The waiter looked bemused.

'I mean, the chickpeas. Are they fresh? They're not frozen or tinned, are they?'

'No sir, they come fresh from the suppliers every morning,' replied the waiter.

'And the avocado. How old is it?'

'How old, sir?'

'Yes. Avocados are grown mainly in Mexico, Chile or Peru. When was it picked?'

'I have no idea sir. But I can ask the chef.'

'No... No. It's ok... But these things can be very important... We must always be aware of the prices of wheat and barley,' muttered David.

'I'm sorry sir?' said the waiter.

'It doesn't matter.'

'Anything to drink, sir?'

'Yes... I see thou hurt not the oil and the wine,' mumbled David again.

'I beg your pardon sir... I didn't get that,' replied the waiter.

'What did you say?' asked Louise.

'Nothing,' replied David. 'Just some bottled water. No gas. And please make sure it is fresh. Very fresh.'

'Yes, it is. Very good, sir. Fresh bottled water,' muttered the waiter as he walked away.

'So,' said Sheena. 'Now we know from that Herschel man, that Michael and Sean's deaths were no accident, right? We know that they were murdered by someone who had access to that weird drug.'

'From North Korea,' added Louise.

'Yes,' said Sheena, taking another mouthful of her wine. 'You work in pharmaceuticals, don't you Louise?'

'Yes. In sales,' replied Louise, cagily. 'And?'

'Nothing...It's just the company you work for is an international one, isn't it?'

'Yes... It is. What of it?'

'Oh, I don't know. It's just if you wanted to get something

128

like that, as unusual as that, say, the first place I would look would be someone with access to an international drugs company.'

'And the first place I would look would be a daughter who ripped off her father and is most likely to benefit from the death of her brother,' countered Louise. 'I can't believe it... After all this, I came here to try and smooth things over again, and you're already throwing accusations around.'

'I'm just saying what everyone else is thinking,' snapped Sheena.

'You're drunk,' said Louise, 'How many glasses of wine have you had? Most of that bottle I think.'

'And the other thing... is... What if the murderer got the wrong people?' said Sheena.

'What? What the heck do you mean?' said Louise.

'I mean... What if they didn't mean to kill Michael or Sean?'

'What? Now, you are just being ridiculous. Who could they be meaning to get? Didn't the police say they dropped the drug into their drink or something?'

'Whoever it was could have dropped the drug into any drink. Maybe it just so happened that Sean and Michael drank it.'

'This is just the booze talking now Sheena. I think you should cool off and go home,' said Louise.

'What if it was someone who wanted – say me, you, or even David – dead?'

'Why on earth would anyone want us dead?'

'Why would anyone want Sean or Michael dead? It doesn't make any sense. And anyway, David is always living on the edge of financial ruin, aren't you David?' said Sheena

David was not listening. His head was down, aimlessly pushing his food around his plate and taking no notice of what was going on. He put his hand to his mouth and coughed loudly.

'You know, any one of his 'contacts' could have the means and opportunity to do such a thing,' continued Sheena. 'I know, I've met a few of them. If they took a dislike to how one of David's schemes was performing, well, they're capable of anything, I reckon. I mean it's perfectly likely that they got the wrong brother. Maybe it should have been him rather than Sean...'

'Oh my God, Sheena... Listen to yourself,' cried Louise. 'This is David. This is your brother. He is sitting right here, in front of you. How could you possibly even think such a thing? You are no wiser about this than any of us. How do you even know that it wasn't meant for me, or what if it was meant for you?'

'Maybe it would have been better if it was... Without Sean, there's no point in me even being here.'

Tears began to form in Sheena's eyes.

'Oh, for goodness sake,' said Louise. 'Pull yourself together.'

'It was all going so well. It was all going to plan,' sobbed Sheena.

'What? What did you say?' asked Louise

David let out a low groan. The two women stopped bickering for a moment and looked at their brother. He groaned again and began to retch. A series of loud guttural sounds came from deep within him.

'Oh my God, David... Are you alright?' cried Louise.

'His skin... Oh my God David, you look positively green,' said Sheena.

David retched again. A dark sounding heave came again from deep within his body.

'Oh David. Do you want some water' asked Louise. 'Do you need some indigestion tablets?'

David's retching increased and it became louder and more repetitive. With each bout, he bent over, double with the pain and the effort.

'David... Please. People are beginning to look,' said Sheena
'I'm alright,' gasped David. 'I'll be fine. All I need is...'
'Oh my God!' screeched Louise. 'What is that?'
She pointed to the table.
'What?' replied Sheena. 'What?'
'There...On the table...There...What is that?'
Louise pointed one of her professionally manicured fingers vigorously at the table top. The two women stared as a brown and black mottled cockroach crawled slowly across the white tablecloth.
'Oh my... That's disgusting,' said Sheena. 'That the last time I'm coming to this...'
'Look!... There's another one... Oh, my God... That's just rev...'
David rose up quickly out of his seat and tried to stand upright. He groaned again and grasped his stomach, then broke wind so loudly that it echoed around the terrace. He groaned again and wrapped his arms around his stomach, bending over as the spasms hit him.
'What?' said Sheena, still distracted. 'David... Are you alright?'
'What the hell is going on?' cried Louise. 'Oh David...David...You're not alright. Is this something to do with... Look, come with me. Let's see if we can find somewhere more private.' Louise moved to help her brother and nodding towards the table said, 'Sheena... Can you get the waiter to do something about those...things.'
Retching again, and doubled over in obvious agony, David broke wind several more times. Each time, louder and longer than the one before. He groaned and retched again as he tried to sit back down, twisting and turning in pain. Some of the other diners began to murmur and point.
'Let's get him out of here,' urged Sheena.
'Oh my God... The smell...' winced Louise, scrunching her face in disgust.

'That is just rank,' replied Sheena, gagging on the stench. 'It's him, isn't it... Oh, my God. That is so disgusting...This is so embarrassing. We should get him out of here.'

Two diners tried to come over to see if they could help, but were quickly repelled by the smell, while others began complaining more obviously about the disturbance.

'Your guest seems to be in some distress,' said the Maitre D'. 'Can I help you at all?'

'You could do something about those,' demanded Sheena, pointing to the table.

David could neither stand up nor sit down. He continued to retch and break wind loudly as he bent over, clutching his abdomen. He coughed again and cried out in pain.

'Oh my God,' cried Louise, pointing at the floor. 'Look... Those insects... They're... they're coming from you, David.'

'I'm afraid your guest is disturbing the other diners,' interrupted the Maitre D'. 'Shall we find somewhere more private for him?'

'Yes, well I'm very sorry my brother is putting them off their risotto,' snapped Sheena. 'Only, if you haven't noticed, our table is infested, and my brother seems to be in excruciating pain. So forgive me if our health is more important to me right now than the state of their bruschetta.'

David groaned again, stood up straight, and still clutching his abdomen, he projectile vomited across the table. A huge arcing hose of green and yellow discharge spewed from his throat, down onto the white table-cloth where, with some force, it splattered upwards and outwards, coating Louise, Sheena and the Maitre D' in its path.

Louise screamed.

'Good God...' cried the Maitre D'.

'Get a fucking ambulance, will you,' yelled Sheena.

The vomit was everywhere: the table, over the half-eaten food, in the wine glasses and all over the polished tiled floor. Dozens of coated cockroaches crawled in it. Sheena, Louise and the Maitre D' each had large globules of vomitus over them. Louise's white blouse was streaked yellow and green, as was the Maitre D's dark waistcoat. Sheena was splattered on her face and in her hair. Alone by the table, David stood up again, groaned loudly, and pulled his shirt up to reveal his emaciated chest and stomach.

'Oh my God... What is happening?' cried Louise. 'David...Your stomach...'

The three of them watched the skin of his abdomen churn and roll as if it were alive. Tears of pain rolled down his face, and he fell to the floor, pulling the tablecloth and all that was upon it, down upon him with an enormous crash.

'What the... For God's sake, get some help!' screamed Sheena.

The Maitre D' pulled away the table cloth and threw it to one side. David was now lying on his back, on the floor, caked in his own insect infested vomit, and crying in torment. Grimacing in pain, he began to tear at his abdomen with his fingers, writhing and screaming like a possessed animal as he did so. He ripped at the skin of his shrunken stomach and began to tear strips of flesh from it. His emaciated stomach fell away easily to reveal black and diseased intestines bursting out from the hole he had just created.

'Stop David. Please stop... You're hurting yourself,' cried Louise.

'Oh my God, the smell...' cried the Maitre D'. He tried to cover his face with a napkin while simultaneously trying to pull David's hands away from his stomach. David's blackened intestines now fell from the large hole in his stomach.

'David... For God's sake, stop that... Oh my God... Look!' shrieked Sheena.

A large intrusion of cockroaches streamed from David's abdomen spilling onto the stained tablecloth. Hundreds of them poured out from him, fell onto the table and crawled across the floor. One of the customers shrieked in horror. Others rapidly cleared their tables and made for the exit.

'Do something!' cried Sheena.

'Like what?' shrieked Louise, 'Look at him... Please... somebody save him... Where is that ambulance?'

David lay twisting and writhing in agony on the floor of the restaurant, surrounded by his two sisters and some of the remaining restaurant customers. The insides of his body, were ravaged by malnutrition, colitis and gangrene, the likes of which Sheena had never been seen before. Louise knelt down and cradled David's head in her arms.

'Oh, you poor, poor soul. What have they done to you?' she whispered.

The hole in David's stomach was larger now. His skin was so thin it was almost transparent and could have been torn with the slightest of touches. The rest of his body was emaci- ated to the point of starvation. As he lay in his sisters' arms, he continued to cough up blood, bile, insects, and multi-coloured vomit. And as the exhaustion took hold, he lay back, still twisting in pain, and put his head back into his sisters' lap. He began to breathe more slowly and regularly, with his eyes fixed upwards at a point way off in the sky.

'We love you, David. Don't die... Please don't die,' cried Louise.

But it was too late. David's body was relaxed now in death, in his sisters' arms. He had all but decomposed and disinte- grated in front of their very eyes.

'It's happened again, hasn't it?' said Sheena through a cloud of cigarette smoke. The tracks of her tears remained etched on her face and her mascara had run down both cheeks. Her top was still smeared with David's bodily fluids. Her hands trem- bled as she held her burning cigarette.

'Why us? Who would want to do that to us?' She pointed towards the emaciated body of her brother, which was now surrounded by police Scene of Crime officers (SoCo's).

'I'm scared, Detective Somerset. I'm really, really, scared,' said Louise, shaking as she pulled the emergency foil blanket tightly around her.

The scene around them was one of chaos and confusion. Dozens of police officers and paramedics had descended on the restaurant after the call was made. They were too late to save David, but they entered the establishment with as much zeal and gusto as before. Armed officers stormed the restaurant from the outside to secure the area, quickly followed by the paramedic first responders. Those customers who weren't met by the muzzle of a Heckler & Koch, and some considerable police force as they climbed the stairs, were taken to one side for questioning. The police helicopter hovered noisily above the scene. The Maitre D' was interviewed by one of the police officers, with his hands clutched to his face in disbelief.

'You are safe here now,' said Somerset. 'Nothing is going to harm you.'

'It doesn't feel that way,' said Louise. 'You didn't see what we just did... It was,.. just,... awful... I feel sick.' She began to sob. 'I can't bear to look at him.'

David's skeletal body, now being inspected and photographed by the police officers, lay in a crumpled heap of vomit, blood and dark bodily fluids. His whole abdominal area had disintegrated, revealing a hole so large that the lower part of his spine was visible. Remnants of whole and trampled cock-roaches were being carefully collected by the forensic officers.

'Well, it's all over now.. Are you able to tell me anything about what happened?' said the Inspector.

'I don't know...It all happened so quickly,' replied Sheena.

'Did your brother... I mean... Was he angry in any way? Like Sean and Michael?' asked the Inspector.

'No, No. Nothing of the sort. He seemed ok at first. He was

late, which isn't unusual, and he said he hadn't been sleeping well, but apart from that,' said Louise.

'Yes, but he wasn't himself, was he?' said Sheena. 'I hadn't noticed how painfully thin he had become. And he didn't touch any of his food.'

I saw that,' said Louise. 'And he was even fussier than usual about what he ordered.'

'So... What.. happened?' asked Somerset gently.

'Well, everything was fine. We were sitting at the table, just talking, when he suddenly became ill. We tried to get him somewhere private, but he deteriorated so fast. He became very ill, very quickly, and well, then he fell down, and that happened,' said Sheena, as she looked over to her brother.

'What was it Inspector? Do you have any idea?' asked Louise.

'It's hard to say at this stage, I'm afraid,' replied Somerset. 'It doesn't look like what happened to your brothers. At least not on the surface. We'll need to do more tests, and consult with the experts, but from what I can see, it looks like he had some kind of infestation that ate him from the inside out.'

'Oh my God!' cried Louise, sobbing with her face in her hands.

'So was this murder again, Inspector? Or something else?' asked Sheena.

'It's impossible to tell at this stage,' said Somerset. 'But trust me, we'll definitely get to the bottom of it.'

'That's another one of this family dead, Inspector,' cried Louise. 'There is definitely someone out to get us, and I don't know why.'

Louise buried her head in her hands again.

'Yes... You need to start thinking about a serial killer here Inspector Somerset,' said Sheena. 'Three of the five of us are now dead, and you are no wiser than you were after Michael and Sean. You need to get some serious resources onto this case and solve it pretty damn quick... and we are going to need around the clock protection. I have no intention of being the next victim,' ordered Sheena.

'What about Herschel? Does he know?' Louise asked as she looked up from her hands.

'He has been advised, yes,' said Somerset. 'And we'll get all the forensic material and the reports over to him as soon as we can. Ok?'

'I know...' said Louise.

'What?' said Somerset.

'I bet you...' said Louise suddenly.

Sheena and the Inspector looked at each other. Louise jumped up and walked over to where the forensic officers were still inspecting David's body. She put her hand over her nose and mouth, and knelt down beside her brother's body.

'What... What are you doing?' asked Sheena.

'You really shouldn't be contaminating the...' said Somerset.

Trying very hard not to look directly at him, Louise felt around and inside her brother's jacket pockets.

'Aha,' she said, 'Just as I thought.'

'What... What is it?' asked Sheena.

'A clay horse. It's a small clay horse. It's a... Black one,' said Louise.

'Oh my God, not another one,' exclaimed Sheena. 'Show me...'

8

DENIAL

'So, there's another clay horse,' said Herschel, as Louise, Sheena and Somerset sat down in the police conference room.

'Louise found it on David's body', said Sheena.

'I knew it would be there... I just had a hunch,' said Louise

'A hunch? That's interesting,' said Herschel. 'Tell me more about what you were thinking and feeling before that hunch came to you...'

'What?' said Louise

'Look... I think these two have had enough troubles for one day,' said Somerset. He sighed as he sat down and dumped another huge pile of papers on the desk. 'Why don't we stop messing around with all the psychology-babble and get to the point? You know, the clay horses themselves?'

'Forgive me, Inspector,' said Herschel, 'but I actually think that it was Louise's state of mind that led her to realise there might be a clay horse somewhere on her brother's body. And that is significant... It could be very significant... I wouldn't classify the investigation of the psychology of a witness to a murder as 'messing around.' Louise obviously had a series of specific thoughts, admittedly after, and probably because she witnessed her brother's demise, but it may be of some benefit in investigating this case if we walked our way through it. Don't you think so, Inspector? If not, well, feel free to fill in some of your forms while I attempt to solve this case... Now Louise, talk me through what you were thinking.'

'Er... Well,' said Louise. 'We had just seen David die in that awful, awful way... And I suppose I was in some kind of shock...'

'Like a trance?' asked Herschel.

'I guess so... I don't really know what I was thinking. I was just there with Sheena, and I could see his horribly thin body... It was just lying there, so tiny against the black and white tiles... Oh, God...' said Louise, wiping a tear away. 'And then I remembered what David had said just before that awful thing, whatever it was, took a hold of him...'

'Yes...'

'He turned up late, which isn't unusual, but he acted strangely from the start... He just wasn't himself. He takes such pride in his appearance... He's normally so very well dressed – always appropriate for the occasion – and his clothes are always high-quality and very well selected. He has... had, an eye for fashion. But today he didn't look anything like he normally would. His shirt was hanging out, and his chinos weren't pressed. His trousers hung very badly on him... But, I don't know – maybe that was because he had lost so much weight. Why didn't we notice it? He must have been in so much pain. The main thing I noticed was how fussy he was about what he was going to eat.'

'I thought that too,' said Sheena.

'David was normally a fussy and faddy eater,' Louise continued. 'He's been a vegan for as long as I can remember and he suffered with an eating disorder as a child. When he was little, he found it difficult to swallow, and so couldn't eat much in the way of solid food. It was all psychological and stress related, and he had to have counselling to help him over-

come it which he eventually did. All his life, he found it difficult to eat in front of people. And he was always embarking on
one new diet or another, and yet he didn't need to – he was
always so painfully thin. We're all a bit narcissistic in this
family, really. But today he was different. It was something he
said... I can't quite remember.'

'Yes... That's right,' said Sheena. 'He said something to the
waiter when he ordered... He was even more fussy than
normal... What was it?'

'Do you remember what he ordered?' asked Herschel.

'He wanted to know where the avocado came from... How
fresh it was. It was an avocado and chickpea salad he ordered,
wasn't it, Sheena?'

'I think so.'

'And he only had water. Bottled water. And he wanted to
make sure it was fresh.'

'Fresh, bottled water?' said Herschel.

'I know,' said Louise. 'But then as he was ordering his
salad, he said something... It sounded a bit church-like to me...
But I just can't remember...'

'Ok,' said Herschel. 'Let's try this another way... Just relax
now... And breathe deeply and slowly. Imagine you are there at
the restaurant... You, Sheena and David...'

'Ok,' Louise took a deep breath and closed her eyes.

'The waiter is standing by you. He has his pad in his hand,
and he is taking David's order...'

'Yes... avocado and chickpea... wheat and barley... That's
what he said. Something about wheat and barley...'

'Ok... Keep going... What else do you see and hear?'

'He said... 'We must be aware of the prices of wheat and
barley'... That was it. He confused the waiter when he said it.'

'Revelations,' said Herschel. 'Did he say anything else?'

'Yes... One other thing that we didn't notice, or didn't listen
to... So we ignored it... He said something about oil and wine...'

'Do not harm the oil and wine?' asked Herschel.

'Yes... that was it. 'I see thou hurt not the oil and the wine.'
I only half heard it, but it has come back to me now... What
does it mean Herschel?'

'It's from Revelations 6:6,' said Herschel. 'Michael hears a
voice in the midst of the four living creatures saying 'A quart of
wheat for a denarius, and three quarts of barley for a denarius;
and do not harm the oil and the wine'.'

'I've never heard that before. Is it significant?'

'It could be. Did he mention anything about horses?'

'Horses?'

'Yes. It could be important... Anything like that?'

'No. I don't think so. Do you Sheena?'

'I don't remember any of this,' said Sheena.

'But then for some reason... You thought to look in your
brother's pockets, right?' asked Herschel.

'Yes.'

'How much of the Bible did you study as a child, Louise?'

'Well, the same as anyone else growing up in a Catholic
family, I guess.'

'And you don't remember those lines at all? They don't
remind you of anything?'

'No? Should they? What does all this mean, Herschel?'

'Well, I'm not sure. I'll need to do some more investigations, but I think that you had some kind of deep childhood
memory that, when combined with what David said, caused
you to think about the horse. The clay horse that you eventually found in his pocket... It's very interesting.'

'Interesting to you, maybe,' replied Sheena. 'But terrifying
for us.'

'Yes. I know. I'm sorry,' said Herschel.

'What does this have to do with how David died, though?'
asked Sheena.

'Well clearly the clay horses on Sean, Michael and David
would indicate some kind of purpose from the killer.'

'The killer?' said Louise. 'So David's death wasn't accidental or self-inflicted?'

'No, I don't think so, and the clay horses are a clue to who and why. I need to do some more work and look more closely at Revelations 6:6'

'Revelations?' asked Sheena. 'You think there's a biblical angle to all this? And the clay horses? Isn't Revelations all about the rapture and the end of days?

'So,the horses? Are you thinking what I'm thinking?' said Cassandra.

'I'm not sure,' said Herschel. 'What are you thinking?'

Louise, Sheena and DI Somerset had left, and Herschel was now on his own in the conference room.

'Well.. I have in mind a biblically obsessed serial killer with a vendetta against the family,' said Cassandra.

'Hmmm, I'm with you part of the way, but I still don't think we should rule out either Sheena or Louise as suspects. They both have far too much to gain from their brothers' deaths.'

'I'm not so sure. They just seem far too upset. I don't think either of them could put on a show like that for as long as they have.'

'They both have enough motive to kill. What if they're in it together? In some kind of femme-fatale plot?'

'But I still don't see how they would benefit? Louise especially. She isn't named in the will. She would stand to benefit from Sean and Sheena's death, but not from David's. And she was close to David. Why David? What benefit could it be to either of them? Or anyone else for that matter.'

'Well, I guess we'll find out...'

The door to the conference room opened and Inspector

Somerset poked his head round. Herschel twisted his head around to look at Somerset.

'Is everything ok, Herschel?' he asked.

'Fine, thank you, Inspector Somerset.'

'Only I thought there was someone in here with you.'

'No. No. Just me and my thoughts... You know me... Sometimes I like to go over what I have just heard after speaking to a witness. I often find it more useful if I vocalise it... You know, speak it to myself. Review it... That kind of thing. I can set it like a play in my head... and I can better sense the motivation behind what the witness has said, and maybe what they might be covering up. You should try it some time... Do you, er... need this room... or?'

'No...No. Feel free to continue... vocalising, as you call it. Interesting. Do you need anything else from me?'

'No. I'm good. I have the three clay horses for the time being, and your team's forensic reports, the photos and the witness statements. I'll let you have the clay figures back when I leave. I just need to do a bit more scenario analysis, if that's ok?'

'Feel free. Vocalise away. I'll be downstairs if you need me.'

'Thanks,' said Herschel. Somerset closed the door.

'Now, where were we?' said Herschel.

'How about we look at the horses and what Louise said about David?' said Cassandra.

'Ok. So what is your take on it? Revelations?'

'Yes. Let's have a closer look. Part of Revelations 6 tells of a book held in God's right hand that is sealed with seven seals. The Lamb of God opens the first four of these seals which summons four beings that ride out on White, Red, Black and Pale Horses. They are described as, 'the ones whom the Lord has sent to patrol the earth'. Ezekiel lists them as War, Famine, Plague and Righteousness.'

'The Four Horsemen of The Apocalypse...'

'That's right. The Four Horsemen figure in the New Testaments' Revelations as well as the Old Testaments' Book of Zachariah and Ezekiel, where they are named as punishments from God, and are a sign of the Antichrist, the End Times, or the last judgement of God. It is said that they were each given authority over a quarter of the earth to kill as they saw fit as a pre-curser to the end of days.'

'Oh, right,' said Herschel. 'So the killer is sending a message that the end of the world is coming, at least as far as he is concerned? And the clay horses are a symbol of that?'

'In his or her mind, almost certainly. The figures found with Michael and Sean were Red and the one found on David was Black.'

'And which one is which?'

'Ok. Let me think... The Red Horseman – he rides with a flaming sword, and represents all War on earth. The Black Horseman is a food-merchant, yet he represents Famine.'

'War and Famine? Well that kind of fits,' said Herschel. 'Michael and Sean battled each other in an act of rage, or War, at least, between the two of them. And as far as we know, David died as a result of his body being unable to process what little nutrients he put into it, and he rotted from the inside out. The killer somehow ensured that no matter what he ate, he still starved to death. So Famine, right?'

'I think so,' said Cassandra. 'And the words that Louise said he spoke relate directly to Revelations 6:6 and refer directly to the Black Horse. She said that he said, 'Do not harm the oil and the wine,' and, 'We must be aware of the prices of wheat and barley'. These are both predictions in the Gospel of Michael for the coming of the Black Horseman.'

'Do you think he knew?'

'David? More likely that in his malnourished, addled state, he had repeated the lines over and over in some kind of subliminal way.'

'Poor guy. It must have taken months to get him to that condition.'

'Probably, but as his sisters said, he was susceptible to it. You know, all those peculiar diets he was fond of.'

'So... That leaves the two other horsemen,' said Herschel.

'Correct,' replied Cassandra. 'The Pale Horse and the White Horse. Revelations has more to say on them. It reads, 'Come and see. And I looked, and behold, a Pale Horse. And the name of him who sat on it was Death.' The third, the Pale Horse is actually a pale green in colour and it is said that it will bring what the Greeks referred to as a great thánatos, or pestilence as we know it.'

'Nice. And the fourth?'

'The fourth is the White Horse – the Righteous Horse. He is associated with cleanliness and purity. He usually carries a bow as a weapon of war. The rider of the White Horse is given a crown to wear, which authorises him to go to war, after which he goes, 'out conquering and to conquer' – the implication being that his entire purpose is to conquer, to dominate, and to subjugate the people's of the earth.

'Ok. So we now know that the murders are linked, and that the killer is trying to send a message of some kind. Probably religious. It's possible, if we assume two remaining horsemen, that he is planning to kill at least two more times.'

'Yes, or at least in two incidents' said Cassandra. 'Do you think he might be aiming for Sheena and Louise?'

'I think that is pretty likely,' said Herschel. 'We'll have to get Somerset to increase their police protection.'

'That would make sense and it will give us an opportunity to keep a closer eye on them.'

'I would have said that Sheena was the most likely suspect after Sean and Michael's deaths, given the inheritance, but now it's got a whole lot more complicated. Perhaps we should consider that the perpetrator might be female?'

'Do you think? Someone with a grudge against accountants, surveyors and architects? Possible, but unlikely. No there must be something else... What about the will?'

'Go on,' said Herschel.

'Well, it's just that that was the last time they were all together, under simpler circumstances - and wills are always a point of contention. And no more so than this one. Didn't Louise say something earlier about the will being stored in a strange way?'

'Yes, I think she did.'

'She said it was housed in a mahogany box that they had to chisel open.'

'Do you think they had to break a seal of any kind on it?

'Like one of the Seven Seals?'

'Exactly,' chirruped Herschel. 'I think we need to make a visit to the solicitor's office and take a closer look at that box.'

'Definitely,' said Cassandra.

Satisfied with his afternoon's work, Herschel got up from his table and walked out of the conference room and turned out the lights.

'A serial killer? Targeting our family?' said Sheena.

'Yes,' said Herschel. 'And we think they have some kind of religious vendetta.'

'Against us? Why on earth would anyone want to kill our family? And for religious reasons? I mean it's not like any of us practice anymore.'

'I suppose it could also be money. The lure of the inheritance, perhaps. If it's common knowledge,' said Herschel. 'Or maybe they have some crazed idea about what your family stands for. To be honest, at this stage their motive could be anything.'

'I haven't told anyone about the inheritance, have you?' said Sheena.

'Of course not,' said Louise. 'Why would I?'

Riding in the taxi together, Herschel, Louise and Sheena

headed towards the solicitor's office. The journey gave Herschel some time to explain his thinking.

'So, we, I mean... I, think that the murders are linked. The clay horses tell us that.'

'I think we kind of knew that already,' said Sheena.

'Yes, but the horses and the verses from Revelations are linked. Have you heard of the Four Horsemen of the Apocalypse?' said Herschel.

'Er... Not really. Maybe... Are they in the Bible? In Revelations?' asked Louise, leaning forward.

'Yes,' said Herschel. 'They are. In that they are part of the scripture that predicts the End of Days.'

'End of Days?' asked Louise.

'The prophesy of the end of the world,' said Sheena. 'Is that what this is all about?

'We think so,' said Herschel. 'We think that the killer is trying to send a message. By killing in a way that imitates the Four Horsemen, we think they are trying to draw attention to the Church by saying that they believe that the end of the world is coming.'

'How have they imitated them with us?' asked Louise

'Well, we discovered the red horses on Sean and Michael. In Revelations, the Red Horseman predicts War. David had a black horse, didn't he? The Black Horseman prophesies hunger and starvation.'

'Oh, I see,' said Louise. 'But what about the other two?'

'The White Horse and the Pale Horse,' said Herschel.

'Are those meant for us? Are they going to try and kill us? Oh my God,' said Louise.

'Please don't worry. I have asked DI Somerset to increase your police protection,' said Herschel.

'Increase? From what? I only ever see a policeman when I go to the station,' complained Sheena.

'Well, it's not always obvious. Anyway, I would ask that you try not to worry about it. With increased coverage from the police, the killer will have absolutely no chance,' said Herschel.

'Oh, that's alright... I feel so much safer now,' said Sheena sarcastically. 'What kind of protection are they going to give us?'

'More non-uniformed officers and unmarked cars, I believe. Plus an armed presence within thirty feet at all times. You won't be aware of it, but trust me it will be there. You'll be treated like royalty,' said Herschel.

'And what about about when I'm at home?' asked Louise. 'And my family? How will they be protected?'

'Unmarked police cars and armed officers are stationed outside,' replied Herschel. 'We can put a police officer inside your house too if you wish.'

'No thank you, very much,' said Louise. 'I don't want some plod living with us and freaking us out any more than they already have.'

Herschel laughed.

'You didn't tell us about the other two horsemen, did you Herschel?' asked Sheena, pointedly. 'What delights does the killer have in store for us?'

'Please don't joke about it, Sheena,' replied Louise, clearly nervous.

'Ah yes,' said Herschel. 'Well, the two other horses are the White Horse and the Pale Horse. The White Horse is the horse of righteous judgement, and is associated with cleanliness and purity.'

'Well, that doesn't sound too bad,' said Louise.

'It's not quite what you think... He is tasked with purifying the souls on Earth at the End of Days. It is his job to remove those whose souls are impure or tainted.'

'Remove? Oh,I see... I was hoping for something different... What about the fourth?'

'The fourth is the Pale Horse. He is depicted as pale green in colour and is the bringer of pestilence and disease.'

'Lovely,' said Sheena. 'For those who have survived War, Famine and Righteous Judgement, we are then left with the plague to deal with.'

'I don't know how you can be so flippant about it, Sheena. Aren't you scared?' asked Louise.

'It's just some religious nutcase. I'm sure Herschel and Somerset will find the perpetrators pretty quickly,' said Sheena.

'Yes, of course...just some religious nutcase who somehow got access to a weapons grade nerve-agent and infected our youngest brother with some kind of vile infestation,' said Louise. 'I don't think you are taking this nearly seriously enough.'

'Well, that's where you're wrong... I take every part of this whole mess very seriously,' said Sheena. 'I'm as scared as you are, Louise, but I'm not going to let some crank make me change the way I live.'

'Well, I hope that works out for you. I'm going to take all the protection I'm offered, but I'm not prepared to change my routine for the police, a killer or anyone. They'll just have to work around me.'

'Well,' said Herschel. 'I would suggest that you don't put yourselves into any risky situations. Don't go out alone, and always let people know where you're going to be,' said Herschel. 'Now, the solicitors...'

'Yes,' said Sheena. 'Why are we going there again?'

'You both said that your father's will was sealed in a wooden box, correct?'

'Yes, that's right,' said Sheena. 'It was a dark wooden one.'

'And to open it, did you have to break something on it? Like a seal?' asked Herschel.

'Yes. It had a kind of clay-ceramic seal on the top of it. Otley had to hit it very hard with a chisel to get it to open,' said Sheena.

'Interesting,' said Herschel. 'Did it break apart, when it was hit?'

'Good God yes... And it made sparks,' said Sheena. 'Otley had to hit it really hard to get it to open.'

'Hmmm... Well, let's hope he still has it and we can piece it back together.'

'Is it some kind of clue, Herschel?' said Louise.

'I'm hoping so. I just need to get a closer look at it to find out.'

'Good to see you all here again,' said Earl Otley, as he shuffled behind his desk. 'I'm so sorry to hear about your brothers... Terrible business.'

The offices of Taylor, Otley and Snyde had improved none since their last visit. Otley's desk remained covered in piles of dusty papers, folders and legal boxes. The office wallpaper was still brown at the edges and the carpet remained exhausted.

'Well thank you for seeing us so quickly,' said Sheena. 'Let me introduce Mr Damien Herschel. He is assisting us and the police in the investigation of our brothers' deaths.'

'Very nice to meet you, Mr Herschel,' said Otley. Herschel nodded.

'We... I mean Herschel, has some questions pertaining to our father's will,' said Sheena.

'I can assure you that everything has been carried out exactly as your father wanted,' Otley replied firmly.

'No... No. It's not that. It's just that the wooden box that contained the will...'

'Yes... What about it?'

'Do you still have it?'

'Er... I think so... I rarely throw anything away.'

'Well,' said Herschel. 'Do you think you could magic it up?'

Otley stopped, turned, and looked at Herschel for a moment. Herschel looked straight back.

'Er, yes... I'm sure... One moment,' said Otley. He pressed his intercom button.

'Miss Dench... Miss Dench,' he shouted. 'Can I have the Gerald Allen material please?'

'Certainly, Sir,' came the distorted reply from just outside his office. 'One moment...'

'You know this is most irregular,' said Otley. 'It's not normal for us to provide the container to the will. Normally it would have been destroyed by now.'

'I do hope not, Mr Otley,' said Herschel, drily. 'Only nothing about this investigation is anywhere near normal. You are in possession of some material evidence that, may, as you say, have been disposed of, which I'm sure you are aware could be considered as tampering with evidence. I'm sure that you wouldn't want to be charged with any crime relating to this investigation, now would you?'

Otley looked at Herschel again for a moment, then hurriedly pressed the button on his intercom again. 'Hurry up, will you please, Miss Dench,' he urged.

Moments later, Otley's assistant bustled into the office carrying a cardboard box containing files and papers, as well as Gerald's mahogany box.

'Oh, thank goodness,' sighed Otley. He cleared his throat. 'Thank-you, Miss Dench.'

Herschel took the box and inspected it closely. He rolled it around in his hands, inspecting each side carefully and tracing his fingers down each face and edge.

'Hmmm... This is a highly crafted piece of workmanship,' said Herschel. 'Look at the invisible jointing and the intricate pearl inlays. Somebody spent a lot of time constructing this. The wood is top quality...mahogany and ivory... Probably from Brazil or Mexico, I would say. The copper hinge is secreted away so it looks like a single block of perfectly carved wood.

Very nice... I would estimate it to be at least fifty to a hundred years old... I was expecting some religious symbology of some sort to be on it, but I see none. There was a seal of some kind on the top here?'

'Yes,' said Sheena. 'It held a large ribbon in place tightly around the box. Mr Otley had to hit it very hard to break it free.'

'Ah, yes. That would explain the damage on the top... Where is the seal now?'

'Inside the box,' said Otley.

'Ah ok. Is it ok if I?' said Herschel. He made a gesture as if to open the box.

'Yes, of course,' said Sheena. 'Do whatever you need to do.'

Herschel lifted the lid. It opened smoothly and moved gently away from its base. He looked inside.

'Beautiful,' he said. 'Just a wonderful piece of crafts-manship.'

Looking inside he saw the remains of the seal.

'We... We, put Gerald's will in the company safe... for er... safekeeping,' interrupted Otley.

Herschel picked out the pieces of broken seal and the purple and black ribbon. He placed them on the table.

'Hmmm... And this is all of them?'

'Yes... When it was struck, the seal broke into several pieces and ended up scattered across the room,' said Otley.

'This room?' said Herschel.

Otley nodded. Herschel placed the pieces of seal onto the desk and arranged them so they formed their original shape.

'This is made of bronze bonded with clay. You must have had to hit this very hard in order to break it.'

'He did,' said Sheena. 'It sent sparks and fragments all over the room.'

Herschel looked closer at one of the pieces.

'Hmmm...though from what I can see, it looks like it was designed to split into a number of pieces... See? There were lines etched into the bronze and it has broken along them. Interesting.'

Herschel pulled the pieces together, clay side up, and arranged them back into their original shape.

'Is there something on it?' said Louise looking closer. 'I don't think I can make it out... Is it an animal of some kind?'

'It's a horse,' said Herschel. 'The clay was fired with an etching of a man on horseback.'

'What? Like you said? Like the Four Horsemen?,' said Louise. 'How can that have anything to do with Dad?'

'We should have taken more care and attention when we broke the seal in the first place,' said Sheena.

'Yes,' said Herschel. 'Too much of a hurry, perhaps? It's definitely an image of a man on horseback. And more interestingly, it has broken into seven pieces.'

'Interestingly?' said Sheena.

'Well, as I said, I think the bronze has been etched to break exactly in that way... Into seven separate pieces... See?' Herschel moved his finger over the pieces and counted them. 'One, two, three, four, five, six... and seven. Its separation was designed in advance.'

'Is that significant?' asked Sheena.

'I think so,' said Herschel. 'I think it might be a reference to the Seven Seals.'

'The Seven Seals? What are they?' asked Sheena. 'Is that more Revelations?'

'Actually, it is. The Bible describes the breaking of the Seven Seals... The act of which marks the second coming of Christ and the beginning of the End of Days, or the Apocalypse. Upon the 'Lamb' opening the seal, a judgement is released and apocalyptic events begin to occur. The first four seals release each of the Four Horsemen. The fifth seal releases what is called 'The cries of the martyrs' for the 'Wrath of God'. The sixth seal prompts earthquakes and other cataclysmic events, while the seventh and final seal brings on the seven angelic trumpeters who in turn cue what is called the Seven Bowl Judgements and more cataclysmic events prior to the End of Days.'

'Oh my God,' said Louise. 'And this has all started because we opened Dad's will?'

'Well... Perhaps in the eyes of the killer, yes. But that just reinforces my theory that he is just a religious extremist. Unless you believe in the literal interpretation of the Bible, then I don't think we're going to see the End of Days. Whoever it is, they are creating these events as an excuse to follow some weird kind of protocol.'

'But what have we ever done wrong?' said Louise. 'We've never hurt anyone.'

'Sadly, I don't think that is going to make any difference,' said Herschel. 'There could be something in your family history or background that they just don't like. Maybe some interaction with the Church, or something connected to the Church...'

'Total nonsense,' interrupted Sheena. 'What reason could anyone have for doing what they have done to our family? Just because of some mumbo-jumbo you have cooked up from reading a few verses in the Bible? I don't believe a word of it. I don't see any connection with Dad's will and Sean, Michael and David's deaths. There is a killer, sure... But if you ask me, all this stuff you've given us is just circumstantial claptrap, and I think you're just making it up to scare us...'

'Oh dear,' sighed Louise.

'Well, you are welcome to believe whatever you like,' said Herschel. 'But I can tell you that this is not circumstantial, mumbo-jumbo, and it is certainly not claptrap. We have given this a great deal of thought and research...There is definitely someone out there with a deep-seated grudge against your family, which now means for you and Louise that your lives are in danger... If you don't believe me, then that's your prerogative ...time will tell... But I urge you to be very careful...

Take advantage of the police protection offered to you, keep your wits about you and don't change your daily routine too much.'

'Sheena...You're scaring me,' said Louise. 'I think Herschel is only trying to help. He has our best interests at heart. Please listen to what he says. You will protect yourself, won't you?'

'Is now a good time to draw your attention to our outstanding bill?' asked Otley.

Louise's phone rang.

'Hello Sheena,' she said.

'Hi. Look, I don't have much time, but I just wanted to talk to you about what happened at Otley's office with Herschel,' said Sheena.

'Ok.'

'It's just that I'm really not sure that he really knows what is happening. All that talk about the seal and the End of Days. Don't you think he's complicating matters?'

'What do you mean? I thought he was trying to help us.'

'I don't know. It's just all of the religious stuff. Do you believe all that? It all feels a bit too Old Testament and vengeful God type stuff to me... A bit far-fetched for this day and age.'

'You were very rude to him you know.'

'Ah well, I'm sure he can take it.'

'And he has done a lot of work on our behalf, especially researching everything and using his contacts. He's the only one that has any idea as to what might be happening.'

'I'm not really sure if he is a one-man band or he has a team behind him... It's a bit confusing.'

'Yes. I know what you mean,' said Louise.

'And all this scaremongering about police protection. Do you really think that you need it?'

'Well, yes, I think I do. I want to protect my family. But I don't think they have the resources to protect us all properly. I mean, you have seen them...'

'But nothing is going to happen to your family, now is it? They're not involved.'

'How could you possibly know that, Sheena? Three of our siblings are dead. Each dispatched in the cruellest and most horrific manner... and you don't think we need protection?'

'Only if you believe what Herschel says... I mean, religious nutcase... Really? And the other thing is I'm not prepared to cower while the killer, whoever they are, makes our lives a misery. The only message people like that will understand is one of strength. If you hide in your house, well, you're just a sitting duck inviting them to come in and attack you.'

'Oh really? Do you think so?' said Louise. 'I hadn't thought about that.'

'Of course you are. If we put on a united front and refuse to be frightened by him, it could throw them off. Two strong women together, eh?'

'Oh, I don't know,' sighed Louise.

'Theres another thing,' said Sheena. 'Do you think there might be a gender element to this?'

'What do you mean?'

'Well, only the boys have been targeted. And let's be honest, none of them were exactly saints, now were they? They all did their fair share of drinking, gambling, drug taking and womanising. What if the killer was simply trying to purge the men in the family for their sinful ways? What if it's a woman?'

'I hadn't thought of that.'

'I mean, if that were the case, then there would be no danger for us, would there?'

'I suppose not.'

'And it's not as ridiculous as you might think. No more far fetched than what Herschel is proposing.'

'I guess not,' replied Louise. 'So what do you want to do about it? Do you want to fire Herschel?'

'No... I don't think so, not yet... Let's see how he does over the next few days. He might come in useful. What I'm saying though, is that we should present a united front, and act normally when going about our business. The police can do their thing, but don't let them get in the way. How does that sound? I mean, what have we got to hide?'

'Well, it sounds good to me,' said Louise. 'I like the idea of not being scared.'

'Excellent. Let's do that then.'

'But there is one thing I am worried about.'

'What's that?'

'Well, you said that we have nothing to hide? I mean is that true? Is that really true?'

'Of course. I've got nothing to hide,' said Sheena. 'I have nothing to be ashamed of.'

'Really Sheena? Really? Even in the eyes of a religious extremist we have in our midst? What might he think about some of the things you have done in the past?'

'Like what?'

'Do you really want me to spell it out?'

'If you must... Go on... Go ahead.'

'Ok. But don't blame me. I'm just trying to explain how a crazed Christian fundamentalist might see things.'

'I am all ears.'

'Well, firstly, you are divorced. You were married for less than a year and then sought an annulment. Does the Church recognise that? I don't think so. Secondly, your liking for married men isn't going to go down well, now is it, either with their wives or the Church. And finally, well we both know that you have had several terminations in the past. Maybe they weren't entirely your fault, but they still happened. And the Catholic Church does not look favourably on that kind of behaviour. So what do you think our killer is going to think of that?'

'Oh, fuck off...'

'I knew you wouldn't like it. But maybe this person thinks differently from others. For all we know they are going to be comparing us with his version of the Virgin Mary.'

'I didn't know you knew about the abortions... I thought Mum and Dad had kept that quiet.'

'Oh, the open secrets?' said Louise. 'In this family? Hah! Nothing was ever sacred. Anything you said to Mum went straight to Dad, and then soon enough, everyone knew. We just didn't admit it, did we? It's funny how we all thought our misdemeanours were safe with Mum and Dad, like a kind of blindness, yet we all knew something about the others that they probably wouldn't have wanted us to know.'

'Like the magazines?' said Sheena.

'What?'

'You posing in men's magazines when you were younger?'

'Oh my God. You did know about that.'

'Didn't you do some videos as well?' continued Sheena. 'It doesn't bother me, but if we're washing our dirty laundry...'

'Oh. My. God. I can't believe you know about that. How did you find out? I was young. I was put up to it. It was just supposed to be a little bit of fun... But it got out of hand, and became way too popular. And now these days, with the internet, well nothing is secret anymore. Thank God I didn't use my real name. How was I to know?... Mum and Dad didn't know did they?'

'I don't think so. They never mentioned it. But the boy's knew.'

'Oh God, No... What am I going to do?'

'So it would seem that neither of us have an unblemished past,' said Sheena.

'Right, but let's not forget... There was the thing that you and Sean were up to with the will,' said Louise.

'What? I... I don't know what you mean.'

'Oh, come off it, Sheena. If we are going to be honest with each other, let's cut the crap. You and Sean conspired to empty Dad's bank accounts all the while you were caring for him. Sean stripped the place of valuables and most of the furniture and sold them. I mean, the place was an empty shell by the time Dad died. Do you really think we didn't notice what was going on?'

'Er...' stammered Sheena.

'And then... not happy with taking most of Dad's cash, living off him for at least seven years, you and Sean tried to forge the will, didn't you? Only you couldn't pull it off because Dad had sealed everything in that mahogany box. You thought you could switch it though, didn't you?'

'Louise...Hold on...'

'But at the will reading, you both realised that you couldn't.'

'I... I really don't know what you are talking about,' stuttered Sheena.

'And then came the most amazing surprise, right? Amazing to everybody... but not as much as you two... Dad had left it all to you and Sean anyway. And it was so much more than you expected. You thought you could swindle the rest of us out of our inheritance of the house. But what happened? We found out that Dad was worth nearly seven million pounds... God only knows how he managed to amass that much. And because he worshipped the ground the two of you walked on, he decided to pass it all to you and Sean. How do you think that made the rest of us feel?'

'Louise... Please.'

'Don't please me, Sheena... You're the one talking about openness and honesty. And yet all the time you've been trying to swindle me out of my rightful inheritance. And now Michael, Sean and David are all dead. Do you think it has been worth it? Do you? Do you think I didn't know? There have been far too many secrets in this family, for far too long. Herschel was right. You are the one with the most to gain from their deaths and you've probably got the most to gain from having me out of the way too.'

'Louise... No... How can you say such things,' pleaded Sheena.

'Because they're all true. You can't deny any of it can you? That was your plan, wasn't it? But now it's just you and I, and it's not quite what you wanted... But you can't give up, can you? You can't simply come clean can you? Even after all this you can't be honest with me. You know, I really don't know why I bother...'

'Louise, please...'

'Goodbye, Sheena. I hope you get everything you deserve.'

Sheena's earpiece clicked.

9

ORPHAN

The small, slender figure walked across the common carrying what could easily have been mistaken for a bag of rags against her chest. She crossed the lane, opened the wire gate, and entered the church grounds, furnished with a large white cross. She stopped briefly to look up at the statue of Jesus Christ. The figure was tall, white and bearded, with his hands placed lovingly onto the heads of two adoring children. She hurried past the statue and up towards a row of terraced houses attached to a larger, more imposing three-storey building, all with steep sloping roofs. Built quickly and cheaply, in the early Victorian period from local calp-limestone, the building was neither imposing nor impressive. In need of some repair, there were sections of the external wall where once there were doors, but had since been repaired rather cheaply with cinder blocks and cement, and left un-plastered. The window sills were peeling and the chimney pots were either broken or cracked. Set opposite the common and nestling alongside a large wood, St Vincent de Paul orphanage was located just south of Dublin, and was designed to house up to 120 children. Originally built as part of the nineteenth century programme for 'fallen women' or those who were deemed to be at 'moral risk', St Vincent de Paul had been converted in the early twentieth century to look after the offspring of some of these very women.

The novice nun, still clutching her package tightly to her breast, was out of breath and a little tearful. She carefully brought one hand out from under her package and pulled on the chain to ring the doorbell. Carefully placing her hand back, she waited patiently until the door was opened by another young nun dressed in a crisp white habit.

'Ah, Sister Julia. There you are,' said the nun. 'We were beginning to wonder. Surely you haven't been running?'

'No, no... not running, Sister Alison, just trying to make sure we get home before the blackout.'

'Ah well, I don't think the Luftwaffe are going to be interested in you tonight, eh? Now then... Let's take a look at the little thing.'

From within the ball of rags, Sister Julia pulled a tiny little face topped with a mop of light brown hair. A pair of minuscule hands held the cloth beneath his face. His eyes were firmly shut.

'Awwww. Isn't he beautiful. How old is he?' asked Sister Alison.

'Just the five days.'

'Aww look at him. He so sweet. Does he have a name, or are we going to...?'

'Connor,' interrupted Julia. 'He's called Connor.'

'Sister Julia,' came a loud voice at the top of the stairs. 'Are you going to come in, or are you going to continue to dawdle your way through your entire life?'

'Just coming, Reverend Mother,' called Sister Julia.

'You had better go,' said Sister Alison. 'Mother Superior has been in a right mood all afternoon.'

Sister Julia made her way up the bare-board stairs to the

second floor, past the confessional booth and into the Reverend Mother's Office.

'Come in...Come in,' hurried Mother Superior. 'So... What have you brought us?'

'This beautiful baby,' said Julia, holding the child up for her to see.

'Hmmmm... Poor child. Boy or Girl?'

'Boy, Reverend Mother. His name is Connor.'

'Is it now? And where did that come from?'

'Ah well, I made a solemn promise to his mother that we would keep the name she gave him.'

'Did you now... And how are you going to keep that solemn promise, Sister Julia? You know very well that we have a policy...'

'Oh please Reverend Mother... Look at him. He looks just like a Connor, now doesn't he? Don't you think? And just this once, perhaps we can allow something of his mother to continue? Surely it can't do any harm.'

'Let me have a closer look at him.' She peered over her tiny half-moon glasses to take the child in. 'Pass the little mite, here.'

As Sister Julia passed the baby to her Mother Superior, he began to cry. The crying became louder and more insistent until the Reverend Mother could bear it no longer, and she handed him back.

'Alright... Just this once, and since it is you, Sister Julia. I will permit you to name him. Connor you say? That is your choice?'

'Yes, Reverend Mother,' said Sister Julia, as she comforted the child.

'Well let it be so... No sign of the father I suppose?

'No, Reverend Mother'

'Hmmm... And his mother, a mere child herself, yes?... How is she?'

'She is physically very well. Very strong...'

'But?'

'She is distraught about having to give him up. I had to tear him away from her. It was horrible. She is so young. She was in tears. Howling, in fact.'

'Well, perhaps she should have thought about that nine months ago...'

'Perhaps... But I told her that we would take good care of him.'

'Well, that's it and all about it now,' said Mother Superior. 'He is our responsibility, and we shall look after him to the best of our abilities, since she is clearly unable. Another one for God's devotion. We shall pray for them, and their mortal souls.'

'Yes, Reverend Mother.'

'Now take him to the nursery and see that he is fed and bathed well.'

'Yes, Reverend Mother.'

'And don't go getting attached to him now, young lady. I shouldn't have to remind you that you are a servant of God, and you are to do God's will here on earth. Do you understand? Beware. Nothing good ever comes from getting too close to the Devil's spawn.'

The postulant nun stopped for a moment, then thought better of it.

'No, Reverend Mother.'

Sister Julia headed out along the dark corridor and back down to the nursery where she put Connor down into a steel-barred cot with three other small babies.

'So, who do we have here?' said a voice from the far side of the nursery.

'Ah Sister Roisin, I didn't see you there... I... I'm just back from Dublin... This is a new addition to our happy brood. His name is Connor.'

'Connor, eh?' said Sister Roisin. 'No Mammy or Pappy for him, den?'

'No... Not now.'

'She's not dead, is she?'

'No... Just very young.'

'How young?'

'Fourteen, I think.'

'Oh, right... One of those tarts who opened her legs too early, eh?'

'No, I don't think it was quite like that...'

'No? When is it not like that Sister Julia? That is what has to happen, you know, to get that...' Sister Roisin pointed at Connor, now sleeping peacefully in his cot. 'I bet you're secretly jealous, now aren't ye?'

'Good Lord No,' said Sister Julia. 'I have dedicated my life to the Lord, as you well know.'

Sister Roisin moved closer. 'But I bet, late at night, when 'de lights are out, and everyone else is asleep, you can't 'elp but have those 'toughts now can ya?'

'Sister Roisin. Please stop.'

'Tinkin about some handsome American airman, I bet...'

'Roisin. Stop!'

'Tinkin about him inside yer... You do, don't ya? 'D'ya miss it? Or have you never...'

'That is none of your business, Sister Roisin. And if you don't stop immediately, I will have to report you to Mother Superior.'

'Hahaha,' Sister Roisin cackled. 'Go ahead. See what happens... It would be twenty lashes fer you jus' for suggestin' it... Our Reverend Mother don't do dat sorta thing, now does she... Ooh, look... You've gone all red an' blotchy.' Sister Roisin laughed again and headed out of the nursery.

Sister Julia loved her work at St Vincent de Paul. She loved the children. They were so happy and vibrant and sweet. She loved to help them just as much as she could. She also wanted them to experience love and his eternal grace. She knew that they were only there because of circumstances in which they played no part. Poverty, ignorance, stupidity, and in some cases, just pure evil. She tried hard to understand how these wonderful children's souls could become infected with the sins of others, and how it was God's will that they were destined to suffer. She wanted to hug them and love them, and yet for some reason, God wanted to punish them. It seemed so unfair.

There was a strict routine at St Vincent's. The Mother Superior saw to that. The nuns rose at 5am to clean, cook, and prepare the orphanage for the day. The children would rise at 6am. They had to be awake, clean, and dressed for Mass at 7am. A thin breakfast was served by the older children at 8am, which was followed by nursery and lessons. All teaching was carried out by the nuns and centred around Bible stories and allegories. It was mostly New Testament gospel tales, but occasionally the Old Testament fire and brimstone stories were brought out to maintain order. English was taught as well as French for some of the older, more talented pupils, but virtually no attention was given to mathematics or science. A lunchtime Mass was followed by more spiritual instruction for the children in the afternoon, finished by prayers. By 4pm the children were allowed to play in the yard, or out in the woods, but they were expected to attend confession with one of the priests at least once a week during this time.

There were three priests assigned to the orphanage. Father Murphy lived onsite and carried out the majority of the services and confessions. He was usually available for a chat in his office, if needed. Father Walsh lived in the village, and also carried out duties for the village parishioners. He would, however, regularly be found helping out at the orphanage, or more often be with Father Murphy in his office. Father James, a younger priest in training, would cycle down from Dublin on a weekly basis to assist with lessons or any other of the ecclesiastical duties.

Failing to attend evening Mass was a punishable offence, according to the Reverend Mother. Unless there was a very good reason – illness, or a doctor's appointment, all the nuns and all the older children were expected to attend Mass every day. Father Murphy always took evening Mass, and Sister Julia really looked forward to it. The smell of incense in the air made her feel as if she had arrived. Father Murphy was a very charismatic speaker. She loved to listen to his voice, no-matter what his sermon was about. The Reverend Mother always took a seat of importance nearest to the priest and close to the pulpit when Father Murphy was speaking. You could almost see her mouthing the words as he spoke them, and she would nod vigorously when he made a particular point.

The orphanage could have as many as 150 children sometimes. You could never say they were really cared for though. Their basic needs were met, but the warmth and comfort they might get from a real family was all but absent. Sister Julia always wanted to fill this particular gap, to give her love and attention freely to the children, especially those who were in the greatest emotional need. But the Reverend Mother strictly forbade any 'unnecessary expressions of emotion', as she called it. This, the postulant nun, found the most difficult. She was a kind and caring person, who naturally bonded with the children. She had been brought up on a farm in rural County Sligo with lots of brothers and sisters, so she was not afraid of hard work. Although she wasn't the cleverest in the class, her open and affectionate nature brought her lots of friends. Like all children growing up in Ireland, she was expected to adhere to the Catholic doctrines. Confirmed at the age of fourteen, Julia took a deep interest in the faith. Her natural piousness, combined with a desire to escape her overbearing and brutish father, drove her to commit herself early to a consecrated life, and to join the convent aged only seventeen. She jumped at the chance to work at the orphanage, and loved every minute of her days there, even though she felt the regime could, at times, be a little harsh for the children.

Father Murphy was something of a rising star with the Catholic hierarchy. He had developed a name for himself on the fund-raising circuit, and this was beginning to be noticed by the bishops in the area, as well as the Cardinal. Father Murphy seemed to be able to conjure up donations, almost without trying. The fund-raising events he held were always well attended by the best-connected people in the area, and the contributions were always extremely generous. The number of people Father Murphy seemed to know, and the increasing interest from senior clergy, really impressed Mother Superior. For her, Father Murphy could do no wrong. Most of the other nuns at St Vincent's were in awe of his easy-going charm too. He loved to hug the children and play with them. He was something of a pied piper around the orphanage. He loved to create an adoring crowd just by his very presence, where the children would compete for his attention. Such was the power of his reputation and personality, that parishioners in the village would even stop and bow their heads as he walked by. To them, he was God's minister upon the earth. Father Murphy would always choose two or three of the older boys to be his unofficial lieutenants. This was a very sought-after role in St Vincent's, and the boys would compete aggressively for Father Murphy's goodwill in order to secure a place. They would carry out odd jobs for him around the village, as well as helping with the fund-raising activities. But more importantly, they would keep him informed as to what was going on at the orphanage, especially when he was away on other duties. The children were always wary of these boys since they were clearly Father Murphy's eyes and ears in the dormitories, the classrooms and the dining room. As much as the children loved him, they feared what his chosen ones might say, and what could result.

Father Murphy always volunteered to conduct the confessional sessions each afternoon. Situated in the booth up on the second floor, each child over the age of six was required to confess. Outside of the booth could be found a pile of printed papers upon which the child could check off the sins to which they were confessing this week. Once inside, the child would pass the paper to Father Murphy who would read it, perhaps ask some questions and then request the appropriate penance be carried out. Murphy was insistent that the penance be carried out without delay. Any child who failed to make the appropriate atonement would be subjected to Mother Superior's severe tongue, or sometimes something worse.

The commotion started upstairs.

'No Father, no... I won't,' came a loud voice, followed soon after by a deeper, more insistent but unintelligible whispering.

'I don't care. I'm not going to,' came the voice again.

The whispering continued, louder now and more insistent. This was a Father Murphy whisper.

'No Father... It's not that... It's just that I...'

'Yes, you will...' bellowed Father Murphy, for all in the orphanage to hear.

Sister Julie and Sister Alison were in the dining room, serving lunch, and Father Murphy's roar from the second floor made them both jump.

'What on earth is that?' said Sister Julie, 'Is that Father Murphy?'

'I wouldn't,' said Sister Alison.

'He sounds upset. What is going on?'

'No. I really wouldn't. He's taking confession, and you know how he doesn't like to be disturbed.'

'But I think that was young Liam's voice I heard?'

'Yes... I think so.'

'But he sounds really upset.'

'Sister Julia... Sister Alison... Do you not have work to be getting on with?' The Mother Superior's voice cut through their conversation like a precision blade. The two nuns put their heads down and continued silently with their tasks.

'Father Murphy?' called Mother Superior from the bottom of the stairs, 'Is everything alright? Do you need any assistance? Father Murphy?'

The Reverend Mother began to walk up the first few steps towards where the noises had come from, listening intently.

'I told you Father... I don't care who you are, or what you say,' Liam's voice was firmer now.

'Liam. Please calm down. I really don't know what you are talking about,' replied Father Murphy.

'Father Murphy...Father Murphy... Can I help at all?' called Mother Superior as she made her way up towards the second floor. 'What is going on Liam... What is this noise and commotion all about?'

Liam and Father Murphy were standing outside the confessional booth. Liam was almost in tears, with his eyes welling up. He was breathing heavily and his fists were tightly clenched.

'He... He... I can't do this any more,' blurted Liam.

'Confession? Liam? We all have to go to confession,' said Mother Superior. 'We all need forgiveness, my poor child. If you're not forgiven, then you will end up in damnation. And we can't have that, now can we?'

'He was getting unnecessarily upset,' said Father Murphy, 'It was just a straight-forward confession.'

'He's... He's...' cried Liam.

'I'm what Liam?' said Father Murphy, sternly.

'Yes what, Liam?' asked Mother Superior.

'He's... He's... Oh God...' Liam buried his face in his hands.

'Do not take our Lord's name in vain, Liam. Perhaps we

should find out what the problem is in private,' said Father Murphy. 'Let's go into my office.'

Father Murphy, Mother Superior and a still snivelling Liam moved into the office and closed the door behind them. Sister Julia and Sister Alison, who had been listening quietly below, crept up the stairs to try and hear more of what was going on.

'He was really upset, wasn't he?' whispered Sister Julia. 'I've never seen him like that before. It's not like him at all. He's usually very robust. I guess he's been a bit withdrawn lately, but he was really angry and upset, wasn't he?'

'How long have you been here, Sister Julia?' asked Sister Alison.

'Not long. Six months or so. Why do you ask?'

'Have you never thought that strange things sometimes happen here?'

'Strange? No... Not really. The Reverend Mother can be a bit strict at times, but she's only doing her job. What do you mean?'

'Don't you ever wonder why Father Murphy insists on carrying out all of the confessions?'

'I've never thought about it. No, why? Should I? He is a priest, and that is part of his job.'

'Or why Father Murphy and Father Walsh have their favourite boys?'

'Favourites? Well, yes... but just to do the odd jobs, and to help with the jumble-sales and concerts and stuff. I don't understand. What are you trying to say, Sister Alison?'

'Well, let me put it this way. Father Murphy and Father Walsh both have their favourite boys, and Liam used to be one of them.'

'Oh, so that's it... Is he upset because he's not allowed to help Father Murphy anymore. I wonder why not?'

'Probably because he is too old now,' said Sister Alison.

Julia put her ears closer to Father Murphy's Office door.

'We shouldn't be doing this,' said Sister Alison. 'If we get caught it will be solitary confinement for us.'

'They wouldn't,' whispered Sister Julia.

'Really? You haven't been here long enough. You'll find out.'

'Wait... I think I can hear them talking... Shhh.'

'I won't do it anymore,' said Liam. 'I don't care what he says, I'm not doing it.'

'Well, I'm sure that whatever Father Murphy asks of you, he has a very good reason to ask it of you. So why won't you help?' said Mother Superior, trying to calm things down.

'You... You... know exactly what I mean..' said Liam looking directly at the Mother Superior.

'I'm sure I don't. I think you need to give Father Murphy here a bit more respect. If it wasn't for him, then I doubt there would be any food on the table tonight. Why aren't you more grateful, Liam?'

'Grateful? Grateful? Do you know what he wants me to do? Do you? Shall I tell you? Shall I tell her, Father? Shall I?'

'Look, I'm sure we can all calm down now,' said Father Murphy. 'You are just upset because you haven't been asked to help with the fund-raising, isn't that right, Liam?'

'Fund raising? What the feck has fund raising got to do with anything? All I know is that if I don't do what you ask, then you're just going to choose a younger boy, aren't you. One that won't fight back.'

'Then what is it that you want Liam?' asked Father Murphy.

'I... I want... you... to stop doing those feckin' things you do to me... That you do,' spluttered Liam.

'I think we've heard just about enough from you young man,' intervened Mother Superior. 'Don't you realise you are talking to a very senior priest here? Where is your respect?

And not just any priest young lad. This is Father Murphy. He is a valued member of St Vincents, of this parish and the of the diocese. I will not hear some jumped up little culchie besmirch the good name of this place and our beloved Father Murphy.'

'But you haven't... You haven't even...'

'The best thing for this little toe-rag is to teach him a lesson, don't you think, Father Murphy? Then perhaps he'll keep his lying little stories to himself.'

'I think I do, Reverend Mother,' said Murphy.

'You hold his arms, then Father and I will get the crop.'

'They're going to beat him,' hissed Sister Julia. 'I can't let this happen.'

Sister Alison grabbed the novice's arm and held her firmly. 'Whatever you do, do not go in there...'

'But this isn't right.'

'Neither are a lot of things here, but you'll do no-one any good if you break in there and try and stop them. It would be worse for Liam and much worse for you...'

'But... but...'

Tears began to well up in Sister Julia's eyes, 'Poor Liam...'

The two nuns stood by the door arching their heads closer trying to hear what was happening inside. Sister Julia's fingers turned white as she grasped the door-frame.

'What's goin' on?' said Sister Roisin, as she appeared behind them. They both jumped.

'Shhhhh,' hissed Sister Alison as she pointed to Father Murphy's office and put her fingers to her lips.

'Ahhh... Is it a beatin' for that lad, Liam? I 'tought as much. He's been headin' towards 'dat for some time. He's getting' a bit too old, and a bit too headstrong, if you know what I mean. Father Murphy prefers 'em younger and more pliable.'

'Be quiet Roisin, or you'll get us all into trouble,' hissed Sister Alison.

'Ah well, it's not de first time, an' I'll be sure as sure can be, it won't be de last. Is Mother Superior in there 'elpin 'im?'

Sister Alison nodded.

'Lookin' de other way, I guess? Well, I suppose he'll survive. He might not be walking straight fer a few days 'tho...'

Sister Roisin laughed her little cackle as she walked away and the first crack of the cane was heard, followed soon after by a muffled screech.

And the tears flowed down Sister Julia's face.

10

SECRETS AND LIES

'The results from the other brother's autopsy and toxicology have come through,' said Somerset.

'David?' replied Herschel.

'Yes. Can you hear me over this line? It's not very good.'

'One moment.'

Herschel, sitting back in his office chair with his feet on the desk in his townhouse study, sprang forward and placed his mobile phone next to the computer system on his desk. The computer screen immediately sprang to life, rendering a perfectly realistic image of a three-dimensional hand which moved rapidly across the screen towards an equally faithful image of a mobile phone. The hand lifted the phone to the side of an image of Herschel's head. Suddenly the room was filled with the sound of the Inspector in his car, with all the subsequent background noise. The screen immediately signalled 'Noise Cancelling', and the line became crystal clear.

'You're on speakerphone now,' said Herschel. 'I can hear you fine.'

'Ah, good... Yes, so can I now.'

'What news?' asked Herschel, getting to the point.

'Well pretty much as we thought. This was clearly another

murder, and we suspect by the same hand as those responsible for Sean and Michael's.'

'Really? Yet the mode of operation was so different.'

'Well, Yes and No. The killer didn't use a toxic agent this time, it was more biological?'

'Biological? How do you mean, biological?'

'Well, according to his sisters, David was very prone to pursuing... well, let's just say, alternative diets. They say he was always trying one new foodstuff or another – always looking for that perfect combination of healthy living and sustainable consumption. His latest passion was for what they called the Stone-Age Diet.'

'The what?'

'It's where you eat only what a stone-age man would eat.'

'You mean only mammoths and sabre-toothed tigers?' laughed Herschel.

'Haha... You may mock, Herschel, but it's a thing. It's more about eating only natural, unprocessed and unadulterated food. So, lots of fruit and vegetables and lean, if not raw, meat.'

'With no pesticides or herbicides?'

'You're ahead of me as usual... Yes... The Stone Age Diet encourages you to eat untreated foodstuffs as much as possible... and to refrain from cooking wherever you can. The more raw and untreated the foodstuff is, the better.'

'I see... And that contributed to his condition?'

'Yes, It would appear that his untreated diet somehow introduced cockroach eggs into his system. They must have laid dormant in his gut for weeks before something induced them to hatch... and then to er... feed.'

'Eurgh... And that was it? That is what killed him?'

'No, apparently not. He also had severe Crohn's disease. You know Crohn's disease? It's a type of bowel disorder that causes inflammation of the digestive tract. It can lead to severe diarrhoea, fatigue, weight loss, abdominal cramps and in extreme cases like his, malnutrition... So, when combined with the infestation, it led to a deadly combination of atrophy and severe sickness. He was literally eaten from the inside out...'

'Oh the poor fellow,' said Herschel. 'But I'm confused... You said this was murder, like we all assumed, but I'm not hearing that.'

'Well, that's where it gets a bit complicated,' replied Somerset. 'Luckily, the toxicologist looking at the case is one of our best. She is very thorough. She carried out extensive tests and was able to link the two symptoms together as a cause and effect.'

'How?' asked Herschel.

'The murderer had to use some kind of biological catalyst to induce the cockroaches and get them to hatch and grow... And what she has found, and forgive me if I'm light on the technicalities here, but she believe's he was given a biological compound of some kind, to do that... You know, to kick the little fella's off. But she also discovered that prolonged exposure to this particular compound will magnify the symptoms of chronic Crohn's disease as well... Something of a double whammy.'

'What is this compound?'

'Well that's where you come in, Herschel... We need you to send the results to your contact so that we can confirm our hypothesis. Although we have the chemical fingerprint, we don't have access to your resources, to determine its exact provenance.'

'I can do that,' said Herschel. 'Can you send me the chemical breakdown?'

'On it's way... Our bets are on it being from Russia or North Korea again.'

'Ok. How long does this compound need to be in the system for it to start having an effect?'

'I'm told between one and six weeks... But your guys can probably confirm that.'

'So if you are correct, you are saying the murderer

somehow slipped this compound into David's food or drink, over an extended period of time, to create the conditions he wanted?'

'Yes, exactly that. He would have to be calculating and persistent. Though, it's our belief that the substance would need to be administered in small but regular doses to achieve the desired effect. It's really powerful stuff.'

'A bit like the Arythmodref-P given to Michael and Sean.'

'Exactly...'

'Ok...I see the connection now. Get the material over to me as soon as you can and I'll get my people to confirm. Good job. Your toxicologist is a smart lady.'

'She certainly has been on this occasion... Speak later.'

The line clicked, and Herschel's computer animated the action of putting down the phone and disconnecting the line.

Herschel sat back down at his desk. He leaned back in his chair again and crossed his feet on top of the desk in from of him. He brought the fingers of each hand together and gazed upwards to the ceiling and slightly to the left.

'That's an interesting development, said Cassandra. 'Looks like we have a confirmed serial killer on our hands, like we thought. Who are you going to get to look at the compound, Zlawitkowski?'

'Yes, said Herschel. 'He isolated the Arythmodref-P, so I'm sure he'll know about this one... But right now, it strikes me... We have been assuming a male killer for this, but, you know, I'm beginning to wonder...'

'You mean poisoning? A female?' said Cassandra.

'Yes... It's just not a male way to do it. Much more Femme Fatale'

'Ninety-three percent of murderers are men,' said Cassandra. 'In total, more men kill with poison than women, but it accounts for only just over 0.3% of killings by men, whereas women use it in more than 3% of murders. Ten times greater per capita.'

'So, do you still think it could be either Louise or Sheena?' said Herschel.

'I'm afraid I do... But why? Why would they want to do such a thing? Money? I don't think that can explain David's murder... There's no monetary benefit to it. It just doesn't add up. No, there's something missing. Have you found anything in the family's background at all?'

'Yes,' said Cassandra. 'I have been doing some research.'

'Ok... Great. What do we know about them?'

'Well, I have been searching for things they might not want to be made public. You know,... dirty linen...'

'Well, I guess we all have some of that... Go ahead.'

'Well, let's take Sean. Although he was a well-known surveyor in the area, and worked for many of the major building firms, construction was not his main source of income. His surveying business was just a front for a fairly large-scale drug distribution business in the area.'

'What kind of drugs?' asked Herschel.

'Nothing like he and Michael were given. Sean was much more into the recreational substances, cocaine mostly, but some ecstasy and amphetamines for the clubbers. He used his contacts to dominate the supply for miles around. You might say he was something of a local kingpin. He had fingers in many pies, especially in the building trade of course. Most of them illegal, including the supply of second-rate building materials and suspect building control safety certificates, blackmailing of local businesses and of course the supply of narcotics. His methods often extended to extortion with menace.'

'Violence?'

'If necessary, yes. He was implicated in the beating of a young, shall we say, 'entrepreneur' who had set up his own supply business. Soon after, the poor chap spent four months in hospital and has never worked again. Nothing was ever proven, but everyone knew who was responsible. Sean had a team of goons to do his dirty work. 'Collections', they used to call it. They would arrive at a premises and refuse to leave until the owner paid his due. I guess you could say he was small-time Mafia.'

'It's surprising then that the killer was able to get to him, especially if he was surrounded by protection?' said Herschel.

'Yes, but this was with family. Maybe he didn't see a threat, and as we have discovered, the murderer didn't arrive swinging a baseball bat, now did he?'

'No... So not expected? His guard was down?'

'Probably,' replied Cassandra

'But Sean must have had plenty of enemies?'

'Oh, plenty. He pushed out all the other small-time dealers over twenty years ago, and much of the resentment from those quarters still remains. There are lots of shop-owners and tenants who are only too happy to see the back of him. Given his reputation, some of his employees and ex-employees may well have had a motive... He also had an ex-wife, who, although they split reasonably amicably, liked to 'be kept in a manner to which she had become accustomed', if you know what I mean. However, her coke habit and liking for expensive shoes, champagne and younger men, meant she was always demanding even more money from him.'

'So would she want him dead, too?' asked Herschel.

'Well perhaps. She is still the main beneficiary in his will.''

'Really? Was he independently wealthy too?'

'Yes, but it was all dirty,' replied Cassandra. 'Much of it held in offshore accounts, or as cash in huge security shipping containers around the country. His problem was that he couldn't get to it, at least not so he could make himself legitimate. He certainly couldn't spend it. It would have attracted far too much attention.'

'So the inheritance from Gerald would have been useful?'

'Very. He could have used the probate process to clean his dirty cash. It would have made him a very wealthy man, and legitimate too, as long as you didn't look too hard. The more money he inherited, the more he could launder.'

'Double the benefit.'

'Exactly. Which kind of makes you wonder why Gerald bequeathed it all to Sean and Sheena.'

'Could they have been carrying out some kind of probate fraud?'

'Well, there's motive, and he had the contacts to make it happen... But if that is the case, they, and I mean both Sean and Sheena, would have had a problem with Gerald's will and the way it was stored. You know, in the box with the clay seal?'

Herschel leaned back further into his chair. 'Aaahhh... Of course... And yet Gerald's money still went to Sean and Sheena.'

'Yes. Amazingly. It was probably as much of a surprise to them as it was to the rest of the family. But crucially, in order to fulfil their plot, to deliver them from their sin so to speak, they still had to break the Four Horsemen's seal, and do it in front of their siblings.'

'Unleashing the Wrath of God?'

'Yes... At least upon Michael, Sean and David.'

'Interesting. Fascinating in fact. Any more?'

'Well that's all we have on Sean, but there is plenty more on the rest of them,' said Cassandra. 'How about David?'

'Ok,' said Herschel.

'Mild-mannered accountant from the Midlands?'

'So it would seem.'

'Nothing like it... What would you say to a maths prodigy, international gambler, poker player and stock market day-trader. Always using OPM.'

'OPM?'

'Other People's Money.'

'Wow... He gambled with other people's money?'

'Exclusively... He was well known on the highest stakes poker tables all around the world – Monte Carlo, Hong Kong,

Las Vegas, San Remo. He only ever flew first-class or by private jet in order to play.'

'Did he win?'

'He used to... But lately he's had a run of bad luck. He was down several million dollars and was trying desperately to recoup his losses before his demise. News travels fast in that rarefied atmosphere, and he was fighting a rear-guard action against some pretty heavy creditors. People you really don't want to upset.'

'David... Wow... You would never have thought it. He seemed so, well, bookish,' said Herschel.

'Maybe that was part of his conceit. I had to dig very deep to retrieve information about him. He covered his tracks very well. Only those who played against him knew his face. He always played under a pseudonym, and he always wore dark glasses at the table. His whole raison-d'être was to gamble with his clients' money. So he was always living on the edge of huge success or monumental failure. His entire existence was something of a double life.'

'No wonder he was a nervous wreck. Would he not have been susceptible to influence from an outside agency, like someone wishing to do him harm? You know leverage of some kind?'

'Almost certainly. And also, with the low-calorie intake he insisted upon, he probably wouldn't have been thinking straight,' said Cassandra.

'So all that stress might explain how he got himself into such a poor physical and mental state. He probably thought he could ride it out, and not for the first time. So he was at a low ebb. Easy pickings for our killer?'

'Yes... But he hid his problems so well, didn't he? No-one suspected that he was so ill... Until... well, it was too late.'

'Could his creditors have been behind it?'

'Yes. It's possible, but unlikely that they would have acted in concert. It's possible that one or more could have funded something... Arranged the hit... And they may well have had the international connections needed to source the nerve-agent and bacterial catalyst.'

'Ah... But that's it, isn't it? Sean and Michael's deaths. David's creditors wouldn't have any reason to want them dead, now would they?'

'We've found no connection between them... So it's pretty unlikely,' said Cassandra.

'So it's hard to connect the events, isn't it? Unless there are two killers.'

'Both with grudges against the family at the same time? Not very likely.'

'No, you are right. So we discount any of the people David owed money to?'

'Yes. I still think the lone, crazed killer is the most likely scenario.'

'So that's David, yes? What about Michael?' asked Herschel.

'Well, we have less on him... Eldest child, full of unfulfilled expectations. His main weakness seems to have been the opposite sex. He was a serial philanderer for most of his adult life, especially during his first marriage. He was unable to hold down much in the way of a serious relationship and took little interest in his children, even if they are mostly grown up now. He's not much of one for wearing clothes, and likes an all-over tan, if you know what I mean. He likes to surround himself with like-minded sorts, with, well, shall we say, a more relaxed approach to relationships.'

'Are you saying, he's a swinger, Cassandra?' Herschel laughed. 'You're not blushing, are you?'

'Of course, not... Just reporting the facts as I know them. Now his relationship with his kids is pretty fractured. He wasn't really around much as they were growing up, and as they got older they really needed a guiding hand. Two of them had several brushes with the police – petty drug stuff, mostly, but they were lucky not to be drawn into more serious crime.'

'Ok. But nothing that might warrant a murderous vendetta?'

'No... Not at all. Michael did enter into some kind of financial arrangement with one of his daughters a couple of years ago – an investment in an Asian startup. The details are a bit murky. Unfortunately, and perhaps not surprisingly, the start-up failed and Michael lost his money.'

'How much?' said Herschel.

'Over half a million pounds. Which was pretty much all he had to his name at the time, and then some. Had the failure been the other way round and Michael was investing on behalf of his daughter's family, then there might have been some cause to investigate further, but this just feels like he got greedy and was burned by his naïveté. Having said that, his other children were not happy that he was looking to make a financial benefit through their sister. They think he got everything he deserved.'

'But not enough motive to want him killed.'

'Not really, no.'

'So unless there is a disgruntled husband somewhere who has it in for Michael, and somehow wanted Sean and David dead too, we can probably discount his associates as well, right?'

'I think so,' said Cassandra. 'Unfortunately, that doesn't give us much else to go on with respect to the three of them.'

'What about the sisters? What do they have to hide?'

'Again, not a lot. Louise dabbled with a semi-professional career in glamour and porn for a while when she was younger – encouraged by her then boyfriend. So there are photographs and some videos of her available on the internet if you choose to look for them. I think they serve more as an embarrassment for her and the family, than anything else. Plus, it was a long time ago...'

'Hmmm,' mulled Herschel. 'Good Catholic girl gone bad? Wouldn't look good in the parish newsletter, now would it? And I expect it reflected badly on Gerald and Kitty.'

'Probably... but you know how easily the Church community are able to sweep a sex-scandal under the carpet. They seemed to brush it away without any real repercussions, other than maybe the occasional muffled sniggering from a choirboy or two.'

'Ok, so nothing there... What about Sheena?'

'She has something of a chequered past too. Lots of boyfriends. Many of them still married. Some hint of dabbling in relationships across the Soviet bloc. You know... suspected sleeper agents. But she probably wasn't aware. She was married for a short time... He didn't stick around for long. Her volcanic temper saw to that. She can be very controlling when she wants, and is unedifying company when she doesn't get her own way. But interestingly, she and Gerald had a very close relationship. He bailed her out of just about every mistake she ever made.'

'Really?'

'Yes... university dropout... Twice. Gerald bailed her out. Marriage...Gerald bailed her out. Abortions... Gerald bailed her out. She was even lined up to adopt a child a few years ago. She got cold feet, and guess what?'

'Gerald bailed her out?'

'Precisely. This was close but very, very, one-sided.'

'Do you think there might have been some leverage there?'

'What, as if she had something over Gerald?'

'Yes.'

'Well, I suppose it's possible, but for all those years? What could she possibly have known?'

'Well, this family seems to run on secrets and lies. She could have known something about Gerald and held it against him. Maybe the favouritism Gerald lavished upon Sheena wasn't exactly what everyone thought it was.'

'Some kind of blackmail, do you think?' asked Cassandra.

'Well, it's possible, isn't it? If she knew something that none of the others did. She's the sort who might try and exploit her position, and from what you say, she certainly took advantage of Gerald's generosity.'

'Even to the point of her inheriting his vast wealth perhaps? With the added constraint of Sean as a co-inheritor.'

'Yes, that would make sense. Perhaps you're onto something there. The challenge, of course, is to find out what. What might Sheena have had over her late father?'

'I'll carry on digging, shall I?' asked Cassandra. 'See what else I can uncover...'

'Sure,' said Herschel, breathing a large sigh. 'So... Gerald. He is the one who intrigues me in all of this... Quite an interesting character, don't you think. He is at the centre of all this. He must be.'

'Yes, you're right,' replied Cassandra. 'He is something of a mystery, isn't he? His passing has been the catalyst for all this.'

'So, what do we have on him?' asked Herschel.

'Quite a lot really, but nothing that you would call dirty laundry. However, there are quite a few gaps that need to be filled in. He lived a pretty interesting life.'

'Ok. Go on...'

'Well, he was in the RAF during the Second World War. Decorated in action for his service over the Middle East... He came from pretty humble stock though. Made a lot of himself. His father was a greengrocer and his mother was a housewife. However, he showed some considerable mathematical ability as a child, extraordinary actually. He would have been labelled a maths genius these days. Indications are that he was an Asperger's sufferer. Borderline autistic, though never diagnosed.'

'Really? How interesting,' said Herschel.

'It was his mathematical skills that got him into the RAF

towards the tail end of the war. He was a Spitfire pilot, with multiple kills to his name.'

'So an Ace?'

'Yes... More than five kills. He wasn't really that sociable though, and never really mixed with the other officers or men. According to our records he kept himself to himself. That could have been his Asperger's though. They tend to find social situations threatening and find it difficult to interact with people. They often have trouble reading people's emotions and so can make horrendous mistakes without even realising it.'

'I know how he feels,' grumbled Herschel with a smile.

'Isaac Newton is thought to be an Asperger's sufferer – a towering genius who had trouble making friends and influencing people. Yet, when left to their own devices, these people can display extraordinary powers of concentration and focus. Albert Einstein, Mozart and Nicolai Tesla are thought to have been sufferers too.'

'And they achieved a thing or two, didn't they?'

'Quite. Having said that, Gerald had a big family around him growing up. Two brothers and a sister, so he must have got used to social situations. He wouldn't have had much of a choice.'

'Catholic, obviously? Are any of his siblings still alive?' asked Herschel.

'Yes, all very Catholic, but only his younger sister has survived him. I'll come onto his religion in a moment. I think it is significant. After serving with distinction in the RAF, he was demobbed and, like many who served, ended back where he started before the war. Gerald went back to his father's greengrocery, but with a burning ambition to become an airline pilot.'

'Right...Which he fulfilled?'

'Eventually, yes, after meeting Kitty.'

'Kitty?'

'Yes. Kitty, his wife. From Tipperary, Ireland.'

'Oh, I see.'

'They met at a local dance. She had been sent over to England to find a husband and pave the way for her four sisters. She and Gerald were married not long after they met, just before Gerald began his training with BOAC. The children began to arrive soon after that.'

'Michael, Sheena, Sean, David and Louise,' confirmed Herschel.

'Correct, and in that order.'

'Ok. So there's probably no significance in their relative ages?'

'No, I don't think so. Gerald carved out a successful career as a pilot with BOAC and then British Airways. He flew DC10's, 727's, 737's and then long-haul Jumbo 747's.

'Pretty amazing for a spitfire pilot.'

'Yes. He rode the boom of international air-travel that exploded after the war.'

'So, he got to travel a lot?'

Yes. He visited pretty much every continent. America's, South Africa, the Far and Middle East. He was one of the first pilots to fly a commercial airline to Australia.'

'Ok. So he had quite a career, and got to travel the world. No wonder he was able to invest his wealth internationally. But the key question is how did he amass such a huge fortune? Surely not on an airline pilot's salary, especially with a growing family?'

'Maybe he was very good at maths? Asperger's sufferers often are,' said Cassandra.

'But nearly £7m invested in property and trusts? He would have to have been both very clever and very lucky to ride the property and stock-market booms. No, there's more to this... But that also makes me think. Any other family abroad? No girls in foreign ports?'

'No, nothing like that. He was devoted to Kitty and his family his entire life.'

'Really? Well good for him. Devoted, but secretive.'

'So it would appear. He was also devoted to his faith,' said Cassandra.

'Aaah... of course.'

'Yes. Now Kitty did most of the social climbing in the parish, but as a couple they very soon became the local power-family for the diocese. Three of Kitty's four sisters married Englishmen and settled locally, increasing their influence in the parish very quickly.'

'They were big cheeses, then?'

'Very much so. The family was highly respected. They always secured the best pews in Mass. They could choose when and where they saw the priest for confession - and if they wanted a special occasion, like a wedding or a christening, well, all the stops were pulled out. No facility was closed to them. They were even given special rights to call upon the Bishop whenever they chose.'

'Wow. That influence doesn't come cheap. They must have donated a lot of money over the years.'

'Yes. I don't have the exact figures to hand - they're not easy to get hold of, but many, many thousands over the decades.'

'They were good business then,' said Herschel with a wry smile.

'For the Church? Yes.'

'Which, when you think about it, and after what you say about their influence and status in the community, makes it odd that Gerald should only have the local priest conduct his funeral.'

'What do you mean?' asked Cassandra.

'Well, you would have thought that someone of Gerald's reputation would have attracted a higher authority than the local priest to undertake his funeral duties.'

'I hadn't thought of that. You're right. Why wasn't it

conducted by the Bishop? I mean, given his status, he might even have attracted the Cardinal,' said Cassandra.

'Hmm... It's strange. Surely he deserved a better send-off than he received.'

Herschel removed his gaze. He stood up and walked towards the large panoramic window and pulled down one of the metallic slats in the venetian blind with a loud snap to look out over the city ...

'You know, I think there is more to this than we are seeing right now...'

Billy's cafe was busy with customers all wanting to be served at the same time. The queue to pay at the till snaked back from the front of the cafe to the back with a mixture of retired couples, mothers with children and singletons looking to move on and out quickly. Sheena had managed to find a table in the corner. She had arranged her coat and bag on the spare chairs so no-one would make the mistake of trying to sit at her table. She rummaged in her bag for her lighter and cigarettes, put one in her mouth, then quickly realising where she was, tutted to herself, sighed, and returned it back to the packet. Drumming her fingers on the table, she sipped at her coffee, stared at the other customers, and waited.

The cafe began to thin out and the waiter and waitress were able to clear some of the tables and make the place more presentable. This was a very popular cafe in the centre of town, where the views were cheap but the coffee was expensive. A favourite of Louise and Sheena's for many years, it was however, now looking a little tired. The popular, shabby-chic style of the 1990's had been allowed to deteriorate even further, such that some of the tables and chairs looked like they might collapse if you put too much weight on them. This didn't bother the cafe owners, who revelled in the cost-effective retro-cuteness of the place. It didn't bother Sheena or Louise either, since they had such good memories of the place. So many times, they had found themselves at Billy's as teenagers, drinking coffee, smoking, and being chatted up by the local boys. To replace anything would have been a sacrilege to the place.

'I'm sorry I'm late,' said Louise as she arrived and sat down. She was dressed in a tight-fitting business suit with a skirt and white blouse that revealed a little lace from underneath. 'It was a bit difficult to get away... Are you ok?'

'Fine,' replied Sheena, tersely.

'Ok, I see,' said Louise. 'So, er... Look... Sheena... We're not going to get anywhere unless we are together on this. Michael, Sean and David are all dead. If we're not united in how we deal with this thing, then we could end up the same way. We need to work together to help the police and Herschel find the killer. You know, you said some pretty nasty things on the phone, but I'm prepared to overlook them if you are...'

'Alright,' said Sheena stoically.

'We need to be much more honest with each other from now on,' continued Louise. 'We've both done things we aren't proud of, and we probably have kept things from each other which hasn't helped, but from now on, let's be proper sisters – you know, like we were in the past. Like we were when we used to come here... You remember, don't you? Sheena, my big glamorous sister, with your fabulous outfits, your year-round tan, your perfect hair and make-up and all the hunky guys chasing you.'

Sheena smiled.

'I was in awe of you. Did you know that? I was only twelve or thirteen and you were so mature and sophisticated. You were so grown up. I really, really wanted to be you. Did you know that too? You made such an impression on me as a kid. I tried to copy every mannerism you had, every flick of your hair, every batt of your eyelashes.'

'I never knew that,' said Sheena.

'No, you probably didn't. I was just your annoying little sister who was always hanging around, right?'

Sheena laughed.

'See, I told you,' laughed Louise. 'But now... Now, I'm a grown woman with my own job, my own house and my own family. I'm not that irritating sister anymore. I have a place in this family, and I intend to keep it and make sure I get what I deserve. But I don't want for us to fall out any more. We are very much in danger, and it can only be to the killer's benefit if we fall out. The police are as close to useless as they can possibly be. If we don't do something he'll take us out, one after the other. We should pool our resources and work together to help catch this madman, even if it is just for Sean, Michael and David, and their memory.'

'Ok,' said Sheena. 'You are right. I'm sorry. It's just you and me now. Me and my big little sister against the world,' she smiled. 'So what do you want to do about it? Either one of us could be next, and I really don't think the police can protect us.'

'Well, that is exactly it. It's protection that we need.'

'What are you suggesting then?' asked Sheena.

'I think we should hire some proper protection – some professional security. Someone who can be there to protect us all the time.'

'What, like bodyguards?'

'Yes, I guess so... We'd probably only need them when we go out...You know, in the car, in town...whenever we are out of our homes... What do you think?'

'It could be expensive,' said Sheena.

Louise looked her sister. 'How much is your life worth Sheena? One, two, three bodyguards? I mean it's not like you're short of cash now, is it?'

'Ok, ok... But who do we approach to do it? Do you know anyone?'

'I might do,' said Louise. 'There's someone I know from a previous life. His name is Matt and he runs his own security firm. I'll ask him and see what he can offer.'

'Do I know him?' asked Sheena.

'No, I don't think so. But I have known him for a long time, and he's been doing security for clubs, shops and other businesses for years. I don't know if he offers personal security, but I'll ask.'

'Ok. Thank you. Who would have thought we'd end up having to hire bodyguards... I don't want the ugly one though. I want the beefy one in a tight-fitting suit.'

They both laughed.

'I'm not sure we can be that picky,' said Louise. 'We're going to need someone quickly, so we might have to take what's available.'

'Ok, I understand. But also thank you. I hate us not being good friends and proper sisters. And I have to admit to being really scared after what happened to David. So scared, I've hardly been out.'

'Me too, pretty much. Just to go to work, and sometimes to do some shopping. But I'm always looking over my shoulder... just in case.'

'But Jim is there isn't he?'

'Well, yes, he's at home, but not all the time. He can't follow me everywhere, and it's not as if he's a trained security expert or anything, so I'm not sure how much good he'd be anyway.'

'No, but at least he's there at night. Someone to keep you company. All I have is an empty house to go home to.'

'And whose fault is th...' Louise quickly stopped herself from finishing the sentence. '...Well, a security guard would make even more sense for you then,' she countered.

'You are all I have left, you know,' said Sheena. 'Mum and Dad are gone. David, Michael and Sean... They're gone... At least you have your family. I have no one...'

Louise drew another tight-lipped breath.

'But you have had all the the opportunities. You could have had anything you wanted. In fact none of us wanted for anything growing up, really, now did we?'

'Yes, but,' said Sheena.

'I think we were brought up really well by Mum and Dad. Good little Catholic family. Mass every other day, Holy Communion of course, and even confession if you could make up something to say. Every festival, we were there weren't we? Christmas, Easter, Stations of the Cross. Every wedding and even some of the funerals. Do you remember your first Holy Communion?'

'Oh my God, do I remember it,' said Sheena. 'We were dressed up like little brides, weren't we? All in white – White dress, white veil, white shoes...'

'Like the Brides of Christ,' said Louise, pulling a face. 'Creepy, wasn't it?'

They laughed together.

'You remember Brother Connor though don't you?' said Louise. 'I didn't recognise him when he came to the house. He was always around. He loved all of the rites, didn't he? All the pomp and the...'

'Ceremony?' added Sheena.

'Yes... He liked to play with us after the services didn't he? He used to make us laugh.'

Sheena's face dropped a little... and she began to stare across the room again.

'There was never any funny business from Brother Connor though, was there?' said Louise. 'I don't remember anything like that.'

'No. Never. Not from him,' replied Sheena flatly.

'Come on... Let's face it,' added Louise. 'Any position we find ourselves in now is largely down to our own decisions, isn't it? I mean, even before finding out about Dad, we were the richest family in the parish. Mum and Dad always wanted us to make a good impression to the priests and of course the Catenian Mafia. So we can't really feel sorry for ourselves. I mean they gave us every opportunity in life. It's just that some of us took greater advantage of those opportunities than others, right?'

'What are you saying?' asked Sheena. 'Are you saying I failed?'

'No, of course not... I think I'm just trying to say that some of us are better at standing on our own two feet than others...'

'You mean better than me?'

'Well maybe a little... Look, Dad spoiled you, didn't he? Whatever you wanted or needed, you were given. You never had to struggle.'

'And you did?'

'Well, yes, actually I did,' said Louise. 'When Ross and I were first married it was really tough. Ross didn't want to take any financial help from Mum and Dad, so we had to do without quite a lot at first.'

'But there was still the safety-net if you needed it... You always knew that.'

'Maybe, but we didn't think of it like that. We wanted to stand on our own two feet.'

'And I didn't? You know I tried Louise, don't you? I tried really hard. But it never works out for me, does it? It never does.' Sheena began to well up a little. Louise reached over across the table and touched her arm.

'It's going to be different from now on, Sheena, I promise. We only have each other, so we're going to have to rely upon one another. I can't rely on you more than you upon me, and vice versa. I can't be Dad's replacement. You know that? You're going to have to learn to be more self-sufficient.'

Sheena pulled her arm away and looked back out of the cafe window.

'Why didn't he tell us what he was doing?' she sniffled. 'Why? It seems so useless now. What good did it do him if he simply sat on it all his life. Why didn't he use what he had? It seems so pointless. Surely, he could have had a more comfortable old age. I mean, in the last years of his life, he hardly went out and he hardly saw anyone. It could have been so different for him.'

'Yes, and for you,' said Louise dryly.

11

ST VINCENT DE PAUL

'Are you going to stay up there all day?' asked Connor, looking up into the tree.

'I might well do that,' replied Ben, looking down on him from one of the topmost branches. 'Look at that... 'An' no one can get to me up here... I can see to the end of the world...'

'If you get caught, Mother Superior will cane your arse.'

'She'd have to climb up here 'an catch me first,' said Ben, bouncing and swinging on the topmost branches. 'I don't think she's got the legs for it... Hahaha!'

'No but she'd wait at the bottom here for you to come down, and she'd be dusting off her switch just for you...'

'She'd be waitin' a good long time then...'

Ben bounced from one branch to another without even looking. He swayed from side to side, hooking his ankles around the branch and waving his hands in the air in a double V-sign. 'Whoooo Hooo! Take that, Mother Superior... Whooo Hooo.. And that, Father Murphy.'

Connor laughed with his friend and wished he could climb as well as him. He could make it up a few branches to about half-way, but he wasn't nearly as fearless as Ben. His friend seemed to be born to climb and scramble. He could climb any building, tree, or wall. In the summer, he liked to climb to the top of St Vincent's and relax on the rooftop, where he knew no-one else could find him. He loved exploring the passages that ran under the floors in the orphanage. If you were small enough, you could make your way around without ever being noticed. Ben was small and scrawny, like many teenagers, with thin arms and legs that belied their power. A small angular face, large nose and small pointed teeth gave him a rodent like appearance. This, and his habit of finding tiny hide-aways from the nuns in the most unlikely places got him the obvious moniker of 'Ratty'. Connor never called him that though. He always called him Ben. Even though he knew he would answer to 'Ratty', Connor preferred to be polite and proper, and to respect the name God had given him.

'So, are you coming down or not?' said Connor. 'Cos the bell for dinner will ring soon, and you probably won't hear it up there. Then there will be a search, and we all know how that will end...'

'Ok... Hold on,' shouted Ben as he scrambled down the huge birch tree that grew at the bottom of the garden, just on the edge of the wood. He swung, monkey-like, on the last two branches and dropped with a gentle thud on the grass next to his friend.

'Had ya goin' for a while there didn't I,' he laughed.

'Oh yes... I was truly fearful, for you,' mocked Connor.

'Here, d'ya want one of these?' Ben pulled from his tattered trouser pocket a small packet of Players cigarettes.

'Where did you get those?' asked Connor.

'Oh, I have my connections'

'Oh connections now do ya? Who'd you steal them from?'

'Haha... I found them in one of the sisters' dormitories. I reckon they are Sister Riosin's.'

'I didn't know she smoked?'

'She doesn't now... Hahaha...'

'What if she finds out?'

'What if she does? She won't know where they've gone. She won't know who's got 'em, and she sure as hell can't ask if anyone has found 'em. It is, as they say, the perfect crime. And more importantly, I'll be saving her from a nasty habit... Habit? Ha! D'ya gettit?'

They both laughed.

Ben and Connor had been friends for years, ever since Ben had arrived at the orphanage, only a year or two after Connor. They had grown up together. They learned how the orphanage worked, and how they might take advantage occasionally. They had eaten together, prayed together, played and cried together. They had slept in the same dormitory for many years as other boys came and went. Now as they both approached their fifteenth year, they were two of the longest-serving of all the children at St Vincent's.

'So, d'ya want one?' asked Ben

'No... I'm trying to give them up,' replied Connor.

'Are you heck... You've never even had so much as a puff... Well, I don't care if you don't... More for me.'

Ben took out one of the stubby little cigarettes, found a match in his shirt pocket, struck it against the bark of the tree, lit the cigarette, and took a long drag.

'Ahh... that's it. They're good for your throat, don't you know? Smoother and better...'

'And make you smell like an ashtray. I don't know why anyone would want to do that to themselves. God gave you a perfect body, why do you want to pollute it with all that stinky smoke?'

'You're right, now you come to mention it. Jesus didn't smoke, now did he? And neither did any of the disciples. I don't think John the Baptist smoked, and I'm pretty certain Mary Magdalene didn't either... Though I bet she would've if she could... Hahaha.'

Ben took another drag and let the smoke billow around the tree.

'So how'd you explain Father Murphy then? He smokes and he drinks. He likes all the vices now don't he? And yet he's a big-shot Monsignor, loved by the whole world, and maybe soon to be a Bishop, so I hear.'

'A Bishop?'

'That's what I heard the Reverend Mother telling her coven last week. If he keeps his nose clean and continues to raise money like he does, then it's in the bag.'

'Crikey,' said Connor, 'Bishop Murphy... Fancy that.'

'I suppose he's been here long enough, both him and old cranky-nuts Superior. They're part of the furniture ain't they? Barking-mad old Mother Superior will have to find someone else to adore once he's gone, eh?'

'She's supposed to have dedicated her life to God,' said Connor.

'Yeah, right... As long as he wears a dog-collar and is called Father Murphy... Hahaha.'

'Do you think we'll get another priest if Father Murphy goes?'

'Bound to, ain't we?'

'But that might mean that...'

'Yes... Exactly. No more of Father Murphy's 'special confessions', eh? No more having to pretend you're asleep when he sneaks into the dormitory at night. No more having to go to his office, 'for a chat'.'

'No more beatings, do you think?'

'Hard to say on that one, 'cos the Reverend Mother just loves 'em don't she?'

'But with Father Murphy gone?'

'Maybe... But who knows who comes after him... They could be worse.'

I always liked Father Walsh. I never knew what happened to him.'

'Ah Father Walsh... Yeah, he was nicer than most, but still fucked-up. They say he had to go for 'special training'.'

'Really? Where?'

'It was a place called The Order of the Paraclete. A special retreat for, well, you know, those kind of priests...'

'He was always nice to me.'

'Yeah? Maybe you weren't his type. I heard he was really fucked-up, which is why he had to go. Too much gossip, and too many angry towns-folk.'

'But Father Murphy has never had to...'

'No. You're right. But he's smart ain't he. He never leaves any marks. And he always chooses those boys who are never gonna tell. Plus, he has old Superior and the rest of the gargoyles to vouch for him.'

'I guess... They know, right?'

'Mother Superior and the rest of them? Of course, they know. They also know which side their bread is buttered. No nun ever got anywhere by grassing up a priest. It just don't happen.'

'Sister Julia isn't like that.'

'No, but what can she do? If there is ever a fuss, all that happens is that some big cheese from Dublin comes along, and whoever in the village that's complaining gets some money and has to sign a form. Then it's all over. Never hear from them again...'

'Unless you're an orphan.'

'Yep. Unless you're an orphan, 'cos nobody ever believes an orphan, do they?'

'Especially not one from St Vincent's.'

'Nope.'

'D'ya remember a couple of years ago, when Stonehouse came?'

'Kinda. He was only here for a short while.'

'Yes. But oh boy, was he the big cheese. He was here to cover something up, I'm sure. I don't know what, but that's what he was here for, but I'm certain of it. He was definitely here to make sure something got smoothed over.'

'D'ya think it was when Jacob went missing?'

'Jacob? I doubt it.'

'Or Benjamin? Or Frankie?'

'Don't think so. The likes of Stonehouse only come to places like this to make sure the things that the Church don't want to come out, don't come out. Did you know that all the priests, when they become priests, have to sign an oath of secrecy to the Church? An oath that is above all else. Above the Law. Above everything... So, there you go. Stonehouse drops in, money changes hands, and everyone keeps schtum. Stonehouse never stays and he don't get involved if an orphan or two goes missing. I mean...'

The two boys looked at each other glumly.

'So what's the way out of here?' said Connor.

'Well, it's not like we're gonna get proper parents, now is it?' replied Ben. 'We're too old and nowhere near cute enough to get adopted. And anyway's, no-one's got any money around here. They have enough trouble feeding their own families without 'aving another mouth to worry about.'

'So, what you gonna do? You can't stay here forever.'

'Hmmm, Dunno... What about you?'

'Me? I'm going to take Holy Orders.'

'What the fuck. No... You?'

'Yeah. Why not?'

'Well, I know you like going to Mass and all that pompous shit, but Holy Orders?'

'Don't you think I'm up to it?'

'No, it's not that. It's just... well... do you really want to become one of them?'

'They're not all like Father Murphy'

'Or Father Walsh, or Father O'Brian?'

'Ok, Ok. It's just, I think I might be a true believer and I think if I'm given the chance that I can bring the true message of the Lord to the people that need it.'

'You've got to be off your feckin' rocker...'

'Ok... Well if you're so smart. What's your idea?'

'Oh, I've got mine all worked out...'

'Oh, right. You've decided now, have you?...'

'Yep. I'm going to escape. I'm going to leave here when no-one is looking and I'm going to get to Dublin, and I'm going to... Going to...'

'Going to, what, Ben?'

'I'm going to... join the Merchant Navy,' blurted Ben.

'The Navy... Wow.'

'Yeah... And get as far away from here and Father Murphy, and the rest of them as I can.'

'And when are you going to do that?' asked Connor.

'Soon, I reckons. There's no point staying around here any longer. It's summer, I'm good with my hands, and I reckons I could get myself a boat pretty easily.'

'Shame they don't have rigging anymore, you'd be straight up into the, what do they call it? The birds nest...'

'The crows nest...'

'Yeah. That's it. The crows nest... But you'll have to be quick and careful, they don't like runaways. Remember what happened to Jack.'

'I'll be fine. I know this place like the back of my hand. I'll be gone before they'll even notice.'

'I'll miss you Ben,' said Connor.

'No, you won't. You'll be too busy lah-de-dahing it up with all the priests and the bishops. Getting all the secret knowledge an' all that...'

'I don't think being an altar boy is going to be enough to get them to put me forward for the seminary. And Father Murphy won't recommend me.'

'No, you're right. So what'cha going to do?'

'The Monastery... I'll be able to get in there. That would be a start, and it'll get me away from here...'

'It's not a priest tho' is it?'

'No, but I could start there and maybe after a few years... I know others have done it.'

'Brother Connor...' Ben mocked. 'You'll be 'Brother Connor. Hahaha.'

'Yes, I guess I will,' said Connor.

'Connor... Connor... Wake up,' hissed Ben.

'Wh... What...What time is it?'

'It's two in the morning. Wake up. I need to talk to you.'

'What? At this time? Talk to me in the morning...'

'No, now. It's important. I need to show you something.'

'Really... Why?'

'Come on... Wake up... Get up.'

Connor propped himself up onto one elbow and peered out into the darkness. All he could see was the green glow of the emergency exit sign above the door to the dormitory.

'Where are you?' asked Connor.

'Here.' Ben flashed his torch against his face. The bright light shining upwards against his thin, rodenty face made him look like a ghost-rat.

'Oh my good lord. Put that down. You'll raise the dead with a face like that.'

'Come on... Get up,' he insisted.

'Ok... Ok... Just give me second. Keep quiet... What is it?... What do you want to show me and why does it have to be in the middle of the night?'

'It's amazing... You're going to love it...'

The boys' dormitory held about twenty bunks. The older, more senior boys usually occupied the lower bunk, as that was easiest to get in and out of, and it was easier to get to your stuff. The younger boys, be it by order or by design, were usually consigned to the upper bunk, which was presented as a treat at first. It was only later, when trying to get in and out without disturbing the lower occupant, that they found it was not as attractive as first sold, and infinitely more painful if you received a kick from the occupant of the lower bunk.

The dormitory was full, and all the boys appeared to be asleep.

'I didn't hear anything,' said Ben. 'I don't think Father Murphy did his rounds tonight.'

'Makes a change,' said Connor. 'I guess we should thank the Lord for some things.'

Connor slipped into some clothes and followed Ben out of the dormitory and into the corridor.

'Where are we going? And why does it have to be now? And why is it so important?' said Connor.

'I've been out huntin',' said Ben.

'Hunting?... What do you mean hunting?'

'Huntin' and collectin'...'

'I don't know what you are talking about, Ben... But this better be good.'

'Follow me,' said Ben, encouraging his accomplice forward.

The two boys headed out of the corridor and down towards the main entrance. The light from a full-moon was strong enough to show them the way. Without it the whole orphanage would have been in complete darkness.

As they proceeded, Connor noticed that Ben was becoming more excited, hopping from one foot to the other. He slipped the lock on the interior door, then pulled a set of keys from his trouser pocket.

'Care of the Reverend Mother,' he said, and opened the main door with one of the keys. The door was heavy and had to be pushed back carefully so as not to make any sound. The pair tip-toed over the driveway gravel, trying not to crunch, and arrived at the entrance to the orphanage chapel. Whereas it would normally be enveloped by darkness at night, Connor noticed a bright glow coming from the building.

'Is this your doing?' he asked.

'Come, come... Come and see,' said Ben, urgently.

Ben opened the chapel door and the pair entered. The chapel was fairly small and plain, but Connor loved it. He loved the majesty and the miracle of all the services he attended there. He loved the dressing up and all the pomp and ceremony. He loved the Mass, all five stages – Kyrie, Gloria, Credo, Sanctus and Agnus Dei. But most of all he loved the eucharist. He could swear that he could feel the presence of God as he took the wafer and the wine into his mouth.

He looked down the nave at the altar, where Ben had lit every candle he could find. They were on the altar, on the window ledges, on the tables and many more on the floor. Ben had placed dozens of them across the far end of the chapel which was now bathed in a strong, pale colour, but warm glow.

'Wow,' said Connor. 'That looks amazing. You must have spent ages collecting and arranging all of those.'

'Yes, I did...' said Ben excitedly. 'But can you smell it, too?'

'The incense? Oh yes... It reminds me of Mass. Oh, I love that smell.'

'There is the largest stack of incense you have ever seen alight just under the altar... It's amazing...'

Ben was obviously very pleased with himself.

'And there is more, Look...' he said dreamily. Ben grabbed Connor's hand and pulled him down towards the altar.

'Look,' he said, 'I have collected the offering for the day.'

There, pinned out across the large altar table, were at least a dozen dead animals. There were several rabbits, a badger, two or three squirrels, a cat, a blackbird and two foxes. Each one of them had been surgically incised and opened up to expose their internal organs. Some of the organs had been removed and placed next to the body. There was a lot of blood staining the altar cloth, dripping down from the table and onto the marble floor.

Connor stood in front of this scene of carnage, open-mouthed.

'Oh my God, Ben. What have you done?'

'It's beautiful, isn't it?'

'But, these animals, Ben. Did you do all this?'

'They are my sacrifice to Selene. My beautiful Selene – so that I may be granted good favour on my journey. Do you think she will look upon me favourably?'

'Selene?'

'Selene, the Goddess of the Moon. The Moon, Connor. Do you see it? It's a sign for me to go...'

'But this is horrific, Ben. All these poor animals. What do you expect to achieve?'

'It is necessary and it is required by the Gods, so I might have good favour...'

'Ben, you're acting really weird. You're scaring me. Are you feeling alright?'

'It's the power of the Moon, Connor. Don't you feel it? I feel Selene filling me up. Filling everything up. I hope she sees that I have done good for her. Only for her...'

'But all the blood, Ben. And for God's sake, this is a Church...'

'Pah to the Church,' spat Ben. 'What are they? Eh? They're just a bunch of queers, sadists and pedo's. And they lie to us, Connor. They do nothing but lie to us...'

'But Ben... Look at what you have done. What will the Reverend Mother say?'

'I don't care about any of them anymore, Connor. Father Murphy, Mother Superior, the rest of them. They're all just fucked-up liars, or fucked-up believers who spend their lives being controlled. And for what? I'm going to be free. Free of all this bullshit. Free of all this pain.'

'But how, Ben... Surely not like this?'

'Oh yes... This is the way, don't you see? The freedom you get from the true Gods – Jupiter, Juno, Minerva, Neptune and Venus. They all work together. Not like the Christian God we are forced to worship. One true God... Really? How does that work? God the Father, God the son? And God the Holy Spirit? Which one is it? There's only one God, right?... It makes no sense? And who was the first to die and be resurrected? Well you know it wasn't Jesus, if he even existed? No, Mithras... He was around centuries before Jesus was even invented. Mithras was born of a virgin, celebrated a last supper with his followers, died on the cross and was resurrected after three days. Sound familiar? It's all lies from them, Connor. And then there's the Ten Commandments, eh? The Second Commandment says, 'Make no graven images', Well look around you? What do you see? Jesus on the cross, everywhere. An image of God. A graven image of a God being tortured on a cross. And we worship it... Lies... It's all lies Connor, it's all lies... It's just there to control us... You know what I mean - every aspect of our life is controlled at St Vincent's... All by their one and only excuse for a true God... And it's not just here, is it?... All throughout this country those poor little beggars are giving their last pennies to support a Church that bullies and controls every aspect of their lives. It's sick, Connor. It's sick because we all fall for it.'

'We all have doubts, Ben, from time to time.'

'Doubts? Doubts! Did you have doubts when Father Murphy was feeling under your bedclothes last night? Or when the Reverend Mother was caning your arse for some stupid thing? What about Jacob, or Benjamin or Frankie, or the dozens of others who have gone missin'? Do you think they didn't have doubts? Look, what good did it do them? Nuttin'... No, I'm going to stick with the Gods I can see, and are real for me. The Sun, the Moon and all the earthly forces... They'll protect me. They'll make me whole again.'

'So what do you want me to do, Ben?' asked Connor.

'I want you to bear witness to this sacrifice as a testament to my devotion to the true Gods. I want you to know who made this offering, and why, so that when Murphy and the rest of his lot see this, you will know that it was me, but he never will.'

'Ok... I will know,' said Connor, 'And I won't tell anyone... That's what you want, right?'

'Yes. It's my little parting gift to Murphy and the rest of those lying blasphemers. I want them all to know that they will never get me.'

'So you're leaving?'

'Yes... Tonight. Wish me luck. This will be the last time you see me.'

'Heading to Dublin and the high seas?' asked Connor.

'That's right, just as I said. By this time tomorrow, I'll be on a ship bound for the other side of the world.'

'Well... I wish you the very best of luck. This is some parting gift, the likes I have never seen before. Remember I will be here for you if you ever need me. And, you may not want it now, but Christ will be here for you as well. He is filled with love and forgiveness.'

'There's nothing I need from Jesus any more,' said Ben. 'Least of all, his love and forgiveness.'

The two boys hugged. Ben handed the large key-ring to Connor and skipped out of the chapel. Connor heard his feet on the gravel, and then nothing. There was just silence and the flickering of the candles.

Connor looked at the massacre in front of him. Regardless of what he had told Ben, he really didn't know what to do. He was shocked and horrified. He was so confused and so conflicted. What Ben had said kind of made sense to him, but how could anyone reject the Lord Jesus Christ, our saviour? How could he have ended up preferring the heathen Gods, rather than the one true God? What did it all mean? He looked at all the dead animals laid out in front of him, knelt at the altar and began to pray...

'Dear Lord God above... Our holiest Father, I beseech thee. I pray for the soul of my very good friend, Ben. He thinks he is lost to you, but I know that you are the saviour, the light and the truth. So I implore you, oh Lord, that you make your presence felt in his heart. Shine your light of truth onto his misguided ways. Help him to find the one true path and bring him back to us, safe, sound and full of love for you.'

Connor paused for breath and thought for a moment. He looked up past the dead animals and into the eyes of Christ on the cross at the head of the church.

'But dear Lord, I have to admit, at this hour of my greatest need, I do have difficulties too. Could any of what Ben said be true? How close is the Kingdom of Heaven really to what we have here on Earth?.. Why is there so much suffering in the world? Why are there people like Father Murphy? Is this of your making? Is this what you want here on Earth? Are you truly happy with what you have created? Does your Church really tell your message here? Your message is of love and forgiveness. But I don't see it... Have we missed something? I am really having trouble here, oh Lord. I am trying to understand what is right and what is wrong. Please... Lord, I need your help.'

Connor put his head down and prayed. He kept his eyes tightly shut, just like he had always done from when he was a kid. He had always felt it was a blasphemy to open his eyes while praying. He was never sure that if he did open them, what he might see – angels dancing around the heads of the priests perhaps, or the image of Jesus in front of a burning bush. The thought scared him, so he always kept them tightly shut. But suddenly today he felt different. The trauma of the sacrifice, and the sadness of Ben's departure, along with all his doubts, all began to fade away. He began to feel a strange sense of calm and serenity. A sudden warmth and peacefulness gently came upon him. He then went against every urge in his body. He felt compelled to... open his eyes.

There before him, Connor could see something strange in the darkness. A vision of a kindly looking man in a dark cloak and with a small white goatee beard, with a dark black peak-less cap upon his small, wizened head, with wisps of blonde hair peeping out. Connor looked closely and then looked around this figure. Everything else seemed normal – the church, the candles and the cross before him, but the figure appeared other-worldly, as though he was present, but not from this place or time. Connor looked again, and the figure smiled at him. A gentle, welcoming smile. Connor was heartened by the man and he was not afraid.

'Hello, my son,' said the figure.

The apparition spoke, but his lips did not move. The voice seemed to be present only in Connor's head.

'Hello, my Lord,' replied Connor.

The figure laughed quietly. 'I am not your Lord, my child. But I am here on my master's behalf and I am here to guide you. I am Vincent de Paul.'

'St Vincent!' exclaimed Connor.

Embarrassed, he averted his eyes downwards and then closed them again. The voice continued on.

'You are troubled, are you not, my son? You are finding it difficult to find your place in this world. You have doubts? Am I correct?'

Connor reopened his eyes, 'Yes, my Lord. I am scared. I don't know where I fit, and I have doubts, serious doubts, about myself, my friends, and my faith.'

'This is all very normal, my child. Remember, he was tested for forty days and forty nights. We tempted him many times and put him under many trials.'

'Does the Lord have faith in me?' asked Connor.

'He does. Your Lord has faith in you. Very much so. He knows you can achieve great things.'

'That makes me feel better.'

'But he does have a task for you.'

'He does... Me? What kind of task? What can the Lord have with me?

'You are very important to him. But he wants you to understand your purpose here on earth. This is an important task.'

'It would be an honour to serve him. What is his bidding?'

'It is very simple, my son. Firstly, you must reject these heathen ways by which you are surrounded. You must reject them with all the strength you can muster.'

'You mean Ben's path?'

'There is only one true Lord and Master and he has found you, through me. The heretical paths only lead to everlasting frustration, pain and crushing hypocrisy. But your Lord does not want this for you. He wants you to find his true path. He has other plans...'

'I can do that... With your help, I think I can do that...'

'Good. I believe you can. And the second thing.'

'Yes...'

'He wants you to devote your life to him.'

'Devote my life? How?'

'You are special Connor. You have been chosen. It is in his plan that you will deliver his message. It is his wish that, in due course, you will enter the Monastery, and you will devote yourself to his true teachings and to his way.'

'Chosen? But I am not worthy.'

'You are more than worthy, my son. But you must have true faith in him. You need to truly discover your faith for yourself. Those around you are unimportant compared to your life's task. You must learn for yourself. But you must never speak of this to anyone. It must remain just between you, me and our Lord and Master. Can you rise to this challenge?'

'It would be my honour.'

'In good time, you will move from the Monastery and enter

the seminary to carry on his work from within the Church. You can spread his word inside the Church.'

'Yes... To spread his word,' repeated Connor. 'That is my challenge.'

'Keep to the true faith and you will be rewarded in his Kingdom.'

'I shall do my very best,' replied Connor.

'Bless you. You will see me again.'

The vision that called himself St Vincent made the sign of an inverted cross in front of Connor, and was gone.

Connor looked around, to see if he had moved somewhere else in the chapel and slapped his face to check that he wasn't dreaming.

Dawn was now breaking, and the thin, watery beams of light seeped into the little chapel. Connor tried to understand what had just happened. What had he just witnessed? Who was this apparition? Who or what was this person? Was it a miracle? He couldn't be sure. But it was something. And he felt reinvigorated. He felt as if he now had some purpose. He knew what he needed to do and he knew exactly how he was going to do it.

'I haven't seen Ratty around for a while,' said Julia. 'Is he doing one of his hide-away tricks again?

'Errr... Yes... I guess so...' mumbled Connor. 'You know what he's like... He likes his solitude.'

Julia looked out of the kitchen window into the back garden where some of the children were playing after lunch. She looked further into the woods as she dried up the plates from lunch.

'Usually at the top of a tree or lying on the church roof, eh?' said Sister Julia.

'Yes.. That's right.'

'But I haven't seen him for a while. He normally turns up after a day or so. Do you think he's alright?'

'Well...'

Sister Julia looked closely at Connor in that mock concerned, but playful way. Her mouth went down at the sides and then her eyebrow twitched.

'Oh my good Lord,' cried Sister Julia. 'The Chapel... That was Ben, wasn't it?'

Connor looked at Sister Julia as blankly as he could muster, but he found it impossible to lie to her.

'Well... Er,' he said.

'Oh, Connor', said Sister Julia. 'That was awful. What happened? Has he run away? You know what happened in the Chapel, don't you? It was horrible... It was him, wasn't it?

'Shhhh,' said Connor, putting his finger to his lips. 'No one knows...'

'The poor lad... So it wasn't vandals. What happened?'

Connor took Sister Julia to one side of the room and moved into a quiet corner of the adjoining corridor.

'Do you promise to keep a secret? Only, if they find out it was him... well, you know...' said Connor.

'Of course, I wouldn't say a word... You know me better than that. I'm just worried that something bad might have happened to him. He could be hurt, or something worse. Did he do that to those animals? Was that him?'

'Yes, it was. But you've got to promise that you won't say anything to anyone. If Father Murphy finds out about this, we'll never hear the end of it. He's mad enough about it as it is.'

Sister Julia made the sign of the cross. 'As Jesus Christ is my witness, you have my solemn word, I will not tell another soul.'

'Ok... Ben took me to the chapel two nights ago, when it was a full moon, and showed me what he had done. It was gruesome. I was horrified, and I haven't been able to think about anything else since.'

'Why did he do it? Was he put up to it by someone?'

Connor moved around and looked down the corridor to make sure there was no-one listening.

'No, it was all his own idea, and he wanted me to see it. I think this place had finally got to him. He was all agitated and excited. But it was what he said that bothered me the most.'

'What? What did he say?

'Well... After all these years, he had come to the conclusion that he had rejected God. Completely. And I mean completely. I think everything that has happened to him over the years, and the way things are here, tipped him over the edge.'

'Well, I suppose we all have our doubts from time to time.'

'That's what I said. But with Ben, well you saw what he did. He had just gone off the rails...'

'Why?'

'I don't think he believed he was a Christian any longer. He kept saying that everything we are told is a lie, and that all the Church does is control us, and take people's money.'

'But there would be no orphanage without the Church,' said Julia.

'Maybe so, but we all know there are things that go on here that really aren't right. He said it was all hypocritical. You know, worshipping a loving God and yet having to live here.'

Sister Julia sighed. 'Oh Connor. It's so difficult... You know what happens if people speak out. I mean, I have always done my best to...'

'Yes, I know... to protect me... and the others. I know... Ben said what he did was part of pagan rituals and rights. I didn't really understand. He said he was now going to worship the Goddess of the Moon.'

'Oh my Lord,' said Sister Julia. She made the sign of the cross.

'He killed all of those animals... He called it a sacrifice... It was disgusting.'

'Oh, I'm so sorry that you had to see that.'

'It's ok. He's my best friend here, well, apart from you...but that's different isn't it...'

Sister Julia smiled. 'But I still don't understand why he did it.'

'I think it is this place,' said Connor. 'You know what it can be like. We are told that Jesus is a loving God, and that we should forgive our enemies and turn the other cheek. I don't think Ben saw that here. I think he saw people in power taking advantage of the weak and the dispossessed and he saw the deceit, and it pushed him over the edge.'

'Perhaps. You know that they are out looking for him. I don't know what will happen if they find him.'

'I just hope he is far away from here by now.'

'Let's hope...'

Connor looked around to see if anyone else was in the corridor. 'Sister Julia?' he said. 'Can I ask you a question.'

'Of course... anything.'

'Have you ever... ever had doubts?'

Sister Julia thought for a moment, and ran her finger under her wimple to push back some stray hairs.

'Of course I have, Connor. Life can be confusing and you wouldn't be human if you didn't have doubts sometimes. But you have to have faith too, that things will always be right in the end.'

'Do you think that our way is the one and only true way? And that God, Christ and the Holy Spirit are the one and only true God?'

'I do Connor, with all of my heart... Do you? Are you having doubts? Has this business with Ben made you question your faith?'

'I'm very confused, Sister Julia. Yes, I am questioning my faith, but not in the way you might think,' said Connor.

'What do you mean?'

'Well... Have you ever seen anything? Anything that might make you think?'

'Like what?'

'I don't know... Maybe an apparition, or a vision?'

'You mean a spook? A ghost?... Whoooooh!' She pushed him in his chest and made a face... and then laughed.

'Have you ever seen a picture of St Vincent?'

'St Vincent, of this orphanage?'

'Yes.'

'Hmmm... I think there may be a small one in Father Murphy's office. He has lots of pictures of saints in his room. But I wouldn't recommend you go looking. And anyway, why such strange questions Connor? Why do you ask?'

'Oh nothing, I just wondered what he looked like. Let's see that the others are alright in the garden.'

Sister Julia put her hand against Connor's shoulder and looked him in the eye.

'You know Connor, you will make a very good priest. You can right these wrongs.'

Looking from his dormitory window, Connor saw the two Guardai police cars arrive. Two guards climbed out of the first car and a further two from the second. The second two held a small boy by each of his arms, behind his back. As they headed towards the front door, Connor saw both Father Murphy and Mother Superior come out to greet them. Father Murphy shook the hands of each of the guards as they brought their delivery inside.

'It's Ben!' Connor shouted. 'They've found him...' He ran to the top of the stairs to see Ben being taken, handcuffed, by two of the guards, into one of the ante-rooms on the ground floor. The door closed loudly behind them. Rushing down the stairs, he arrived at the door just as Sister Julia and Sister Roisin arrived. Unfortunately, the sight of two Guardai cars and their contents had attracted the attention of most of the children, who immediately gathered behind Connor and the two nuns to see what was going on.

'It's Ben,' said Connor

'Yes, I saw,' replied Sister Julia.

The children began to make a noise, so the nuns had to shoo them away. Just as quiet was being restored, the door opened and Father Murphy emerged.

'I would be grateful if you could keep the noise down,' he said.

'I think we have it under control now, Father... Is everything alright?' asked Sister Julia.

'Everything is fine thank you. You can all get back to your business now.'

Connor peered over and around Father Murphy and tried to see what was happening behind him. He could see one of the guards standing with his back to the door, and the outstretched feet of the other one beyond that. He could just make out what he assumed was Ben's feet next to the guard's as if he were sitting.

'I said, you may get on with you business now,' said Father Murphy, firmly. He turned and closed the door behind him, and the group slowly dissolved away.

'What did you see?' asked Sister Julia.

'Not much. I thought I could just make out Ben's feet.'

'What do you think has happened? It took four guards to bring him back,' snickered Sister Roisin.

'I have no idea. I'm just glad that he's safe,' said Sister Julia.

'Safe? 'Ere?...' said Sister Roisin. 'After dat stunt, he'd be safer in de station. Murphy will put him in solitary, you watch.'

'Solitary?' said Julia.

'Yep...In d'basement. 'Dey'll put him in one of those,' said

Sister Roisin.

'We have cells in the basement? Oh my good Lord. That is barbaric,' replied Sister Julia. 'Do the guards know about them?'

Oh, I reckon so,' said Roisin. 'Dey'll put him in there.'

The three of them tried hard to hear what was happening on the other side of the door, but all they could hear was muffled conversation.

'Well, at least Father Murphy isn't shouting,' said Sister Julia.

'Not yet,' added Sister Roisin.

The voices stopped and the door opened, giving the three of them just enough time to move away and look like they were doing something useful.

'Thank you, officers,' said Father Murphy. 'I'm sorry if we have been a trouble to you. We can handle things from here.'

'No trouble Father,' said the officer. 'I'm sure you have things under control. And don't go hard on the lad. We were all fifteen once.'

'That is true,' said Father Murphy, smiling as he let the four guards out. 'I'll see you at Mass next Sunday, will I?'

Father Murphy turned and Connor, Sister Julia and Sister Roisin all saw his face as he returned to the room. It was as black as thunder.

'Get on with your work!' he shouted as he slammed the door.

'Oh, no,' said Sister Julia. 'This isn't right. What can we do?'

'Well if yer value yer 'ealth, den you'll look d'other way,' said Sister Roisin.

'We can't do that. We can't just sit back and watch. We have to help Ben somehow.'

'Look,' said Connor. 'If they put him in the basement. In the... the cells, I can get to him. I know a way.'

'The tunnels?' said Sister Julia.

'Yes. There's a small passageway that could take me there... So, I could see him.'

'What about me?' said Sister Julia.

'You're too tall, and besides, if you were caught, you'd be beaten black and blue too. And then where would you be? Leave it to me. I'll get to him.'

It was then that the first crack of the cane sounded from inside the room, followed shortly by a cry that was unmistakably Ben.

'Oh, my goodness,' cried Sister Julia. She moved towards the door and grabbed the handle. Sister Roisin caught her arm and pulled it away. 'No Sister. You won't be doin' anyone no good by going in 'dere and creatin' hell,' she said. 'He's goin' to have to take his punishment for d'time bein'. He's a strong lad. He'll be alright.'

'But poor Ratty...Poor Ben. They can't do this to him. It's inhuman.'

Another high-pitched thwack came from the other side of the door, followed by a cry from Ben.

'I can't listen to this,' said Sister Julia. 'Connor... You have to get to him. You have to show him that he is loved... That we care about him... Can you save him?'

'I can only do my best,' said Connor.

———

Connor shimmied down the last section of the tiny passageway that led into the basement. He pushed firmly at the mesh screen that faced out into the empty corridor. Making a reassuring crack, the entire frame came away in his hands and he was able to drop down the few feet onto the walkway. With his flashlight in his hand, Connor made his way along to the end of the corridor, passing several steel-fronted doors until he saw a light sneaking from under one of them at the far end.

'Ben?' he whispered. 'Ben? Are you there?'

A low moan came from behind the door.

'Ben? Is that you? Are you alright?'

The low moan repeated itself.

Looking around, Connor found a small wooden chair, and dragged it in front of the door. With his torch in his mouth, he stood on the chair and felt around for a hatch of some kind. He ran his fingers around the square edges of steel plate and found a catch. Pulling at it, the hatch slid open to reveal a tiny cell, maybe 8ft by 6ft, with no window, just a dim electric lamp high on the wall, a low wooden bunk, a bucket, and a washbasin. Ben's small figure was prostrate on the wooden bunk.

'Ben... It's Connor... Are you alright?'

The groan repeated again.

'Ben... Look at me... It's Connor. I've come to help you. Are you injured or hurt in any way?'

'I can't move... My arse hurts,' cried Ben into his pillow.

Connor could make out the outline of his friend on the bed, face down, his arms over his head. He was still wearing the ragged old trousers and shapeless top Connor had last seen him in the chapel.

'They beat you didn't they?' said Connor.

'Oh yes... They did me over, well and truly.'

'Murphy and the Mother Superior?'

'Oh yes... They took turns in beating the Christianity back into me.'

Ben raised his head up a little and looked over towards his friend. His face was bruised and lacerated. His lip was swollen and he had a nasty looking distended black eye.

'Oh my God Ben. Your face? Did they do that to you too?'

'No, no... That was the Guardai.'

'What? The guards? They beat you up?'

'Yep... Who'd have thought it... They kept calling me a heathen, an occultist, a Satanist.'

'Oh... I'm so sorry Ben.'

'I don't even know what a feckin' Satanist is. I guess it's not good.'

'Can you get up? Can you get over to the door? Sister Julia gave me some food for you and some ointment for your wounds.'

'Hold on', moaned Ben, and he slowly hauled himself out of the bunk and limped slowly over to the hatch.

'Here...' Connor passed a small package through the hatch. 'There's some bread and some cheese in there as well as the ointment. You have water?'

'Thanks, pal. I'm ok for water, but I haven't eaten in quite a while.'

'Are you ok to talk? Sister Julia and I want to get you out of here, as soon as possible.'

'Well I haven't had much conversation in the last few days... other than with Murphy and the Police. But I guess I'm the lucky one.'

'The lucky one? How can you be the lucky one, Ben?'

'I'm still alive...'

'Alive? Yes, you're alive. But how does that make you lucky? You're black and blue...'

'Well, the plan didn't really go as I wanted, now did it? There wasn't any way I could get to Dublin on foot straight away without being picked up, so I thought I would lie low in the woods for a day or so before seeing if I could hitch a ride.'

'Ok. Did you make it any further?'

'No. Not really. And I'll tell you why. It'll make your blood run cold.'

'Oh, Jesus, Ben... You didn't kill more animals, did you?'

'Naah, nothing like that! Though I wish I had been able to, cos I got truly hungry in that wood. I couldn't make a fire for fear of being discovered, so all I had was the little trench I dug. I filled it with leaves and covered it with ferns. So it was ok. Cold and a bit damp, but it did the trick.'

'How long did you stay there?'

'I was planning on just a night or two, until everything had quietened down, you know?'

'Well there was a lot of noise. Especially from Murphy.'

'Hahaha... Owww,' Ben held his sides and grimaced.

'He went ape when he saw what you had done. But he had no idea it was you...'

'No, not until he beat it out of me...'

'I didn't say anything... And I only had to tell Sister Julia when she guessed.'

'Really?'

'So what happened?'

'Oh my God Connor... it was terrible. If anything was going to make me more of a Pagan, or a Sata..'

'Satanist, Ben. Someone who worships the Devil... Satan.'

'Oh... Well, I'm not one of those...'

'But, I have to ask Ben. Do you still reject Christ?'

'You don't understand... What I have seen in the past few days would turn even the Pope against Christianity.'

'Good Lord, Ben. What has happened to you... What happened?'

'Well, I was hiding out in my little den, waiting for a chance to head off towards Dublin, as I said. From my camp I could see the outbuildings of the orphanage. You know, the low flint ones, where some of the gardening equipment is kept.'

'Yes, I know the ones.'

'I've never really taken much notice of what goes on in those buildings. I guess no-one does. They're just there aren't they... with the rakes and the forks for the leaves and the spades and the wheelbarrows for gardening, right?'

'Right.'

'But what I saw... Well... Every night I was there, and sometimes during the day, I would see some of the nuns go in there. Sometimes two together and sometimes one with Father Murphy, and sometimes one with Father Whelan. One time, I took a closer look, and through the old chipped windows I could see them...'

'See them?'

'Yeah. See them...at it... You know... Fucking... Sister Barbara, Sister Karen and Sister Roisin mostly. But sometimes Sister Rachel too. They must have been in and out there twice a day. And Father Murphy with Father Whelan too... on their own sometimes...'

'Oh my Lord!'

'I knew Murphy was a deviant, but it would seem fiddling with boys isn't enough for him...'

'And this was day and night?'

'Yes. Sometimes they'd have a little party, depending on how many there were. They'd be drinking and smoking and ...well, you know... fucking each other... On the old brown settees that are in there. It was a right free for all, sometimes. That Sister Roisin let them do everything to her... Everything!'

'What about Mother Superior? Didn't she stop them?'

'Stop them? Stop them! Hah!... Twice I saw her go to one of the buildings, knock on the door, apologise in that way she does, and call for Father Murphy to come out... She knows everything about it.'

'You didn't see... er, Sister Julia?'

'No, no... never. But Sister Roisin, yes, many times.'

'This place,' said Connor, and he shook his head.

'But that's not all Connor... if that wasn't enough. It's worse...'

'Worse? How could it possibly be worse?'

'I saw them giving whippings and beatings to some of the children. Even some of the smaller ones. I reckon they were even using cold water on some of them.. You know, to make 'em feel like they were drownin', an' all...'

'God they are brutal... Why don't we know about this?'

'And this was every day Connor... Every day I was there, I saw it...'

'Those poor children. They don't deserve anything like that...'

'Murphy and Mother Superior and the rest of them are just evil, evil, bastards. No wonder so many try to escape. Like me...'

Ben's voice trailed off, and he began to sob. He began to sob really hard.

'I'm so sorry Ben. I suppose in the back of our minds, we knew that the beatings went on. I thought it was just the older kids that got it.'

Ben's broken face suddenly appeared right at the hatch, bloodied and swollen.

'They killed them Connor... They killed them... dozens of them!'

'What? What do you mean?'

'I saw them do it. I saw them... The babies... The new ones. The ones just arrived.'

Ben's face was covered in tears. His eyes were both simultaneously swollen and shrunken... Snot and spit oozed from his nose and lips.'

'The poor little babies... The mothers came and delivered them... They were always in tears... Always... And the girls, they were always so, so, young. Our age, sometimes even younger. And they handed them over to that witch... I saw it. With my very own eyes. They didn't want to... But they had to... They were told to... Why? Because we say it's a sin, and because some fisherman hundreds of years ago told us to love each other... They've twisted it all... They've taken it, and fucked it up for their own selfish purposes... And you know what?... It's our fault... We let them... We let them get away with it... We all knew things here weren't right, but who... who had the courage to stand up to them? Not I... Not you... No one in the village... No one in Dublin... The Church... It's just too strong.'

Ben burst into more sobs, his chest heaving up and down. Connor's eyes welled up with tears at what he was being told.

'Murphy and Mother Superior are killing the new-born

babies? Beautiful little babies. Their mothers never know what happens to them. They probably think that like you and me, they'll be brought up in the orphanage. Not a perfect life, but at least it's something... But they're not Connor... They get rid of them straight away... They put their bodies down the well... After they... you know... They wrap them in little blankets and they drop them into the well. I saw them do it... Many times, in just two days.'

'Good God... Someone needs to know about this...'

'Hah... What's the point? They won't believe us..'

'We should tell the guards.'

'What do you think I've been trying to do for the last two days? When I saw what was happening, I couldn't just leave. I headed into town and went straight to the station.'

'And you told them?'

'Yes, of course I did. I told them everything. Everything I had seen. Murphy, Mother Superior... The beatings, the torture, and the babies...'

Connor looked at his friend. 'They didn't believe you did they?'

Ben sobbed even harder.

'Not a word. They told me to stop making up stories about the priests and the Church... They told me I was evil and deranged... They put me in a cell... And when no-one was looking, they beat me up... And then they told me I was a Satan...ist, and that I would burn in hell... For eternity. And then when they had finished with me, they brought me back here...'

'Oh my God...'

'It makes no difference, what we do... They won't believe us. They'll carry on doing this and they'll get away with it. God only knows how many are at the bottom of that well... They have all the power... None of us are safe... None of us can ever escape this place...'

12

THE ONION RING

The sign read, 'The Onion Ring - Dr Felix Parker BSc MSc MRCPsych MBBS RCPsych - Psychiatrist.' Herschel stood for a moment looking at the sign. He smiled and pressed the buzzer next to the door... and waited.

'Hello,' came the robotic voice from the intercom.

'Herschel...'

'Ah, Mr. Herschel... Do come in...'

The door buzzed. Herschel pushed and stepped into the wide entrance hall. The lobby stretched back some distance to a desk at the far end of the hall. Its surgical white walls and floor were punctuated only with a series of large paintings hung at regular intervals on each side, and a series of objet d'art on plinths in glass cases down the centre. Herschel walked towards the desk but took his time to look at some of the paintings and art on display. The first item he stopped at was a pair of ornate golden pouring vases sitting inside a glass box. At about twelve inches high, they were Greco-Roman in style, with a thick triangular-footed base – solid gold, elaborately carved, and decorated with three ornate snakes that entwined the handles and the body, giving the impression of a heavy, substantial utensil.

'Beautiful,' said Herschel. 'Pax Romana, I would say... Do these belong to you?'

'Sadly not,' said the receptionist from behind her desk. '... Good morning Mr. Herschel. How are you today?'

'Ah... Apologies,' said Herschel. 'I'm being rude. Good morning, Melissa. I am very well. How are you?'

'They are beautiful, aren't they? They are as light as a feather, even though they don't look it... Sadly they are only on loan to us. From one of Dr Parker's more appreciative clients. Have you seen the egg over there?' She pointed towards the nearest plinth.

'Oh, my goodness,' said Herschel as he quickly moved towards the display. 'Is this what I think it is?'

'What do you think it is?' smirked Melissa.

'It's a pink Fabergé egg, isn't it?'

'You are correct.'

'Wow... It is beautiful. How old?'

'I am told that it was made in 1843 for a Russian Princess.'

'Romanov... I don't think I have seen a pink one before. It really is quite exquisite. I love the beautiful golden feet, the pearl inlays and the delicate leaves and flowers creeping gently around it.'

'It's so romantic, isn't it? Are you an expert, Mr. Herschel?' asked Melissa.

'Oh, not really... I just admire the workmanship... A bit like your two artists here... Is that a Diebenkorn? And that one a Jenny Saville?' Herschel pointed at two of the paintings on the wall.

'I'm very impressed,' said Melissa. 'Normally I quiz the patients while they're waiting, to see if they recognise the artists. The trouble is, Dr Parker likes to change the paintings around quite frequently, so then I have to re-learn them.'

'Not an art lover yourself?'

'I think I'm becoming one... So what time is your appointment?'

'Three o'clock... I'm a little early.'

'Not a problem. Ah, yes. That's right. Please take a seat. Make yourself comfortable. There's an iPad in the drawer beneath the cushion if you need it. You can watch the news...play a video game, do a crossword? But you know that already, Mr. Herschel. There is fresh tea and coffee available if you would like me to bring you something.'

'That would be very nice. Some green tea please.'

Melissa rose from her seat, poured the tea into a delicate china cup and saucer, and brought it over.

'How long has it been?'

'What?' said Herschel. 'Since my last appointment? Oh, I don't know... I usually try and see Felix at least once a quarter... But you probably know that already.'

Melissa smiled and sat back behind her large white desk.

'Yes... It's been thirteen weeks since you last saw him,' she added.

'Ah, how I have missed him...'

'Herschel...' A soft Scottish brogue came from behind the reception desk.

'I thought I heard your voice... Has it been that long already? How are you? Lovely to see you again.'

The voice appeared from a small room behind the reception – attached to a tall, slim man in his mid-fifties. Dr Felix Parker was dressed in a well cut soft-grey checked suit with a feint blue line across each check, giving it a subtle but unmistakable tartan effect and complimenting a light blue open-necked shirt. The ensemble was topped off with a pair of highly polished black brogues and a pair of sixties-style glasses that gave him a stylish, academic look. Dr Parker strode over and shook Herschel's hand vigorously.

'How have you been? Well, I hope? Anything interesting going on in the world of global espionage?' he asked, laughing.

'Ah...Nothing new,' replied Herschel. 'Just the run-of-the-mill international terrorists and crazed serial killers.'

'Well you're in the right place then... Ha! Do you like our new art collection? I managed to twist a few arms to enhance it.'

'Yes, I was admiring your Fabergé egg... It is quite exquisite.'

'It is isn't it... Although it's not ours... One of my clients had it sent over from St Petersburg. The insurance was insane... But when he first showed me a picture... well, I had to display it. So of course, when he wasn't expecting it, I put him in a deep trance...and, well, here it is. Haha! Only borrowed, sadly, but I'm looking for an opportunity to suggest to him that he never lent it to us... Ha!'

Dr. Parker stroked his chin with his thumb and forefinger through his tightly cut beard and then ran his hand through his greying, swept back hair.

'Shall we head up?'

'Of course,' said Herschel.

Dr Parker skipped up the stairs next to the reception, towards his office, so fast that Herschel could only just keep up with him.

Dr Parker's office was large and airy. The room comprised of a wall-sized window behind a large polished desk which looked over the city, two stories below. The outside light streamed into the office to give the room a bright and spacious feel. The carpet was off-white in colour, but thick and luxurious. The walls were a similar colour and decorated with more art down each side – a combination of classic portraits and modern. A sturdy black conference table that could seat at least eight was positioned opposite two office-style sofas that were set in an L-shape on the far side. A longer, more traditional leather couch for a single occupant, set at a high elevation, sat near the window to one side of the desk.

'Come in, come in,' said Dr Parker enthusiastically. He pointed to one of the sofas.

'Do sit down, Herschel... Can I get you something to drink?'

'I'm fine, thank you Felix,' replied Herschel as he sat. 'Melissa gave me some green tea.'

'Ah, yes. She's a wonder, isn't she? I don't know how I ever did without her. She practically runs this place now.' Felix sat down on the opposite sofa.

'She certainly knows what she is doing. She's even becoming something of an expert on your art pieces I see.'

'She certainly is. Whatever she turns her hand to...'

'Exactly.'

'Now, enough about the lovely Melissa. You'll have plenty of time to talk to her after our session. So...How have you been?'

'Structurally sound... Thank you.'

'Ha! That is such a Herschelian answer. Answering the question, but giving almost nothing away. Come on Herschel... You know the drill. Let's try again... How have you been? How are you feeling?'

'Ok. Just fine thank you Felix, really. Nothing out of the ordinary. Things are pretty balanced right now.'

'Ok. That's good to hear. Is your work giving you any unnecessary stress?'

Herschel tilted his head and looked at Felix with an eyebrow raised.

'Ok. Stress is part of the game, I know,' said Felix. 'But we both know you are different. So stress can affect you differently, and sometimes, not very well, right? Do you have any active cases right now?'

'I'm just finishing off a case with the Israeli counter-terrorism bureau. We had a nice result there. We managed to head off what could have been a very nasty incident in Jerusalem. And I'm also looking at a rather interesting serial killer case. Three members of the same family, murdered by somebody with a religious vendetta of some kind.'

'Religious? Interesting... Something of a new area for you, I guess?'

'Two sisters of a family of five siblings are the only ones left. They are scared witless they might be next, so there's a bit of a race on to try and catch him before he can do any further harm.'

'Are you sure it's a him?' asked Felix.

'Ninety-seven percent sure. There have been only three confirmed cases of female serial killers worldwide, in the last forty years. So yes, pretty sure.'

'And do you think you will catch him? Are you getting the right assistance?'

'I think we'll get to the bottom of it yes. I just hope it is in time.'

'Ok. Well, I'm glad to hear it... Keep pressing on... And what about the others? How have they been?'

'Well, of late, it's only been Cassandra. But that has been good because she is so knowledgeable, especially on religious matters. She has been really helpful providing details about the Four Horsemen.'

'Four Horsemen?'

'The serial killer... He's imitating The Four Horsemen of the Apocalypse, in his MO.'

'Oh, I see... What, you mean?'

'Yes... War, Famine, Pestilence... The whole Old Testament thing. He's been pretty sophisticated in his methods. We think he must have international, possible Russian or North Korean military connections.'

'Nasty... Three dead, then?'

'Yes... And I want it stopped there.'

'So... Cassandra? She's been helping?'

'Very much so. Her analytical skills are beyond anything from anyone I have ever met.'

'Is she listening now?'

'Of course... She's always listening. She is one of the few that do. She is aware of all of us.'

'Ok. I'm just conscious of your history, Herschel. I don't want you taking on anything that might put you under unnecessary strain. When you came to me all those years ago, you were something of a mess, now weren't you?'

'That was a long time ago, Felix...'

'Yes... But not only were you untreated, you weren't looking after your health at all. I know I sound like some whining old doctor, but I'm trying to protect you and your condition. I remember that first time I saw you, I thought, "Good God.." You were deep in psychosis. You were delusional, paranoid, hallucinating, and close to complete dementia. You were only moments away from being fully sectioned.'

'Well, I had been burning the candle at both ends, rather.'

'Yes, but you were only a teenager... Living on your own, undiagnosed and unsupported. It's amazing that you turned out as well as you did. If it hadn't been for Dr. Jarvis at the asylum calling me... well, you might still be there.' Felix motioned with his arms wrapped around himself as if he was in a straight-jacket, with his eyes rolling and his tongue lolling out of his mouth.

'Haha,' laughed Herschel. 'I have always been grateful to you, Felix. You know that, don't you?'

'Of course. But I just want to impress upon you how serious your symptoms could become if left unchecked. That's why these visits are so important. You need to keep a close eye on your mental and physical health at all times. You're taking your meds regularly, yes??'

'I am.'

'Good. There aren't that many cases of multiple-personality in the world, and not many of them are lucky enough to have the high-functioning character mix that you appear to enjoy. I mean Cassandra, wow, she really is something of a blessing.'

'She says hello, by the way...'

'You are such an interesting case... Oh, hello Cassandra... She can hear me right?'

'She hears everything.'

'But it's strange how she never takes over... I mean.. You are always you, aren't you?'

'Yes... As far as I'm aware. At least for now. I think she just likes to know everything that goes on. She's a gatherer of information, not a control freak. She likes to know things. And the things she knows, I have no idea how she knows them. God only knows how she discovers them. But there we are. Most importantly, we are friends, a bit like you and me Felix, except that she is with me all the time, and I can call upon her anytime I need her.'

'I'm pleased to hear that,' smiled Felix.

'But like you just said, my case is unusual. I hear the voices and I can speak to some of them... though I don't think they can read my mind. I just see Cassandra and the others like a different part of myself... We're different people. It's just that, well, we happen to occupy the same brain.'

'It's wonderful really,' said Felix. 'Astonishing.'

'I'm used to it, really... Although I often get caught talking with Cassandra. The Inspector on the case I'm working on walked in on us mid-conversation at the police station. It can be a bit irritating because it feels like someone crashing unin-vited into our conversation, a bit like someone bursting in on this one. We'd be a bit annoyed, right? Usually I just brush it off as me talking to myself, which I suppose is exactly what I'm doing... And that usually works, though they say it is the first sign of madness, don't they? Ha! If only they knew. But it's a bit frustrating because it's an interruption, and it can be hard to find our way back to where we were.'

'So Cassandra doesn't talk to you in your head?'

'Oh, yes... But she only comes to the forefront when she wants something or needs to tell me something really impor-tant. And then I have to speak to her, for her to hear and understand me. I guess it's a kind of compartmentalism. You might think it's weird, but over the years, I have become really quite used to it.'

'Brilliant,' said Felix. 'She's like your guardian angel.'

'She's laughing now... And I have to tell you, it's not with you,' said Herschel.

'Have you ever wanted to share the knowledge of your gift with anyone?'

'What? As in tell other people about it? No. Never.'

'Why not?'

'I don't think society is quite ready for my kind of psychosis just yet. I mean we're only just getting to grips with celebrities jumping on to the mental health bandwagon with their anxiety and depression.'

'Is that what you really think?'

'I do. And of course, we only ever hear about it after the fact... The usual tabloid headline – 'My Depression Hell', by – insert name here... It's become the alternative to 'My Drugs, Sex and Booze Hell', now, hasn't it? To me, it kind of debases the whole issue. It shines the wrong kind of light on mental illness and mental health. Nothing good will come of the rich and famous endorsing it.'

'But don't you feel you want to share your innermost feelings with someone close?'

'I'm sharing them with you, aren't I? No... it's my condition and it will stay private. I doubt if I will ever share it with anyone else. I'm not sure what MI6 and GCHQ would say if it were common knowledge anyway. So, no. I don't think the world is quite ready for multiple personalities on the front pages of their breakfast newspapers. And I'm not ready to be the twenty-first century's equivalent of the Elephant Man.'

'Ok. Fair enough... What about the others?'

'The other identities?'

'Yes. Anything from them?'

'Well, actually they have been pretty quiet recently.

Perhaps all my energy is going into Cassandra and solving this murder case.'

'But they used to bother you sometimes, didn't they?

'Oh, the noisy ones like, Ansel and Alessandro? Yes, they used to. They would keep me awake at night sometimes with their shouting and hollering but nothing of late. They're still there. I can feel them. But they're not like Cassandra; they're more vivacious and energetic and far less cool and cerebral. I mean Alessandro speaks so fast, it's a wonder that I understand a word he says, especially his Spanish.'

Felix laughed.

'No,' continued Herschel. 'Most of the others are different. I don't think they are aware that they are sharing.'

'Do you think they have a purpose?'

'Purpose?'

'Yes... In that you may have created them to help you with a particular problem that you were facing at that time?'

'I suppose it's possible. But I don't explicitly conjure them up. They arrive of their own accord. The right personality just seems to come to the forefront at the right time, either quietly and calmly like Cassandra or noisily and rudely like Alessandro, but I can never tell. It's not like I'm in control of it, now is it?'

Felix laughed again. 'Ok,' he said. 'I'm going to have to give you a quick examination. Is that alright?'

'Of course,' replied Herschel.

Dr Parker pointed towards the couch by the window. 'Pop up on there for me, will you? You know the drill. Lay down and put your arms by your side.'

Herschel jumped up onto the couch, which was curved to support his head, back and torso, and was set at a high elevation. He swung his legs round and settled back into the soft black leather.

'Comfortable?' said Felix.

'Very... I love the view from your office. Very metropolitan.'

'All the better to get you into a calm frame of mind... Now just lay back, relax, and let me take a closer look at you.'

The doctor moved behind the couch and placed his hands on Herschel's temples. He rubbed them gently in a small circular movement.

'How does that feel?' he said.

'Very relaxing.'

'Good. Now I want you to shut your eyes and empty your mind for me...'

The doctor continued to massage Herschel's temples. After a few moments, he moved around beside him. He took a penlight from his jacket pocket, switched on the beam and held the light over Herschel's closed eyelids.

'I want you to really relax now. Imagine you are walking down a flight of stairs... One at a time. That's right. And with each step you fall deeper into a very deep sleep for me. Can you do that for me?'

'Steps... Deep sleep,' replied Herschel, lazily.

'Yes... Step down another step. Deeper into your sleep...'

'Deeper...'

'Good... Now you find yourself at the bottom of the stairs, in the deepest, most relaxed sleep you can imagine. How do you feel?'

'Goood,' replied Herschel.

Felix gently lifted Herschel's right eyelid with his fore-finger and thumb, and ran his penlight across his exposed eye.

'Excellent,' he said. He then repeated the procedure for Herschel's left eye. 'Good... You are the most relaxed and comfortable that you could ever be. You are completely safe and you are very calm... Now, tell me your full name, please.'

'Damien Vasilis Herschel.'

'How old are you, Damien?'

'I am thirty-five.'

'And what is your profession?'

'I am born of English nobility. I am an aristocrat.'

'Haha...Ok... And what do you do?'

'I dabble...'

'In what do you dabble, Damien?'

'I like to help others. If I see people in distress or danger, I like to help them.'

'Are you helping people now, Damien?'

'I hope so... They are so scared... I'm the only... the only one who can. I've got to catch him... I've got to...'

'Ok... Ok. Keep calm, Damien... Relax... You are safe here. You know you have it within you to solve this case, don't you. You have the intellect and the abilities required to catch your killer...It is only a matter of time... You will do it.'

'I will do it...'

'Now... Is there anyone else there? Is there anyone else who wants to speak?'

'Yes, there is. Cassandra... She wants to speak.'

'Excellent... Can I speak to Cassandra, please? Can you let her come forward please.'

Herschel squirmed on the couch for a moment... His features twisted a little, then his chin rose and his cheeks reddened...'

'Hello, Dr. Parker. How are you?' said Cassandra.

'Cassandra... So good to speak to you again. I am very well, thank you. How are things with you?'

Herschel's eyes were shut and his face impassive, yet his voice sounded lighter and higher.

'Pretty good thank you, Dr. Parker... I'm glad he let me through. I do need to talk to you.'

'Ok... That's what I am here for. Is there something wrong?'

'I am worried about Herschel. I think he is overdoing things.'

'That was my suspicion too,' said Dr. Parker. 'He seems a bit wrung out to me.'

'Yes... He has been working very hard on this case. But it's not just that. Herschel and I speak regularly, and I am glad to be able to give him assistance where I can.'

'Well you heard how much he appreciates your insights.'

'Yes, I did... But he would do better to listen more.'

'Really? Does he not?'

'No... Not enough. Not by a long way. You see, when he is under pressure, like he is now, I act as the gatekeeper for the others. I make sure that they can't get to him unless it is really important. I filter and pass on any information they have to him. That's why he hasn't heard much from the others recently, and also why he thinks I am a fountain of knowledge.'

'Ah, so the others are working in the background to help him, and you keep him up to date... Yes?'

'Yes. Exactly that... Only, sometimes he doesn't pay attention.'

'How come?' said Dr. Parker.

'Well only the other day, I was passing on something we had noticed about one of the crime scenes, but he didn't want to know. He was absorbed in something else and just ignored me. And I think it might be material in solving the crime.'

'Oh... I see. Have you tried again?'

'No... But I will, of course. I'll try and catch him when he is more receptive.'

'I think that's a good idea. But is all this gatekeeping effort putting a strain on you too, Cassandra?'

'Probably... But I can handle it, especially if it means he has more space to think.'

'I know you are very capable, Cassandra, but please don't take on too much. I don't want you becoming stressed as well. That wouldn't do anyone any good.'

'I'll be fine Dr. Parker. To be honest, the biggest effort generally, is keeping some of the others, especially the more excitable ones, quiet and focused on the task at hand. They each have their special skills, but of course that comes with certain demands. My strength is in co-ordination, and getting the best out of each of them. It's just when we have put a lot of thought and effort into presenting something to him, and then he just ignores it. Well it's not only frustrating, but it could be dangerous.'

'I understand,' said Dr. Parker. 'He has no idea the amount of effort that is going on in the background?'

'No, none at all.'

'Keep persisting with him. Don't take no, or him ignoring you, for an answer. You are doing an outstanding job. And between you all... well, you make Damien Herschel what he is... And you know he is a world-class private investigator and international espionage expert.'

'Thank you, Dr. Parker,' said Cassandra.

'So...Shall I wake him up now? Is that ok? Are you happy to go back?'

'Of course. Thank you for the advice... Maybe next time you can meet some of the others as well.'

'Well,' said Dr. Parker. 'I have met quite a few already... Some no longer with us, I'm afraid to say. But yes, if that is something you can organise then I would be happy to.'

'Organising is my middle name,' said Cassandra. 'Ok, I will recede... You can wake him up now.'

Felix watched as Herschel's chin lowered towards his chest and his face slowly returned to his normal complexion. The doctor moved behind him and began to gently massage his temples once again.

'Right... Now Herschel,' said Felix. 'When I tap your index finger you will begin to awaken from your sleep. You will imagine walking back up the stairs and when you get to the top you will wake up feeling fit, healthy and refreshed.'

Herschel's face began to twitch and twist, and his once still arms and legs began to move slightly. After a few seconds, his eyes opened and he looked up at Felix. The doctor was now standing next to him and was smiling broadly.

'Fantastic,' said Herschel.

'What?' replied Felix.

'The view... Like I was just saying. The view from your office window is just fantastic. I am very jealous.'

'Oh... Yes... of course, It's the main reason I opened this office. Nothing quite like it... So how are you feeling? Refreshed I hope?'

'I feel great, thank you Felix... Though I sometimes wonder...'

'Wonder? What's that?'

'Well, when I come here, and of course I know that I have to, but each time I do, I only ever spend a few minutes chatting with you on the sofa, and then thirty seconds on the couch. I spend more time talking to Melissa than I do to you. It seems like a bit of a waste of your time, Doctor.'

'Oh, that's perfectly alright,' said Felix. 'Time flies when you're enjoying yourself.'

'It certainly seems to... Are we done?'

'Yes. All done. Shall I show you out?' said Felix. 'Next appointment in three months? Remember not to overdo it now... Oh, and remember to listen to everything and everyone, right? Two ears. One mouth. Remember, you are a valuable asset.'

'Er, right,' said Herschel. 'Will do. See you next time.'

13

SANCTUARY

'm so pleased that the two of you have come to see me,' said Brother Connor. 'This has been such a terrible business... Terrible...Shocking in fact. We should do everything we can. We... I... should help... So...er... how can I, er... help?'

Brother Connor tripped through what he imagined in his head were words of reassurance for the two sisters. He leaned back in his chair, which creaked at the joints as he did so. Looking around, Connor's office was rather outdated and tired. Assorted paper cups and sandwich wrappings littered his desk. His waste-bin was filled with similar detritus, while his overflowing ashtray was equally disregarded. A thin film of dust clung to his large wooden desk which, when disturbed, would shed its haul of fine particles, adding to the powdery haze in the room.

The two sisters sat opposite, on stiff wooden chairs and looked back at him impassively.

'You know, a great evil is at work here,' he continued. 'You do know that don't you?... Your poor brothers should never have met their end in that way... It really is shocking... Terrible, in fact... Just terrible.'

Brother Connor was dressed in his normal daytime attire – black trousers, black shirt buttoned to the top, and a black jacket. As usual, his dog collar was too tight for him. His neck spilled out over the top giving a strange, two-tiered effect that made his head look as though his chin was balancing directly upon his shoulders. His thick, horn-rimmed glasses sat neatly on the bridge of his nose, in the crease intelligently-designed for the purpose. They gave his eyes a wide-angled, tunnel effect that made them look smaller and further away than they really were. His hair was cut tight to his scalp, where it almost circumnavigated the southern section of his head, leaving a smooth monk-like tonsure at the top that in certain conditions, reflected the light from the fluorescent lamp above, giving the impression of a halo.

Louise broke the silence.

'We were hoping that the church could help us, Brother Connor,' she said. 'After what has happened, we are both very frightened, and we want to know if there is anything you can do... You said you could help.'

'I shall do my very best for you,' replied Connor.

'You have to understand that it's just the two of us now, Brother,' continued Sheena. 'And given what happened to Michael, Sean and David, well, we don't want to face the same fate.'

'Of course not,' replied Connor, leaning back further in his chair.

'We are two women, pretty much on our own, now,' continued Louise. 'And in light of the amount of support our family has given the Church in the past, well...We were hoping for...'

'Of course, of course... it's my solemn duty to assist my flock. I can help bring the forces of the Lord to bear here...'

'What?' said Sheena. 'What forces?'

'Oh yes,' replied Brother Connor. 'You have no idea...

There are forces here and within the church that are more powerful than you can ever imagine.'

'Powerful? What do you mean, more powerful?' said Sheena. 'More powerful than what?'

Sheena looked at Louise. 'I told you this was a stupid idea...'

Brother Connor leaned further back in his creaking chair and brought his fingertips together in the shape of a 'steeple' in front of his chest. His brow furrowed a little further...

'There are more things in Heaven and earth than are dreamt of in your philosophy,' he quoted, while lightly strumming his fingertips, raising his eyebrows and attempting to make his eyes look as surprised as he could.

'But what does that actually mean? Brother Connor?' asked Louise, pacing back and forth. 'Does that mean that the Church will help us?... Can you help us?... Can you protect us, even? What can you do? What forces, as you call them, can you bring to bear? Can you catch the killer? Can you stop him from killing again? Can you protect us?'

'Relax, relax,' said Brother Connor as he leant forward. 'It's probably best that you don't know the full details, but just let me say that this two-thousand-year-old organisation with over two billion followers has some pretty good contacts around the world... And if necessary, we can mobilise at a moments notice...'

'Wow,' said Louise. 'Really? Mobilise... And you can do that for us?'

'If necessary,' said Brother Connor.

'But this is necessary, isn't it?' pressed Louise.

'Almost certainly,' said Brother Connor.

'Almost certainly?' cried Sheena. 'Our three brothers have been brutally murdered by some crazed maniac. How much more certainty do you fucking need? And mobilise? Mobilise! You talk about mobilising. What are you going to mobilise?

Angels? Jesus? The Holy Spirit?' Sheena's knuckles were white as she gripped the edge of the priest's desk.

'Relax... Relax... Please relax,' impressed Brother Connor, trying hard to calm Sheena down. 'You are in safe hands... Very safe hands... But this is a highly unusual situation. I will make some calls and see what we can marshal to provide you some protection and keep you safe. I will be sure to let you know.'

'Thank you,' said Louise, exhaling loudly.

'In the meantime, let us just take a moment perhaps..? A moment of silence...'

The cleric paused while the room calmed, and after that moment, when he was ready, he brought his palms together, and bowed his head. The two women automatically did the same.

'Let us pray,' said Brother Connor.

'Poppycock...'

'Excuse me?' said Brother Connor, looking up.

'Poppycock. Absolute poppycock,' repeated Herschel from the far side of the room. He stood in front of a wooden panel etched with the words, 'God is Love', under which hung a large classical painting of an unknown religious figure dressed in a red cardinal's outfit atop a stallion with several over-flowing pots of coins at its feet.

'Oh... I'm sorry if praying in a house of God upsets you Mr Herschel,' said Connor.

'Oh, it's not the praying I object to Father... It's the moun-tains of horse-shit.'

'I beg your pardon?'

'Can't you see these women are desperate for your help? Your guidance. Your protection. Sanctuary, even. They have spent their whole lives deeply ingrained in the ways of the church. Their family has been a pillar of this community for years. They have supported the Church for decades, through their regular attendance at Mass and all the other ceremonies. They have supported many church-run events as well as contributing very generously to your coffers. And all I hear is what? Promises and prayers? That is what I see and I call it plain old horse-shit.'

Brother Connor unclasped his hands and sat upright in his chair.

'I'm sorry Mr Herschel, I'm really not sure why you are here. I fail to see how you can help these two women, especially now in their most desperate hour of spiritual need. It appears to me that you are a source of some division and doubt in their minds, and that is exactly why they are here now. Prayers and consolation may be poppycock to you, but for many, they can provide much comfort.'

'Is that right?' Herschel retorted. 'And who have they got to rely upon? Who can they trust? You? God? Which God? Your God? Or perhaps the God of one of the thousands of other religions, eh?'

'There is only one true God, Mr Herschel,' replied Connor calmly.

'Is that right? And I ask you Father, what is it that makes your God the only one true God? The really true God? Is it because it says so in the Bible? All the other Gods are false prophets, aren't they? Peddling their untruths? Is that right?'

Connor sighed and moved awkwardly in his seat.

'So how many Gods do you not believe in?' continued Herschel. The other one-thousand nine-hundred and ninety-nine, eh?... Is that right?'

Connor moved again, uneasily.

'It would seem to me then, that I simply believe in only one less God than you, Father...'

The priest stared into the distance. He cleared his throat.

'So that probably makes me a heathen in your eyes,' Herschel continued. 'A heretic? Maybe a pagan? A blasphemer? And if so, what do I deserve? To be excommunicated? Disavowed perhaps? Tortured? Burned at the stake? Or any one of the multitudes of horrific acts that have been carried out in the name of your one true God.'

Brother Connor's mouth was now clapped tightly shut as he was forced to listen to Herschel. The two sisters looked on. Louise was tight-lipped with embarrassment. Sheena remained stoic, but seemed to be trying to cover up a 'told-you-so' smirk.

'And what about this one God of yours, eh? Perhaps we should examine exactly what kind of God he is. What kind of God it is that you hold in such high-regard that you pray to him three times a day. Isn't this the same God that demanded Abraham sacrifice his son Isaac to prove his devotion? Isn't this the same God who banished Adam and Eve from the Garden of Eden, and sentenced all mankind to everlasting sin... after failing to tell them why he had put them there, and what his rules were? Isn't this the same God who decided that even though he had bestowed free will upon his greatest creation, that after a while he didn't like how things had turned out, so decided to murder almost all of them in a terrible flood?'

Connor was now stony-faced and silent.

'Should I continue?' said Herschel... 'Only it seems to me, Father, that your one true God, at least the one described in the Old Testament is arguably the most unpleasant character in all fiction. He is jealous and proud of it. He is a petty, unjust control-freak; a vindictive, bloodthirsty ethnic cleanser; a misogynistic, homophobic racist; an infanticidal, genocidal, filicidal, pestilential, megalomaniacal, sadomasochistic, capriciously malevolent bully. I mean, why would a truly all-loving God threaten to send those he went to so much effort to create, to eternal damnation in Hell?'

'My Lord is the one and only truth,' recited the priest softly. Then, thinking he might have revealed too much, composed himself and raised his voice to a more controlled, authoritarian tone.

'I see. Thank you very much Mr Herschel for your views. Now if you have finished and if you don't mind, I have many things to attend to...' Connor waved his arm towards the door.

'Oh really? You think it is as easy as that, do you?' pressed Herschel. 'Only we haven't finished now, have we? Don't you see that these two women are throwing themselves upon your mercy? They are begging for you and your Church's assistance. I have no idea why. But then I wasn't brought up a Catholic. But they were, and they want your safety and security. Only a few moments ago you were promising...what was it... The powers of the almighty. They were coming to you for that very help out of desperation. For help, or maybe sanctuary, if you will, that only a moment ago you were promising in spades. What was it you said? 'There are more things in Heaven and Earth'. And now, because your Old Testament bubble has been dented by a few home truths, your embarrassment sends you running, and you turn your back on them...'

'Herschel... Please...' pleaded Louise.

'Please? Please for what? It's true isn't it? You are both here because you are desperate for help. The police are failing you. I can only do so much, and so you are falling back on what makes you feel safe. Neither of you have been to Church in years, yet religion is seared so deeply into your character you can't help it. It's not your fault. And now, even through all of the empty promises and mumbo-jumbo, you still can't see what this so-called man of the cloth stands for... for what it really is...'

'Look,' said Louise. 'It is all very well listening to how you feel, Herschel. But that doesn't really help us. Sheena and I came here in good faith. We were brought up with the Church in our lives, and if Brother Connor can help us, or bring the power of the Church to bear to help us in some way, well I for one am willing to listen.'

'I suppose so,' said Sheena, reluctantly. 'I don't care about history, or politics, I just want to hear what you can do to help us. Please Brother Connor. Please continue...'

It seemed it was now Herschel's turn to listen. Patently unwilling to subject himself to yet another sermon, he turned and headed towards the door.

'Please don't leave us Herschel,' pleaded Louise. 'Please stay and hear what Brother Connor has to say. You might learn something... Please...'

Herschel raised his hand as if to respond, but on seeing Louise's face, he thought better of it.

'Ok,' he said. 'I'll listen. But don't expect me to agree with anything.'

Louise smiled. 'Go ahead, please Brother... '

Brother Connor looked triumphantly at Herschel, and then back to the two women in front of him.

'Well, we can probably help you from a pastoral and spiritual perspective. But in order to do so, I will need for you to cleanse yourselves of your sins... through confession.'

'Confession?' said Sheena. 'It's been years since I have been to confession... I don't think you'll live long enough, Brother.'

'Nonetheless, it is important that your souls are properly cleansed and that you take a penance before we can even begin to call upon the forces of the Lord.'

'And who do we confess to?' asked Louise. 'You?'

The priest nodded.

'And what kind of penance can we be expected to pay?' asked Sheena. 'Like I said, it's been a long while since my last confession. A lot of water has passed under the bridge. I'm not sure I'm really ready for any more trauma.'

'There is no other way, I'm afraid. I can only help you if you have taken absolution... And in good faith,' replied Connor.

'Ok,' said Louise. 'How do you want us to proceed?'

Connor put his palms together. 'Well, first of all... Let us pray,' he said.

'Oh, good grief,' said Herschel.

The two women bowed their heads and put their palms together. Brother Connor began.

'Dear Lord, we beseech thee... to help these two poor wretched souls...'

'Wretched?' complained Sheena. '...Don't you mean fearful?'

Brother Connor looked up at the the sisters, cleared his throat and continued.

'Dear Lord, We beseech thee... to help these two poor fearful women. They have suffered a dreadful misfortune and are in fear for their lives from despicable forces. Forces that without your help, may overcome them. Their brothers were not fortunate to be in the bosom of your love when they passed. Let us not make the same mistake with them. Lord, they know they have not been good Catholics. They have been tempted away from the righteous path many, many times. They have led selfish and hedonistic lives. They have sinned many times... and they have taken your name in vain...'

'Brother Connor...' asked Louise. 'Is all this really necessary?'

'My dear Louise,' said Connor. 'If you are to benefit from the sanctuary to be offered by the Church, then you must arrive at its door with a pure heart and a cleansed soul... And this is where that cleansing begins... If you feel you cannot endure a deep examination of your actions over many years, then perhaps...'

'No... No... I understand. Please continue,' said Louise.

'A deep examination of our actions?' asked Sheena. 'What do you mean?'

Connor raised his head up and looked hard at the crucifix on the wall at the end of the room.

'Your confession will need to be extensive and complete.

Nothing can be overlooked... Nothing. Everything you have done over the years will be examined very carefully. The good, and... well, the not so good. I will need to be sure of your genuine contrition, and your willingness to return into the loving arms of the Lord. But before you can even begin that journey, you will have to undergo a penance... something appropriate to begin to cleanse your soul of your sins... I hope I have made myself clear...'

'Oh my God,' said Louise. 'What kind of penance? What do you mean?'

'I suppose it is you who are the judge and the jury in all of this cleansing and penance, right?' added Sheena.

'Well, it is you who have come to me,' replied Connor. 'I can't stress strongly enough that this is about the saviour of your eternal souls and your everlasting life with the Lord...'

'Ok... Ok. I think I understand,' said Louise. 'What do we have to do? Please just tell us...'

'Well, there have been a few changes in the way we can go about this now. I was specially chosen for some intensive training only a few months ago. So there is a way I can expedite your penance.'

'Expedite it?' said Sheena. 'Ok, great... How can we do that?'

'Well, it is very new and advanced... And a bit unconventional... Some might say that it skirts the edges of Canon Law... and you might think what I am about to ask is a bit strange,' said Connor.

'Just tell us what we have to do,' pleaded Louise. 'Anything to get this over with.'

'Well, ok,' said Connor. 'But you know this is highly confidential... What I'm about to say to you must stay between us. It must go no further. And that means you too, Mr Herschel.'

'Oh, this just gets better and better,' muttered Herschel from the darkness.

'I mean it,' said Connor as he moved around in his seat.

'This is largely uncharted territory for you, me and the Church, and if taken in the wrong context it could make all of our lives very difficult. But it must be done.'

'Just get on with it,' implored Sheena.

'Ok... What I need from each of you is a sacrifice. We need to show that you are genuine in your desire to cleanse your tarnished soul and that you are both full of contrition in the eyes of the Lord,' said Connor.

'Sacrifice?' said Louise. ' You mean like giving up something? Like, for lent? Oh, that's easy, I can do that.'

'What do you want us to sacrifice?' asked Sheena. 'I mean, I suppose I could give something up. But it better not be for long. And it better not be smoking.'

'I can give up chocolate if you like? Is it for like 40 days?' said Louise.

'It's not that kind of sacrifice that I need,' replied the priest. I need something much more tangible, more authentic. I need the two of you to make a sacrifice.'

'Yes, like you said,' said Louise.

'I'm sorry' said Sheena. 'I don't think I follow. What do you mean? We've already said...'

'I need you to choose something... Something living... and sacrifice it to show your devotion to the Lord... Just like God demanded of Abraham. I am asking you to show how devoted you are by presenting him with your own personal sacrificial offering,' added Connor.

'A live sacrifice!' cried Louise. '...You want us to murder someone?'

'Good Lord no,' replied Connor. 'No... of course not. What I'm asking is much more... More... less... I mean... But you are required to demonstrate a proper sacrifice, just like Abraham showed to God.'

'If you think I am going to sacrifice any of my children,' exclaimed Louise.

'No... No... No... That's not what I mean... It needs to be something,... Something else...'

'Do you mean... like an animal? An animal sacrifice?' asked Sheena.

'Yes... Yes... Yes... That's what I mean,' hurried the priest. He bounced rapidly backwards and forwards in his seat.

'To show your love and commitment to the Lord... You must make... er, ...a sacrifice... It doesn't have to be large... unless you want it to be, of course... It could be a mouse... or maybe a rat... nobody likes rats, do they... Or maybe a fox... I mean, they're vermin aren't they? We hunt foxes... Or if you wanted to... a, a cat or even a dog... Yes a dog, hahaha... That would do... Do either you have a dog? Or could you get a dog?'

'This is insane,' interrupted Herschel. 'I can't believe I'm hearing this. Are you really asking these two poor frightened women to carry out some kind of ritual slaughter of an innocent animal, just to get the reassurance and protection of the Church? This is complete nonsense... I've never heard of anything so ridiculous? What kind of a priest are you?'

'Well, I, I... I said it was unconventional,' spluttered Connor, suddenly stopped in his tracks.

'Unconventional? It's completely crazy... I have heard enough. I'm not going to stay a moment longer... And if you two had any sense at all you would leave this place too. This so-called priest can do nothing for you... I suggest you make your own arrangements for your own safety...'

'You are beginning to frighten me, Brother Connor,' said Louise '...I don't understand... I don't know what it is you want from us anymore... Can you help us? Or can you not?'

'Just go...' shouted Connor... ' I shouldn't have taken you into my confidence... It was a mistake. I'm sorry... But I really can't help you any more. You will have to find your sanctuary elsewhere.'

Brother Connor stood up from behind his desk and once again motioned his hand towards the door.

'Goodbye...' he said, his voice and hand shaking.

Herschel headed out towards the door of the office, shaking his head slowly. Just before he left, he stopped, brought his hand up to his chin, looked at the door and turned.

'Hold on just one second,' said Herschel. 'As much as I want to, I can't just leave like this... You, a representative of the Church really cannot be allowed to treat these two women like this. You have a... and I can't believe I am actually saying this, a moral duty to help them.'

'I've tried the best I can,' said Connor. 'Please... if you don't mind.' And he gestured towards the door again.

'No. No... I'm not having it.' Herschel stepped forward into the the centre of the room. 'It's about time you realised the harm you are doing... You should realise you and your Church are not a force for good.'

'Oh really,' answered Connor. 'And what makes you the arbiter of good taste in these matters? What makes you the judge and jury of all you survey, eh? I see no spiritual or moral leadership from you, Mr Herschel.'

'Oh, I am just a spokesperson for the moderate wing of atheism,' countered Herschel, quickly. 'Believe me, I have friends and colleagues that would make me look like a play-school outing when it comes to criticism of organised religion.'

'Oh, I'm sure of that,' said Connor. 'But you are yet to see the true power and the stunning magisterial glory of our Lord and master... I understand that you are yet to have that wonderful, life-changing, joyous experience. And I suppose the absence of that knowledge makes you the man you are... But I have a question for you, Mr Herschel. Perhaps you can help me with it? Can you answer me this one simple question... from a non-believer's point of view?'

Herschel paused and looked at the priest. Louise and Sheena

remained seated and looked on, fascinated. Everything in his body was saying, 'Go... Leave... Do not engage with this idiot'. But then his competitive streak kicked-in, and over-rode all his reservations. He couldn't just leave and let this charlatan win.

'Ok. I'll bite,' said Herschel. 'Go ahead... Ask away...'

'I have a simple question for you... And I would ask that you answer it with a simple Yes or No,' said Connor.

'Ok... Well, I'm not sure I like being cornered into a binary answer, but I'll give you the benefit of my doubt, and of my curiosity, and go along with it...'

'Ok. Good,' said Connor. 'Now imagine for me, for a moment, that you are in a strange city... Night is falling. You are with no friends... you are all alone... and you see twelve men coming towards you.'

Herschel smirked a little, and then furrowed his brow.

'Ok... I'm there. And I have to tell you, it's nothing new. I've been in just such a situation many times. So go ahead with your question.'

'So, there you are... in an unknown city... all alone. No family. No friends. And twelve strange men coming towards you... Now, what if I were to tell you that those men were just returning from a prayer meeting.'

'Ok. Interesting,' replied Herschel.

'So, here is the real question. Now that you know they have come from a prayer meeting. And it matters not which religion. Would you feel more, or would you feel less safe?'

'Ahhh... Very good,' smiled Herschel, his intellect piqued. He thought for a moment.

'I like the premise. And I like the way you try to force a yes or no answer. Trying to close down my options at the beginning and making me choose a side.'

'I don't really think so,' said Connor. 'It's just a hypothetical situation to elicit your true feelings.'

'Is it? Is it though?' replied Herschel. 'In that even if I were to be in that position... and I came across twelve men returning from a prayer meeting, and I knew that? Well, there are so many other factors that would influence how I really felt. Safe or not safe?... I mean... Is it daytime? Are there other people around? Are the men calm and serene or are they boisterous or even aggressive? What are they wearing? Are they armed? Do they look like they might be armed? Are they intoxicated or under the influence of narcotics? You can't just boil it down to one simplistic factor. Otherwise, it is just a puerile thought-experiment designed to drive a preconceived answer. What is more interesting, well more interesting to me anyway, is the real purpose of the question... The intent behind it...And I'm afraid, as is true with many challenges in real life, reality is so much more nuanced and complicated than that. Your question fails to provide me anywhere near enough information for me to make a proper, informed decision. And for that reason, I refuse to answer it.'

'I see,' said Connor. 'You may believe all that, but do you not think it gets to the heart of the issue of faith and of your own deep-seated prejudices?'

'Prejudices? Prejudices!' replied Herschel. 'Let me tell you something about prejudices... I have been in those cities... In that very situation. Confronted by friendly and not so friendly faces... And I have felt both safe and at other times very unsafe. And it's not the fact that these men have been to a religious meeting that is, for me, the deciding factor. I mean, I have seen so called religious people act in ways that Satan himself would applaud, simply based upon what type of religion they are... That is, the wrong type of religion. Acts of unspeakable cruelty carried out for this one single reason, and on no other basis at all.

There are parts of this world where people live in the grip of what can only be called religious fanaticism, not so dissimilar to what I have witnessed today, who are actively encouraged to kill, murder and destroy others who are of an almost the same, but not quite, version of their own sect, simply because they don't have the right version of their own faith. They risk homelessness, death, and mutilation on a daily basis because of this... A simple and irrelevant difference in their religious history. In these countries people are defined by their religion, not by their citizenship.

Religion is not presented to us by revelation. It doesn't come from the heavens. It doesn't come from beyond. It doesn't come from the divine. It is wholly man made... And it shows. It shows very well that religion is created, invented and imposed by a species only half a chromosome away from a chimpanzee...

I say we should oppose the religious impulse itself, and oppose strongly at every opportunity. We should endeavour to identify and criticise it in ourselves as well as in others. It is a stain on our humanity. We should believe in humanity, in evidence, scepticism, and reason. We should hold on to those values with as much conviction and principle as any God-fearing person would, but we should remain open to the argument and the fact that evidence and the truth, can and does change. To constantly question our values is healthy and progressive. We should never believe those who say that they know 'God's will', and that they can tell you what it is... For I tell you this now... They are our enemies...'

Herschel finally moved towards the door, turned and looked at Louise and Sheena before he left.

'...And they are your enemies too.'

'Ah... Brother Connor... So good that you could come and see me again.'

The Cardinal was once again working in his office with its imposing surroundings, this time dressed in a simple black cassock with a dog collar, a silver crucifix around his neck and a purple cincture around his waist. Standing behind his desk, he looked slim, tall and athletic, unusual for a man in his seventies. The assistant priests who were usually there to attend to his every wish had been dismissed, and the Cardinal and Connor were together alone once again.

Connor, although now more familiar with the Cardinal's office and the status that surrounded him, was still impressed by the trappings of office. Every convenience and desire were catered for. Every utterance was seized and acted upon immediately. Clearly, Cardinal Stonehouse was looking to have his own portrait mounted in the hallway at some time, so visitors could see how important he was too. Better turned out this time, Brother Connor's cassock was freshly laundered, his dog collar clean and white, his shoes even more highly polished than before, and he'd made something of an effort to tidy up his fingernails. However, he couldn't help notice the Cardinal's long, delicate and finely manicured fingers as they traced lightly across the wording of the report that he was perusing.

'Do come in... Do sit down.' Stonehouse motioned towards not the sofas, but the desk this time. Connor sat down in the upright chair in front of the desk and opposite the Cardinal and stared up at him.

What news do you have for me, Brother Connor?'

'N... News?' replied Connor. 'News about what?'

The Cardinal paused, made a little sigh and looked up, over his glasses, sternly at the priest.

'The family, Bother Connor? Gerald and Kitty? Their children? You were going to keep a close eye on them for me.'

'Oh... Yes... Of course. I'm sorry. I didn't... didn't understand what you meant. Yes... The family.'

'There have been some developments, yes? Is that right? I heard that there had been another accident.'

'Accident? Well, I'm not sure you would call it an accident. But, that's right your Eminence. The youngest brother this time. David.'

'Hmmm. That is what I heard. That is just terrible. Do we know anything more?'

'Not really, sir. I mean, the police are investigating. It is all very peculiar and rather hard to understand. They have yet to say what actually happened, but they do think foul play was involved. '

'Really? How can that be so? He wasn't murdered was he? I thought it was some kind of stomach problem? There was no assailant or anything like that, is that right?'

'No, your Eminence, nothing like that, but they think that the same person might be to blame for all three incidents.'

'All three? Michael, Sean and David. Good grief. How are Louise and Sheena coping?'

'Well, they are very scared, of course. They came to me for church protection.'

'Excellent. I hope you have offered some kind of sanctuary.'

'Well, yes... I tried. But they have employed this private detective who is making things difficult.'

'Oh really. Difficult? How?'

'Well he's not really a spiritual type... He looks on the church with some animosity.'

'Oh really, why? What is his name?'

'Herschel... Damien Herschel... I have no knowledge of his background or history... or... anything really. He is a bit of a mystery and he just turned up with the two sisters and started trying to undermine me.'

'Herschel, eh? Can't say I know the name... But I'll take a closer look and let you know if we find anything. But more importantly, now after David's sad demise, we really must do something for the two sisters. Notwithstanding this Herschel fellow, do you think you have their confidence?'

'Oh, er... I... No... I, er... really don't...' stammered Connor.

'Well you should have by now,' snapped the Cardinal.

Connor flinched, and, after edging forward during the conversation, retreated back into his seat.

The Cardinal looked down at the priest.

'Oh I'm sorry...' he said. 'It's just... just that I think we have a duty to the family. After all they have done to support the church. And to these two women, especially after what has happened. They must be terrified. I really think that we can be of help to them... and I want you to be the instrument of the Church's help in doing that.'

The Cardinal paused. 'You do think you can do that, don't you, Connor?'

'Y... Yes, of course,' stammered Connor. 'I have been trying, but it's not as easy as I expected.'

'Yes, I know... I know,' replied the Cardinal. 'But I think we're going to have to try a little harder here, now, aren't we? I mean, we need to protect these two women and make sure nothing unnecessary is propagated. Their safety is paramount of course, but it is also very important that we protect the Church.'

'Yes, of course. Protect the Church?' repeated Connor. 'But from what?'

'Well it's hard for me to be explicit, Brother, but let me just say that there are other forces at play here. Forces that you are not aware of. But trust me, it will be to both our benefit, and the church's of course, that no harm comes to Louise or Sheena. They must be kept safe. And away from prying eyes like those of Mr Herschel. Do you understand?'

'I knew it. I knew it...' said Connor. 'Things are happening, aren't they? It's the dark forces, isn't it? They are in play now... all around us... That's it, isn't it?'

Connor sat forward in his chair and clapped his hands together, excitedly.

'No No No... Calm down Brother Connor... It's not quite like that.'

'It's the End of Days, isn't it?' exclaimed the priest, almost jumping out of his seat. 'I knew it. We are living in the End Times...'

'End of Days? End Times? What on earth are you talking about?' scoffed the Cardinal. 'Of course not. Where did you get that idea? For goodness sake, man, don't be so ridiculous...'

Connor stopped bouncing and slumped back into his chair.

The Cardinal paused again. 'No... look... This is just a little local difficulty,' he added. 'It's something that you and I should handle quietly and discreetly ourselves. And you are, what do they call it? My main man to do it... You are my eyes and ears on the ground. You are acting as my secret emissary. Do you understand? I need you to keep calm and act like an agent of the Church. Do you think you can do that for me?'

'Your main man,' repeated Connor. 'Yes, of course... Your main man... Yes... I can do that.'

'Good...There is more to this family than meets the eye at first... Some things that perhaps Gerald wanted to keep confidential. Certain sensitivities, if you understand me? And he has used his influence to try and protect what was dearest to him. His family. So we must be discreet... If not for Gerald's benefit, then for the memory of Michael, Sean and David...Louise and Sheena, and of course the good name of the Church.'

The Cardinal stopped and looked straight at the priest.

'What more have they said to you?'

'Who?' said Connor?

'The two sisters... now that David... well... you know...'

'Nothing more than I have explained, your Eminence.'

'What? Nothing at all? After all this time? I thought you were getting closer to them...like I asked.'

'I have... But, it's not so easy with that private investigator in the way.'

'Hmmm. I need to know what they know, Connor. I really need you to lean in to them. Do whatever you need to do to get that private investigator out of the way... And see if you can discover if they know any more about what Gerald might have told them... you know... anything... about the family, you know...'

'Ok,' said Connor. 'But I have tried already...'

'I know... But I need you to try a little harder... I can't stress to you how much it would please me for you to learn more... All so that we can protect the Church, of course...'

The Cardinal made a gesture with his left arm to indicate that the meeting was coming to an end, waving gently towards the office door.

'I will do my best, your Eminence,' said Connor as he rose.

'Excellent. And while you're at it...' said the Cardinal, 'See if you can find out what is happening with the... er,... inheritance...You know...now that the boys are, er... you know...'

'Inheritance... Ok. I'll try. What do you want to know?'

'Well, as I have said, Gerald was more than generous during his lifetime, but I haven't heard if he wanted to bequeath any of his estate...'

'Oh, I understand,' said Connor.

'And now that Michael, David and Sean have passed, there may be an opportunity ...to, er...Well, you know...'

'Yes, of course,' said Connor. 'I'll see what I can find out...'

'I mean, there may be clauses in Gerald's will that come into play if one of the recipients should die unexpectedly.'

'I'll do my best for you Father,' said Connor as he backed out towards the door.

'Thank you, my son. You know, Connor... You are an excellent emissary for the Church... and I respect your commitment and your devotion... and of course, your discretion in these matters. I think you could really develop from this. I can make things happen for you, if that is what you want... You know that don't you. If you are successful with this, then the rewards could be, well... considerable.'

Connor's face reddened again. He looked around at the now more familiar surroundings in which he found himself. He wondered how he could possibly have found himself here. He thought about the centuries of history surrounding this Church and those who had filled its hallowed halls. He thought about the influence it had over kings, queens and presidents. He thought of the amazing power that it could wield. He also wondered why this time he had not been offered a glass of the Cardinal's fine Irish whiskey, nor had he been invited to pray with him.

'Thank you, Father. You are very kind. You have, as always, my total devotion.'

'So, have you come to any conclusions?' said Herschel, as he leaned back lazily in his office chair, feet up comfortably on the desk in front of him.

'Well,' said Cassandra. 'It's quite complicated. I've been spending a lot of time researching, you know, behind the scenes, so to speak... I have talked to some of the others and I have tried to assess who else might have an axe to grind against the family. Unfortunately, we now have to remove David from the list of suspects, and I've used the reverse quantum-axiom algorithm across the local populace to try and eliminate any outliers, and reduce us down to a cohesive sample of potential perpetrators.'

'Ok. Excellent,' said Herschel. 'What have you got?'

'Well, there are a number of factors to consider... Motive, means and opportunity of course, but then there are the psychological drivers too... and, as we have already discovered, the religious perspective.'

'Correct.'

'But David's death has shed some more light on the means of murder, and it has complicated matters considerably.'

'Oh really. How?'

'Well, we've heard from Zlawitkowski in Israel. He has confirmed that the poison used on David was not Arythmodref-P, as was used on Michael and Sean, but as the police suspected, it was a binary biological agent that acted as a catalyst inside him over a period of time.'

'A binary catalyst?'

'Yes,' said Cassandra. 'Two substances that are each benign on their own, but when combined in the right dosage and in the right circumstances, can turn into a powerful agent. And in this case, a fierce toxin to induce disease.'

'That's pretty sneaky.'

'It's even sneakier when you think that one of the binary agents was mixed with microscopic freeze-dried cockroach larvae, that were awakened by the second agent.'

'Wow,' said Herschel. 'So, the larvae in the first dose could have been administered many times and without his knowledge. And this could have gone on for some time before the second dose was used to kick things off?'

'Exactly. Zlawitkowski said that he could have been being fed the first agent for months without any knowledge, and then at the moment the murderer wanted to strike, he or she simply supplied the second non-toxic, tasteless and odourless catalyst to the victim.'

'Wow that is brilliant. Untraceable?' asked Herschel.

'Almost,' said Cassandra. 'But it's even more sophisticated than that. Zlawitkowski has told me that the speed at which the reaction occurs could have been controlled by the murderer, depending upon the volume and concentration of the catalyst. He said that it could be tuned to take effect between a few weeks to twenty-four hours.'

'So the culprit is nowhere to be seen when the effects finally take place, like at the rooftop restaurant.'

'Exactly,' replied Cassandra.

Herschel pushed further back in his chair to digest these new facts. He glanced momentarily at the computer screen on his desk to check some of the real-time data and video feeds coming into the Hive. As he stretched back, with his arms over his head, the door opened quickly and Mrs Cambridge bustled breathlessly into the room.

'Hello Damien... I'm sorry to burst in on you like this... phew, those stairs... but I've kind of finished everything down-stairs, well almost... you know... just a little left to do... you don't mind, do you? And I wanted to let you know what was in the fridge and the pantry for you before I left. You know I'm not going to be around for a couple of days... Me and hubby are going away... He's taking me to Brighton. That's nice isn't it? Always wanted to go to Brighton... Although I might have been there as a kid, not sure... You're not busy are you? Only you're here all on your own again... Don't you get lonely up here all by yourself? It's not right you know Damien...You really should get out more...'

Mrs Cambridge's stream of consciousness stopped abruptly as she saw Herschel staring directly at her.

'I'm not interrupting anything am I?' she asked, looking quizzically around the office. 'It's not like you're in a meeting with... anyone... or anything?'

She put her hand on her hips.

'You're staring at the ceiling again, aren't you Damien? You are, aren't you... Tsk... I've told you about this before, it's not good for you, you know... You're never going to find a Mrs Herschel if you spend all your time staring at the ceiling and talking to yourself, you know.'

Herschel sighed and got up from his chair.

'Thank you, Mrs Cambridge. I would appreciate it if you were to knock once in a while before interrupting my train of thought... I have my methods, as you well know, and I know that you and perhaps others would consider them unorthodox, but they work very well for me... So I'd appreciate it if you could show a little more discretion and tact... especially when you know I'm working... This is a very important case...'

'Ooooh,' cried Mrs Cambridge as she pursed her lips together and pulled a face.

'Just remember,' she said in a high pitched voice, 'I've known you a long time, Damien... There's very little that I don't know about you... And anyway, who else would put up with the peculiar hours you work, and the strange way you go about it. You never eat properly. You're in and out at all times. Always up when everyone else is sleeping. Always asleep in the middle of the day. Don't think I'm not aware of all the pacing and chatting to yourself that you do up here... If I didn't know better, I'd think there was a whole troop of you in this room, sometimes... What with all the arguments, shouting and all that... Tsk.'

Mrs Cambridge threw her head back dramatically with the back of her palm against it, swoon-like.

'You know,' she continued. 'In fact, I think you should feel very lucky to have me... I work very hard for you, and have done for many years. I never complain about the strange goings on here. I cast a blind-eye most of the time you know...'

'Yes ...Yes. Yes. Mrs Cambridge,' said Herschel agitatedly, now trying to gently usher her out of the room. 'I'm sorry...You are right... I'm sorry about the peculiar hours and my strange way of living. You are very much appreciated, Mrs Cambridge. Thank you for the... what was it? What did you say was in the fridge? Or is it the pantry?'

'Yes... I've left you something for while I'm away... Make sure you eat regularly, now.'

'Yes, that's right. Thank you Mrs Cambridge...You are right, I don't know what I would do without you... Have a nice time in Eastbourne.'

'Brighton...'

'Yes. That's right... See you when you are back... Thanks so much again. Have a lovely time...'

Herschel pretty much pushed her through the doorway, closed the door, and leant his back heavily against it, as if to prevent any further invasion. He sighed heavily.

'I'm sorry about that,' he said.

'Why don't you tell her about us?' said Cassandra. 'I'm sure she would understand.'

'Understand? Do you think? How do you think I would explain it to her? Eh?'

Herschel began to play out his imaginary conversation with his housekeeper.

'Well Mrs Cambridge, I thought, after all these years of excellent service, that I'd just let you know that all that noise you hear in the office above you, and all the comings and goings and strange hours kept by your client, is because he, unfortunately, suffers from something of a mental disease. Yes, Mrs Cambridge, I'm sorry to have to tell you that you are the housekeeper to a whack-job schizophrenic. A nutcase with a headful of multiple personalities. Not one. Not two... but at least fourteen at the last count, each with their own individual ways of living, their own demands and desires, their own appetites, their own sleeping patterns and even some with their very own language. Yes, I'm sure Mrs Cambridge, a woman who has travelled no further than Eastbourne, would be able to comprehend such a thing. She'd understand it perfectly well, I'm sure...'

'I didn't quite mean it like that,' said Cassandra.

'Though, thinking about it, I don't know if the main problem would be explaining it to her... She's a rational woman. She knows the world, if only through what's on the TV. No, the main problem wouldn't be getting her to believe that I live with all these people in my head. No, the biggest problem would be trying to get her to keep it to herself. The moment she knew, it would be all over the city. She wouldn't be able to help herself.'

Herschel began impersonating Mrs Cambridge, contorting his face to make it the way he saw her.

'Herschel's a nut-job... who talks to all his other personalities while staring at the ceiling in his office and pacing up and down... He's got so many in his head we don't know who is who. You can never tell.'

'If she only knew,' added Cassandra.

Herschel continued with his imitation.

'...And another thing... He allows some of them take him over to carry out specific tasks when needed, like mathematics, or history or archaeology, while others just sit in the background and comment... or criticise... or...'

'Ok Herschel, you've made your point,' said Cassandra calmly. 'Probably best not to let her in on our little secret just yet.'

'No, so I don't think she, nor I... nor we, for that matter, are quite ready for that.'

'You don't think she might have some idea already?' said Cassandra. 'I mean she said as much, ...didn't she? She probably just wants you to admit it.'

'I think we've explored that enough. Best to leave things as they are, right? Shall we carry on?' said Herschel.

'Ok,' replied Cassandra. As you wish. Where do you want to go now?'

'Well, we've covered the means of all three of the murders,' said Herschel. 'And there's certainly a pattern. What about the Q-A Algorithm results? What did they show up?'

'Ah, yes, of course. I nearly forgot. Well as you know, the algorithm allows us to ingest and analyse huge amounts of data across the UK spectrum, gleaned from multiple sources: Governmental, Social, Police, Military and Secret Service. And we can overlay upon that data our profile based upon the facts we have to date and cross-match against the data-lake.

'Ok. Good.'

'Well, other than the usual list of nut-cases and sex-offenders that it always throws up...there is one outlier that you would be interested in.'

'Who?'

'Teresita Arbolasiné'

'Teresita?'

'Arbolasiné... It's an alias for Sheena,' said Cassandra.

'Sheena? Really? Now you do have my undivided attention,' emphasised Herschel.

'Why is she using an alias? And more to the point, what is she using it for?'

'It's what she used when previously married. Her husband was Spanish, and she adopted the Spanish-sounding first name.'

'Hmmm... So does that mean she is hiding something?'

'It could do... We found out a great deal more about Teresita Arbolasiné than we did about Sheena Allen.'

'Like what?'

As Cassandra spoke, a revolving image of a younger, very sun-tanned Sheena appeared on Herschel's large computer monitor. The full-sized image was low in resolution at first, but developed into a very high-definition image as the packets of data arrived and span around her in the opposite direction, like the ball on a roulette wheel as the dataset grew.

'Well, some very interesting revelations. For example, she's not the university drop-out we thought she was. She graduated from Exeter University with a First Class Honours in Virology and Immunology... Which she then extended with a Masters in Tropical Diseases at Cambridge.'

'Virology? Tropical diseases? Wow... Why didn't we know that before? I'm confused. Surely she should have built a career on those kinds of qualifications. What happened? How did she end up as Gerald's carer?'

'Well, that's what she did do,' said Cassandra. 'But she has a deeper, and more chequered past than we thought. And much, much, more sophisticated.'

'And she has kept this information very much to herself?'

'She has... And she also omitted to tell us that she worked for Texas-Beechurst Pharma in their research and development department for 17 years.'

'Tropical Disease and Virology Research?' said Herschel.
'Exactly.'

An image of a large industrial facility and a map showing its location appeared on the monitor next to that of the image of Sheena. The factory bore the sign of Texas-Beechurst, in red lettering.

'Well, well, well,' sniffed Herschel. 'That puts a completely different perspective on things. Does she have any international connections?'

'Many... Perhaps not now, but in the past, she published multiple scientific papers on the effects of combining certain hallucinogens with viral agents such as varicella-zoster, chikungunya, measles and rubella. Our investigations have revealed that she invested a great deal of her time, and the company's money of course, researching the effectiveness of a combined LSD/Ebola drug. She originally focussed on mammals...mainly apes...at first...to discover the effects of a group drug consciousness experience...'

'Really?... Wow... That sounds very advanced. Administering LSD to groups of people?'

'It was very sophisticated. She even expanded into human subjects. She developed a mechanism to use Ebola as the delivery tool for LSD, in an extraordinarily efficient manner, to the serotonin receptors in the subjects' brain. But not only that, she extended the model to encourage the virus to mutate, grow and re-transmit quickly, from one host to another.'

The monitor began to show a grainy image of three people in a room clearly under the influence of the hallucinogenic drug. One was twisting and turning in a chair. A second stared and pointed into the corner of the ceiling, while the third lay prostrate on the floor, eyes wide open with enormous pupils.

'What? Wait. Hold on. Let me understand this better,' said Herschel. 'She worked out a way to infect people with LSD?'

'Yes.'

'And the LSD is delivered, and people then 'catch' it?

'Yes. That's quite correct,' said Cassandra

'Amazing...,' Herschel's synapses were firing furiously now.

'So she could turn an individual's experience of an LSD trip into a mutual, shared experience?'

'Yes... That's right,' said Cassandra.

The monitor showed the same treatment room, but now with between ten and fifteen people, each clearly experiencing the effects of the LSD.

'Amazing. Imagine... 'Catching' LSD. Wow! That sounds attractive, don't you think?'

'Well yes, perhaps' said Cassandra. 'But eventually the research had to be shut down as it became far too successful. The Ebola agent was found to be extremely virulent. It had an R number of well over 100 and it was impossible to contain. There are reports of experiments that ended up running completely out of control, with the subjects, all the scientists and all the support staff, tripping for hours on end.'

'Haha... Really?'

'Yes, and with only a single tab of acid used as R0. The virus was able to manufacture the LSD as a payload as it mutated and spread itself between the hosts. And not only that, it was so efficient, that a room of fifteen or twenty people could go from totally straight to completely tripping in less than five minutes.'

'Wow... That's really amazing. So I guess the challenge was regulating the growth of the 'infection'?'

'Right. But there was no control mechanism. None at all. And by the looks of her reports, she tried pretty much everything.'

The monitor briefly showed a blurry image of a scientific report, which quickly changed to an ultra high-definition picture, with the words 'Classified' written in red letters upon it. Herschel looked at it briefly, flicking across the pages with his index finger in mid-air, before dismissing it.

'Ok,' said Herschel. 'Go on.'

'There was no means by which to limit its transmission and re-infection,' said Cassandra. 'Every trial got out of hand. During one experiment, the only way they were able to stop the entire plant from being infected was to seal the subjects inside the facility until they had come down... And because the virus was able to reproduce the LSD to such a high level of purity and at a phenomenally effective dose, that took several days. The air had to be pumped out of the test facility over a three-week period... And that air has been liquified and is sealed in containers in underground vaults. Some of the test subjects were never the same again.'

'This is excellent,' said Herschel, clearly excited by the prospect. 'How come we have only just found out about it?' asked Herschel.

'Well, she covered her tracks very well. Admittedly it was quite a few years ago, when records weren't so easily digitised, detected, or ingested into the Hive... and she was using a pseu-donym that sort of related to her married name...It seems like after her short-lived marriage that she chose to revert back to the original style of her name. She went back to a normal job, and of course, covered her tracks so that her digital footprint was almost untraceable. But only almost. We managed to find her by using some complex cross-functioning endo-analytics using an enormous dataset – petabytes, and not an insignificant amount of quantum computing power.'

'GCHQ or NSA?'

'Both.'

'Excellent. Very good work,' said Herschel. 'I'm proud of you. And you said you almost forgot... Cheeky.' He waved his index finger in the air.

'But there's more,' said Cassandra, calmly.

'More? How could there possibly be more. Surely that's plenty...'

'The religious aspect?...'

'Oh wow, really? There's a religious angle as well? That

makes it even more interesting. Did she get involved in some kind of cult or something?'

'Bullseye... After her marriage fell apart, she left Texas-Beechurst, under some kind of non-disclosure agreement, of course. She and Michael got involved with the Church of the Children of James, a quasi-Christian cult run by a charismatic leader by the name of Emiliano Casellas out of Leon, Spain.'

A two-dimensional image of a swarthy, bearded, long-haired latino man appeared next to the others on the monitor. After a moment or two the image took on three-dimensional proportions and began to spin slowly next to that of Sheena.

'Oh, my good grief...Is that right.'

'Do you know him?'

'No, but it is beginning to all make sense.'

'Casellas used a well-trodden mode of operation, of course. He claimed to have regular conversations with a vision of Jesus, who he said had instructed him to become a prophet and a preacher, and to gather his flock around him before the world came to an end. He used the standard inverted spiritual-guilt model – non-conformist and anti-capitalistic, unsurprisingly. Members had to eschew all worldly goods, in that they had to donate them to the church community. They were forced to work ungodly hours either in the commune, or sent out into the towns selling the cheap rubbish they had made the day before. You know, clothes-pegs, mouse-traps... that kind of thing. Polyamorous relationships, of course. Casellas encouraged female members to 'show Jesus' love' through sexual relationships with other church members. He, of course, choosing the pick of his followers as his own personal disciples.'

'They never learn do they?'

'No, of course not,' replied Cassandra. 'Sheena became one of Casellas' most trusted lieutenants. Not only sharing his bed, but she became so close to him that he put her in charge of recruitment.'

'Chief Quartermaster, eh?' said Herschel.

'And she was very successful. The Church of the Children of James grew from a couple of dozen converts to over five hundred in less than two years.'

'Impressive and scary at the same time,' said Herschel.

'Their mode of operation was mostly to prey on the pilgrims walking the Camino to Santiago de Compostella in Northern Spain. Knowing that they can be susceptible to religious influence, the Casellas' members were pressed to raise money and would walk parts of the Camino as if they were Peregrinos. They would look to befriend vulnerable pilgrims on their way westward.'

'For what? Recruitment?'

'Well, yes, either to recruit, or to rob them of what little they had. Those that they managed to recruit were expected to donate their belongings to the Church anyway, so it was larceny on two levels.'

'Don't you just love organised religion?' said Herschel. 'And I guess they got away with it?'

'I'm afraid so. The authorities were never going to take much notice of a poor, penniless pilgrim with a sob story. So the Church of the Children of James grew considerably. They built a village just outside Leon, from where they managed their operation. Over fifty dwellings, with a conference centre, a school and small hospital... A real community.'

'So what went wrong?' asked Herschel.

'Ah...well,' said Cassandra. 'The usual...'

'Sexual impropriety by the leadership?' quizzed Herschel.

'Yes... Reports of under-age sexual contact began to leak from their compound. One or two whistle-blowers began to disclose some of the community's practices. Religious prostitution, for example, where female members were encouraged to lure new male members with the promise of 'free love'. It was only when the police could no longer ignore growing reports of child abuse and incest, that they finally acted and raided the site. Casellas and the rest of the leadership, including Sheena, fled the compound. Casellas was never seen again, though there have been some unsubstantiated sightings of him in Buenos Aires. The cult was wound up, with the usual fallout and court cases by victims claiming that they had been abused and mistreated.'

'And what happened to Sheena?'

'Well, she disappeared for several years; we presume either living with Casellas, or keeping a very low profile in Spain. She was never charged with any impropriety, and eventually she reintegrated herself back into society, changed her identity, and worked hard to cover her trail.'

'That's a bit convenient,' said Herschel. 'She couldn't have managed all that on her own'

'No, she had help,' replied Cassandra. 'Gerald came to the rescue, aided by the church. He mobilised a team of priests in Northern Spain to spring her from Casella's grasp.'

'What, like the SAS?' laughed Herschel.

'Well, you may scoff, but yes, kind of. A small team comprising negotiators and what they like to call 'intervention-ists' were dispatched to effect her escape. Led by a young priest called Stonehouse. After ten days or so, they succeeded in negotiating her release from the cult.'

'Hmmm... Interesting. Doesn't that tell us more about Gerald's influence in the Church than anything else?'

'That is what I thought,' said Cassandra. 'And Stone-house has done rather well for himself in the subsequent years.'

'Que sorprisa,' replied Herschel, smiling.

'Sheena eventually returned to the bosom of Gerald's protection, and changed her name back to Sheena Allen to follow something of a random career afterwards. She settled down to look after Gerald in his latter years, after Kitty's passing.'

'Excellent, work Cassandra,' said Herschel. 'So this is

enough, right? By what you are saying, we've got enough to link her to all three murders?'

'Well, she certainly has the most to gain from her siblings' deaths,' said Cassandra. 'She was heard shouting that she wished Gerald was dead, only hours before he passed. She has a background in virology, immunology and tropical diseases. She was involved in a pretty dubious drug testing programme in the past, and she has a history of religious extremism. Do we need anything else?'

'Ok, point taken,' said Herschel. 'I think we need to mobilise the troops.'

'Bring her in?' said Cassandra.

Herschel clicked his fingers and the spinning images on the monitor dissolved into nothingness.

'Yes. I'll call Somerset,' he said.

'Ok, Ok... Settle down... Please. I'm sure you all find it very amusing. But let's get serious... We need to finalise things,' said Detective Inspector Somerset.

'I know you have been over it several times already, but I'm going to go through it one more time, so there are no chances for a cock-up, right?'

An audible groan came from the thirty or so police officers. The briefing room was pale and shabby, with no discernible means of natural light. Its low ceiling was painted the same pale vanilla as the walls, with a single door in the far corner. The only relief from the mundanity came from the black skirting board that ran the perimeter of the room and the whiteboards and poster boards on the wall at the far end of the room. A plain white digital clock mounted on the end wall blinked 3:17am. Opposite, a large flat-screen TV displayed two pictures of Sheena. One, younger and very dark skinned – ebony almost, during her time in Spain, and a second, more recent image with her mass of dark hair covering her cheeks and forehead down almost over her eyes.

The officers were seated in rows of metal chairs that scraped loudly when moved. The Tactical Offence Team was at the front, fully kitted-up, wearing their protective gear, but with their helmets and night-vision goggles by their sides. Other teams filled the room. The Dog Squad, a large group of Tactical Support Officers, SoCo's, Forensics, Drivers and Special Incident Photographers. At the back sat the Biological Threat Team, suited in their layer-1 cotton hazmat outfits, ready for the extra protective outer layers needed for the assault.

'So, now... to re-iterate, this lady is a potential high-level threat,' said Somerset. 'We believe she has access to military-grade biological compounds, that she has used very recently. Our primary objective this morning is to effect a safe and secure identification, arrest, and rendition of our primary suspect, Sheena Allen.'

Somerset pointed to the photographs displayed on the TV screen.

'She is about five foot three tall, dark hair and dark eyes. We believe she is the sole occupant of the property. 'H' hour is 05:00. Now, we believe this woman to be extremely dangerous, and capable of inflicting serious injury or death, through her extensive knowledge and use of toxic compounds. So I do not want any officers having any bare skin exposed to the air while on the premises. Not until we receive the all-clear from the bio-hazard team. Understand?'

'Sir... Is she a witch, Sir?' Came the question from some-where in the room, followed by muffled laughter.

'Very funny,' said Somerset. 'No, I don't think she is a witch, well at least not in the medieval sense, but we do think she is capable of wreaking something very nasty if given the chance. Remember, we believe that she has killed three of her siblings already. Her means are odourless, tasteless and symptomless until the very last moment. So be careful. You won't know until it's too late.'

'A quiet chant of 'Hubble, bubble, toil and trouble...' murmured its way through the room, followed by more sniggering.

'Alright, that's enough,' said Somerset firmly. The room quietened again.

'The tactical team will be first in. They will gain entry via the front and rear entrances. This will be a forced entry from the start. There will be Stage-2 teams waiting to enter once the primary team has secured the premises. We will be using the dogs to clear out any suspicious rooms or cellars, and we have authority to use deadly force if so required. The plan is to immobilise the suspect as soon as possible to prevent her from responding with anything nasty. She must be placed into the restraining jacket with a full face-mask, before removing her from the premises on a tied-stretcher. No matter what she says or does, the jacket, mask and stretcher are non-negotiable.'

A low murmuring undertone came from the assembled police officers.

'I don't give a damn what you think,' said Somerset. 'She is a potential terror risk, and I'm taking no chances. Remember, there will be a helicopter overhead equipped with full thermal imaging, as well as six backup dogs, should things go awry. Now, finally, this will only succeed if we all work together, exactly as we have trained, and with the timing we have perfected. Stay on the comms, and be clear with your instructions and your confirmations. I want this executed swiftly and professionally. We have trained for every kind of situation, and you are more than prepared, and more than capable.'

'Any further questions? No? Ok, Let's go...'

14

THE WHITE HORSE

'Herschel... Herschel! Can you hear me?' The sound of Somerset's voice was largely drowned out by the sound of shouting and a helicopter in the background.

'Herschel... Are you there? Can you hear me?' urged Somerset.

Herschel sat up, wiped his fingertips across his eyelids and looked blearily at his bedside clock. It read 6:17am. Babbage was curled up, comfortably asleep on the bed at his feet.'

'Good grief, Somerset... Why are you calling me this early? What on earth...'

'It's Sheena... It's not her...'

Somerset's voice was drowned out again by loud shouting and the sound of accelerating vehicles in the background.

'Look...I'm trying,' said Somerset... 'Can you lot just pipe down for a second...'

'What?' said Herschel, still half asleep.

Somerset's words faded in and out on the line... drowned out by the continued shouting of his men, the sound of engines revving, and the drone of a helicopter.

'Hold on a moment,' said Herschel. He waved his hand

over his mobile phone to engage the secure clear-line protocol. A glowing green bar moved diagonally across the screen and the line became crystal clear.

'Say that again, Somerset. What has happened?'

'Sheena... It's not her. It can't be her... We've just found her.'

'Not her?' said Herschel. 'Of course it's her. We went through all this. You have all the information I provided. There is no doubt that she is the culprit... How can you have fouled up? How?'

'No!' Somerset cut in. 'It's not her, Herschel... She's a victim.'

'A victim? How? What do you mean, a victim?'

'We arrived to make the arrest. The team were fully prepared for every eventuality... or so we thought.'

'Is she alive?'

'Yes... just... But she's not in a good way.'

'What do you mean?'

'We found her in her bedroom. She had been nailed upside-down, to an inverted cross.'

'Oh my good God,' exclaimed Herschel.

'It was lucky we broke in when we did... She wouldn't have lasted much longer.'

'Is she ok? Where is she now?' asked Herschel.

'Well, she's alive... We mobilised the fast reaction para-medics... That's their helicopter you can probably hear... She's being flown to the hospital right now. And Herschel...'

'What...'

'You were wrong about all this...'

'Wrong? What do you mean wrong?'

'All that stuff about Sheena? Her background... The drugs... The religious cult. None of that was relevant, was it?'

'What? How can that even be so?' snapped Herschel. 'Are you sure all this is not self-inflicted?'

'Self-inflicted? Self-inflicted!! How many people do you

know who can nail themselves, upside-down to a wooden cross?' yelled Somerset.

'Oh, I see. I didn't understand. I'm still half asleep.'

'Whoever did this is sick, really sick. They have turned the house into some kind of satanic shrine. Chalk pentangles and animal sacrifices everywhere, upstairs and down. There's a lot of blood.'

'Good grief,' replied Herschel.

'And another thing...when we found her, she had a drip of some kind in her arm.'

'A drip?'

'Yes. We found her upside-down on the cross, crucified, nails through her hands and feet, and with a drip in her arm delivering something into her veins. We have no idea what it might be but it's on its way to Porton Down right now for analysis. Sheena is on her way to isolation and observation at the specialist Centre for Tropical Medicine.'

'Do you think she'll be ok?' asked Herschel.

'We just don't know, it's too early to tell. I mean, I'm sure her wounds will heal fine. She'll probably have some scarring, but we don't really know yet what the bastard did to her, and what the long-term effects might be. Being inverted for so long put a huge strain on her lungs and heart. Not to mention the mental trauma. She is in a bad way right now... pretty delirious. It's a miracle we got to her in time.'

'And the infusion?'

'The drip? We don't know what it is,' said Somerset. 'Porton Down will be able to give us an analysis, and hopefully they can provide an antidote of some kind. But it all takes time... Let's hope, eh?'

'We need to find out what she has been poisoned with as soon as possible,' said Herschel. 'Who is there that will know what it might be, and what effect it might have? We need the best people on it straight away. For all we know, the culprit might have gallons of the stuff. The rest of the city could be in danger.'

'You're right. I'll get onto it straight away. There's one other thing though,' said Somerset.

'Yes...'

'It took some time to get her down from the cross. She was pretty delusional, like I said. We weren't really sure how best to do it... You know, whether to cut her out of the crucifix with parts still attached, if you know what I mean.'

'I don't expect there is a police procedure for this kind of thing,' said Herschel.

'No, in the end we were able to cut through the nails by going in behind her hands and feet, and freeing her that way. It wasn't pleasant. She'll need surgery. It took some time, and she was pretty incoherent. She kept on babbling about what she had done in her past, and how sorry she was about the way she had treated people and her family. She kept demanding absolution. She was so fearful that her sins in this world would be carried over into the next. She was hallucinating that she was at the pearly gates... And confessing her sins...and pleading for God's forgiveness... She kept mentioning her brother or brothers... It was strange really, like she was meeting Michael, Sean or David. Something like that, but she was acting really strange...she was quite venomous towards them all, or one of them... calling him a fake and a fraud... bringing shame on the family...She really meant it... But it was hard to tell exactly what she meant...and who she meant.'

'It's probably the effect of drugs she was given,' said Herschel.

'Maybe, but she was very insistent. Let's hope she remembers some of it when she recovers.'

'Have you sent armed protection for Louise?' asked Herschel casually.

'Louise? What do you mean?'

'What? Don't tell me that Louise is still out there alone and doesn't have heightened protection? Don't you realise there's a maniac on the loose!'

'Oh my God...What with all the frenzy going on here... It just slipped my...'

'Somerset! For God's sake... Get a squad and backup to Louise immediately. Full armed tactical, biological, and full backup. Now! And whatever you do, do not let Sheena out of your sight... I don't care if you have to hold her hand while she's on the toilet... You never let her be alone with anyone but a police officer..'

'Herschel, I... I...' stammered the Detective Inspector.

'Yes, I know... Now move!!'

'We're just looking, sir,' said the police officer. 'We've cordoned off the house and the SoCo's are carrying out a search right now. No sign of anyone yet.'

'What no-one?' said Herschel breathlessly. 'No family?'

'One of the neighbours said they haven't seen them for two or three weeks,' replied the officer. 'And her phone is dead.'

'What about the police protection?' snapped Herschel, angrily. 'Where the hell was that?'

The police officer just shrugged. 'I can't help you there, sir'

Herschel looked around the scene. The large detached house was surrounded with at least eight police vehicles, most with their blue lights still flashing against the thin early morning sunlight. A makeshift taped cordon had been placed around the front of the house. No lights were on, but every now and then a fast-moving beam of torchlight would flash across the inside of one of the windows.

'Is this going to take much longer? If she's not here, then we'll have to widen the search,' said Herschel.

'All in good time, sir,' said the officer. 'They have reported

signs of occupancy. There is definitely someone living there...
So there's every chance...'

'Come on... Come on...They need to hurry up,' urged
Herschel.

'I know, sir... They are moving as fast as they can, but in
the circumstances, and after what has just happened, they also
need to move very carefully.'

'Ok... Ok,' said Herschel. 'Let me know when I can take a
look.'

'Will do, sir.'

Herschel turned on his heels and began to walk away. As
he raised his phone to his ear he heard the officer's radio
crackle into life. The policeman listened for a moment to a
garbled message.

'Sir... Sir... Mr Herschel,' he called. 'They have found
something.'

'Excellent.'

He turned again and walked back towards the house,
straight through the yellow and black tape, stretching it until it
broke, and headed down the path.

'The garage,' shouted the police officer behind him.
'They're in the garage.'

Herschel walked towards the garage at the right of the
house and opened the side door. Inside was large enough for
two vehicles, though there was only one small car on one side.
There was a mass of plastic sheeting covering everything he
could see, with three high-powered floodlights casting stark
white beams into the room. At the far end was an industrial-
sized white chest freezer standing three foot high and six feet
long. The light from the arcs reflected off the shiny surfaces
and created an eerie, sterile, operating-theatre feel, all white
and silver with hard, reflective surfaces.

Two SoCo's, dressed from head to foot in white disposable
overalls, stood close by the cabinet. They were breathing
heavily in their restrictive outfits and tightly fitting face-masks.

'She's in here,' said one.

The policewoman lifted the lid to reveal Louise laying on her back, on top of the packets of frozen food, with her eyes wide open and her arms crossed across her waist. She was covered in a thin white frost and was frozen completely stiff.

'Oh, my good God,' said Herschel as he put his hand up to his face. 'She's... She's?'

'Yes, I'm afraid so,' said the officer. 'Please do not move the body or touch anything... She is very brittle... Rigor mortis and minus twenty degrees. We don't want any breakages, if you know what I mean. The forensic teams are on their way.'

Louise looked far from serene. Under the covering of frost, her eyes bulged and her face was contorted, etched with her last moments into a silent, desperate scream, as she had tried desperately to fight off the inevitable. Her cheeks and forehead were heavily grazed and bruised, and both her lips were split.

Herschel pulled a torchlight pen from his jacket pocket and clicked the top.

'May I?' he said as he leaned in towards the freezer.

He shone the thin bright beam of light into Louise's unresponsive eyes. Then he moved down further over her body. She wore a short tight white dress, the skirt of which finished above her knee. The top was plunging and revealed a substantial amount of cleavage and part of a lacy white bra. Herschel looked towards her feet to see her shoes, but they were not on her feet. Her high black stiletto heels were lying halfway down beside her body on top of many large packs of frozen meat. Herschel looked closer. One of the shoes was scuffed and badly damaged, with the leather peeling from the point of the stiletto right up to the back of the heel. The top of the shoe was flattened and distorted and the toe was sunken and scraped. Herschel looked up quizzically at the SoCo officer.'

'Her hands,' she said, pointing downwards. '...Look at her nails.'

Herschel looked closer to see her hands were bruised and grazed, with her trademark long red nails broken and split.

'She tried to fight her way out?' said Herschel.

'Looks that way... You can see where she used her shoe on the inside,' said the officer. She pointed her green laser-light to show thin black vertical stripes alongside blood stains and dents in the surface of the white metal.

'She hadn't a hope,' sighed the officer. 'Someone shut her in and padlocked it shut.' She pointed her light towards the remnants of the thick metal clasp on the side of the cabinet.

'What are those?' said Herschel pointing towards what looked like a number of papers spread out underneath the body.

'We haven't been able to look closely yet, because we can't move the body, but we think they are adult magazines... You know, top-shelf stuff.'

'Really? Who buys those anymore?' said Herschel. '...Why?'

'They feature her... If you look closely you can see a couple of pages with pictures of her on them.'

Herschel looked closer and gently teased one of the pages out with his pen. 'Meet Amber Dare' said the bold yellow headline above a picture of a much younger, and much more naked Louise on a couch, with a provocative look on her face, welcoming all viewers.

'Ah, I see,' said Herschel. 'These aren't recent, are they? Do you think these are hers?'

'Either hers or the murderer's,' replied the officer. 'If you look closely there are also some old polaroid photos amongst all this stuff. You can't make out much right now, but it looks like somebody had quite an extensive collection of 'Amber Dare' photos. We think there are some VHS tapes further underneath her too.'

Herschel leaned over and picked up one of the Polaroids. A

very youthful Louise stared out, smiling and laughing, happily naked, and posing without any inhibition.

'Something to show the grandkids, eh?' smirked the second officer.

'Perhaps,' replied Herschel.

'To be honest sir,' said the officer, 'she was quite well known to most of the male officers at the station, especially those of a certain age. We all knew Amber Dare, even if she thought no-one recognised her any more. Even after her notoriety faded, we knew where she lived. She was something of a celebrity in her time. I mean, we all had copies of her magazines when we were younger. I've probably still got some of her video tapes in my own garage. She was amazing, especially at the height of her fame. She did Page 3 and Playboy at least twice.'

'I think we have a fan,' said Herschel.

The police officer continued undeterred.

'She was always in the magazines... We used to follow her exploits... She had a fan-club and everything... All good clean fun... Quite wholesome really. She even had a letters page where she would help people out with their relationship problems. It was hilarious... She had a very particular and no-nonsense way of dealing with their issues. She was, shall we say, very straight to the point. She didn't mince her words.'

'And usually embellished with pictures of her in various states of undress,' chuckled the first officer.

'But she didn't deserve this,' said Herschel.

'No... No... Of course not,' replied the first officer quickly. 'Er... There are a couple of other things you should be made aware of.'

'Oh really, what?'

'Well firstly the puncture wound in her arm... There.. See?' The officer pointed her laser pen at Louise's right arm, where just in the shadow, where her arms crossed, could be seen a small puncture wound and some bruising just above the inside of her wrist. Herschel carefully lifted her arm to look more closely with his own torchlight.

'Hmmm.. Looks like the murderer attached a canular... She's been drugged.'

'That's what we thought... But what with? Same as her sister?'

'Could be. We'll have to wait for forensics. But she wasn't drugged enough for her to be unconscious when she was put in here, now was she?'

'No... So sad,' said the first officer.

'So beautiful,' sighed the second.

'And the other thing?' asked Herschel.

'Well,' said the officer. 'If you look closely, just beneath the neckline of her dress. There is something there. It's only small, but you can see it breaks the line of her dress.'

'Oh yes... Let me have a closer look... I bet I know what that is.'

Herschel pointed his torch down Louise's dress.

'Ah...Yes... I can see it... May I?'

Herschel took two pencils from his inside pocket and formed them parallel, in his fingers.

'Sir, I'm not sure we should be...' said the second officer.

'It's ok,' replied Herschel. 'If this is what I think it is, we'll need to see it straight away.'

'What do you think it is, sir?'

'Well, let's see...'

Herschel reached inside, and with the dexterity of a man very experienced with chopsticks, pulled the small white clay horse from under Louise's dress. He held it up to the light and inspected it closely.

'I thought so...A White Horse,' sighed Herschel. 'It's the Third Horseman.'

'I just can't believe it,' said Cassandra. 'I was sure we were onto the right person. It had to be Sheena. Where did we go wrong?'

'Spectacularly wrong. Louise is dead and Sheena is in a coma in intensive care,' said Herschel.

'I'm so sorry,' said Cassandra. 'This should have never happened. We were so sure... It had to be Sheena... I feel so responsible now.'

'Well, everything pointed towards her... So don't feel bad,' said Herschel. 'Maybe we got a little carried away with the information.'

'Maybe... We should think twice next time. Oh, I was so sure it was her.'

'Never mind...'

'So, where does this leave us?'

'Well, I don't want to be there when Sheena comes round. That is going to be a difficult story to explain. Somerset and the Commissioner are none too happy. A lot of police time and resources were spent on the raid – all of it based on our evidence. And of course, the newspapers have got wind of it all. The vultures are circling. They don't have all the facts yet, but they are piecing them together, especially the juicy parts... So the pressure is on to get a result quickly. And it's on everyone.'

'Ok, message received...We need to up our game, but it's just that all the evidence...'

'I know,' interrupted Herschel. 'But we have to accept we were wrong. We have to put all that behind us now. We need to focus on the future... and find a solution.'

Herschel slumped into the black leather sofa in his office. He stretched his arms out wide across the back of the Chesterfield, he closed his eyes and tilted his neck back to rest it on the back of the sofa. He put his feet up on the small table in front, looked straight up at the ceiling and sighed.

'So, where are we?' he asked. 'What do we know for certain? We should check our facts.'

'Ok, that's probably a good idea. Let's re-group, and review what we know and see if there are any gaps or incorrect assumptions,' said Cassandra.

'So... five siblings – three men, two women. Each the offspring of Gerald Allen, a respected pilot and upstanding member of the local community. A good Catholic family, with strong links into the parish and perhaps higher. Gerald dies...'

'Of natural causes,' said Herschel.

'Yes... but leaves an unexpectedly large inheritance to only two of his five children.'

'Who are then mysteriously murdered... or in Sheena's case, nearly murdered, in the short period following his passing,' added Herschel.

'So let's investigate what we know for certain for each incident... Murders one and two... Michael and Sean, the eldest brothers... one due to inherit a lot of property and money,... the other without two farthings to rub together, killed each other in the most violent way as a result of a weapons-grade poison administered by person or persons unknown.'

'Our first horseman... The Red Horseman - The Horse of War,' declared Herschel.

'Murder number two...'

'Well three, actually,' corrected Cassandra.

'You are right. Murder number three – David. Killed by an atypical poison combination. This time a binary biological toxin, the first of its kind in the world, as far as we know.'

'Our second, the Black Horseman - The Horse of Famine. Again, by person or persons unknown...'

'Then Louise... Yes? Toxicology says that she had large quantities of ketamine in her system, enough to render her malleable but not unconscious, before she was locked into the freezer.'

'Ketamine? Of course... The horse tranquilliser,' said Herschel. 'A favourite of clubbers the world over.'

'It has a strong anaesthetic affect,' added Cassandra. 'In the right quantities it can reduce feeling in the body so that you can lose all sense in your extremities.'

'So she wouldn't have felt anything as she tried to beat her way out?'

'Probably not... It just prolonged the torture...'

'Ugh. It's hard to contemplate,' grimaced Herschel. 'The White Horse, right? The Righteous Horse.'

'Yes... Which might explain the accompanying material and the fact she was encased in frost and ice. The Righteous Horse brings high-minded, principled and noble actions to a sinful and wicked world. It is the horse of revenge in a blasphemous and godless world. The White Horse is bestowed with the power to smite down the wicked and sinful in whichever way he chooses.'

'The wicked and sinful world in which Louise participated...'

'So it would seem,' added Cassandra.

'And how about Sheena? Is she talking yet?'

'No... She's still in a drug-induced coma. But we have had the toxicology reports back from Porton Down. Other than the injuries to her hands and feet, which are superficial, she suffered heavy compression to her internal organs. Her lungs and heart are damaged, such that she needs life-support at the moment. Once she regains her strength, she will be taken off the machinery. With the right physiotherapy and physical and mental support, she should make a full recovery.'

'And the drip?' asked Herschel.

'Yes... I was coming to that. They analysed the contents, and found that it contained a mixture of saline and Bubonic Plague.'

'Bubonic Plague? What? As in Fourteenth Century boils and pustules?' asked Herschel.

'The very thing. Surprisingly, people don't realise that it is still prevalent in some parts of the world. It has never really gone away. We just don't see it much in developed countries anymore, unless it is brought back by a traveller.'

'But I mean, plague... Ugh... Is there an antidote? A treatment?'

'Fortunately, she was taken to the Centre for Tropical Medicine. They diagnosed it pretty quickly and were able to treat her with a neutralising agent but its effect can be variable. Her records suggest that if she responds, then she should not experience any harmful effects. But there is an increased risk of secondary infections. It's going to take her some time to recover, and if all goes well, she should pull through. But she'll need a lot of support.'

'Hopefully, she'll remember something to help us once she is aware of her surroundings.'

'Don't expect too much, especially after what she has been through,' said Cassandra.

'So Bubonic Plague... Pestilence of course. The Pale Horse. They found another clay figure, yes?'

'No.'

'What? Really?

'No. Not this time.'

'That's hard to believe... It has all the hallmarks... Surely... Do you think the Police were thorough enough? Could they have missed it?'

'The report says not.'

'That's weird,' said Herschel. 'We should get them to check again... There must be one somewhere.'

'I'll get on it,' replied Cassandra.

'So, that's three of the four of them, right? I'm not sure if it's a relief or not,' said Herschel.

'At least we have one survivor,' replied Cassandra.

'One survivor,' sniffed Herschel. 'From five siblings... And she's only surviving thanks to a life-support machine. I'm not sure I'd call that much of a success, would you?'

'Well, when you put it like that, I suppose not.'

'We're not really any further forward now, are we?' sighed Herschel. 'To be honest, I'm not sure where we are.'

'Well, let's try and look on the positive side... We have a means of operation and the religious intention is clear.'

'But do we?' said Herschel. 'Do we really? I mean, other than us grasping at the idea of some religious crank on a murder spree for no apparent reason... If it's the inheritance, there's no one else left alive to receive it, now is there?'

'What about the Church?' said Cassandra.

'What do you mean?'

'Well... What if the Church was to benefit if all of the siblings were dead?'

'Oh, I see... We haven't thought about that, now have we? Do you really think it is something an organisation like the Catholic Church would... No strike that, of course they would... But aren't they rich enough already? Don't they have enough? I mean, it would be a small win, given their vast wealth. Why would they stoop that low, just to get hold of Gerald's money?'

'Maybe it's not the money,' said Cassandra. 'Maybe it's something else? What if this is an attempt to cover things up? Something they didn't want the siblings to reveal.'

'Hmmm... That's an interesting thought... Such as?' said Herschel.

'Well, it could be anything... The Church has a pretty unenvious history when it comes to concealing truths. Maybe the five siblings knew more than they realised?'

'Or maybe Gerald did?'

'Exactly,' said Cassandra.

'But what? And how do we find out?'

'It's a difficult one. They are notoriously protective about their records. Even though they have centuries of material, none of it has ever been digitised, which means it's impossible for our software-crawlers to access.'

'Paper is safer,' chuckled Herschel.

'They have crypts full of documents, and whole teams to curate and manage it, but these stores are impossible to access unless you have proper authorisation. And sometimes that authorisation has to come from the Pontiff himself.'

'So this means we need to do some good, old-fashioned detective work, then. See if we can find someone on the inside.'

'Do we have someone?' asked Cassandra.

'No one that will let us have the kind of access we're going to need.'

'We're at a bit of an impasse. Where else do we have to go?'

'Nowhere,' said Herschel, glumly.

15

REVELATIONS

'What the hell is going on, Connor!' bellowed the Cardinal. 'I thought I told you to look after them and protect them?'

Stonehouse strode angrily around his desk, pacing up and down... hands first on his hips, then held aloft in exasperation. He ran the fingers of both his hands through his hair, then stretched out his arms imploringly towards the leaded window, shaking in fury.

'I mean... I explicitly told you to keep a close eye on them... To use all the resources you needed. Nothing... Nothing was supposed to happen to them... And now, because of you, another one is dead and the other may never recover.'

Brother Connor sat at the Cardinal's desk, his head in his hands, rocking forwards and back rhythmically, while mumbling under his breath. Sweat poured from his flushed head and puffy neck. It seeped through his fingers, dripped down his neck and ran into the off-white of his worn dog collar. Outside the Cathedral, the sun was setting, while large cumulonimbus clouds formed on the horizon, drawing a distinct line between the bright blue sky of the daytime and the menace of a tempestuous night.

'I tried,' wept Brother Connor. 'I did everything I could... But it was so difficult... I couldn't keep an eye on both of them all of the time. It was impossible. I'm so sorry... It's all my fault.'

Connor threw his head back into his hands and sobbed. As he sobbed harder his mumblings grew louder and his rocking back and forth became more pronounced.

'For God's sake, man,' said the Cardinal. 'I gave you one simple job, and you failed me. You failed me...And not just me... You failed the Church, and you failed yourself... You really should be ashamed... I just don't know how I'm going to be able to protect you anymore.'

'Protect me?' whimpered Connor.

'Oh, get a grip of yourself!' Stonehouse shouted. 'We'll never get anywhere if you insist on snivelling like this. Show some backbone man. I would have thought that with your background, you would have had more character than this.'

The priest flinched at each of the Cardinal's hard syllables, reacting as if each word was physically striking him. His tears, moaning and rocking continued. Foaming spittle began to appear at the sides of his mouth.

'Have I not been a true and faithful servant, Father? To you and to the Church?' mouthed Connor through the tears and the phlegm. 'Have I not done everything you have asked? Have I not been a dedicated and loyal instrument for you? Please tell me it is so...'

Connor looked up at the Cardinal through red, swollen eyes and saturated fingers. And the Cardinal looked at the broken mess of the man before him.

'Ok, ok, I know... I know...' said the Cardinal, as he placed his hand on Connor's head. 'I suppose you have tried your best. That's all I should have expected of you. Perhaps the error was mine. Perhaps I asked too much of you. But I really thought you would be the right person... Maybe I thought you were made of sterner stuff... That you were from more robust stock,' sighed the Cardinal.

'What do you mean,' snivelled the priest. 'More robust stock?'

'I don't mean anything,' replied Stonehouse. 'I... I just meant that with your background, you know... Perhaps you would have been more... more... determined.'

'More determined? With my background?' asked Connor, straightening his back and regaining his composure somewhat. 'What about my background?'

'Well... er, you know...Your background in, er... Ireland... I mean... The orphanage... Tough upbringing.'

Connor's tears had stopped now, and he was sitting upright.

'Yes... That's right,' he said. 'You know about the orphanage in Ireland. But what do you mean? Is there something I should know? Are you holding something from me? What do you know? What is it you know about my background?'

'I... I... don't know any more than you have told me...'

Connor paused for a moment, leaned back in his chair, his demeanour visibly changing. He looked directly at the Cardinal. 'I think you do, Father... I think you do.'

'I really don't, Connor,' replied Stonehouse. 'Shall we move on?'

Connor's composure had begun to return. He had more of an air of determination in him and his curiosity was piqued.

'You knew my real parents, didn't you? You knew my mother and father, didn't you Cardinal Stonehouse?' said the priest, flatly.

'I beg your pardon,' replied Stonehouse. 'I don't know what you are talking about. I know nothing of the sort...'

'I think you do, Sir... I think you know more than you have said.'

'Utter nonsense,' said Stonehouse. 'You and I only met for the first time a few weeks ago... I couldn't possibly have...'

'That's not correct now is it, Sir. We have met before, haven't we? Only it was a long time ago... You must remember? I mean, if I remember, and I was only a small child, you surely must remember.'

'Remember? I suggest you remember who you are, your place, and who you are talking to, Brother Connor... I really don't have time for this... As, as far as I'm aware, you are just another unfortunate Irish bastard child given away by his teenage mother who couldn't keep her legs closed.'

'Liar!' shouted Connor as he stood up to face the Cardinal. 'Don't take me for a fool...You know exactly who my parents were. You know it all... Shall I tell you? Shall I refresh your memory, Cardinal? You know that Kitty was my mother and that Gerald was my father... You know that...You have known that all my life...'

'Gerald?' said Stonehouse.

'And they abandoned me into that hellhole they called an orphanage. They gave me up as a baby to be preyed upon by those creatures that call themselves Godly. I hope they all burn in Hell... But I survived didn't I? That wasn't expected, now was it? How? I have no idea. The beatings... The starvation... I was lucky not to end up in the well... But, but why am I telling you?... You already know all this.'

'I... I... I,' stammered Stonehouse.

'Don't feign innocence with me, Cardinal... Your fakery won't wash with me any more. I know all about it. All the backstage deals... All the payments... All the blackmail... That's how Gerald got to be so rich, wasn't it?' continued Connor.

'What?' said Stonehouse.

'He demanded money from you, didn't he? All those years ago... To keep quiet about all the things that went on with Father Murphy and Mother Superior at the orphanage. He knew... didn't he? He knew... And you knew... And he forced you to give him money. He blackmailed you and the Church didn't he? He threatened to report you and the rest of them to the authorities didn't he?'

'No... It wasn't like that...' pleaded Stonehouse.

'I have had years to work it out. Years in St Vincent's... Years in the monastery. I have known for a long time. You paid him for his silence, didn't you? So the Church could carry on with its despicable crusade... Exploiting the poor, and ennobling the rich and the powerful. Rich and powerful people like you, eh? Gerald and Kitty and the rest of that family got rich and powerful from you and the Church, and you got rich and powerful for keeping its secrets? All off the back of people like me... Like me...'

Connor was standing up now, face red, eyes bulging, anger bursting with every word.

'No Connor...' said the Cardinal. 'You have it all wrong... Nothing like what you have described happened. You don't understand...'

'You have no idea of the kind of life I have had to lead to get me to here... I had to claw my way out of St Vincent's, with no help from you or the rest of them. I had to fight all the way. We all did. But some are better at fighting than others, aren't they? My best friend Ben. Well, he couldn't fight anymore. He gave up. When he couldn't fight any longer, he took the only way out available to him. What a terrible waste...Another wasted life... Well, that wasn't going to happen to me. I had a mission to fulfil. I was always going to fight. Never give up. They did everything in their power to stop me from becoming a priest. It was only when Murphy was old and frail that I took my chance and escaped. I arrived with nothing and I left with nothing... I had to throw myself on the mercy of the Brothers just to survive.'

'Yes,...I'm sure it must have been very hard for you,' said the Cardinal

'Hard? Hard! Nineteen years I toiled in that monastery. I

worked from the ground up... I looked after the animals, I tended the gardens, I spread their shit across the fields. I ate in the barn every day with the goats and the sheep. I was nothing. But I did everything that was asked of me. And I watched... and I learned. Oh...The happiest day of my life was when I was given the keys to the crypt and discovered the library within it... Oh, what a treasure trove that turned out to be... Books and learning going back hundreds and hundreds of years... so much of it never seen before. So much lost to civilisation. There were basements full of ancient scripts and teachings... Some might call it witchcraft. So I read... and I learned... and I experimented... and I read...and I learned more... and I watched...and I waited...'

'Good grief,' cried Stonehouse. 'Joachim... Joachim!... Where are you?'

Connor seemed now to be towering over the Cardinal.

'There's no-one to help you here, Father. It's just you and me now. And for once in your life, you are going to shut-up and listen to what I have to say. You might learn something... Sit!'

Connor pointed at the Cardinal's large black office chair.

'You still have no idea what I had to do to get here. The sins I was forced to commit and the disgusting acts I had to perform. I clawed my way up and, step by little step, out of St Vincent's and the monastery. I started by being kind and tried to help people, but that got me nowhere. And I soon learned how the Church worked. I found that blackmail and extortion are much more effective for career development... But I don't have to tell you that, now do I? I mean, just look at this place... Look at all the finery, the valuables, and precious things that have been stolen from your poor dedicated followers. Look at the paintings of all the cheating, lying individuals here that came before you. I mean it's quite a gallery of villainy, isn't it?'

'Those are all highly respected, humble men,' replied Stonehouse.

'Pah! They're fraudsters. Fakers... abusers and murderers... the lot of them. They just had the power of the Church to hide behind. They don't believe in God any more than you or I do...'

'But you worked your way up to be a man of the cloth... Your holy vows? Do they not mean anything to you?' asked Stonehouse.

'It just means that we are part of the same club that I can use to get what I want... No different from you, Cardinal Stonehouse,' Connor spat out his name venomously across the desk.

'When Gerald died, I thought this was my chance... My chance to put all those wrongs right... All those family occasions that I was denied. All those birthdays... all those Christmases. All I needed was the right opportunity to tell them... To get the acknowledgement I deserve... To explain what had really happened. They would understand, wouldn't they? They would realise... And then they would welcome me into their lives as part of their family. That's what would happen. And I was slowly getting into their lives... I had befriended Sheena and I was getting to know Sean better... It was all going according to plan... But then you had to make it difficult for me. You told me to keep a closer eye on them like a priest... To protect them from some deranged killer... And, of course, what am I to them then? I'm their kindly priest. Brother Connor... Their protector... Their saviour. Their deliverer from all their evil... That's a laugh. Oh, and there is so much evil here... So much... We're surrounded by it... So how can I possibly tell them who I really am to them, eh?'

'Look... we were very young,' interrupted Stonehouse. 'It was so different in those days. An out of wedlock pregnancy would have had such a bad effect on both... I mean, there was a career to think of... and of course Kitty's reputation. It had to be kept very quiet... I... I... Just did what I thought was right to protect both you and Kitty.'

'Yes... and what you thought was right was to dump me in

that shit-hole of an orphanage, with all of the other unwanted bastards, and hope that even if I were to survive, that I would keep quiet and not find out...'

'No. of course not...'

'But that wasn't just an orphanage I was left in, you know... It was a prison. A prison worse than any of you could imagine, where the guards were free to do anything to you. Anything they wanted... Beat you...abuse you... Rape you... Even murder you... and no-one would do a thing about it... No one. Not the Church. Not the police. No-one. They all knew... We were just there to be exploited, or to be left to rot and to die... All in the name of Jesus Christ... The best we could do for them was to die quickly and quietly, and not make any fuss.'

'You know I visited St Vincent's as often as I could... I tried to keep an eye on you as you grew up,' said Stonehouse weakly.

'Oh really? What for? What was I to you anyway? Some interesting little experiment? You didn't watch over me at all did you? Well, even if you did, what good was that? Did it stop me being abused every night by Father Murphy, stinking of tobacco and alcohol? Did it stop me being raped? Did it stop me from being beaten into unconsciousness by sadistic nuns with a whole cupboard full of canes? No. No, it didn't? And anyway, what did you care? You were probably only checking on me to make sure that the secret never came out... and so you could keep me and Gerald just where you wanted us.'

'Connor...Please, it wasn't like that at all. I wanted... I needed... to make sure you were alright... You were my fle...'

'Oh, go to Hell!...' snapped Connor. 'Go to Hell with the rest of them... Then you can come and join me... I've been in my own hell for decades... And you know why? Because, just like you said, I was just a little bastard like the rest of them – unchristened and unwanted. Beyond salvation, stained with mortal sin... and destined to spend eternity outside the Kingdom of Heaven. What kind of Church does that to a

young child? What kind of a Church is happy to see poor innocent children treated in such a way? Is that a loving Church?
A loving God? I don't think so... Well let me tell you, I like
hell... I've grown used to it... I've been here for so long... And I
enjoy it here... You will be most welcome.'

'Oh, my good God, Connor,' said Stonehouse. 'I'm so, so
sorry that you have ended up like this... And I so regret that I
couldn't have been in your life more, or to have helped you
more... But you can't take your frustrations out on that poor
family...'

The Cardinal paused for a moment in thought.

'You haven't... You're not?' asked the Cardinal.

'Haven't what?' asked Connor.

'You... You haven't done anything stupid, have you?'

'Stupid? Oh no... Nothing stupid at all. Everything I have
done has been carefully thought out, planned and prepared
over many, many, years. And it's going very much to plan...'

'Connor...are you responsible for?' asked the Cardinal.

'I just wanted them to accept me,' said the priest. 'I just
wanted to be part of the family... To have a life with a family... I
don't care about the money. They can keep it. That money is
dirty, anyway. It means nothing to me. But the retribution, the
retribution for their dreadful sins... Oh, that belongs to me...
That is mine to enact... For them, I am a true and just God... I
shall forgive those who are truly sorry for their actions... But
those five were never sorry for their dreadful, despicable lives.
They were never devout or fearing of the one true Lord. They
took advantage of the weak, and the vulnerable at every
chance they had. They exploited anyone who came into contact
with them... And so, they, one by one, will ride on the back of a
horseman, and join with me and my father in the depths of
Hell ...'

'You can't talk like that, my son,' said the Cardinal. 'I fear...
I fear for you and your everlasting soul...If you have done
something... Something that you need to... That you might

need to confess? I am here for you, my son. You will feel better once you have shared it with God...'

'God?' shouted Connor. 'What has God ever done for me? All I ever got from God was fear, pain and torment. Just look... Open your eyes... His sins are everywhere... You see it in the eyes of the poor and the sick... The pain he delivers unto those desperate souls... And yet the likes of you have convinced them to accept it and come back for more... You see it in the eyes of the rich and famous, constantly trying in vain to reclaim their lost direction. Their lost integrity... No, my one true Lord is a much more benevolent and loving being to me. He provides and he nourishes. All that we need. Ille verus dominus est. Ille verus Deus.'

'The one true lord?,' replied Stonehouse. 'I don't think you really mean that Connor. You are mistaken. You are misled... And I truly believe your soul is in mortal danger.'

'My soul was delivered into the arms of my one and only true Lord many years ago, by the Church itself. They did this... It is their work... They are responsible... I hope they are happy... I hope you are happy.'

Connor began to clasp himself with his arms wrapped tightly around his torso. He threw his head back and started to twist and turn his body and while chanting under his breath.

'Ipse est dominus meus et dominus meus... Sequar vocantem...'

'Lord God... Don't do this, Connor... Please,' cried Stonehouse. But the Cardinal's words had no effect. The priest began to twist and turn his body with each incantation as if being spun by an invisible hand.

'Ego sum verus filius dei... Te amo satanas... Deus meus es tu...' he mumbled.

'No Connor... No... That is not right... You cannot worship the Devil... You are a man of God... You have been seduced... Satan will only bring chaos, confusion and eternal torment. You must turn away from him...'

'Turn away from him? That's a joke... You sent me here... My beautiful Lord has been nothing but true and honest with me. He never lied to me. He never deceived me. He has always shown me the one true path. Ever since he revealed himself to me in the chapel at St Vincent's, he has been by by my side. Guiding me. Teaching me. Loving me. Long ago I learned that his way is the one true way... not your twisted, depraved ways of your Nazarene... Satanas te amo.'

Connor's twisting and turning continued, and he began to chant in a deep, guttural growl.

'No Connor... No! This is wrong...You cannot love Satan!' cried Stonehouse.

The Cardinal went to embrace Connor, and wrap his arms around this turbulent Priest to try and break him from this spell. But Connor was too strong. He twisted hard and broke away from Stonehouse's grip. With his bloodshot eyes, and his face even more swollen than before, he launched Stonehouse into the air with a single push. Then, with super-human strength, he threw the Cardinal across his desk and onto the floor. As he fell, he heard his wrist snap with a loud crack. The Cardinal cried out in pain and rolled onto his side, clutching his arm. He lay panting on the floor and could hear Connor moving roughly about his office, noisily opening and closing cupboard doors, rummaging through drawers, and scattering books and papers everywhere... Stonehouse laid his head on the floor and peered under his desk. He could just make out the priest's feet as he moved from one side of the office to the other, rummaging through things. Every now and then the Cardinal could see Connor's silhouette illuminated by the silent flashes from the approaching storm. After several more minutes he heard further loud scrabbling followed by the creak and slam of a door. At that moment Stonehouse knew that Connor had left through one of the concealed exits.

'So you say you've managed to get more information on the priest?' said Herschel.

'Yes,' said Cassandra. 'One of the others spent some time researching the family in more detail...as well as the priest... I think you'll be interested in what we've discovered.'

The lighting in Herschel's office was low. A cool blue light emanated from somewhere in the bottom corners of the room, from behind his chesterfield, and dissipated gradually up to the ceiling. In this light, the covers of his vast library of books that spread across the length of the side wall, appeared as though they were next to a swimming pool, flickering gently in the mottled blue and white light. On the far wall of the office hung two large paintings – one, a twelve by four Kandinsky, stretched over half the wall and showed an abstract set of circles and squares juxtaposed against one another. The image enticed you into its weird vortex of balance and imbalance. It was Herschel's favourite, and one in which he found something new every day. Mounted next to this abstract masterpiece hung a more traditional sea-view of a bay in Cyprus, at sunset. Painted in shades of deep brown, red and yellows, it depicted a broad, open seascape with a schooner anchored in the centre, with a small rowing boat of about four people nearby. These two pictures provided Herschel with a simultaneous view of his past and of his present.

Herschel was seated alone once again, feet up on his desk in front of his super-sized computer monitor, upon which was displayed multiple windows, each being driven by a multi-gigabit stream of invisible data, while other windows displayed rapidly changing and rotating images of faces, three-dimensional heads or buildings. Each of these agents was being analysed in multi-threaded real-time by the artificial intelligence software connected to the vast network that made up the Hive.

'So what have you got?' asked Herschel.

'Ok,' said Cassandra. 'Let's start with the psychological

profile of our killer. I know we've been here before, but it's worth revisiting. Following the recent attacks, we have been able to generate billions more data points and have collated and crossmatched them before feeding them into the Hive. We have recalibrated the AI agents and run over twenty-five billion separate scenarios, with some interesting results... We are pretty certain of the main attributes that the killer, statistically speaking at least, is likely to possess.'

'Excellent... What are they?'

'Ok... Firstly, and go with this... male, white, aged forty-five to sixty, as we previously thought. Likely to be orphaned or adopted at a young age and very likely to have been exposed to regular ritualistic religious services, but not necessarily the occult. He would be a fairly gregarious person in public. He probably enjoys the ego-boost of public speaking or officiating over public ceremonies, but underneath, is an extreme loner who would probably not align with conformist policies and procedures. He would actively seek to undermine them, but not publicly. He is deferential to authority figures in public, but subversively hates them and looks to undermine them whenever he can, as long as he is not implicated.'

'Interesting... Sneaky with a chip on his shoulder?' said Herschel.

'He really would not want to connect to the modern world,' continued Cassandra. 'No fancy cars and mobile phones for him. He doesn't trust technology and prefers traditional values and mechanisms like word of mouth and pencil and paper. He likes things simple and very orderly, yet he has an enormous thirst for knowledge. Highly intelligent, but you probably wouldn't realise it. It wouldn't be obvious.'

'So what sort of person...What profession?'

'Top three would be... One, college professor in something like virology, ecology or environmental studies. Two, a rural parish Priest or Monsignor, maybe even a Bishop who has come from very humble, rural beginnings and has a background in liturgical studies as well as microbiology or botany. And three, is a farmer or farm labourer, but one who has an ecological background, or might even be an eco-warrior type, with an extensive knowledge of plants and toxicology.'

'Have we done a search for those who might fit this profile?'

'We have, but more than that. We have had something of a breakthrough too on the data ingestion side. We have been able to hook the Hive into an even richer set of data repositories that have just recently become available in Europe. It has given us access to an additional sixty petabytes of data and has allowed us to make something of a breakthrough. It has proven very useful. The most interesting dataset for our purposes turns out to be a large and complex unstructured repository that records information across thousands of classifications, going back for nearly two hundred and fifty years, in Ireland.'

'Ireland? What's the connection?'

'Like I said... go with this... We'll get there.'

'Ok, but I'm beginning to get impatient,' said Herschel.

'By crossmatching and filtering against our profile, we have discovered that our very own Brother Connor matches the profile very well.'

'Really? The priest? Why? I just thought he was being pushed about by the Church to provide protection to the sisters. Fat lot of good that did.'

'Connor was born in Ireland.'

'Right. Of course, he was.'

'He was raised in an orphanage just outside Dublin. It only closed down a few years ago.'

As Cassandra continued to explain, a large black and white photograph spun into the centre of the monitor screen showing a rather typical school-type photograph, clearly old and somewhat blurred. Three rows of young children between the ages of four to fifteen were flanked each side by four nuns in dark habits, while at the back stood two priests clearly identifiable by their dark jackets and shirts with dog-collars.

'There were rumours of malpractice by the staff, mostly nuns and at least two of the priests,' said Cassandra. 'A group of nuns calling themselves 'The Daughters of Charity' were implicated in unethical and unlawful behaviour at St Vincent de Paul and several other orphanages in Ireland. Two priests were sent for 'retraining' and were excardinated to other parishes. The Vatican ordered its closure but no criminal charges were ever brought, though.'

'Ok, but that doesn't mean he's our killer now does it? I'm sure lots of priests have started life in a Catholic orphanage.'

'No, but we think there is a strong connection between him and the family.'

'Connection? What connection? How?'

'Kitty was born and raised in Ireland... In Tipperary, not such a long way from Dublin.'

'Ok, but I'm still struggling...'

'We don't have access to the exact records, but there is a strong correlation between what we do have access to, plus the orphanage records, that Kitty was forced to leave behind a child at the St Vincent de Paul orphanage.'

'A child? You mean Connor?'

'Exactly that. She would have been unmarried and under-age, so clearly an embarrassment to be hushed up. There was a long applied policy of forced adoption, and worse, at that time in Ireland. Kitty was lucky not to have been put into an asylum, as many were. The Church took a dim view of 'way-ward' girls and sought to remove them from society. Some spent their entire lives in institutions as a result. The orphanage register shows that dozens of children were left there each year but we have no record of what happened to the mothers.'

'So Connor is the sibling's brother?'

'Exactly.'

'Connor... Brother... Connor... Yes... Of course... Brother Connor! Brother Connor is the brother to Michael, Sean, Sheena, David and Louise...'

'Well, half-brother...'

'Half Brother? Gerald wasn't the father?'

'No. He couldn't be. The dates don't match up... Kitty didn't leave for England until a year or two later. She didn't meet Gerald until she had been in the country for another year. Of that we are certain.'

'So if Gerald isn't Connor's father... Who is?'

'Well, this is where we have to rely heavily on statistical data and the machine learning algorithms to determine a best fit. But we know from the recently released datasets that Cardinal Stonehouse, just a simple seminarian at the time, visited St Vincent de Paul regularly.'

The photograph zoomed into one of the priests in the back row to show a rather blurred and faded image of a young Stonehouse. As the image settled, a number of visible data-points appeared over his face, joined up and turned from grey to green and began to blink.

'Stonehouse's visits increased significantly, immediately after Connor arrived,' added Cassandra. 'At the time this picture was taken, Stonehouse was still training to become a priest, in... and I'll give you one guess where?'

'Tipperary.'

'Correct...'

'So not only is Connor the five sibling's brother, but he is the son of a Cardinal,' said Herschel.

'The secret son of a Cardinal,' added Cassandra. 'And he would be the eldest son too. So he would be first in line.'

'Good grief. The illegitimate son of a Cardinal. That is big.'

'Yes... The Church wouldn't want that to become public knowledge.'

'No... So was there a cover up?'

'Almost certainly... And one that has lasted for over fifty years.'

'Fifty years... How?'

'We have traced large, regular transactions going from Stonehouse and the Church to...'

'Gerald!' exclaimed Herschel. '...Of course...Gerald was blackmailing Stonehouse and the Church.'

'Well done... You have got it... Gerald was using Stonehouse's indiscretion of over fifty years previously to leverage money out of the Church on an industrial scale.'

'Wow... They must have really loved Cardinal Stonehouse.'

'Yes. Though it's difficult to know how much of those funds were Stonehouse's personal finances and how much were the Church's, especially at first, but the amounts were regular and substantial.'

'Enough to build up a portfolio of £6.7m?'

'Over that time period? More than enough.'

'Wow-wee!' cried Herschel. 'Brother Connor, eh? And Gerald managing to turn the screws on the Church over all these years.'

'Well, Stonehouse is very well connected across the Catholic community, and in many countries. He has even been tipped as a potential future Pope, so perhaps the powers in the Vatican were willing to protect him. I mean they have form, don't they?'

'But wait a moment,' said Herschel. 'We were just talking about the killer; do you mean to say that Brother Connor is...'

'That's exactly what I am saying,' said Cassandra. 'He is our Four Horsemen killer.'

'How on earth did he get hold of the toxins? Weren't they supposed to be North Korean or Chinese?'

'We're still working on that one. Unless he had some international contacts or access to the formulas, we don't know right now. But the rest of it fits, now, doesn't it?'

'Certainly seems to... And gives him a whopping motive.'

'The inheritance?'

'Yes,' said Herschel.

'No, his motive is not money. We think it is something else?'

'Such as?' said Herschel.

'We don't know yet... Recognition maybe? Acceptance into the family? Maybe acknowledgement by Cardinal Stonehouse of his paternity.'

'But Stonehouse hasn't been attacked or harmed in any way... Just Gerald's family. That doesn't make sense. Surely Stonehouse would be the first person Connor would go to...'

'Unless...' said Cassandra.

'Unless what?' said Herschel, suspiciously.

'Unless he doesn't know?'

'What?... Doesn't know? What do you mean?'

'What if he believes that Gerald was his father? It would be an easy mistake to make. I mean, we very nearly made it.'

'I'm sorry, I don't follow,' said Herschel. 'Stonehouse is Connor's father, but Connor thinks that Gerald was his father?'

'Yes... He has put two and two together and unfortunately got five. We expended several billion permutations on the possibility, but the dates simply do not, and cannot fit. Short of obtaining DNA material to run an exact match, Stonehouse is Connor's father.'

'That makes perfect sense,' said Herschel. 'Because then his retribution would be mis-directed towards Gerald and his family. If he's so desperate to be their brother... He would want to be a brother within the family of the person he thinks is his father.'

'Exactly.'

'And if he can't achieve it, would he seek to destroy it?'

'That's what our psychological profile strongly suggests,' replied Cassandra.

'So what happens now?' asked Herschel.

'I think we should get Somerset to gather his army and bring him in.'

'Yes, but from where?'

The dark and once distant storm cloud was now casting an ominous shadow over St Elegius and the rest of the city. Lightning flashes could be seen within the heart of the storm, but no resulting thunder could be heard. Even though it looked angry and aggressive, no lighting forks emerged from the anvil-shaped cloud, and none came to strike the ground. It formed an eerie, silent, darkness over the Cathedral, like an enormous visiting alien craft. The storm cloud brought the low-light of dusk to a premature end before the elegant, cast-iron streetlights could illuminate the grounds with their dim glow.

The dark silence of the courtyard was harshly pierced by the clamouring sirens and blue flashing lights of four police cars as they squealed around the corner and came to an abrupt halt in front of the Cathedral. The Inspector was the first out of the first police vehicle, whilst behind him his men spread out along the walls of the Cathedral.

'Secure the area!' ordered Somerset into his communications set as he headed towards the front door. 'Under no circumstances should you enter the building, unless on my command. No shots are to be fired if anyone exits the building – only as a last resort. I want no more deaths. Now, set up an outer and inner perimeter and make sure the press is kept as far away as possible.'

Somerset made his way to the small access door cut out of one of the large oak panels of the main doors. He pushed, and was surprised when it opened to his touch. He stepped inside to find himself at the far end of the transept, looking straight down the length of the Cathedral towards the altar. Throughout the Cathedral every candle that could be, was lit.

The light emanating from each side was full and warm, while the altar was ablaze with a full white light. At the far end, just in front of the altar, Somerset could see a tall angular figure, standing gazing at the figure of Christ on the crucifix.

'What took you so long,' said the figure.

'Christ... You got here quickly, Herschel,' panted Somerset. 'How... How did you know?'

'Oh, police radio communications were hacked decades ago, Somerset. I probably knew before you did,' quipped Herschel.

'Oh... So you heard the Cardinal's message? Where is he? He said he was injured.'

'I don't know... I have only just got here myself... But Connor is here... somewhere.'

'And he is our man?'

'I'm afraid so... I'll explain it to you later, we don't have time now... But he is extremely dangerous and mentally very unstable.'

'I've setup a cordon... He won't be going anywhere.'

'Let's hope not... But first we have got to find Stonehouse. His life may be in danger.'

'Who lit all the candles?'

'I don't know... Connor, probably... I think he wants to make a statement.'

As the two men talked, an enormous crash echoed high above them. They looked up.

'What was that?' asked Somerset.

'It sounded like it was in the roof,' said Herschel.

'I can't see anything...'

A second, even louder crash sounded further along, nearer the altar, followed by some maniacal laughter.'

'It's Connor... He must be in the passages.'

'Passages? What passages?' asked Somerset.

'The maze of passages that allowed the priests to move, through the Cathedral... They were put in when the Cathedral was first built... But really put to use during the Reformation. They allowed the clergy secret access to the Cathedral and its ante-rooms and external buildings. Priests could move around without being seen... Connor is in them... It's a bloody rats nest... He could be anywhere... And he could get anywhere...'

'So how do we apprehend him?'

'I have no idea right now. Let's see if we can find Stonehouse...'

Herschel turned and began to march back down the aisle towards the Cathedral entrance.

'I'm here, Mr Herschel. It's good to meet you. I have heard a lot about you,' said the Cardinal, emerging from the shadows of a side chapel. 'I saw the police vehicles arrive and thought I would find you all here. I came straight down. And you are quite correct... Connor has discovered the Cathedral's passageways so he could be anywhere.'

'Are you ok?' asked Somerset. 'Your arm?'

'It's ok... I fell. I've made a makeshift bandage for the time being. I'll get it looked at later. But for now we have to see if we can entice Connor out in some way... We need to put an end to all of this.'

Another loud crash came from high above the nave, followed by running footsteps and loud scraping sounds. The three men peered high up into the Cathedral ceiling, trying to locate the source of the noises.

'I can't see a thing up there...but I sure can hear him,' said Somerset.

'There is a whole labyrinth of passages in the loft space, all connected to corridors and secret stairways leading up to them,' said Stonehouse. 'Plus, there's a network of passages running underneath the grounds... He could appear from anywhere.'

'As I said,' replied Herschel, '...anywhere.'

As the three men were considering their next actions, a mighty scream pierced the echoey silence. It was so high-pitched and sudden that the three men cowered briefly while covering their ears.

'What on earth was that?' winced Somerset. 'That didn't sound human.'

'Watch out!' shouted Herschel as he pitched himself forward and caught Somerset square in the chest with his left shoulder forcing the two men horizontally across the aisle and landing in the footwell of the pews, with Herschel on top of the Inspector, in a mess of arms and legs. Simultaneously, and reacting to Herschel's shout, the Cardinal leaped the opposite way, as, out of the darkness swung a shrieking and screaming Connor, in a huge arc, Tarzan-like, astride an oversized thurible from the far end of the Church.

The three-foot high, heavy silver censer was attached to a sixty-foot length of rope, and swung from the Cathedral ceiling. St Elegius liturgical censing ceremony was famous the world over, and attracted thousands of the faithful to the Cathedral. Used in spectacular ceremonies, where it would take five or six priests to swing the huge burning incense container, like a heavy, fast-moving pendulum, up and down the length of the Cathedral.

Connor, screaming at the top of his voice with a piercing, child-like pitch, held on to the thick rope with one hand, while in the other he swung a huge medieval sword. As he reached the lowest point of the arc, he narrowly missed the diving Cardinal. Swinging past the men, his arc drew Connor forwards and upwards to an apex thirty feet above the altar. Just as he reached his maximum height, Connor leapt from the rope, only to fall towards the balustrade, and land just above the altar. Crashing hard against the metal and stonework, but managing to cling on, Connor seemed oblivious to any pain. His rapidly darting eyes were bulging almost out of his head and his mouth frothed, thick with spittle. Breathing heavily, and with his chest moving rapidly up and down, he looked back down the Cathedral.

Herschel, Stonehouse and Somerset were slumped down behind the pews on each side of the aisle as the heavy vessel swung back towards them. The three rose to their feet once the danger had passed.

'Connor!' shouted Stonehouse. 'What the hell are you doing? You could have killed us...'

'AAahhahhhaa... HAhhaaAhAhhaa,' howled Connor with a weird inside-out laugh, as he hung from the balcony.

'Get down from there immediately,' ordered Stonehouse. 'You are going to injure someone.'

'AAhhaa AahahhHhHhaAahaAa,' wailed Connor, as he brought the huge metal sword crashing against the metal balustrade. The clang from the clashing metals echoed throughout the building.

'We've got him,' reported Somerset into his radio.

'I don't think so,' replied Herschel.

'Get down from there, Connor. Be sensible, man,' shouted Stonehouse.

'Fuck you... Cardinal' shouted Connor. 'You are nothing but the bitch of that Nazarene-pussy-Pope. The one and only Anti-Christ! So fuck you! I piss on you and your fuck-stick of a Church.'

He ran the sword loudly across the railings while gesticulating towards his crotch.

'I've told you enough times, Connor. You are a man of the cloth... Start acting with some dignity,' shouted Stonehouse as he ran towards the altar followed by Herschel and Somerset.

'Cloth? Cloth! Me? A man of the cloth?' shouted Connor. 'Don't make me laugh. Isn't it you who is a man of the cloth? A very important man of the cloth... though, aren't you? With your finery...and your rings, and your wealth... and your adoring flock... and your hypocrisy... and your paedophilia... and all your murders... That's what it means to be a man of the cloth.'

Connor swung low from the balustrade and scraped his

sword hard across the wall behind the large statue of Christ on the crucifix that dominated the altar.

Connor pointed at the effigy of Christ.

'Do you think he will forgive you, Cardinal? Eh? Do you think he will forgive you your terrible crimes... Car - Dee - Nal?' Large globules of saliva fell to the altar floor as Connor spat out each individual syllable.

'When you finally meet your maker... St Peter at the pearly gates perhaps? But I think it is more likely to be my true Lord at the steaming gates of Hades for you... Do you think you will be met... met by all of those children... All those beautiful children... Kids... toddlers... babies... THAT YOU FU-CK-ING MUR-DER-ED!'

'Good grief... What do you mean?' said Stonehouse. 'I don't know what you are talking about Connor... I mean... I have never...'

'Don't fucking lie... You snivelling, cock-sucking, old bucket-boy... You knew what was happening... You orchestrated the whole fucking thing... The secret visits every night to get fingered and fucked by Father Murphy... Or beaten by Mother Superior...You knew... You all knew, didn't you? But those poor babies... Were they too expensive? Did they drink a little too much milk, or eat a little too much bread? It was you... It was you all the time... They were nothing to you... Sweet, innocent little children, free of sin... Such beautiful, beautiful children...You snuffed them out... You extinguished them ... And didn't give them a second thought... They are waiting for you Cardinal Stonehouse... They are all waiting for you... At the bottom of that well... The stinking, cold well, full of little bodies... They will lead you to the gates of hell... Ahahghaaahhaahhhaaa...'

Connor leapt from the balustrade and landed squarely between the Crucifix and Stonehouse. Stonehouse put his arms up, expecting a blow that didn't come. Tears were streaming down his face.

'What have I done? What have I done...' cried the Cardinal. 'I never thought it would end like this... Do I really deserve this? Was it me? Am I really responsible? Oh my Lord, please forgive me... If it be your will, my Lord, please take me. Please take me now.'

Connor pushed the point of his sword towards Stonehouse's face.

'Kneel, you pathetic brownie-queen fuck-faggot... Get on your knees... and pray to your anti-christ for something resembling redemption...'

Stonehouse knelt, closed his eyes, brought his palms together and began praying under his breath.

'I hope you are asking your God for forgiveness...' snarled Connor. 'Because you fucking need it...'

'I'm praying for your soul,' said the Cardinal.

'AHahhAhHHaaa... that's a laugh... Don't pray for me... My soul is with my one true master... My Lord. ... I have no trouble with that... Pray for your children... Pray to your Nazarene for the souls of the dozens of infants you sent to their deaths. Pray for your vicarious redemption... For your immoral teachings... Pray for him to take all of your sins. Pray for the children...'

'I am praying for my children... I am praying for my child... I am praying for you... Connor.'

'Yes...The children...'

'No Connor... I'm praying for my child... For you...'

'What? The children that you saw die? No... Don't pray for me... Not me. Why would you pray for me?I am lost... My soul is lost... I am damned forever. You and your hypocrisy saw to that. My soul is with my exquisite dark Lord... Why would you bother praying for me?...'

'I am praying for my child Connor... My child...You... You are my child Connor... I am your father... Your real father... And you are my son... My flesh and blood.'

'What!' shouted Connor... Never! That's not true... No...
You lie... Kitty was my mother... Gerald, my father...'

Connor began to pace around the Cardinal, back and forth,
swinging the blade of the sword by Stonehouse's head...
swishing it dangerously close to his ears.

'I swear to you Connor. It was a long time ago. We were so
in love,... but I was a young priest... We had no choice... We
had to give you up... I'm... so... so... sorry.'

'No... No... That can't be right,...' screamed Connor. 'That
can't be true... Gerald is my father. Sheena, Michael, Sean,
David and Louise...They're all my family... They are my family... They are my real family... They're all as fucked up as me...
I loved to see them all beautifully seduced by the darkness...
Drugs... Avarice...Greed... Lust... Crime... Cheating and
lying... They are just like me... They are mine.. And I will join
them all in Hell...'

'No, Connor. You are mine... My son,' said Stonehouse
quietly.

'It's true,' interjected Herschel. 'Gerald could never have
been your father. He didn't meet Kitty until after she reached
England. After you were born... And can I just suggest that
you put that sword dow...'

'Nooooo!' cried Connor. He swung his sword in a wide arc,
hard against the bottom of the crucifix. Shards of wood and
plaster flew into the air with a huge ear-splitting crunch.
Stonehouse remained on his knees, still, and with his eyes
closed as the dust and splinters covered him. His lips moved
imperceptibly as he prayed under his breath.

'Fiat mihi secundum verbum...' whispered the Cardinal.

'It can't be true... You can't be my father...' screamed
Connor as he paced backwards and forwards. Connor's permanently reddened face was now a mess of tears, snot and spittle
foam. His bloodshot eyes darted back and forth around the
Church, left, right, up and down, his pupils enlarged to
grotesque proportions.

'You... a snivelling streak of arrogant, entitled, gay piss... I can't possibly be your flesh and blood.'

'Connor. It is true... I am your father. That's why I tried to look after you in St Vincent's,' continued Stonehouse, his eyes now fixed upwards on the crucifix. 'I did the best I could... I tried to make sure you were looked after. I tried to ensure no harm came to you.'

'No Harm! No Harm!' screamed Connor. 'Well you didn't try very hard did you, because I, like most of the abandoned kids, was abused, raped and beaten almost every day. Do you have any idea what it was like? We grew up thinking it was normal... That it was normal for a priest to want to fuck you...That's what they did... That's what we were for... That it was normal for a nun to want to beat you until you bled. And... and when they had had enough of you, they would get rid of you, like another piece of unwanted shit'.

'Agnus dei, qui tolis peccata mundi,' whispered Stonehouse. 'I am the Lamb of God... I am truly, so sorry... It was up to me to take away the sins... I have failed... I have been so selfish...I should have atoned for your sins...And I didn't.'

'My sins? My Sins!... Oh my lord... Give me strength... By Sanguis Christi - fiat mihi secundum verbum... How could someone as pathetic as you possibly atone for my sins. You have no idea the depths of depravity that I have inhabited... Dies Irae – It is the End of Days. Today is Judgement Day.'

'Oh Lord, let me start anew,' Stonehouse whispered to himself. 'Let me start a new life in the power of your Kingdom.'

Connor, turned away from Stonehouse and looked up to Christ on the cross before him as he held the sword in his hand. He looked and stared... perhaps hoping for some kind of divine intervention. Smiling and nodding, he moved one step away, then swung the cleaver high above his head in a wide reverse arc, simultaneously spinning on his toes like a samurai to bring the blade down vertically upon the Cardinal's skull in a single swift movement, splitting the man almost in two, dividing him from his crown to just above his groin in a single blow, that left the sword buried three-quarters of the way down his body. Like a perfect anatomical exhibit, he had been bisected down the middle. The Cardinal's face remained serene and intact for a moment, until the two halves slipped away from each other, and with all the force of an over-ripe fruit, burst upwards and outwards. The blood and entrails exploded high over Connor's head, colouring both him and the crucifix scarlet.

'Oh, my good God!' exclaimed Somerset.

Herschel and Somerset ran forward. Stonehouse was kneeling, leaning forward, unpeeled, with the blade deep within him, and with the curved butt of the sword now resting against the ground preventing him from toppling over. His body was surrounded by an enormous pool of blood and entrails, leaving the steps of the altar dripping red with his remains.

'Christ!' said Herschel.

'Get an ambulance...Now!' Somerset barked into his comms set.

'I think it's too late for that,' winced Herschel, as they looked at the body.

'...Somerset? Where has he gone?'

'Who?'

'Connor...'

'We've searched everywhere sir. No sign of him in the Cathedral or the grounds,' said the police officer.

'He's running rings around us Somerset,' said Herschel. 'He's coming and going as he pleases.'

'I can't believe what just happened,' said the Inspector. 'In all my years, I've never seen anything like it. He just cut him in two, with a single blow... Almost superhuman... And his own father... Terrible... And who would have thought it... Cardinal Stonehouse, Connor's father.'

'The Sins of the fathers,' replied Herschel. '...Are usually visited upon the children. But in this case they have been returned with interest.'

'You can say that again... Poor man.'

'Who? Connor?'

'No... I was thinking of the Cardinal.'

'Pffft!' scoffed Herschel.

'Connor is clearly insane,' added Somerset. 'All of this has pushed him over the edge.'

'Perhaps, but I think he might have been sampling his own concoctions.'

'Concoctions? You mean drugs? Like what he used on Sean, Michael and David.'

'More like hallucinogens and maybe other stuff. I think Connor is smarter than we gave him credit for. In fact, a lot smarter...'

'So are you saying it's going to take more to catch him? I mean, I've got teams of officers on it.'

'I don't know. But he clearly has the run of this place, and unless we apprehend him soon, who knows what more he could do.'

Somerset reached for his radio. 'All units... Be aware that our suspect could appear from anywhere, and I mean anywhere... From below ground or even from above.. I want you all to keep your eyes peeled for our man, and to report immediately. But I repeat, I want no shots unless explicitly authorised by me.'

Herschel looked at Somerset quizzically.

'This weird light doesn't help much,' said Somerset. 'Look at that storm cloud. Eerie isn't it? It's kind of dark before it should be.'

'Apocalyptic?' asked Herschel. '...End of Days?'

'Ok. Ok,' continued Somerset. ' I think we've had enough premonitions for one day. We've got the spotlights out to help catch him if he appears, and there are dozens of officers posted in a double cordon around the Cathedral, but we can't follow him if he uses the tunnels. The Tactical Squad are searching, but there are miles of them. I've called for ground radar, but they're going to take a few hours to get here.'

Herschel and Somerset stood outside the Cathedral. Night was approaching. It was much darker than normal and the air was thick with positive ions. Three roaming searchlight beams penetrated the evening sky and lit up the Cathedral and its spire like St Paul's during the Blitz.

'That storm does look angry,' said Herschel. 'But it's weird. No noise from it at all... Very strange. Have you seen the lightning? There are big flashes, but no bangs... Dry lightning...It's very rare and peculiar...What about the helicopter?'

'They can't get close because of the storm... The nearest they can be is five miles away, so they're not going to be of much use.'

'Ok... So we'll have to rely upon our boots on the ground. We need to know, the instant he appears.'

'But it could be from anywhere, Herschel. I've got a lot of officers deployed, but we can't possibly cover everywhere.'

'What if he slips through the net? We just can't have that. I won't be responsible for letting a serial killer loose in the...'

Somerset's radio crackled into life. 'There he is Sir. He's on the roof...'

The three spotlights immediately moved to focus on a single point high above them on the Cathedral. Connor, still dressed in black was scampering across the apex from the bell-tower.

'Hold your fire,' ordered Somerset over the radio. 'I don't want any more fatalities... He's heading for the spire.'

Connor ran along the extended ridge from the bell tower. The bright spotlights picked him out of the darkness like an escaped convict. He jumped the parapet and began to climb the spire, using the lighting conductor to guide him up.

'What the hell is he up to?' asked Somerset

'Maybe he wants to get closer to God,' answered Herschel.

'Is he climbing to the top? Is he going to jump?'

The two men watched as Connor climbed higher and at some speed. At first he looked as though he was heading for the summit, but stopped about three-quarters of the way up.

'Get me a loudhailer,' ordered Somerset.

Herschel cupped his hands around his mouth and shouted. 'Connor... Stop... We can talk about this. You're just making things more difficult for yourself...Come down. You can't go any further...We have snipers all around you...'

'Go to Hell!' shouted Connor, as he leant confidently out from the building. He had jammed his feet hard against the sloping roof tiles and was holding on with his hand wrapped tightly around the metal lightning conductor.

'This is Detective Inspector Somerset,' shouted Somerset through the loudhailer.

'Owww,' cried Herschel as the speaker screeched its feed-back. 'Too loud...'

'That's weird,' said Somerset.

'It must be something to do with that storm cloud sitting over us. It must be creating some strange atmospheric condi-tions,' said Herschel. 'I don't think we'll need that.'

Connor, silhouetted against the building, was lit up with each lighting flash, like a strange black gargoyle etched onto the Cathedral spire.

'I had to do it. I had no choice,' cried Connor. '...They had to die... It's the only way we will ever be together... As a proper family... I should be sorry about him, but he... he was the reason for all this... I thought it was Gerald's fault. But it never was... it was that Anti-Christ Stonehouse all along... I should have realised... He'd never have acknowledged me. I would only ever be an inconvenience... Much better to hide me away.

So he had to pay the price... But I know we'll meet again... We'll be together soon... All of us...The whole family.'

'What?' said Herschel. '...Don't do anything stupid.'

'AhhaahHHaaaaha... My true Lord will decide my fate... It is now up to him... My wonderful, seductive, dark Lord,' cried Connor. 'To my true Lord, I am a hero... His hero. I have united this family for all eternity... And in the sweet beauty of damnation. I am a Master Demon now... I have succeeded... I will live for all eternity with my Lord...He will decide what is to happen... He has been with me for so long... I trust him with my ever-lasting soul... He will decide when I am to come unto him... When I meet him and the others... He has helped me...He has made it all possible...'

'His dark Lord?...Does he mean?...' asked Somerset.

'It's the Occult... He's completely deranged. He thinks he's being directed by Satan.'

'Hearing voices?' said Somerset.

'Well, probably yes. Voices, hallucinations... The whole shebang, I expect... I guess if you're not hallucinating with the ones from upstairs, then it's probably going to be the ones from down below,' sighed Herschel.

Connor's ranting continued.

'So maybe I was born a sinner... in God's eyes... An innocent child born into a world of sin... Oh, and I have truly sinned... He can strike me down for all I care... But will he? Can he? Where is he? Where is this all-loving, all-powerful God? Have we seen anything of him for the last two thousand years? Does he really exist? Is he hiding? If he never shows himself, how can we possibly believe in him? I think God is dead. God is dead to us all... There is no redemption... No absolution... Nothing... There is only eternal and exquisite pain and darkness...'

'Connor...' shouted Herschel. 'This doesn't have to end this way. If you come down now, we can work something out. There needn't be any more of this.'

'Fuck you Herschel,' cried Connor. 'You are nothing but a dull and boring philistine. You have no soul. You believe in nothing. Your eternity will be nothing but a grey monotony of eternal blandness in a cheerless world of drab mundanity. You believe in nothing Herschel, and nothing believes in you.'

'It doesn't matter what I believe in, Connor,' called Herschel. 'Five people are dead because of you. Don't you think we deserve an explanation? People will want to know your story... They'll want to know why you did what you did. What drove you...How you suffered... I'm sure people will be interested... There will be sympathy for you.'

'Herschel...' said Somerset quietly.

'Isn't it fucking obvious?' shouted Connor. 'I mean just look at this world. The world that he created... What a complete and utter fuck-up. Surely it can't be what he wanted? It's the liars, cheats and hypocrites that are in charge. Success in this world is measured by how much we cheat and steal from one another and by how much torment and misery we can inflict. Pain and suffering are just the rungs on the ladder of success. We reward the swindlers, the con-men, the paedophiles and the genocidal maniacs with power. We honour them with riches, with sex, with drugs... and most significantly, we reward them with our unwavering adulation... Don't we? And what does that tell you? What does that tell you about this world he created? It tells me he's no longer here... He left a long time ago...God is dead! He died centuries ago... and look... No-one fucking noticed... And no-one fucking cares... After the deluge he said he would interfere no longer... that that precious commodity – free will – was ours... Ha! That was his big mistake... His infinite power failed him just when he needed it most... His arrogance was all my sweet Lord needed. And he has relished every moment since. He has changed the world to his likeness, exploiting all of our irresistible human weaknesses. Playing on our fears and conceits. And he has had such fun... So let me tell you... what I do, and what I have done has no relevance... God is dead. And he died in despair, broken-hearted at his dreadful mistake.'

'Oh my good God,' said Somerset.

'And my Lord gave me the honour of insight into his oh so beautiful plan... His grand plan... He believes in me... He found me at my lowest moment. He took me under his wing... He took me into his confidence... And he revealed it all to me. In all its magnificent torment... And it's now time to finish what we started... To end it all now... Who said this should go on forever? No one... Now is the End Times... The seal was broken, and the Horsemen were unleashed to rip their revenge upon the cheaters, liars, pushers and fornicators. They had to go first. They must be first alongside me when the gates are opened to us all. We will savour the rapture together... And it is just the start... There is so much more to come... So much more agony, suffering and pain in his beautiful plan. There is such pleasure in its delicious elegance. Just you watch... The fun is just beginning...'

'Hang on Connor... We're sending someone to help you,' called Somerset.

In his excitement Connor began to sway harder while he gripped onto the copper lightning conductor. As he moved more animatedly, the rivets holding the rod above him began to stretch and pop. Connor failed to notice the weakening of the fixings until it was too late. A large section of the rod came away with a loud metallic snap, and fell away from the building. Still gripping on, Connor dropped several feet, downwards, outward and jerked to a halt as the rod snapped into its new position leaving Connor hanging by one arm and dangling high over the edge of the Cathedral.

'Nooooo!' screamed Somerset as he watched Connor drop and then come to a sudden halt.

'AhhaaHhaaahaaAaahaaAa...' laughed Connor hysterically.

'Hang on... We'll get you down,' shouted Somerset. The

inspector reached for his radio and barked into it angrily. 'We need that fucking helicopter!'

Connor laughed maniacally as he swung back and forth in the spot-lit darkness, like some strange religious fruit.

'This is perfect,' he shouted. 'At last... This is his chance. He can show himself now... He can prove all his doubters wrong after all these years... I demand my right for full judgement in front of God... Come on you sickening old horror, come on... Show yourself... This is your last chance... Save me... Or punish me. Whatever you want... I don't care... Redeem me, or smite me with your lightning bolt... I dare you. Come on you miserable old fucker!'

Somerset and the Police team watched as the priest ranted and raved from his precarious position, half expecting some kind of celestial intervention. Herschel however, did not.

'Oh you can't do it can you,' continued Connor. You can't possibly judge me... Can you?... Why? Because you have been dead for centuries... Well let me tell you, if you can't judge me, then I will judge you ... And I judge you badly... You have failed your creation...You have let us all down... We had such high hopes for you... and you have left us wanting... Come on, show yourself... Prove to us that everlasting love and forgiveness is the light and the truth... Come on you desperate old goat... Show yourself... I don't care how... Go on! Do it!!'

Herschel and Somerset watched open-mouthed as Connor's swaying intensified... and his grip loosened. But neither his redemption nor his damnation arrived.

'Watch out,' cried Herschel. '...He's going to fall.'

Connor made one last twisting motion with his body before his grip finally failed him. He dropped feet first vertically, slamming into the side of the flaring spire. The priest ricocheted off the Cathedral roof, bouncing and somersaulting sideways, with broken tiles and debris falling after him. He dropped hard and struck the top of the flying buttress with a bone-crunching crack. Connor's high-pitched strangled laugh echoed across the quadrangle as he smashed into the stonework. Lying face down, he spat out a huge ball of blood and groaned before gravity got the better of his convulsing body, pulling it inexorably downwards for a second time, where the long, polished spikes of the iron railings were waiting for him. The barbed fence simultaneously ripped into the priest's chest, head and torso as he landed, exploding him on impact in a bloody, sopping mess. What remained of his torso was left hanging and dripping in a twisted, ugly, red heap, between, in and over the black ironwork.

'Oh, my good God,' cried Somerset. The Inspector ran forward to check on the priest. He grabbed what remained of Connor's arm to try and get a pulse.

'It's over,' he said. 'Get the ambulance over here... Good grief. The poor fellow. Did you see how he fell? Even after all that he had done, he didn't deserve that.'

'Fell? Or jumped?' said Herschel. 'It could have been either. Who can be sure?'

'Did you hear him crying out for his redemption? Maybe he felt some remorse.'

Herschel looked down at the bloody, dismembered remains of the priest.

'No... I think he got what he wanted...'

'Do you really think so?' asked Somerset. 'I don't think he ever got what he wanted.'

16

THE PALE HORSE

Herschel looked out of the conference room window onto the drab police station car park below. Drops of rain slid down the outside of the window forming long transparent lines against the plated glass. He absent-mindedly drew his finger vertically down the window, tracing one of the streaks as it meandered down the pane. He tutted as he looked at his finger-tip covered in a thin silvery film of dust. The electrical storm had passed, leaving in its wake, an oppressive grey drizzle that had lasted more than two days. Herschel looked around the conference room and sighed. The beige walls and office furniture remained the same, while in the doorway the carpet was still worn to an off-white colour.

'Is Somerset coming?' asked Cassandra.

'Yes,' said Herschel. 'He's going to debrief us here. He's bringing some of his team too.'

'Not much to debrief about really, now is there?'

'Maybe not,' said Herschel.

'I think we probably have more information than he does. So I suggest we are prudent with what we share... and how we came to be in possession of it.'

'Hmmm... Ok. But we can share some of it, though... right?' said Herschel.

'Only what they need to know,' pressed Cassandra firmly.

'So with only Sheena left alive now, I suppose she will inherit everything. At least that has been saved. Someone can benefit from it.'

'Would the Church not want it back? The proceeds of blackmail?' asked Cassandra.

'Hmmm. Unlikely, I think. They'll want to draw a veil over this affair as fast as possible. They won't want to get entangled in a messy legal wrangle. They won't want the publicity.'

'Ok... So how about we take a look at the case before Somerset gets here,' said Cassandra...'Motive?'

'Sure... I mean, that was pretty clear... Revenge against his family, the orphanage, the Church...Pushed over the edge by his treatment as a child and the family that ultimately rejected him, despite his deluded expectation of their acceptance. Eventually, his only safe place was the occult and his distorted belief that the end of the world was imminent, and that by murdering them he could bring them all together in his version of Heaven.'

'Yes... Hell,' said Herschel. 'It's hard to believe that people still believe in all that mumbo-jumbo.'

'Well, they do, Herschel... Many more people than you might imagine. For some, all they have in this life is the promise of what might be in the next.'

'I know... I know... It just seems such a waste of time and energy.'

'Well, it gives some people comfort... Is that such a bad thing?' said Cassandra.

'Only if it introduces false hope,' said Herschel. 'And I think it does... And then, what if that false hope is abused? Can't that lead to exploitation? Just like Connor suffered? I struggle to see where the good is in it. Dashed hopes will only ever lead to frustration, anger... and as we have just seen, murder and ultimately destruction.'

'And you think that is what drove him to do what he did?' asked Cassandra.

'It's complicated, but ultimately, yes I do. I think responsibility lies within our institutions.'

'Which ones?'

'Church, State and Establishment of course... In that order.'

'How come?'

'Well, these organisations have been in place for hundreds, if not thousands of years. So we take them for granted. We see them as the status quo. And we tend to see their principles and policies as unquestionable. But the problem is that every organisations' first objective is to maintain that organisation, at the expense of everything else. So those within it are allowed, even encouraged, to act in a way that maintains that very status quo within the organisation. Sometimes to the point of criminality.'

'Can anything be done?'

'Probably not... They are entrenched in our psyche... And we, as a society, have come to rely upon their permanence. Connor suffered a tragedy and a travesty which our institutions will only ever view as a collateral side effect.'

'I know. It was utterly pointless,' said Cassandra. 'Even after all his ranting... And all this death, what did he achieve?'

'The Church will cover up the incident. They'll close ranks and in doing so, Stonehouse, Gerald, and the rest of the family will be absolved of any responsibility.'

'And all the blame will be heaped on Satan?'

'Of course... Again,' laughed Herschel.

'So, next... Means?' asked Cassandra.

'Ah, the poisons. Well, we missed a trick on that one.'

'Yes. I guess we underestimated the breadth and depth of Church knowledge.'

'Quite. It's quite awe inspiring really when you think about the amount of scientific knowledge they might hold in secret archives across the world.'

'But aren't willing to share,' said Cassandra.

'Exactly. Or maybe aren't even aware that they have it. I wonder if Connor just happened upon that research. Did he seek it out or was it just an accident?'

'We'll never know... but more importantly, what other gems might they have, hiding in their vaults?'

'I know. It defies explanation really,' sighed Herschel. 'There could be a cure for cancer or the elixir of everlasting youth, and no one would be any the wiser.'

'That's true... But there's one other thing that still troubles me though,' said Cassandra

'Oh yes? What's that?'

'The Seal... On Gerald's will? The one with the inscriptions and the horse on it? How did that start all of this? I mean, it couldn't have been Gerald, could it? He knew nothing about the horsemen, did he?'

'I'm not sure we'll ever know,' replied Herschel. 'Clearly Gerald was an unusual and secretive character. I mean he had that fortune squirrelled away and told no-one. And he never seemed to spend any of it.'

'But if he had been responsible for the seal, then he would have had to collude with Connor, wouldn't he? Which would make him an accessory. That can't be right... It doesn't make sense,' said Cassandra.

'Is it possible that Connor got to the will before anyone else?'

'What do you mean? How?'

'Well, the solicitor did say that Gerald had changed it only six months before and had the box especially made.'

'I wouldn't trust that solicitor as far as I could throw him. Nasty piece of work. He'd sell his own grandmother, that one.'

'Interesting... What if Connor was the craftsman that built the box and the seal?'

'What? You mean when Gerald had it recommissioned?' said Cassandra. 'Of course... And that's what prevented Sheena and Sean from tampering with it.'

'My, my... Clever old Connor,' said Herschel. 'I suppose he could have posed as a craftsman through a front company and offered to do the work cheaply for Otley...'

I wonder if he changed the contents of the will too?'

'I think that was sealed in the envelope, but I guess we'll never know...'

The door to the police conference room opened and Somerset walked in, laughing and joking, followed by three uniformed officers.

'Ah... Talking to yourself again Herschel? You're making a bit of a habit of that,' said Somerset. The Inspector smiled broadly. 'You remember Sergeant's Sayers and Chalk... and Special Officer Nash?'

'Yes. Hello again,' replied Herschel, ignoring the jibe. 'You sound very pleased with yourself Inspector.'

'Well, I suppose we are a little. I mean this is a major one ticked off the list.'

'Crime?' asked Herschel.

'Well, yes. Five murders solved in one go.'

'I see,' said Herschel. 'And in what way do you think you solved them?'

'Well,' hesitated Somerset. 'We know who the perpetrator was and why he did it, and that's good enough for our crime stats. This will go down as five solved murders which is excellent for our numbers.'

'I'm sure it will be,' replied Herschel drily. 'So why did he do it? And more importantly, how did he do it? Anything from your statistics on that?'

'Well, it was obviously because of his family and the inheritance. He was just after the money now, wasn't he?'

'What?' said Cassandra, her voice echoing in Herschel's head. 'What is he talking about? Connor wasn't interested in the money at all.'

'Yes,' said Herschel, ignoring her. 'You are quite right, Somerset. That's exactly what it was... But how did he do it? How did he get access to those powerful toxins?'

'We're still investigating that,' replied Somerset. 'But as you said, there's a probable link to North Korea. It's just that we can't prove it yet. Maybe that's something you and your contacts could help with?'

'I'll see what influence the Church might have in North Korea,' said Herschel. 'We'll need to check their involvement with the NK security services and how far advanced the Church's research is, in pharmacology and toxicology.'

'Thanks. That would be really helpful,' said Somerset.

'Herschel,' said Cassandra. 'Stop it... You are just winding him up now.'

'I do have a couple of questions, though,' said Somerset.

'Go ahead,' replied Herschel.

'The Four Horsemen... We only seem to have had three. The Red Horse - War. The Black Horse - Famine, and the White Horse - Righteousness. What about the fourth? The Pale Horse? Pestilence?'

'Wasn't that Sheena? He filled her with Bubonic Plague?'

'That's true, but we searched her house with a fine-tooth comb and we didn't find anything. I mean, that was his calling card, now wasn't it?'

'It's bound to turn up somewhere,' dismissed Herschel.

'I hope so,' replied Somerset. 'It just seems strange that it wasn't obvious. The other three were.'

'Maybe one of your officers has taken it as a trophy,' suggested Herschel. 'Perhaps you should ask them?'

The two Sergeants and the Special Officer looked at each other quizzically.

'I'll check with them,' said Sergeant Sayers. 'But if I find out that there's been some souvenir hunting, there'll be hell to pay.'

'Good choice of words, officer,' said Herschel.

'And there is one more thing,' asked Somerset. 'Stonehouse as Connor's father. I get that, but why would that turn Connor into the murdering maniac that he became?'

'His time at the orphanage,' replied Herschel. 'They really were dreadful places, especially in Ireland. Thank goodness they have been closed down now. Lord only knows what he suffered. They are still finding mass graves to this day and no-one has ever apologised or been held accountable. There have been inquiries, reports, investigations and the like, but never any charges, prosecutions or convictions.'

'That's terrible,' said Somerset.

'It is, and from all accounts, it went on for many decades. Unwanted children, wanted children and unmarried mothers were taken into Catholic orphanages and institutions across the country and simply forgotten about. They were put to work in laundries or tending crops and they quickly became institutionalised. The conditions were appalling. They were often starved and beaten, and of course sexual abuse was endemic. They would even incarcerate young girls who they considered to be too high-spirited and wayward. These were young women who had committed no crime, moral or other-wise, even in the eyes of a strict, authoritarian Church. They were simply deemed likely to do so, and so, in order to protect the moral integrity of society, they were imprisoned, illegally, sometimes for decades.'

'That is more than criminal,' said Somerset. 'How did they get away with it? What about the authorities?'

'I don't think you understand the power of the Church in Ireland, Somerset. In most towns and cities in the nineteenth and twentieth centuries the Church was God and God was the Law. No one was above God. Not the police. Not the judiciary. Not even the establishment or the gentry. A parish priest in rural Ireland was untouchable. They could do anything they wanted. And we are finding out now that that is exactly what they did. No one would ever question it. How could they? So, for an up and coming priest like Stonehouse, anointed as a future leader by the Vatican, he was God incarnate. No one would ever question him. Whatever happened in St Vincent de Paul orphanage would turn even the most hardened police officer to tears. Connor spent years there so one can only imagine how he felt. The things he would have had to do to survive. It must have been like living in the gulag. Survive or die. It hardly bears thinking about.'

'Good grief,' said Somerset.

'And it is only recently, after some of the child-abuse cases that have come to light, that the Irish authorities have been able to break free from the religious dogma, taken it seriously, and conducted proper investigations. We are still waiting for genuine reconciliation and restitution for the victims, whoever they might be.'

'God help them,' said Somerset.

'Amen to that,' replied Herschel.

The ambulance pulled up slowly in front of the small terraced house. The driver and a paramedic jumped out the front and walked around to open the back doors. Inside, a second paramedic gently helped Sheena down the stairs of the ambulance. Looking frail and weak, she was dressed in a loose-fitting tracksuit. With her hands and feet bandaged, the drip attached to her arm snaked its way to a colourless bag of liquid carried by one of the paramedics. She walked slowly and unsteadily towards the door, supported by one of the medics. The ambulance driver fitted the key into the lock and let them in. The house was dark and dismal. The carpet was worn and some of the wallpaper corners were peeling away where the wall met the ceiling. The furniture was functional but quite cheap and dated, and some of the fixtures and fitting were broken.

'Put a light on,' commanded Sheena.

One of the paramedics felt for the light on the table in the hallway and switched it on to reveal the ground floor of a house in some disarray. Clothes, shoes, makeup containers, food wrappers, tins and other detritus were strewn across the floor or abandoned on the furniture. The two paramedics looked at each other. One of them tried to disguise a wince.

'Oh dear,' said the paramedic. 'Looks like you could do with some help around the here...'

'Don't fucking start,' said Sheena. 'This is my house. I'll live just the way I like. I'm not going back in Dad's house. Not after...'

'But Sheena, this is unhygienic. I'm not sure you are in any state to live here, especially after what the consultants said...'

'Look... I don't care what you or any of the doctors think. I'm not staying in that hospital a moment longer. This is my home and I'm comfortable here. I'll get someone to clear up for me later.'

She waved her un-dripped arm over the living room scene.

'Ok,' replied the first paramedic with some uncertainty. 'But maybe we should get in touch with Social Services too. They can come and check on you in a day or so.'

'Yeah... Whatever,' dismissed Sheena.

'You know how unhappy the doctors were about you discharging yourself, don't you? They only agreed because you kicked up such a fuss. You know how irregular this is... And how worried everyone has been about you. Do you know how close you came to dying?'

'Yeah... Yeah... I know,' replied Sheena. 'But another minute in that place and I would have thrown myself out of one of the windows. And probably taken one of you lot with me.'

'But here Sheena? I mean... Really?' asked the paramedic.

'I'll live, how I fucking want to live... So stop judging me... I had enough of that from that lunatic priest.'

'Ok. Ok... How about we get you into bed. Settle you in. We can give this place a tidy up. Then we can be certain that you are comfortable before we leave you... Ok?'

'Yes... Fine,' answered Sheena through tight lips.

'Oh my good God,' called the other paramedic from the kitchen.

'Do you mind,' yelled Sheena. 'What the fuck do you think you are doing in there? Get out.'

'I'm not happy about this,' said the paramedic from the kitchen. 'This is not good, Sheena. You really should be able to look after yourself better than this. I mean there's all sorts of...'

'Do you mind,' she hissed. 'Why don't the two of you just do your jobs. Drop me off. Make sure I'm ok... Leave me alone, and get the fuck out of here. You're just pissing me off now... Don't you understand? In the last few weeks, I have lost every member of my family, and you're expecting me to be interested in home economics...'

She stopped and took a breath. 'Look... Please... I beg you... Just go...'

'Ok ok... Let's just get you upstairs,' said the first paramedic. 'Do you need some help?'

The two medics held Sheena as she gradually stepped up the stairs and into the main bedroom. A thin vertical sliver of light penetrated between the gap in the heavy curtains.

'Let's get some light in here too,' said the medic. He drew back the curtains with a loud screech, but they would only open a few inches.

'Oh dear,' he said, as he looked around.

The room was strewn with empty tins of cola, unwashed plates and glasses, three overflowing ashtrays, at least two cheap plastic lighters, several boxes of matches, opened packets of condoms, and dozens of packets of cigarettes – some open, others not.

344

'Oh Sheena,' said the other paramedic. 'How can you live like this. This isn't going to help you.'

'For fuck's sake... Look, I'm perfectly capable of looking after myself. It may not be an operating theatre, but I have managed to support myself for all these years... I don't think I need lectures from you two. I told the doctors that I would be fine at home... And I will be... I just need some time to rest and readjust.'

'Ok... Ok,' said the paramedic. 'Let's at least change the sheets for you, so you have something clean and fresh to sleep in. We'll tidy up a bit and get someone to clean up properly later... Ok?

'Ok,' said Sheena.

The two medics changed the bedsheets, tidied the room a little and let Sheena settle in her bed. The paramedic stood over her.

'Now, you have to remember you are still very unwell. You're still on some pretty strong antibiotics, your wounds are still healing slowly and your body has had an enormous shock. It's going to take some time for you to recover.'

'I'm happier here, in my own surroundings. I can take my time...'

'And don't underestimate the psychological impact as well... What you were subjected to was horrendous... It's amazing that you survived it at all. You will need counselling before you are even ready to come to terms with what happened.'

'Thank you,' said Sheena. 'And, sorry for my outburst... It's just that I have had to fight every inch of the way to get here.'

'We understand... We're going to leave you now. You look after yourself... And if there are any problems, ring us. You have the emergency number.'

'Yes... I will do,' said Sheena, thinly.

'Someone will be in later today to change your drip. Be careful with it. It's powerful stuff.'

'Yes... Thank you.'

The two paramedics left the house and shut the front door behind them. As soon as they were gone Sheena let out a huge sigh, leaned over the side of the bed and scrabbled on the floor for a packet of cigarettes. She retrieved one, grabbed a lighter and hurriedly lit it. Dragging deeply she drew the smoke deep into her lungs and expelled it forcefully with a satisfied sigh. She then moved over to her bedside cabinet and opened it to retrieve a half full bottle of vodka. With a single, well-rehearsed movement, she removed the lid, put the bottle to her lips and took a deep swig. Sighing again with relief as she rested back against the pillows, she surveyed her surroundings.

'You know...,' she said. 'Perhaps they're right. Maybe I shouldn't have come here. This place really is a dump.'

Taking another drag, she looked closer at the canular feeding the antibiotic into her vein. She ran her hand over the membrane on her arm to feel the bulge of the plastic encased needle. Pinching it a little, she winced slightly but then smiled. She took yet another drag from her cigarette and another gulp from the bottle.

'That's better,' she said.

After a few more moments lying on her back, she finished off the bottle while staring up at her yellowed bedroom ceiling.

'Oowww,' she cried in pain as she rolled over to rummage under her bed. She groaned and gasped, and pulled out an A3 sized scrapbook. Grimacing again, she opened it, and a few papers and photographs fell out onto the bed. She picked up one of the photographs and looked at it.

'Ah...Connor. Dear Brother Connor... Well, well, well... Look what became of you, eh? Well, I'm still here, aren't I? I survived... Where are you, eh? Damned to eternity in the depths of Hell? Ha! It's probably what you always wanted.'

Sheena leafed through the scrapbook. As she did, more pictures of Brother Connor as a child, in the orphanage, and at

Communion fell out onto the bed. She lifted a newspaper cutting of Cardinal Stonehouse as a priest.

'Rising star Priest, Father Stonehouse saves pilgrims from Spanish cult-gang,' she said, reading the headline out loud. 'Well, maybe you did, Cardinal Stonehouse, but you weren't able to save yourself from my father or from your own son, now were you? You're nothing more than a ghost yourself, now... Hahhahhaa...'

She laughed deeply, taking in lungfuls of air to do so. She then started to cough and splutter so hard that she had to stop and compose herself before catching her breath again. Gaining her composure, she drew deeply on the remainder of her cigarette, letting the ash drop onto the clean bedsheets.

She took out a small, faded picture of Kitty as a young teenager from the scrapbook, she smiled and kissed it. She then picked up a more recent picture of Connor and held it out in front of her.

'Oh Connor... Do you think Dad didn't know? Do you think he didn't tell me? Well of course he knew. He always knew... And he was always going to win. And he told me... Of course he did... Even when he told me again just before he died, I already knew... I was his special one... He could always trust me. But I got them all going didn't I, eh? They were desperate to know what I knew. I perfected that act... I knew who you were... Dad told me years ago. I always knew... And his plan worked perfectly... I wasn't going to let the rest of them know though. That would have been foolish. And that's why you could never win... Dad and I were always the perfect team. And we weren't going to let you beat us, now were we?'

She took another gulp of vodka and winced in pain.

'I never thought you would resort to murder, though... That really was a surprise... I didn't think you had it in you. You may have been the firstborn, but Dad was never going to let you and Stonehouse get your hands on his fortune, now was he? He was far too smart for that... You were never going to get close... Surely you know when you have been played? Owww...'

She flinched again as she turned over in the bed then doubled up as the strong waves ran painfully through her. She gritted her teeth and grunted as the spasm ripped through her body. Laughing out loud as the pain gradually subsided, she coughed heavily, took another large swig and looked at her bandaged hands.

'Well I have to admit, it was a close one though... But I think we can agree that the best woman won... It was a high price to pay, but I think you would agree, at least for me, in the end, it was worth it... Haaha.'

She moved again, and a further torrent of pain coursed through her body, snapping her rigid. This time for much longer. Grimacing through tightly clamped teeth, she convulsed and twitched as the episode continued. Finally, as the torment subsided, she threw off the now soaking bedclothes, scattering the photographs and cuttings across the bed and onto the floor. Clutching at her abdomen, she pulled down her pyjama bottoms and kicked them off while simultaneously removing her top to try and find some comfort in the coolness of the open air. Sweat covered her body. She laid back naked, to reveal a torso green, yellow and black with disease. Stretching from her pubis to her collarbone, and across her stomach, the virulent necrotising fasciitis had gradually worked its way through her body.

'Ohhh...Fuck,' she cried, as she suffered yet another flood of excruciating pain. 'Hahahaa...' she cried, squirming left and right to try and get away from the discomfort. The disease was gradually destroying her internal organs and turning her body black. As her suffering intensified, and the pain became almost too much to bear, she began to remonstrate with herself.

'What do the doctors know anyway?'

Dragging hard on the last of her cigarette, she flicked it away, pulled a face and put on her best doctor's voice.

'You're still very unwell... You won't survive without twenty-four-hour care... You shouldn't discharge yourself... But if it's your decision... Sign here... We can't be responsible... Not us... Complications...'

Her face dropped and her head fell back on the pillow as the mimicry left her.

'Really? Well, fuck that... We'll see who's right.'

Sheena had other plans. She always had, regardless of any circumstance. She had never lived her life being dictated to by anyone, and she wasn't about to start now. She surely wasn't going to let her lunatic half-brother get the better of her. Still doubled up in agony, she grabbed the packet of pain-killers on the sideboard and swallowed four with the contents of yet another bottle. She groaned and slumped back again on the bed, breathing heavily and sweating profusely. Her body was framed in the steely low light streaming in through her bedroom window. Her skin cast a soft pale-green colour against the whiteness of her bed-sheets as she slowly slipped into a coma. Her dark hair covered most of her face as it fell sideways against the bed and her arms dropped outwards, perpendicular to her body. As she faded away, her grip loosened on a small pale-green clay figure which she held in her palm – before it dropped and landed softly on the floor.

ACKNOWLEDGEMENTS

Thanks go to:

Adele Newing, Trevor Fitzpatrick, Debbie Sawh, Jane Purbrook, Lisa and Simon Donlevy, Tracy Sayers, and Wayne Prangnell for their help, guidance and outstanding attention to detail.

Edited by : Jessie Raymond
Cover design : Xee_Designs

ABOUT THE AUTHOR

D.B. Cooper was born in Oxfordshire. After an extraordi-narily normal upbringing, he read Computer Science and Technology at Cambridge University before joining the Royal Marines, rising to the rank of Major.

As a full-time intelligence and security liaison officer he found himself regularly operating at the intersection between the military, the security services, and the emerging computer technology business. On leaving the military he developed cryptographic software for a number of international financial institutions where he gained a deep insight into how business and technology can unite to foil organised and disorganised crime. Latterly, he has grown his own technology business to a point where he now has commercial, security, and military clients on almost every continent.

Raised a Catholic, he lapsed many years ago, but he keeps a keen interest, and an eternal optimism for Church betterment. Married for over thirty years, and with a growing family, he now resides on the South Coast of England where he pursues his many interests.

He has never knowingly parachuted from a commercial airliner.

D.B.Cooper.com

Printed in Great Britain
by Amazon

21425644R00210